Dreamseeker's Road

TOM DEITZ

AVON BOOKS • NEW YORK

DREAMSEEKER'S ROAD is an original publication of Avon Books. This work is a novel. Any similarity to actual persons or events is purely coincidental.

AVON BOOKS
A division of
The Hearst Corporation
1350 Avenue of the Americas
New York, New York 10019

Copyright © 1995 by Thomas F. Deitz
Cover art by Daniel Horne
Published by arrangement with the author
Library of Congress Catalog Card Number: 94-46584
ISBN: 0-380-77484-4

First AvoNova Printing: May 1996
First Morrow/AvoNova Hardcover Printing: July 1995

AVONOVA TRADEMARK REG. U.S. PAT. OFF. AND IN OTHER COUNTRIES, MARCA REGISTRADA, HECHO EN U.S.A.

Printed in the U.S.A.

RA 10 9 8 7 6 5 4 3 2 1

TOM DEITZ

"A MASTER"
Brad Strickland, author of *Moondreams*

"A MAJOR FANTASY WRITER"
Booklist

**"FEW WRITERS MATCH PERSONAL CRISIS
WITH EPIC CONFLICTS AS EFFECTIVELY"**
Dragon

**"DEITZ GIVES THE READER
A REFRESHINGLY DIFFERENT
KIND OF MAGIC"**
A.C. Crispin, author of *The Starbridge Chronicles*

"ONE OF THE BEST"
OtherRealms

**"DEITZ HAS THE ENVIABLE ABILITY TO
MAKE CLEARLY FANTASTIC INCIDENTS
SEEM REALISTIC AND SUPERIMPOSE THEM
ON A STORY OF GENUINE CHARACTERS
DEALING WITH GENUINE PROBLEMS."**
Science Fiction Chronicle

**"TOM DEITZ IS WRITING BETTER
THAN EVER."**
Mercedes Lackey, author of *Magic's Price*

For Reid

ACKNOWLEDGMENTS

Gilbert Head
Manfred Jones
Greg Keyes
Nell Keyes
Adele Leone
Reid Locklin
Betty Marchinton
Buck Marchinton
Larry Marchinton
Chris Miller

Prelude:
Invasion of Privacy

(Gargyn's Hold—
Tir-Nan-Og—approaching Samhain)

"Don't dig down *too* far," Gargyn advised his eldest through a puff on his thornwood pipe. "The land runs thin this far out—you *could* chop right on through!"

" 'T'd be more interestin' 'n stayin' 'round *here*!" the lad shot back sourly, pausing to wipe a lock of moss-colored hair from his forehead before continuing his midday hoeing.

"Here's good 'nough for us," Gargyn replied, with a scowl that took in most of the melon patch and half the surrounding woods besides—as well as two more biddable sons beyond range of his tongue: Evvan and Evvell—wheat-thatched the one, cornflower-locked the other; black-kilted and crimson-trewed respectively. "We know who we are; nobody bothers us; don't take much to make stuff grow; an' there's always 'nough to hunt. What else you want?"

"Fun, mostly. 'Citement."

"You think fallin' through the floor o' the World's fun?" Gargyn snorted through another puff. "You wanta see the end o' the World, you march half a day past where I'm pointin' an' you'll find it soon enough! Fresh hole burned through there not a year gone by."

"Fuckin' iron," the eldest—Markon—grumbled.

"That's a quick-folks' curse!" Gargyn snapped. "You don't need t' be usin' quick-folks' curses."

Markon paused again at his hoeing. He had made no

1

discernible progress. "The Littl'un saw a dragon," he offered slyly, lifting a brow for effect.

Gargyn's slanted eyes narrowed beneath his crimson mop. Chills danced across his bare torso and dived beneath his kilt. He suddenly felt ages old. "Where?"

Markon grinned smugly. "Them woods," he replied, sweeping a knobby six-fingered hand toward a copse of feathery trees a good minute's trot away. "Said it was red as blood an' crusted with jools an' silver. Had round black feet an' squinty cat eyes."

"How . . . *big* was it?" Gargyn asked carefully.

Markon leaned on his hoe. "He said it was all crouched down like a wolf does when it's huntin'; said it was ten arm spans long an' twice as tall as he was. Said he was just standin' there chewin' a 'shroom, an' he heard somethin' roar an' saw it flash 'tween two trees, an' then it was gone."

Gargyn gnawed his pipe stem. "Wish he'd tol' me."

"Tol' you what?" another voice intruded—as a welcomed cool dampness pressed between his bony shoulders. He twisted around to accept the mug of cider his mate, Borbin, had brought to ease his tiller's thirst, noting the jug in her other hand and a covey of mugs hung from her scarlet kirtle. Impulsively, he hugged her, tweaked a tawny braid, and would have fondled an ample breast had the boy not been gawking.

"Tol' you *what*?" Borbin persisted, filling another mug for the glowering Markon.

"Dragon," Gargyn mumbled, between swallows.

"Only dragons 'round here's them kind," Borbin muttered, as she pointed to the High Road that formed the far edge of the field. Gargyn had to squint even more than usual, but made out the traveler: elegant gray stallion with silver stripes, sky-blue barding, and a young man astride: gold-haired, slim, and handsome; his every move graceful, the ice-blue gaze he trained on them keen even here, and full of disdain. He stared a long moment, while Gargyn glared back, then set spurs to sides and was gone in a flurry of shimmering cloak. Gargyn wondered vainly why all the Danaans were so tall and sleek and fair, while all male bodochs were as knottily thin as their women were ample. Not that the Danaans minded, sometimes. Why, he remembered his cousin Mev . . .

" 'Least dragons hoard stuff you c'n steal," Borbin sighed. "Them Seelie folk won't help nobody, not even when it's *their* land what's rottin' away."

"I've tried to talk to 'em. We all have—"

"An' got as much hearin' as a cat pissin'!"

"They say Varzi's 'quested audience w' Lugh again."

"Be better off talkin' to Rhiannon."

"She's got no say here, 'cept guest right."

"No, but she's got ears that'll listen to us small folk. That's more'n Lugh'll do."

"Yeah, well, he'd better *learn* to—or he'll wake up one day an' find he's king of an empty kingdom."

"They say Erbo's gonna emigrate."

Gargyn was about to request elaboration—but at that moment, with a rumbling shriek like a pride of cow-sized lions trying to roar and purr and yowl all at once, a scarlet shape leapt from the fringe of the forest and launched itself across the melon patch, scattering Gargyn's brood in its wake. The Littl'un had been right too: it really was all crouched down like a wolf. Real compact, in fact, with its black legs moving faster than he could see, a flipped-up rump but no true tail, and a hint of shadowy gray beneath, that hurt to look at straight.

And then it was rushing at them, narrow eyes wide and blazing; and Gargyn saw with a start that someone rode in a sort of enclosed carriage midway along its back. And then it sprang—and vanished, leaving a wake of wind hot as forge-fire and smelling of iron.

When he picked himself up from where he'd flung himself in fear of his life, it was to see Borbin's eyes as huge as the bottom of her mug. "Dragon . . ." he managed between gasps.

"Dragon . . ."

Fortunately, Borbin was infinitely practical. "Didn't hurt nobody," she observed. "An' weren't no dragon."

"*Fuck* it weren't!" Gargyn spat before he remembered what he'd told the boy.

"Weren't no dragon," Borbin repeated. "I seen a picture in a book one time, what was stole from the quickfolks."

"An' what were it then?" Gargyn demanded.

"Well, I'm not sure, *exactly*," Borbin admitted. "But I *think* it was what the quick-folks call a shev-ro-lay."

Prologue:
Closing Time

(University of Georgia Library—
Friday, October 23—late)

Tana hid behind Edgar Allan Poe.

More precisely, she hid behind a life-size cardboard cutout of the illustrious Virginian some resourceful English major had posted on perpetual lookout just inside the door to the study carrel she'd let herself into half an hour before. That it was not *her* carrel was of no concern, nor that the means by which she had circumvented the lock would have raised eyebrows in security forces more elite than the University of Georgia Police. No, what mattered was remaining undetected five minutes longer.

She'd had a bout of panic just now, when the youthful security guard had paused by the inset window and peered through—to catch Mr. Poe, but not the slim, dark-haired woman who crouched behind him. A sigh of relief whispered from her lips as his footsteps slapped away, echoing among the looming ranks of loose-shelved periodicals that filled half the Ilah Dunlap Little Library's basement.

Braaakzzzkkkk!

The alarm made Tana start in spite of herself. Six months in this country, and she still hadn't acclimated to all those electronic trinkets that festooned every building: warning her away from this, watching while she did that; denying entry to one place, easing access to another.

5

—Buzzing fifteen minutes ago to remind a huge building's worth of would-be scholars that a mere quarter hour remained until closing time.

And again five minutes later, this time with blinking lights.

And once more just now, with lights *and* guard.

Four minutes to go.

Three.

Two.

One.

The fluorescents outside, that had given her sharp pale features a sallow glow, went dark, plunging her into blue-gray gloom in which the only relief was the ghostly silver square of the carrel window.

One minute . . .

Two—Tana eased from Mr. Poe's shadow and turned the doorknob—and was alone with three million books, uncounted periodicals, and more microforms— film and fiche both—than she wanted to consider.

Silently—barefoot beneath designer jeans and a long-sleeved black silk shirt—she crept toward the library's core. No one was about. Then again, few would have noted her anyway, master that she was at moving unobtrusively among these foreigners, among these odd strangers who were so scared of . . . *everything* that they built glass and metal eyes to ward them while they slept.

Eyes that did not, however, see everywhere—or everything. Or everybody.

Abruptly she was there. Steel-toned elevator doors faced double gray-painted analogues across an unlit lobby. Steps angled up and down beyond the second, while an eye-sized light blinked balefully above their juncture: a fiery counterpoint to the moonbeams that worked their way through infrequent windows to paint sea-toned geometries on the floor.

She paused at the right-hand portal, listening, caught steps, but distant and receding, then sharper clicks as master switches were thrown on level after level. Each quenched an acre of brightness; each dimmed the stairwell more, as guards cleared every floor in sequence from top to bottom.

Another breathless minute passed, ears alert for the alarm that would signal a secured zone breached. And then, cracking the profound silence only large buildings can conjure, Tana heard, by means of certain . . . advantages, a young male voice call "all clear."

She'd timed it exactly right.

The red light above the door gained a green accomplice; the trigger was in place. Anyone breaking those contacts now would set off alarms in half a dozen offices. Tana, however, wasn't planning to leave that night—not by conventional means.

Assuming she ever got started.

A quick sifting of her pockets produced a tightly scribbled list in an odd fluid hand and luminous ink. She studied it briefly, then squared her shoulders and padded away from the stairwell and into the waist-high labyrinth of beige-enameled cabinets that housed the vast master archive of the Georgia Newspaper Project—a decades-long attempt at locating and preserving on microfilm the official legal organs of each of Georgia's 159 counties, most of the significant city rags, and all the major dailies. The largest collection in the state, 'twas said, and likewise the most comprehensive assemblage of information about Georgia happenings in existence—with duplicates strewn worldwide, including the Library of Congress.

So where *was* tonight's victim? She scanned the cardboard placards atop the cases. K . . . L . . . M . . . Morgan County . . . Moultrie— But where . . . ? O-kay . . . She squatted, scarcely able to see the drawer labels in the dim light, and at that, her night vision was better than most. M . . . for . . . *Mouth of the Mountains*.

Carefully she slid out the designated drawer. It

moved smoothly on nylon runners—and blessedly did not squeak, as others sometimes had.

Her gaze swept the blue-and-white boxes, each maybe four-by-four-by-two inches, with a range of dates typed on labels. But where to begin? August of a certain year, perhaps? *That* year, in fact—whereupon she snared a spool and rose. The walls around the labyrinth showed more carrels, these housing microfilm readers. Not locked. *Never* locked—as she well knew. She chose the nearest, eased inside, and shut the door. A denser gloom enclosed her, but she found the switch on the machine by practiced feel and flicked it. A square screen of white light promptly appeared, marred by abstract lines and speckles, and illuminating an intricate apparatus beneath. She slipped into the chair before it and threaded the film through a complex of rollers and between two plates of glass. Now what was the first date?

Right.

She twisted a dial. A blur of gray flew across the screen, smudged with darker lines that a more-leisurely viewing would resolve into type—fortunately, this reel was a *positive* image, a welcome change from the white-on-blue negatives she'd grown accustomed to. She slowed halfway through . . . slower . . . Larger words appeared, and squares of pictures. *Slower*, checking dates now: August 7 . . . 8 . . . 9 . . . *Had it!* Now to locate the article . . .

Before she could, however, her gaze was drawn to a pair of grainy photographs to the upper right. Nothing remarkable, really, merely standard yearbook mug shots of two boys in their mid-to-late teens. Handsome one was, by the standards hereabouts, with thick, white-blond hair worn long above what she knew from other sources were blue eyes, the cheeks and chin showing the angles of incipient manhood emerging from the more androgynous curves of adolescence, the eyes displaying the slight squint of one accustomed to wearing glasses and eschewing them from vanity, a not-so-slight grin parting lips she would not have minded kissing.

The other boy, by contrast, was pleasantly bland if a shade too neat, with short dark hair rising in careful spikes above a smooth-jawed face that narrowed to a pointed chin. His lips were thinner than the other boy's, his brows level, shadowing eyes probably gray or green, his expression, self-consciously serious. *Follower,* that face proclaimed. *Eternal runner-up. Vice president. Second-in-command. Jilted lover.*

"Local Boys Win Essay Awards at Governor's Honors Program," ran the caption beneath. She shaped the names silently: *David Sullivan. Alec McLean.* "David *Kevin* Sullivan," she repeated aloud. The blond. From rural Enotah County up in the mountains. Probably the smartest lad his age in his part of the world, the most gifted—and quite possibly the most cursed. Someone whose innocent actions a few years back had caused ripples in his small splash of Georgia that had become tsunamis impossibly far afield. Yeah, that boy, admirable though he was, had launched a shipload of grief. And though he'd been encouragingly quiescent lately, he still bore watching. Indeed, if not for him, she wouldn't be here now.

But she'd wasted enough time pondering facts that could not be altered; it was *her* job to massage their repercussions. And for that she required a certain article.

It took but an instant: four column inches on the lower half of the same page:

FREAK FIRE FRUSTRATES MACTYRIE FIRE DEPARTMENT

That was *exactly* what she sought: an account of a fire that had decimated the camp of a band of Travelers—Irish Horse Traders, as they were sometimes called—who'd set up business on the athletic field of a small north Georgia town. The article was sketchy on details but did note how very difficult the blaze had been to extinguish, how oddly it had appeared, and made reference to a number of unusual-looking characters setting the fire, prolonging it—and escaping on horseback. One in particular was mentioned: a tall, blond man with only one arm.

Not much there that was either informative or incriminating—by itself. But combined with enough *other* references, it could suggest a troubling pattern— which Tana was pledged to eradicate.

From a canvas tote, she extracted an Allstate Motor Club World Road Atlas, a yellow legal pad, and a gold fountain pen bearing swirls and flourishes upon its elegant barrel that might equally have been mindless filigree or writing in an unknown tongue. Holding her hand just *so*, she proceeded to line through certain words and phrases on the screen: those that hinted most blatantly at . . . otherness. The ink did not so much mark the glass, however, as seep *through*, into the image itself.

Revision took longer, as she wrote new words atop the old. "Freak Fire" became simply "Fire." "Difficult to extinguish" became "easily put out." "Seemed to spread by magic," became "spread quickly through very dry grass." And the escaped riders and one-armed man vanished entirely, the missing half column inch being replaced with a scribbled filler couplet by her favorite contemporary poet, John Devlin, set off in a bolder face to further shift attention from the account of the conflagration.

Her editing concluded, she opened the atlas to a certain page, removed the film without rewinding it, stretched the relevant segment on the Formica counter beside the reader, laid her left hand atop it— and stabbed the golden pen through her flesh and into the acetate.

She gasped as the metal slid between her bones, but

only a little, for she was used to the pain by now, and had only a few more days of such work left in any case: mopping up the fringes, mostly, in lieu of the major damage control she'd accomplished earlier—like that mess in the *Willacoochee Witness* two years back, which had required some *truly* creative rewording.

Which was reflection for leisure, not haste.

Her blood was seeping out now: adding its red to the film's blue and white. And at a certain moment—instinct told her when—she raised the wounded hand and slapped it upon the atlas—atop a map of the United States on which all libraries and similar repositories likely to retain copies of the article she had just revised or its microfilm surrogates were marked with tiny stars of real gold. A deep breath, an instant's concentration, and tendrils of blood flowed out from between her fingers and found their way to those miniscule markers. Each pulsed briefly, as though they drank their fill, then dulled back to mundanity. Another breath, when the last bright star had faded, and she was done. Her hand no longer bled, and the map was dry, as was the film.

Quickly, she reinserted the reels, located the suspect article, and read it one last time. Good. Her changes were all there—in print now. Anyone using either the original newspaper or the copies—be they at Emory University or the Library of Congress; the University of Tennessee, Harvard, Berkley, Boston University, Spellman College, the University of Texas at Austin, or the myriad others she'd starred; never mind the National Archives, the British Museum, and the Bibliothèque Nationale—would see a slightly different headline, a subtly altered text.

Too bad she couldn't track down *all* the copies, though, like the ones little old ladies tended to squirrel away in trunks and parents stuck in scrapbooks. Still, this was enough—probably. Besides, some things were even beyond the *Sidhe*.

Nuada, she was certain, would be pleased.

Sighing, Tana recorded the change on her legal pad, then consulted her scribbled list. Her next target was an article about a storm disrupting graduation at Enotah County High School almost a year after the previous occurrence, on which occasion numerous spectators claimed to have glimpsed the ghostly shapes of strangely clad warriors engaged in some titanic battle.

Fixing *that* would be a challenge.

Chapter I:
Autumn Chill

(Nichols Ridge,
Enotah National Forest, Georgia—
Saturday, October 24—morning)

"*Will* you be quiet?" David Sullivan hissed under his breath and over his shoulder at the taller, fog-shrouded form behind him, that *might* have worn a fluorescent orange cap atop spiky dark hair. "And point that thing at the ground or somewhere. Anywhere but at my butt!"

The damp-edged crunch of forest leaves promptly decreased in frequency—but not, so David noticed, in volume, though the shadowing shape faded farther back into the morning fog, movement all that marked it from the gray trunks around it. "I can't yawn and stealth at the same time!" came a muttered reply.

"Put a sock on it, McLean!" David growled back. "Better yet, put one *in* it!"

"It's socks that's the trouble," the soft voice retorted. "*You're* the one made me wear two pairs; they're makin' me walk funny!"

"You *always* walk funny! 'Sides, it's usually cold enough this early this time of year to need 'em!"

"You're *both* gonna be walkin' funny if you don't can it," a third voice broke in, from the head of the three-man file. David froze in mid-stalk, cheeks hot with embarrassment garnished with irritation. The fog was thicker here: a shroud of white around what should be bright-leaved oaks and maples, now orange-pink and mauve and pastel yellow. The ground was steep: a mountainside.

McLean—Alec—disappeared entirely, save for the rasp of his breathing. Silence went before—until suddenly a form solidified a yard from David's nose. He started, jerked his .308 half-around from reflex, then lowered the barrel sheepishly as that shape resolved into a compact, serious-looking youth an inch or so shorter than he. Gold-framed glasses hid hazel eyes, while near-black hair masked the forehead beneath a camouflage cap that was ironic counterpoint to the blaze orange vest Georgia law required of hunters in deer season; wide cheekbones narrowed to a pointed chin below very red lips for a boy. Aikin "Mighty Hunter" Daniels, it was. David's number three buddy after Alec and Calvin McIntosh, Alec's *oldest* friend—and present nemesis.

Black brows furrowed Aikin's forehead as he frowned. "Okay, guys: five minute break, then quiet, okay? *Absolute* quiet! Watch where you put your feet; ease 'em down *softly*, and try to remember that we're *supposed* to be hunting the wariest thing there is 'round here. Something that can smell the soap you washed with this mornin', and hear when you fantasize too hard about Winona Ryder."

David discovered an oak near enough to flop against—which he did. Alec remanifested and claimed its twin, propping the old Enfield Aikin had loaned him against the trunk. "I don't need to *fantasize* about anyone!" David snorted.

"And I don't *usually* have to bitch at you 'bout bein' quiet!"

"Old age," David yawned, as he massaged his thighs through cammo fatigues, surprised his legs were so tight. Alec wasn't the only one having trouble moving, and three miles uphill at o-bright-thirty didn't help.

"Twenty's, old?"

"Two years past your sexual peak," Alec observed.

"Will you get *off* it?"

Aikin rolled his eyes at David. "This is what comes of watchin' *Emmanuel VII* last night 'stead of cashin' in early. Deer can *smell* testosterone."

"So *that's* why you were in the john so long this morning," Alec giggled.

"Put a *sock*— Oh shit! Forget I said that!"

"You wish!"

Aikin simply glowered. "Why, oh why, did I listen when you asked to come along?"

" 'Cause I begged so prettily," Alec shot back sweetly. "You and Dave can't have *all* the fun."

"Yeah, Aik," David broke in, from where he was scratching his shoulders against the bark of his tree, "I mean, you and me made this a ritual when we were what? Thirteen? Now we're college men. That's long enough to hold out on anybody. We—"

"*We* take it seriously," Aikin interrupted. "I don't have to stop every five minutes to *explain* stuff to you!"

David shrugged. "It'll make a man out of 'im."

"Think of it as advancing my education," Alec added helpfully. "I learn how to shoot Bambi. I also learn what the big deal is about shooting Bambi, and thereby learn more about my two—present half hour apparently excluded—best buddies."

"You've been huntin' before," David reminded him.

"Squirrels."

"Killer instinct's killer instinct."

" 'Better A Hunter Than A Gatherer Be,' " Aikin quoted the bumper sticker on his pickup. "And as for the big deal about shootin' Bambi—yucky phrase— you don't seem to mind *eatin'* Bambi—or his mom, or Thumper, or any of his other furry friends when Dave or me serve 'em up pan-fried! And you were Mr. Brave Guy at the wildlife supper last year!"

"Yeah," David agreed with a smirk. "Even *I* won't eat mountain oysters."

"I didn't know what they were, *okay*?"

" 'Sides," Aikin went on, "you've got a vested interest in this one. Whatever I get today's the main course for my Thanksgiving bash."

"Presuming you get *anything*."

"I may *not*, if we don't get on with it!"

"You said five minutes," Alec noted. "We've still got two."

"Anal retentive," Aikin muttered. "And anyway, what *is* this about you wantin' the blood? You never gave me a straight answer last night."

David stiffened abruptly and shot Alec a warning glance. *He* knew exactly why, and the reason was essentially unbelievable. Alec *knew* he knew, but Aik was supposed to be totally in the dark—and hopefully would stay that way. *Watch it!* he mouthed, where Aikin couldn't see. He drew his finger across his throat for emphasis.

Alec patted a thermos-shaped bulge in his vest's game-pocket. "It's for a project." Which was not—quite—a lie.

"You're a computer nerd! What do *you* need deer blood for?"

Alec ignored Aikin's taunt—and David's warning. "I'm also taking Geology 101, in which I have to do a project, which is to test a bunch of minerals with supposed arcane properties against those same properties under scientific conditions—which should be of interest to you, Mr. GameGod! Unfortunately, I can't do like the Romans and drink wine from an amethyst cup to see if it keeps you from gettin' drunk—but I *can* soak a bloodstone in blood, to see if *that's* got any measurable effect."

"So why does it have to be deer blood?" Aikin asked pointedly. "I can get all the beef blood you want from the animal science folks."

"Yeah, well, my assumption is that stuff like that arose with paleolithic hunters, and they didn't *have* animal science folks—or domestic cattle. I figure the closer to original conditions—"

"You're gonna sit naked in the woods with an atlatl?"

Alec reached for his fly. "*Want* me to?"

Aikin grunted, then glared at David. "You got a hidden agenda too?" he asked abruptly.

The question caught David off guard, but he covered with a shrug. "Wouldn't be hidden if I talked about it, would it?"

"What if I invoke the Vow?" Aikin countered so recklessly that David wondered if something was bugging him that he wasn't letting on—besides Alec's presence. Something minor that had caught fire all in a rush, and blazed up past control—which was Aikin's style on those rare occasions when he lost it. Trouble was, the guy had guessed true.

"I would ask that you not do that," David replied carefully. "If there was, it'd be personal—*family* personal."

"One hint?"

David gnawed his lip. Dammit, why was Aik *doing* this? He, who a moment before had been urging silence, the most private of the entire MacTyrie Gang. More to the point, why did he have to invoke the oath he and the other Gangsters had made in ninth grade to always be straight with each other, to always answer sincere questions honestly, to hold back *nothing* that did not violate confidences conferred outside their circle?

Family personal . . .

Without warning, the memories ambushed him:

. . . himself, age thirteen (but viewed from without, as by an observer), sprawled on his bed in jeans and sockfeet, reading Dune *for the first time, in that down time between afterschool chores and supper. The distant knock on the back door he'd almost tuned out; the low buzz of voices; then his mom's, very clearly, gasping "Oh, God, no!" And then his uncle (great-*

uncle, technically) *Dale Sullivan, appearing at his door white-faced, and his strange, calm voice saying, "I just got a call from Beirut . . ."*

And then a fast-forward of others:

. . . a closed-casket funeral in a small mountain church; lots of food, lots of crying; a burial in a hillside cemetery; a pervasive numbness that gave way to a silent, private anger . . .

. . . himself, alone, at sunset, with the mountains at his back and the sanguine smear of the Sullivan Cove Road bisecting the valley before him, and Bloody Bald (too much blood, *he thought,* far too much) *catching the rays of a dying sun* (dying son, *he remembered think-ing*) *to the west. Him in his favorite jeans and sneak-ers, and a T-shirt proclaiming "Hard Rock Cafe: Tbilisi (Opening Soon)," with this very same Christmas gift Remington .308 in white-knuckled hands, firing twenty-one times into the crimsoning sky, as though to slay an unfair God where he sat on an undeserved throne . . .*

"Seven years," David whispered finally, blinking away a tear he hoped no one saw, hoping, likewise, that the reference was sufficiently obscure.

Alec—who clearly caught it—vented a sigh of relief. Aikin nodded. "I guess that'll have to do," he grumbled. "Now, if you guys are *quite* finished, I suggest we stand here, very quietly, and think about nothing but the backstrap you will *not* be eating if we don't let *Homo sapiens neanderthalensis* take over for *Home sapiens . . . IBMis!*"

Alec fumbled for his rifle.

"And for God's sakes," Aikin added, "will you point that thing at the *sky!*"

(*Killing God,* the thought recycled. *Slaying the au-thor of bad news . . .*)

Alec bared his teeth, but Aikin's eyes went wide and wary as he raised a hand sharply, signing silence. Alec looked confused, but David nodded acknowledgment.

He'd caught it too: a rustle of leaves in a certain cadence, a rhythm of step and pause. Deer, almost certainly—large, close by, and approaching.

Stupid, too—or deaf—to have ignored the racket
they'd been making. Normally one climbed a tree, sat
a stand, and waited, silent as the grave, motionless as
the dead. Normally the prey did not come to you.

(*Normally, good people didn't get blown to hamburger at twenty-one.*)

Having noticed it first, Aikin by tradition had first
shot. David, therefore, kept his place, though he likewise shouldered his rifle and drew a tentative bead,
peering through the scope.

Alec gawked.

Aikin was a man transformed. David could almost
see the veneer of civilization sloughing off his sturdy
shoulders as his buddy eased around in place, moving as if in slow motion; so carefully fabric did not
rasp against itself as he leaned against an oak, steadied his Winchester .30.06 against a limb, and with
calm deliberation set his eye to his scope, steel barrel
gleaming damply, poised . . . ready . . . waiting. His
ears, while small, stuck out slightly, and David could
imagine one twitching, as though to catch each loud-
ening rustle.

The softest of clicks, then, as Aikin released the
safety with his thumb . . .

More rustling, closer yet—and a gust of oddly warm
wind thinned the fog upslope to gauze, as if a gate had
opened and set the silent air to dancing. David caught
a blur of movement: a graying of the white; a flash of
ivory above, that was surely sunlight on antler tines
raised above the mist. He held his breath.

The beast was no more than fifty yards away now—
impossibly close, given the ruckus they'd been raising.
Any second the buck—for clearly it was, and a fine
one—would prance into that patch of brightness that
had awakened between those two hickories, and Aik

would have a clear shot: uphill and with no brush between.

Soon . . .

Very soon . . .

A finger eased to the rifle's trigger, though David knew beyond doubt that Aik would never shoot at sound alone, never fire at an uncertain target. He looked back at the shadow in the fog. His eyes . . .

"Shit!" Aikin spat and dropped his rifle.

"Oh shit!" David gulped in turn—as a too-familiar tingle set fire to his eyes, filling them with tears as he lowered his own weapon—

—And they all saw a cervine shape bound into the blaze of light between the hickories and pause there at gaze, coat white as winter snow, dark eyes huge and frightened. And far too intelligent, when the buck stared at them, aloof and accusingly—and with one vast surge of muscle, bounded across the ridge and out of sight.

The wind whipped up at that; the warm air shifted. The burning in David's eyes ceased as suddenly as it had come, but a different fire had awakened in those Aikin turned upon him, as he slumped against his tree. *"Goddamn,* Sullivan; what the *fuck* was that?"

"What . . . do you *think* it was?" David panted, as he caught his breath and backed away—into Alec.

"Wow, did you *see* that guy?" Alec gasped.

"I'm . . . not sure *what* I saw," Aikin managed shakily. "It was white, of course, which is rare as hell by itself; but I thought for a minute that— Oh, never mind."

"What?" David persisted, as a cold clot of sick dread turned to ice in his gut.

"Its rack . . . You notice anything about its rack?"

"Like what?"

"That it didn't curve out and around like a whitetail's is supposed to. That it swept straight back like a . . . like a friggin' *elk!*"

"Elk?" from Alec.

David ignored him. "We don't *have* elk 'round here."

"Of *course* we don't!" Aikin cried. "But if you hadn't spooked it 'fore I could figure out what was goin' on—!"

"It also had stripes!" Alec blundered on obliviously. "Stripes—like a zebra. Faint, but you could see 'em— or *I* could: streams of silver against the white. Like something out of—"

"No it didn't!" David broke in desperately, kicking Alec in the shin.

Aikin eyed him narrowly. "Yes it did. Only I'd say they were more like what you get on a bongo antelope."

"Maybe," Alec mumbled, too late. "I dunno."

"Or *maybe*," Aikin whispered, "on something out of . . . Faerie?"

Chapter II:
Worlds, Tracks, and Blood

*(Nichols Mountain,
Enotah National Forest, Georgia)*

". . . Faerie?"

Aikin's last word was still melting into the thick cool air. And with it, the final vestige of Mighty Hunter vanished, leaving only a frustrated junior forestry jock who feared he'd said too much.

. . . Faerie . . .

He could tell by the way David's blue eyes glittered, the way normally merry lips hardened to a thin grim line as his jawline tightened beneath its well-tanned curves, that he'd struck a naked nerve. And most times that would've bugged him; most times he'd already have been seething with guilt at having deliberately trespassed on taboo ground.

But he'd just flat out had *enough*! They'd been at it for over four years now, Dave and Alec had. Never mind Runnerman and Gary and Dave's girlfriend, Liz Hughes—and that new Cherokee guy, Calvin McIntosh, and who-knew-who-else: disappearing unexpectedly, and not explaining shit when they returned wearing very grown-up shadows on their faces, joy and wonder in their eyes he'd not been asked to share.

And there was no reason he *shouldn't* share those things! No way he was any different from the others—*including* the entire Gang—who'd walked upon the—what did Dave call 'em? Straight Tracks? After all, wasn't his appellation, besides Mighty Hunter,

GameGod? Earned because he was a master at creating fantasy worlds for role-playing adventures. Which was cold comfort when the rest of his buds were having real ones.

Of course they literally *couldn't* tell him—at first, not Dave and Alec and Liz. They'd finally confessed that much: how they'd been bound by a magical geas not to speak of what they'd seen in certain places, done in certain others. But there were ways around injunctions like that, ways to avoid direct questions: to listen without being seen, to pause outside doors or tent flaps or windows, to creep silently back when you'd loudly walked away. Dave himself acknowledged him to be the quietest person he knew, save Calvin. But even Mad David Sullivan didn't know how quiet Aikin Daniels could be, how stealthily he could move when frustration gave him cause.

And so he'd learned a few things, by repute and a scatter of begrudged conversations. But not once had he ventured in the flesh to that mysterious realm he'd just named. "Faerie," he repeated, to force himself to confront it—and further lay the goad to David's soul. "Or *Galunlati*?" he added, louder—though his voice shook in a way he loathed.

"Prob'ly," David grunted, not looking at him, though the resigned slump of his shoulders proclaimed as loudly as words that he was about to relent. Alec would've caved in already, had he not been taking cues from Dave. Once, Aikin admitted wistfully, *he'd* have been calling the shots. He'd never fully accepted his demotion to Alec's number two bud.

Nor did he break eye contact with Alec as he slowly reset the Winchester's safety, folded himself down in place, and with deliberate nonchalance laid the weapon athwart his thighs: a woodland king with his sword of state. "If we're gonna keep on bein' friends," he announced, "we *gotta* talk."

"I thought you wanted to hunt!" David choked—and Aikin knew he'd won.

"I can *hunt* any time. You won't talk about *this* stuff any time, and I don't feel like workin' up nerve to hit you with it again."

"It'd take all day, to tell right."

"I know a bunch of it anyway," Aikin countered, "the stuff about you havin' the Second Sight and seein' the Sidhe ridin' through your dad's back forty one summer night. The magic ring one of 'em gave you . . ."

"Hmmm," Alec mused. "Maybe we oughta ask what *you* know."

Aikin ignored hm. "How 'bout we start with the deer? What was it? More to the point, where'd it come from? What's it *doin'* here?"

David sighed resignedly and slumped back against his tree. "Okay," he began, "first . . . I don't *know* what it was—exactly. Obviously it was *some* kind of cervid. Equally obviously it wasn't any kind that lives in this World—"

"I'd *guess* it was from Faerie," Alec inserted, casting a nervous eye at his glowering friends. "Critters from Galunlati tend to be *our* critters only more so: Pleistocene America and newer—plus odd lots, like the *uktena* or the water-panthers—"

"Hold it!" Aikin broke in. "First things first. What do you mean by World? The way *you* said it, I mean?"

Another sigh. "Don't want much, do you?" David chided. "But the best way to describe 'em, I guess, is to think of *our* World—our primary physical reality—as a toy globe; and then think of the *other* Worlds as pieces of wet tissue paper torn into random shapes and thrown on it. They stick and conform to the globe's shape and depend on it for support; but they also wrinkle, at which points they *don't* touch our World—and they don't cover it all over anyway. Oh, but they *can* land on top of each other; and if our World disappeared, they'd collapse into mush. Somehow our gravity extends there and maintains 'em, even though most of 'em really do have finite edges—you really can walk off the end of the world in some of 'em. But anyway, there're a *bunch* of these Worlds that overlap and interconnect, but most of the ones *we* know about overlap northwest Europe and the eastern U.S. The most . . . accessible ones are collectively called Faerie; and the inhabitants—the human-type inhabitants—all arrived here from one place and settled 'em, but not all at once."

He paused for breath, then went on. "So like I said, there're three main Faerie realms separated by some kind of tenuous quasi ocean that doesn't always exist, as best I can tell. And each of these realms overlaps our World at a different place—and time, so I've been told, which I don't understand at all, since they all exist at the *same* time in their own space. The closest one's Tir-Nan-Og, which covers the present-day southeastern U.S.—I'm not sure where the boundaries are, but they go at least as far south as Cumberland Island, where they've got some kinda port where the ships from Annwyn arrive. Then there's Erenn, which overlaps Ireland in the eighteenth century, and Annwyn, which overlaps medieval Wales. I *think* there used to be one called Norwald, which was destroyed by iron, which is mondo dangerous stuff there 'cause it's supposedly never cooled since . . . the Big Bang, I guess. And there're all kinds of pocket universes and stuff that bud off the big ones, that can be reached from just one point or World. Like, there was a tower on an island *inside* Stone Mountain—"

"Fine," Aikin interrupted. "So what about the deer?"

"Actually, I was sorta gettin' to that by a long road when I started in about the Worlds," David replied. "See, the Worlds connect with each other via something we call Straight Tracks, though I've also heard 'em called Ley Lines and a couple other things. They're apparently lines of 'cosmic force,' or some such. Might be sort of solidified gravity, or they could be related to cosmic strings—that's what Calvin's lady thinks. But what's major is that they connect *all* the Worlds. They can exist where there's literally nothing outside. And they even reach to other stars. The Sidhe—they're kinda the Faerie high nobility—got here on 'em from somewhere else, though they're interfertile with our kind, in spite of it. So anyway, these Tracks run all across our World, unseen—'cept that I can see 'em with my Second Sight, which you know about—"

"The *deer*, Dave, the *deer*!"

"Oh yeah—well, *normally* I'd say it got on the Tracks in Faerie and got off here. 'Cept that doesn't make a lotta sense, 'cause to get on or off a Track requires a certain skill—which nobody *I* know in our World has. Folks in Faerie can do it, and sometimes animals from there. But the thing that's buggin' me about the big white guy, is that there's no Track anywhere near here. Nuada—he's one of the Lords of the Sidhe—showed me where all the local ones were one time—at least the ones that connect with Faerie—and the closest, which is in the woods behind my folks' place, is still more than three miles away. Also, there's the matter of 'the substance of this World' "—David made quote marks with his fingers. "What that means is that beings tend to wear the . . . matter, I guess you could say, of whatever World they're native to, and the farther from their own World they get, and the longer they stay away *in their own substance*, the more that World'll draw 'em back—like a bungee cord, or whatever. Some of the Sidhe can get around this by putting on the substance of our World—in which form they can use iron, but lose most of their magic. And how this connects with old whitey is that animals generally *can't* do that, which means that even if one somehow got on the Tracks in Faerie and got off here, there'd be a draw on its instinct that'd keep it close to where it came in."

"So *this* guy," Aikin exclaimed, "evidently got here some *other* way!"

"And the only one that makes sense is that it didn't get here by the Tracks at all, but came straight through the World Walls, which it shouldn't have been able to do."

"Unless," Alec noted, "the World Walls are weak somewhere nearby, which can happen—'specially where there's lots of iron in our World."

"Which that weird wind we felt right after we saw it supports."

"The . . . World Walls," Aikin mused. "They're the . . . interface between Worlds, right?"

David grinned. "You're in the wrong major, man."

Aikin grinned back in spite of himself. "I puzzled a lot of this out a long time ago, guys. I mean, a lot of it's in books, if you can get hold of the right ones. Some of it's even in gaming manuals."

"Which are not, however, to be trusted," David snorted.

"So what now?" Alec prompted. "Seeing how you've got us started."

"I . . . don't know," Aikin sighed. "Much as I'd like to hear more of this, we've gotta get back to hunting. So how 'bout if we just settle for a promise to talk about it again—like real soon. Or—" He paused, as another idea struck him. "What I'd *really* like is for you guys to *show* me something."

"No can do," David shot back immediately. "Sorry."

Aikin felt his anger rising to a head again, and had to fight to keep his voice low. "Well *goddamn*, guys! What the fuck have I gotta *do*? I mean—"

"We can't access the Tracks," Alec told him. "Shoot, Dave can't even *see* 'em—or sense 'em, or whatever he does—unless they're activated, which means the Sidhe are traveling on 'em. It's like a wire glowing red when it conducts electricity."

Aikin's eyes narrowed suspiciously. "But aren't there

other ways? Can't you guys *look* between the Worlds, or something?"

"The World Walls weaken at the quarters of the day," David admitted. "Sometimes you can see stuff then."

"Except there's nothing to see 'round here," Alec added. "And the sun's already up."

"But—" Aikin began—and broke off abruptly. His sharp ears had caught a rustling in the leaves across the ridge. The white stag returning? Maybe? *Probably?*, he prayed.

Only . . . this didn't sound exactly right. There was something different about the pacing of these steps, something more . . . tentative . . . more uncertain. More mundane. Yet surely a *real* deer wouldn't approach so close to three far-too-talkative hunters, however low their voices.

Unless the remnants of the fog had muted their tones—that and the mass of mountain 'twixt here and the quarry.

And at that exact moment, what he'd taken for a spray of sweet gums along the ridge crest moved—to reveal, sixty yards away, silhouetted against a sky now far more blue than pink or purple, a small spike buck: probably one that had been a fawn last season. And just ahead of it, a much larger doe—both good old American *Odocoileus virginianus*.

Fortunately, Dave and Alec had caught his reaction, if not yet the focus thereof, and quieted obligingly. Barely daring to breathe, Aikin twisted around onto his belly, to sprawl along the slope like a grunt in one of those Vietnam movies he'd obsessed on a few years back. A squint through the scope confirmed the target—the doe, which had lowered its narrow head to nibble along the ground: a perfect profile, with virtually no fog between. Once more he released the safety. Crosshairs found the heart, then slid toward the neck: quicker death that way.

And then instinct took over. He got that odd sensation he always did when prey was in his sights, of a thousand generations of elder Danielses peering over his shoulder as he enacted that most ancient of survival rites. Nor did he choose—consciously—when to pull the trigger.

Yet one instant there was absolute silence, the next, a boom loud enough to wake the world—and a solid slab of fiberglass stock slammed back into his shoulder: a shadow of the pain he'd just inflicted.

But what he saw—not through the scope, not any longer—was the little buck leaping away and the big doe collapsing where she stood, a bullet—*his* bullet—in her spine.

"Way to go!" David cheered behind him.

"Al*right*!" Alec echoed, already scrambling up the slope.

Aikin hauled him back by an ankle, sprawling him among the leaves. "Not yet!" he hissed—for no obvious reason since his shot had just put every critter in earshot on red alert. "We gotta hold off a couple minutes. I could've just stunned 'er."

Alec blinked uncomprehendingly. "So?"

"They've been known to come to when you're right at 'em," Aikin informed him patiently.

"*So?*"

"How'd *you* like to have your throat laid open by a hoof?"

"But the blood . . ."

"Oughta be plenty in the thoracic cavity," Aikin assured him with a fiendish grin, as he reached for his knife, "—from bone splinters, if nothing else. And I tell you what, McLean, *you* can have first slice!"

"You can carry her, too," David chimed in gleefully, with a wider grin of his own.

Aikin suppressed a chuckle. "We *will* talk more," he told them. "And I don't mean about hunting."

Interlude I:
Live Audience

(Banba's Wood—
Tir-Nan-Og—approaching Samhain)

Gargyn took a deep breath and strode from the shelter of head-high ferns onto the gleaming gravel of the High Road where it turned west through Banba's Wood. He wore his best kilt, a fresh white linen shirt, and the black felt hat Borbin had made for special days. Beneath it, his crimson thatch was as neat as could be managed with a broken onyx comb one of the Seelie lords had abandoned; and his face, hands, and knees were as clean as a summer sky. His bare feet could have used some work; then again, they *had* worked all afternoon to bring him here, in quest of a certain meeting.

Bad luck breeds blind hope, he told himself, repeating what Borbin had declared the day before, when he'd finally recovered wit enough to dare the forest where the Littl'un had first seen the wyrm. The one from which it—or one of its kin—had roared out yesterday morn. He'd found no dragon—no bloodred shev-ro-lay—but what he *had* unearthed was far more disconcerting.

A hole.

Not a dirt-walled digging full of decaying leaves and the odd feisty beetle, however, but a full-out *hole*: a strip forty paces long and half that wide, where the forest floor simply *wasn't*. Ragged at the borders it was, and with a few roots and tufts of grass clutching grimly

30

at the edges, where they had not yet dissolved—but mostly simply a patch of *nothing* where a hunk of his hold had been. And even as he'd stood gaping, a stone right at the marge—just by his left foot, in fact—had sifted away to . . . gone.

He'd mumbled a certain Word then, and held his mouth a particular way, and, with one eye open and the other closed, had peered through the World Walls that bordered that troublesome not-place, and into the Lands of Men.

It was iron, sure enough: a long, ripply fence of the cursed ever-hot stuff half as high as he was tall, endlessly long, and fixed to a series of wooden poles set in the earth between two stretches of quick-folks' High Road. A trifling work, for them, Borbin had informed him, something they built beside their roads to keep their shev-ro-lays from grazing—or butting heads. But the World Walls were thin at that point, and with all that new iron there, the Mortal World had simply burned through. Fortunately, most quick-folk were numb as rocks when it came to matters of Power and couldn't look into Faerie anyway. Most would see nothing at all—an instant's disorientation, a breath of too-fresh air, and they'd be none the wiser—save, perhaps, in their dreams. A few *might* glimpse a patch of fog, and the very talented *maybe* the shadow of something old, alive, and rooted—like a tree. Only those with the Sight must needs be wary, and they were scarce as white krakens in the distant sea.

But there were more of 'em all the time: seers, quick-folk, big iron things, and holes in the World Walls, all; and Gargyn was tired of fretting about his clan. Which was why he was here, in his very best clothes, waiting for one of the Seelie folk to ride by and hear his case. One often did this time of day, Borbin's brother had confided over an ale: one who'd harken to even a humble bodach's woes.

He didn't have long to wait—far less time than three

sturdy quick-folk lads took to tote a dead deer two mortal miles—before a subtle pounding began to jolt up through his ankles. And very soon after that, he heard the scratchy thunder of hooves at a steady run.

He almost fled when she careened around the corner, so tall and fair and fey that lady was. But then she saw him, and reined her smoked-silver stallion, and smiled at him like lightning at stormy dawn—and Gargyn could not move, perilous though Seelie folk might be. She wore no crown, nor suffered any escort, yet was she clearly a queen. She also looked dangerously preoccupied.

"Hail, master bodach," she called from the saddle, as her gown of pewter, charcoal, and greenish gray settled around her, like waves beneath a nervous sky. "Is there a reason you assay Lugh's High Road on so fine an afternoon?"

Gargyn felt heat rise in his cheeks and decided to ponder the ground, but the woman's eyes caught his and drew his gaze like a moth toward the flame of her own. Fierce, she looked, and angry, though not, he felt, at him. But sympathetic she likewise seemed, and so he told his tale.

She listened with patience and silence, then nodded when he was done. "Your plight is not rare," she acknowledged, "though your own king does not seem to deem these . . . erosions worth his note. Then again, he has *never* cared much for you small fey, has he? As though you were a blight on the bloom of his oh-so-perfect realm. But Rhiannon of Ys knows your worth and would welcome you to my shores—were there not so many of you so suddenly, all fleeing these troublesome holes. Yet come, if you will, and I will comfort you, for I have found a World where you could dwell in peace forever."

Gargyn chewed his lip. " 'At's as much as we could 'ope for, Lady," he sighed. "But—well, where *is* this place? I can't say I've 'eard of it."

"Ys touches the Mortal World underwater," Rhiannon informed him. "But it overlaps another land on the other side: one in which Power burns more brightly than in the Mortal World. I would settle you small folk there."

Gargyn's eyes narrowed sharply. *"Would?* Does 'at mean you're not sure?"

"Access is awkward," the queen admitted. "Yet a means exists in the Mortal World to erect a permanent gate between my realm and this other."

"But—"

"Enough!" Rhiannon snapped. "You have your dreams, I have mine, and mine require that I mold *another's* dreaming." And with that, she set heels to her horse's flanks and flashed away.

Gargyn watched her as long as he could. And wondered what Borbin would think about moving.

Chapter III:
Rocks and Mages

(Lookout Rock, Georgia—
Saturday, October 24—noonish)

"Well, *that* little grossness is done," Aikin sighed, so
softly Alec could scarcely hear him above the whoosh-
ing jingle of the water that slid down fifty feet of black
rocks into a small pool two yards to his right. "All them
guts be out and gone—*like we shoulda done to start
with*," he added, more loudly, over his shoulder.

Alec looked up warily from where, stripped to his
cammo fatigues, he was attempting to wash everything
above the belt in an escaped tributary of the pond—
one whose normal clarity was clouded with swirls of
red from the abundant supply that stained nearly all
his visible skin.

Blood. *Deer* blood, courtesy of "friends" with
screwed-up senses of humor.

True, Aik was also ensanguined, as was Dave; but
he'd got the worst of it. And he should've known better,
dammit! Should've expected that, as neophyte deer
hunter and default group geek, he'd run afoul of some
stupid initiation rite. With his first squirrel, at age thirteen, it had been smears of blood down either cheek,
marked with David's fingers. He'd expected the same
with the doe, though she clearly wasn't *his* kill.

What he *hadn't* counted on was for Aik to pass him
his Rakestraw hunting knife, point at the dime-sized
hole at the base of the poor beast's neck, and state
bluntly, "It's time you got your hands bloody."

He'd done it, too, had sawed right on in there—with his teeth clenched and his stomach threatening to revolt at the stench of hot viscera. And there'd been God's plenty of blood, sure enough, more than enough to fill the Thermos that sat on the rock shelf behind him with what, just that morning, had carried something's life.

But what he absolutely hadn't anticipated was that David would grab him from behind just as he was securing the cap, while Aik thrust his arms into the wound up to the elbows, and thus begored, tried to smear the yucky stuff across his face—*and* bare belly and chest, which, despite his best efforts, David's deft hands had exposed.

And what his so-called friends hadn't counted on (nor he) was the cap on the Thermos not being as secure as any of them had thought, and that his frantic thrashings (better than quiescent acceptance, though he'd known he was doomed from the start) would unseat it—lavishly anointing all three with the gruesome contents. Dave had caught it in the face; Aik from chin to groin. A free-for-all had ensued. In the end, they'd emptied the Thermos—much of it down David's britches.

At least Aik had been sport enough to refill it.

But what *none* of 'em had counted on—or had forgotten in a year—was how heavy a medium-sized doe was when you had to drag her close to three miles. Hand-rasping, leg-numbing, shoulder-straining numb. Even in two-man shifts.

"*Really* should've field-dressed her where she lay," Aikin persisted, as he skinned out of his T-shirt, squatted to Alec's left, and commenced to scrub his hands.

" 'Cept we'd have scooped up half a mountain's worth of crud inside her," David muttered absently, as he joined them. Behind him, the lately-eviscerated deer dangled by its hind legs from a dying pine between the lean-to they sometimes camped in and the impressive stone outcrop that gave Lookout Rock its name. Like his companions, he'd shed his shirt. Unlike them, he'd likewise doffed his boots. He looked unaccountably grim.

"Yeah, but we had a start on it already," Aikin countered with a smirk. "I mean, given that old Frank Buck here split the friggin' diaphragm so the guts started oozin' out a mile down the trail—and we're *still* gonna have to lug it on down to your house! *Right McLean?*"

"*You're* the forestry jock!" Alec growled. "You're the fool who handed *me* the knife. *I've* skinned three squirrels in my life and dissected one frog and a fetal pig. I don't know crap about deer anatomy."

"You guys got a spare pair of pants?" David asked abruptly.

"Wash what you got or go nekkid," Aikin snorted. "Ain't nobody gonna see but us and your folks."

"Gosh," Alec added, deadpan, "you mean you're not gonna browbeat us into takin' a dip?"

"Pants," David snapped. "Now! If you got 'em. I don't feel like puttin' up with any more shit."

"Gym shorts in my backpack," Alec grunted. "If I had any sense, I'd make you beg."

Aikin eyed him askance. "You bring *clothes* on a half day hike?"

"I have . . . friends I don't entirely trust."

David ignored them, but retrieved the shorts, swapped them for his cammos and Fruit of the Looms, which he left in the pool to soak, and picked his way barefoot to the verge of the overlook, where he stood staring west to where the near-perfect cone of Bloody Bald lifted its quartzite crown above the waters of Langford Lake. Eventually he sat down: silent, still, and staring, shivering every now and then in the autumn air.

Alec stowed the Thermos in his backpack and regarded him dully. It really *was* getting to him this time. Then again, the anniversary of the death of David's favorite, role model, and namesake uncle had never actually coincided with his and Aik's ritual first-deer-hunt-of-the-season. What was it he'd said when Aik had asked what was bugging him? Seven years? Had it really been that long since David-the-Elder's death? Seven years was a long time to miss somebody, a long time to nurse so much pain.

God knew *he* knew about missing somebody, about a heart clogged thick with loss.

For in spite of what logic—and David, all too frequently—told him about how ruthlessly she had used him, he still missed a slim, dark-haired Faery woman he'd only known as Eva. Aife, actually; she'd been a partisan of Ailill's, the Faery lord David had thwarted all those years back. In revenge, she'd disguised herself as a mortal, put on the substance of the Lands of Men, and in that form used his own jealousy of David's newborn love for Liz Hughes as a means of wreaking vengeance on Lugh Samildinach, the local Faery king.

Somewhere in there he'd let her pop his cherry, never dreaming that she'd wanted not *him*, but merely his seed, so as to strengthen her magical hold. He'd felt like singing then—and like putting a bullet through his skull when he'd learned the truth soon after. And for a while he'd hated Eva. Yet there at the last, when she lay dying in Uncle Dale Sullivan's yard (as much as the Sidhe *could* die) she'd admitted that in spite of herself, she'd come to love him too. A flame had awakened then, and that flame had never entirely died.

"You're not the only one who hasn't forgotten," he told David, as he came to stand behind him. Their shadows were tiny before them; it was breathing hard on noon.

"Seven years," David gritted. "Seven bloody years

since the best man who ever lived got blown to pieces on a Middle Eastern street."

"Less than that since the only woman I ever loved betrayed me, redeemed herself—and left me all over again."

"And at the end of seven years the Queen of the Faeries pays a tithe to hell," Aikin finished, as he joined them. "That's what it says in 'Tam Lin.'"

"It's not like that," David snorted. "No more than sex is like jackin' off."

"Don't remind me," Alec groaned.

They ignored him.

"I haven't forgotten," Aikin said eventually.

"Sex?" David wondered. "Or jacking off?"

"That it's noon! That's a *between* time, right? One of the times the World Walls grow thin."

"That's what the books say," David spat. "Why should the truth be any different?"

"Seven years since something hurt you," Aikin went on. "And three since something else hurt Alec. I can't help you guys, but you can keep me from hurting anymore."

David rose explosively. Alec stepped back to let him pass—and saw his friends glaring at each other, chest to chest: fair-skinned blond against dark brunette; gymnast-slim versus wrestler-stocky; blue eyes vying with hazel. The air was taut with incipient violence, though Alec had no idea who would strike first—or why. But then David exhaled loudly, and with that, the hardness of his anger that had made the very earth seem frail and weak melted away, leaving a soft, resigned core. "We'll try the easy way first, if you don't mind," he said tersely.

Aikin looked briefly confused, but nodded.

"Come here, then," David told him, grabbing him by the arm. "Step on my feet—no, both of 'em: yours atop mine, and barefoot would probably work best—skin on skin usually does."

Aikin shrugged free long enough to remove his boots and socks, then eased onto David's feet once more. David wrapped his left arm around him to balance them both. "Okay, now look over my right shoulder toward Bloody Bald."

"What am I supposed to see?"

"I'm not gonna tell you—though you probably know already. Just look at Bloody Bald!"

Aikin did, resting his chin (he was five-five-point-five versus David's five-seven and Alec's five-foot-ten) on his friend's shoulder. David took a deep breath, drew Aikin into a tighter embrace—and clapped his free hand atop the shorter boy's head. "Everything between my hands and my feet is mine!" he cried. "Now see, Aikin; *see!*"

Alec expected some reaction. Probably he expected Aik to go stiff, or cry out in wonder or awe. Instead, he remained as he was: inert in David's arms.

"See anything?" David prompted, when perhaps ten seconds had passed.

"The wind on the water," Aikin murmured, quoting Malory. "Maybe a shimmer on the mountaintop; *maybe* a glittery spikiness up there."

"No castle?"

"Coulda been, I don't know."

David released him. Aikin staggered back, face bitter with disappointment. "You should've seen a whole lot more. The High King of Tir-Nan-Og's got a friggin' *castle* up there."

"Well, I missed it!"

Alec scratched his head. "The World Walls—" he began.

Aikin spun to face him. "What about 'em?"

Alec started. "Oh, uh . . . well, it just occurred to me that we've seen evidence that the World Walls were thin back up on the mountain. So maybe they're *thicker* than usual around Lugh's palace. Shoot, maybe they're in a state of flux."

David scowled thoughtfully: a worried look in lieu of the anger, which seemed to have vanished as quickly as it had appeared. "God, I hope not. The last thing I need's trouble with *them*."

Aikin glared at him. "What's it got to do with you?"

"Nothing—I hope. But trouble in Faerie hereabouts has a tendency to . . . infect me."

"Cool," Aikin said. "I'm game."

"It won't make you happy," David countered. "It never does."

"I still wanta see."

"Tough."

Aikin regarded him steadily, a cold glint in his eyes. "What about that jewel in the pot you think I don't know Alec brought along," he whispered, with a smug grin. "What's it called? An *ulunsuti*?"

"Christ!" Alec grumbled. "What *don't* you know?"

"Tell him," David snapped. "Hell, *show* him. I don't care." He sat down again and stared at the recalcitrant mountain.

Alec puffed his cheeks and likewise sat, motioning Aikin down beside him. "If I'm gonna *talk* about it, I might as well show you," he agreed. Whereupon he reached around to snare his backpack. He held it in his lap while he rummaged inside, finally producing three objects. One was the Thermos of deer blood that had caused so much angst already; the second was an unglazed bowl the size of a big man's brainpan; and the last was a plain clay jar, simply shaped, and closed with a thick bark stopper. The Thermos he set to his right, the bowl in the center of the rough triangle they'd somehow formed, while he pried the lid off the jar and reached inside. An instant later, he drew out a hand-sized pouch of white-bleached buckskin, soft as suede and delicately nappy. Carefully unlacing it, he tipped the contents into his palm.

Aikin's breath hissed as Alec held it there, bright in

the sun, its glitter less hard than diamond, sharper than oil on water. Like amber, perhaps, or some types of plastic. Hand-sized it was, and roughly oval, milky-clear, with a red septum bisecting the center, perhaps to separate its two parts: real and unreal; animal and mineral; comprehensible and insane.

"The ulunsuti," David whispered, for Aikin's benefit—and probably for dramatic effect. "The jewel from the head of the great uktena."

"Which is a giant serpent that lives in Galunlati," Alec explained. "That's the Overworld of the Cherokee, if you don't already know. A shaman-type guy we know over there gave it to me—only I don't want it. It has assorted oracular powers, but you have to prime it with blood to effect anything useful. And once a year you have to feed it the blood of a large animal or it'll go mad—which so far, I'm pleased to say, has not occurred."

"Thus the reason for beggin' along on this trip?"

Alec nodded sheepishly. "Basically. See, I've been feeding it beef blood, but that's . . . not quite working anymore. I can't say *how* I know, but I feel like it needs the real thing: hot from the body of something wild."

"So could *we* maybe try something wild?" Aikin asked carefully. "I mean, given that you've gotta feed it anyway?"

Alec exchanged glances with David.

"I think we oughta cut your ears off," David growled.

"Let's do it," Alec sighed. "You know we're gonna have to sooner or later."

"We'll have to hurry then," David grunted. "We've *still* gotta lug Bambi's mom down the mountain, 'fore the meat goes bad."

In spite of himself, Alec hated what came next. He was a computer nerd—a protoscientist (lodged between chemistry and geology, at the moment). His world of preference was facts and formulae, cause and effect, predictable results, and logical rules—world without end, amen. It wasn't fair that *he*, of all unlikely folks, was saddled with the onus of such preposterous irrationalities as physical places with grounds, skies, and geological features that suddenly ended in *nothing*. Never mind endless tubes paved with golden light and walled with such unlikely entities as vast tangled hedges of thorn, a yard beyond which lay utter void. Never *mind* trying to figure out how the complex of chemicals that was blood, gleaned from a creature of this World, could prompt a clump of quasi crystal from another to peer into other times and places. There was *no* connection there: blood to crystal to vision; not like acid to base to alkaline. Not like $E = MC^2$. Not even like chaos theory and fractal geometry and fuzzy logic. And *absolutely* never mind how the damned crystal—the goddamned ulunsuti—knew the difference between domestic Guernsey and wild whitetail hot off the cloven hoof.

Yet here he was, still suffering the figurative ripples of his friends' near-confrontation; sitting half-naked on a mountainside, with his knees touching David's and Aikin's; pretending he was a shaman presiding at a rite he neither approved of nor understood.

David, to his left, looked nonplussed and bored. Aikin, by contrast, seemed anxious and apprehensive—and was trying very hard to hide both. "Pass the grue," he told the latter, and with that, he set the ulunsuti in the bowl.

And jerked reflexively. It was almost as though the jewel had shocked him, had reached for him in some hungry way, and nipped away an invisible piece of his flesh. Setting his jaw, he accepted the Thermos, unscrewed the cap, and tipped it over both crystal and bowl.

The blood was darker than he remembered, which surprised him, given how much of it he'd seen that day.

It also stank (he thought of it as a stench, at any rate; David and Aik rather liked it). And to his surprise, it gave off a faint warmth: subtle, but noticeable, where it flowed past his fingertips. Already the ulunsuti was filmed with crimson; already it was half-drowned in a sanguine pool.

He could almost feel its pleasure, too, almost hear a soundless purr of contentment, as the jewel drank its fill of whatever empowered it. He squinted at it, saw it slowly begin to glow; and as he did, an idea came to him: a chance for subtle revenge. Aik wanted magic, huh? Well, he'd give him magic. But Aik would also pay the price for being a dweeb.

"Dave," Alec muttered, "give Hunterman your knife. We've primed this thing already, but if it's gonna do its thing for him, *he* oughta provide the fuse."

Aikin eyed him dubiously. And took the weapon.

"Cut yourself," Alec told him. "Enough to draw blood that'll drip. Otherwise, you'd have to touch the crystal with the wound, and that might not be cool. Shoot, it *could* suck you dry, blood and . . . life force both. Right now it's both sated and hungry, so feed it, but don't risk yourself. And when you're done, stare at the septum and try to imagine—I dunno—imagine Bloody Bald with a veil over it, and then imagine that veil lifting. It's kinda hard to say, really; Liz usually does that kind of thing. Mostly it works best when you just sort of worry at it. But this close—"

"I get the message," Aikin broke in, as he drew the gleaming blade along his thumb. "Let's do it."

Though Aikin's attitude pissed him a little, Alec could think of no useful reply. Instead, he nodded at David and likewise stared at the septum, following the instructions he'd just passed on: to visualize the mountain a few miles away, and what lay unseen upon it.

For an instant, he saw nothing. But then the septum pulsed with ruby light—and reality ripped asunder as the whole world became a mass of faceted towers, flying arches, and extravagant gardens rushing at him at alarming speed.

Too fast! Far too fast! He resisted instinctively, tore his gaze away—

"Shit!" David gasped, as Alec met his eyes, neither of them daring to look directly at the crystal that pulsed like a strobe between them, making their skin seem to shift 'twixt dead and flayed.

"Double shit," Alec echoed, as the effect slowly faded. "*That's* never happened before."

"What?" From Aikin, who had likewise wrenched his attention from the stone and was staring at Alec with a mix of joy, awe, and terror.

"That sort of intense reaction," Alec gulped. "Not remote observation, but headlong rush!"

"Probably 'cause we used that kind of blood," David mused. "Or of us bein' so close to the target at what's still pretty near a magical time of day."

"Let's hope," Alec yawned. "And, dammit, I've got a mother-effer of a headache. Stuff like this always gives me one, but this is a real banger—and only from that little time!"

"I've got one too," David admitted. "Seems like I always forget about the side effects." And then he, too, was yawning.

Aikin rolled his eyes. "I wish you'd warned me about that—'cause I've *also* got one."

"The price of knowledge is pain," David chuckled—and yawned again.

"So now you know," Alec agreed. "It gives you a headache and puts you to sleep."

Aikin checked his watch. "Actually, I wouldn't mind a nap. We did get up early, and then we had to lug Bambi's mom—"

"And we've nowhere to be until supper," David finished, rising. "I just wish we'd fixed up the lean-to."

"See you in the Dreamtime," Alec murmured lazily, stretching out where he sat.

"Not if I see you first," David grinned, and sprawled beside him.

Aikin said nothing at all—because he was snoring.

Chapter IV:
Dreamseekers

(Lookout Rock, Georgia—
Saturday, October 24)

. . . a hand smooth as ivory, soft as silk brushing the hair from his brow. His head pillowed on a beautiful woman's lap, his eyes, half-closed, gazing upon a sky ablaze with the stars of Georgia summer . . .

"Alec," she breathed, and his heart skipped to hear his name whispered with that voice, through those lips that had so lately kissed him. He blushed, sure she had seen some sign of this wild inner joy that possessed him. Certainly she could have noted any shift in his face at all, any change in the whole of his body—for he was naked, as he had never before been with a woman. He had no secrets from her now; she knew the whole length of him: his curves and his planes, where he was soft or smooth, firm or rough— hard or hairy. What it felt like to have him inside her.

"Alec, my Alec," she murmured once more.

He shifted as he smiled, and felt the woman's discarded skirt bunch beneath his buttocks, where he lay amid the ruins of a burned-out dwelling on the ridge above the MacTyrie Athletic Field. She smiled back, though he could scarcely see her face, there in the soft summer dark. Only a cloud of hair, each strand backlit by moonlight; only the curve of her cheeks, the arch of her brow, the spark of magic in her eyes as she bent to kiss him once more, while her hands went roam-

46

ing to places no woman had ventured before that night . . .

"Eva," he sighed, when she had finished, and closed his eyes.

"My Alec," she answered, softly as an echo—but something had changed: he no longer lay languid and sated in his first lover's lap, but crouched in the yard of an ancient farmhouse beneath a storm-torn midnight sky. Lightning flickered ominously, limning wind-whipped trees and the billowing cloaks of a host of Faery warriors, who sat coal-black steeds between writhing poplars, then crowded in respectfully to where one of their number lay crushed upon the ground while a blond-haired boy who instants before had been a raging serpent-monster huge enough to coil around a building sprawled dazed and senseless beside her.

Beside . . . Eva! For he had removed that fallen warrior's helm, revealing the face of she who had seduced him and loved him and betrayed him most brutally at last. Except that he was running a few emotions behind just now—which fact he realized bitterly as he stared down at one he now knew was a devious Faery woman with her own complex agenda, which surely did not include loving any mortal, much less skinny, naive Alec McLean.

He should have hated her, should have despised this wretch who had twisted his jealousy and caused such grief to older, more loyal friends. Yet as she lay there, her beauty awash with a pain she could only escape by death, he could not. "Farewell, my Alec," she sighed, and spoke no more.

She was one of the Sidhe, Alec's dreamself reminded him. And the Sidhe could not die—not truly, not forever the way men did. Sooner or later she would return: sooner or later her spirit would build new flesh and Aife would once more walk the fields of Faerie.

They'd be waiting for her, too: Lugh's scouts and soldiers and spies would, they whose purpose it was to maintain balance and justice and order in Tir-Nan-Og. And since Aife had betrayed a king along with her mortal lover, that king would claim first vengeance, in whatever form revenge was enacted among the Tuatha de Danaan. Cursed to wear beast shape, she might be, as Ailill mac Angus had been. Or exiled to some island far from comfort and joy. Perhaps the Death of Iron, even, that severed soul and body past reunion—though that was unlikely, for mere traitors.

Yes, all those were possible options. But what Alec knew far more certainly, felt more passionately, there in the heart of his self, was that he still loved her and wanted one last time to be with her honestly, with no deception on either side. She'd loved him, she'd told him once—and lied. She'd come to love him, she'd said again at the edge of death—and, he sensed, spoken true.

So where was Aife now? How could he, Alec McLean, be with her again?

As if in answer, the ruby-septumed stone that lay less than a yard from his head, that had drunk deep of the blood of wild beasts and tame boys, pulsed with scarlet fire . . .

. . . "My Alec!"

Alec blinked in bewilderment, for though he knew that he still dreamed, something more subtle assured him he dreamed true. And what he saw was the answer to his desire. Not where Eva and he had made love, or where she had died, but where she presently resided.

"Come to me, my Alec, my dreaming boy-man-lover!"

But Alec could only stare—first at the face of his lady, then at her body, where she sat clothed in shadow-gray samite on a padded velvet seat beneath a high, arched window, gazing out at nothing. And then at the larger room around her: rough stone walls and bare stone floor, across which splatters of furs and skins were strewn like storm wrack . . .

And at a thrice-barred door, and a staircase leading to it, that spiraled around an open, dim-lit core . . .

And a tower, ancient, scarred, and broken, in which the love of his life was imprisoned, for whatever space of days Lugh Samildinach deemed just . . .

And a blasted plain around it, and beyond that a border of nothing, beyond which lay nothing save one Straight Track, along which the Winds between the Worlds both screamed and sang.

And one wind found him and caressed him with a touch like a certain lover's and spoke to him with her voice.

"None may come here but through Tir-Nan-Og, my Alec—unless Mortal Men have learned to pierce the World Walls. And because my crime was born of love misguided and buried by love misused, I am doomed to remain in this tower until a mortal man who loves me finds his way here. And since but one mortal man has ever loved me, it is you alone, my Alec, who can accomplish this."

"Eva!" Alec cried to a cool but cloudless sky on an autumn afternoon. No one heard, though close by either hand his best friends likewise dreamed . . .

. . . Bloody Bald, Aikin thought sourly, was simply a mountain—a well-nigh-perfect cone, steeper-sided than most Georgia mountains, and solitary, as most were not—with sheer quartzite cliffs athwart its summit that caught the rays of sunset and dawn and blazed red as the blood that bestowed its name. Water lapped around it, encircling it with cold and dark and a man-made lake: one of those R.E.A. jobs that

*had claimed so many valleys, so many homesteads;
displaced so many folks who were his and David's
kin . . .*

*Yeah, it was simply a mountain, and no more. He'd
been nuts to believe Dave's stories, however elabo-
rately wrought, of a castle that crowned it all unseen,
cloaked from the eyes of men by Faery glamour. A
man would be a fool to believe such crap, and Aikin
Carlisle Daniels was no fool. If there was magic in the
world, he'd know it by now; God knew he'd read
enough on that topic to fill a good-sized library.*

But suppose Dave's tales were true?

*Suppose magic was rampant in the north Georgia
woods and he had missed it? Had missed the Seelie
Court riding in procession four times a year, had
missed Faery critters that watched his friends, and
Faery runners that ran races with them and kid-
napped their brothers and shot elven arrows into
their uncles. Never mind journeys to those other
Worlds, whose names themselves conjured dreams:
Tir-Nan-Og and Annwyn and Erenn; Galunlati and
the Lands of Fire and the Realm of the Powersmiths.*

*He wanted to believe it all, dammit! Did not want
to brand his best friends as crazy, fools, or liars. Yet
to believe, one needed proof, had to see the Faeries
riding, had to hear the horns of Elfland saluting dusk
and dawn.*

*And one odd-coated, queer-horned stag glimpsed in
the woods of a foggy morn was not sufficient.*

*He had to have more; had to see the castle on that
mountain, had to find his way to Faerie and all those
other realms.*

*But how could he? He who, though hungriest, had
longest been denied that wondrous feast?*

But then his subconscious lodged against that most
stubborn and deepest-set desire, and the force of that
soulfelt need set fire in a certain stone.

And so the dreamshape that was Aikin Daniels

stood on the most perilous edge of the precipice that looked on Bloody Bald, and wished most fervently to see what was hidden there.

And Aikin saw: Lugh's mountaintop citadel, and the perilous peak beneath it, and the wide green country that spread about its base, where in the Lands of Men was only mountains and lakes. And he saw a webwork of gold laid upon those meads and meadows, upon those forests and streams. And he found he could follow those strands, away from Tir-Nan-Og and through countless other Worlds that layered 'round it like the chambers of some complex seashell, some more alien than the Lands of Men and some achingly familiar, for he had chanced on them before in less potent dreams.

One Track in particular intrigued him, for it swept farther afield than the mountains. He traced it: south—and east, over hills, over ridges, into the rolling Piedmont. Settlements blazed by—Helen, Cleveland, Gainesville, Jefferson, Arcade—sensed but not truly seen. And then Aikin came upon one particular town.

He pronounced its name. Athens. Oz Upon the Oconee. The place he lived. The place he went to college.

But the magic ran there as well: a glitter of Track far less than a mile from his cabin in Whitehall Forest. He had only to locate it in his World, and somehow, someway, he would walk there.

All he required was a landmark: something to mark it past mistaking.

He sought one, even as the Straight Track vanished save for the merest glimmer, even as the rest of the world grew hard and dirty and . . . real. Real as that lightning-blasted oak beside the maple with the bifurcated trunk. Them he would remember; them he would seek when he awoke . . .

* * *

David dreamed of guns. He dreamed of the rifle he had hunted with that morning, and he dreamed of he who had bestowed it, who had died seven years gone by, and in whose honor he had dedicated that day's kill. David-the-Elder, he'd been styled, after David himself had been born. David Thomas Sullivan: his father's youngest brother.

David-the-Younger's role model, who had taught him how to affect the good-ole-boy facade a guy needed to survive a rural mountain high school—and those more sophisticated skills a college man must possess so as not to be thought a hick or a geek or a dweeb; so that he could ride a horse, drive a tractor, chop sorghum, dig 'taters, pour concrete and weld—*and* run almost forever, swim well nigh that long, hold his own at wrestling in spite of being not very big, drive a twisting road without brakes, and shoot anything that walked, crawled, sat still, or flew. But he'd also read all of Shakespeare before high school—and Malory, Milton, Tolkien, Lewis, and Poe; and could write passable iambic pentameter, transliterate Norse runes and the Hebrew, Greek, and Sindarin alphabets; as well as identify almost every song played on the airways more than twice during the last nine years, and drink anything alcoholic, however foul tasting, without coughing or making a face. All because David-the-Elder had said that was what a man who was really alive should do.

. . . *guns* . . .

He'd rehearsed that awful afternoon once that day already, the one when Uncle Dale had appeared at his bedroom door to proclaim his nephew's death. And he'd relived his private salute after the funeral.

And he'd *certainly* recalled how none of it was fair, that someone as accomplished as David-the-Elder should die so ignominiously. That, in fact, no one should really know *how* he had died at all. No one had seen it—or admitted as much; and the report from the Rangers had been frustratingly vague. But he would find out one day, would write the Pentagon for the full report. Shoot, he'd get Alec to hack into the government's files, as he was perfectly able to do.

But no mere report could relate everything that had transpired; none could fully convey David-the-Elder's final hours.

But a red-septumed quasi stone in a blood-filled bowl beside his head could. And as fatigue and regret clogged David's reason, magic from another World revealed that fateful day . . .

It was like watching TV, David thought, and thought no more, but witnessed.

. . . a young man in the jeans and Nikes and T-shirt that proclaimed him a Ranger off-duty, prowling the narrow cobblestoned length of a Middle Eastern street. His hair, white-blond like his namesake nephew's, was a beacon of difference in the harsh sunlight—and possibly a mistake to reveal; but he'd given his Atlanta Braves cap to a brown-faced street boy in trade for a wide white grin and directions to where the best pomegranates could really be found. Pomegranates: the word had the same root as grenade (as in hand grenade), because the two looked alike. He hoped to buy a couple dozen, ship 'em to a friend in Granada, Spain, and have him send 'em to the younger David, with a note not to pull the pins— which his brilliant nephew would understand and appreciate.

Trouble was, he'd taken a wrong turn somewhere between the barracks and the bazaar, and smiling boy directions notwithstanding, very much feared he was lost. Which was not necessarily cool for tow-haired American servicemen in Middle Eastern cities, however ingratiating their honest mountain smiles might be.

But speaking of smiles, here was that kid again, still with his baseball cap, only now it perched atop one of those complex turban-things the locals affected.

With a flourish the lad removed the latter and passed it to him. "Trade," he said, solemnly. "Trade."

"Lost," the elder David countered, as he gamely donned the headpiece. The boy's grin widened. "Pomegranates," he called, pointing down a narrow side street.

David-the-Elder thanked him and followed his directions, ambling toward a slit of light glimmering at the end of the alley, where a tinkling splash of water and a half-seen spray of palms hinted at pleasantry. His hiking stick clicked upon the cobblestones.

But as he stepped into the brightness, something small and dark thumped to the pavement before him. Rock . . . or—

But he had no more time for thinking, as the world first went loud, then very white—and then traded all trace of noise for a greater, more infinite light.

"No!" the younger David screamed. "No!" But the ulunsuti was not finished, for it knew in its way that what he *really* wished to know was where that grenade had come from, that had erased a good man's life.

And so he saw that small plaza, and centering it the fountain, in which a fragment of undifferentiated human flesh was weeping blood. He did not see the body—what remained; and in that the ulunsuti was merciful. But he did note a splatter of red across yard upon yard of stucco and stone.

And on a balcony one level up and four narrow buildings away, he saw a young man's eyes go wide beneath their cammo and khaki. "Ooops!" that youth exclaimed, his voice as slurred as his eyes were unfocused and his movements clumsy and vague.

"Friendly fire," his companion across a tiny table opined, through a thickening veil of hashish fumes. The voice was ambiguous: familiar and foreign, at once that of man and woman. "One should never treat weapons casually," that one continued, "lest one take friend for foe and fling one in lieu of an orange—

*which you just did. And without the pin, too—or did
you assume that was the stem? What must you have
been thinking? That he wore the headgear of a well-
known terrorist? That the hiking staff he carried was
a gun? They will blame the rebels, I suppose."*

"I'm gonna be sick," the clumsy one announced—
and lurched to his feet.

"No," said the hashish smoker. *"Come, let me heal
you. Let me make you forget that you hated that man
because he beat you at poker, Risk, Jeopardy, and
Joust; and everybody liked him, but thought you were
impulsive and clumsy and stupid and rude. Let me
make you forget that you should never have brought
that weapon with you, for such like do not impress
me, who have witnessed more war than a thousand
like you could ever imagine."*

*The Ranger stared crookedly at the drifting smoke
that rose from the hookah, at the lambs'-eyes-in-honey
in silver bowls upon the table. At the plaza below that
was already clogged with gawkers come to point and
stare at what might have been a young American.
"Nobody can forget killin' a man,"* he spat, sounding
stone-cold sober.

"I can make you forget," the other gave back, voice
more like a woman by the second.

"Nobody c'n do that," said the soldier. *"Nobody c'n
cut a memory outta your mind."*

"No one . . . human . . ."

"Ooops," sighed the soldier. *"I forget."*

"I know!" the other laughed—and drew him away
from the balcony and the noise and the oddly inept
search—and thence to an inner room, where she removed her androgynous outer robes.

"My angel," said the man, when she was naked.

"My mortal lover," the woman replied, and reached
for him.

*And when she turned to face the man who in a
hashish haze had casually slain David Thomas Sul-*

livan, David Kevin *Sullivan likewise saw her*. And shouted where he dreamed on that stony mountainside.

Angel, *the drugged-out man had called her. And so one so fair might seem to such as he. But it was no angel the younger David had seen; no sirree. He had seen that face before, though, far too many times; and he now knew who'd been first cause of his hero-uncle's death. Not an angel, but one of the Sidhe: the flame-haired battle goddess called the Morrigu, some-time advisor to Lugh Samildinach, High King in Tir-Nan-Og, whom David almost called friend. Occasional companion as well to Nuada Airgetlam, whom David did consider one.*

Well, she was bloody well no friend to him! And if those others also knew what she had instigated . . . well, that was downright betrayal!

"*You goddamned bitch,*" David whispered.

And with that last word he blinked into the harsh light of midday.

And for an instant thought he was still in the Middle East. His heart was thumping like mad, and he was hyperventilating, as he briefly lodged between two Worlds. Blue sky there; blue sky here. Stone pavement; stony ground. A fountain tinkling in a foreign land; a waterfall murmuring by his shoulder.

For a moment, he expected to hear the cries of people rushing to see what had exploded. Instead, when his vision clarified, he saw Alec twitch in his sleep, then rouse abruptly, a troubled scowl furrowing his brow.

"Welcome back," David yawned. "Jeez, but that rock of yours caught me off guard."

"It just added to what was already there," Alec replied carefully, as Aikin likewise stirred. "We were already sleepy from gettin' up early, and tired from hiking and lugging the deer. Probably we were too tired to attempt as much magic as we did."

"Yeah," David agreed darkly. "I hope."

Alec studied him. "You dream?"

A shrug. "Nothin' I recall." Which was a lie. Yet the truth was so fresh—and he knew it *was* the truth—he dared not face it.

"Same here," Alec admitted, not quite meeting his gaze.

"Same here too," came Aikin's soft, smooth murmur, as one eye slitted open.

" 'Time is it?" Alec wondered.

"Time to get Bambi's mom off this mountain," David told him.

Time to think about some things, he added to himself. *I wonder how you avenge yourself on an immortal?*

Interlude II:
Freedom of Information

(Sullivan Cove, Georgia—
Sunday, October 25—early afternoon)

"*You* guys work it out, and call me back," David growled into his folks' new portable phone, as he paced around the empty kitchen of the slightly run-down farmhouse he'd called home for most of twenty years. "I don't care where I pick y'all up, but it just makes more sense to make *one* stop."

"Yeah, well, Alec's gone picky-pissy cubed," Aikin retorted. "He's definitely got a rat up his ass about *something*."

"And you *don't*?" David shot back irritably, too pre-occupied by a certain rodent of his own to be polite. "First you were Mr. Curiosity yesterday mornin', then you start actin' like we'd shot off your tongue 'stead of that doe."

"So?"

"So I don't trust you when you stop askin' questions. Not about *that* stuff, anyway."

"And I don't trust *you* when you pick at fresh back-strap."

"I was tired."

"Bullshit!"

David merely grunted. "Look, you call McLean, and one of you call me. I've gotta do some stuff 'fore we leave."

And with that he broke the connection.

The sudden silence enclosed him like a breath of

winter wind. In spite of the midday warmth, he shivered where he stood. Muffled voices floating down the hall from the front porch carried his pa's ill-formed opinions, his ma's indignant protests, and his little brother's careless laughter. Footsteps came with them: slow, calm, and careful; the familiar tread of a man still vigorous in his seventies.

Uncle Dale Sullivan paused in the doorway that cut the kitchen off from the rest of the house. Thin and tall he was, and aged like a locust fence rail, with white hair tied back in a scandalous ponytail scarcely shorter than David's own. He was David's favorite kinsman, his grandpa's oldest brother—and someone who'd seen his share of magic in his time. The old man stared at him a moment, then reached to a back pocket and slid out a hip flask, which he extended wordlessly. David accepted it with a solemn nod, unscrewed it, and drank a long draught of the moonshine it contained. And didn't cough, though its heat flowed through him like a brushfire.

"Wanta talk about it?" Dale asked, not moving.

David took another sip and shrugged. His gaze drifted down to the worn tile floor.

"I won't laugh, I won't yell, and I won't cry," Dale prompted softly.

David did not look up. "I might, though."

"Which?"

"Yell," David muttered at last. "Cry—Fuck, *I* don't know!"

"I got a hanky."

Silence, then, finally a long sigh, and, very softly: "How did David-the-Elder die?"

"Shoulda known that was it," Dale sighed in turn. "Yesterday was the day wasn't it? I guess I forgot . . . or wanted to."

David met his gaze. "But how—?"

"You *know* all this, boy!"

"Tell me anyway."

"He was blown up by a hand grenade in that town I never can remember the name of."

"Any more?"

"What more *is* there? Details won't bring him back. The city, the street; who found him, who investigated—that won't change nothin'. And you don't *wanta* know the rest."

"Wrong!"

"You *wanta* see the autopsy report?" Dale flared sharply. "You wanta know how many pieces he was in? How they identified him? I wanted to know that too, one time! I never told nobody, but I did. I used the Freedom of Information Act and got the fatality report, and it didn't say *nothin'*—'cept that they thought the grenade was one of ours. Somebody stole it, they claimed."

"They *claimed*!" David snapped. "You never told me any of this—and I asked—lots of times. For *years*!"

"You were just a kid, Davy. You were tryin' to hang on. If there'd been anything in there that would have helped you, I'd have told you. I saw you in the graveyard, boy: shootin' that rifle he gave you them twenty-one times. I *knew* you were hurtin'. But there wasn't nothing I could do! I wanted you to remember a good-lookin' boy, not—"

"Chunks of meat," David finished. "That's about it, isn't it?"

"Feel any better?"

" 'Least I've been honest!"

"I *tried* to be."

"More'n the rest of 'em, anyway," David snorted. He slumped against the doorjamb and folded his arms across his chest. "You still got it?"

Dale looked startled. "What?"

"The report. Whatever else there is. I'd just like to see it; see if I can figure out anything 'bout . . . how it really was."

"I'm not sure that'd be good, boy."

Another shrug. "I need to know."

Dale scratched his bewhiskered chin. "I'd have to dig 'em out. It'd take a while."

"Yeah, well, no big hurry."

Dale smiled sadly. "If it'll help kill whatever's eatin' on you, I'll do 'er."

" 'Preciate it."

Dale turned to leave.

"Did he have any . . . buddies?" David asked abruptly. "Somebody who was there? Who might know something that wasn't in the paperwork?"

The old man twisted around where he stood. "Don't reckon," he mused through a frown. "Oh, everybody *liked* him, don't get me wrong; but he hadn't been with that unit long. Oh, but wait: he did write some 'bout meetin' this guy who'd been a Ranger and got out. Said he was a 'stranger in a strange land just like he was, and as fey.' "

David's eyes narrowed. "*Fey*? He said *fey*?"

Dale nodded. "I had to look it up."

"You remember this guy's name?"

"John Devlin."

"Devlin . . ." David repeated. And then realization struck him. "Oh my God! You don't mean the *poet*, do you? I went to one of his readings down at Georgia!"

"Could be," Dale replied. "There was a poem in with one of the letters."

"Oh jeez," David breathed. "Oh jeez. So what—?"

But at that moment the phone rang.

"If I'm gonna find that stuff 'fore you leave," Dale said in parting, "I'd best be at it. If I don't find it today, I'll send it when I do."

David smiled wanly. " 'Preciate it." And spent the next quarter hour fussing with Alec about rides.

Chapter V:
Into the Woods

(Athens, Georgia—
Tuesday, October 27—afternoon)

Aikin felt like Moses—and looked rather like him too.

Though he had not been found among the bullrushes by Pharaoh's Daughter, long days in the sun of a seemingly endless summer had tanned his compact frame as dark as any Egyptian. He already had black hair and dark eyes (hazel, however, not genuine Nile valley-brown), and at the moment—barefoot, and with the sleeves of the white gauze shirt he'd worn to class knotted around his waist above frayed khaki shorts, and a towel draped across his head beneath his University of Georgia Foresters cap for no better reason than funkiness—he even looked the part.

Of course he had no beard to speak of, and certainly not a phony waxed one. And he doubted Moses had sported a black nylon backpack bulged near to bursting with books, or a boombox blaring Tori Amos's latest. But he *had* known something about magic, which was what those books concerned (Ms. Amos, too, he suspected). And the prophet had likewise, by good report, often toted a staff—which Aikin also did: a near-twin to the rune-inscribed, copper-shod hiking items Dave and Alec lugged around. Dave had made all three, in fact; his had been a Christmas present five years back and still showed no sign of wear, though he used it constantly.

He stared at it for a moment and tried to evoke the

62

scene from *The Ten Commandments* in which his hoary analogue had parted the Red Sea. *He* had no such ambitious body of water, of course—was about five thousand miles too far west, for one thing. But he did have the Middle Oconee. In fact, he was standing in the middle of it—but *not* in water up to his neck, or with uncanny cliffs of it towering to either side like so much Jell-O.

Rather, he had the dam.

Forty yards of decaying concrete, it was, and a yard wide at the top: easy enough to walk across if one kept one's balance, and his was very good. Before and behind, water rushed, shushed, and occasionally rumbled through Whitehall Forest, a sprawl of preserved woodland belonging to the University of Georgia School of Forest Resources a few miles south of Athens proper. Deer lived there—and squirrels, coons, 'possums, and chipmunks—as though sixty-odd thousand beings higher up the food chain didn't call the same county home. Yet two miles of ill-paved road to the north put you at the key-card gate behind the brick Victorian jumble of Whitehall Mansion; and just beyond that, you hit Whitehall Road, that a touch of sleight of hand involving road signs transformed into Milledge Avenue—Athens's fraternity row—a few fields and a bypass farther on.

But eschewing a single pull-tab gleaming in the sun, there was no sign of frat folks here. Only the roof of the newish cabin he shared with three other majors up the slope to the left, and beside it, the longer shape of Flinchum's Phoenix, Forestry's assembly-and-banquet hall, hinted at civilization.

And—again—the dam.

Water swirled through at least three breaches in its upstream face, but none actually reached the summit-slab, though the tangle of flood wrack at those places made another kind of barrier. A tumble of blocks, steps, and arches at the north end showed where a mill had been abandoned. The ruins were bloody evocative, too; and more than once Runnerman's sister, Myra, had posed some member of the Gang there, in whatever odd (and usually skimpy—or absent) costume struck her fancy, often as not engaged in mock combat, all as grist for her fantasy paintings.

Aikin's fantasy, however, lay not in any evocation of the parted Red Sea (with the bondage of academia in hot pursuit, more dire than Pharaoh's legions), but in the Promised Land on the farther shore. For there, the dam terminated in a coarse-sanded beach below a wooded ridge, beyond which lay more forest. Of course, it wasn't *that* far to a brace of suburban backyards; but here, at least, the illusion was preserved.

He wondered, though, how long he'd have to wander in the wilderness before he found what he sought. And whether he would receive commandments or confront the golden—well, what he sought was gold, but it definitely wasn't no calf.

Three days had passed since the hunting expedition . . . since the dream. One he'd spent back in the mountains, hanging out with his folks through supper before stuffing himself into Dave's old Mustang for a harrowing ride back here. Rain had caught them halfway down: just above Gainesville. It had not let up until that morning.

Which meant he'd had no chance to scout out the place the ulunsuti had shown him.

Nor did he really have time now; he was cutting botany as it was. But he did have to submit a plant collection in that class; and there were plants in the target zone. And if he just *happened* to find that place the ulunsuti had revealed, so much the better.

And if he didn't . . . well, empty woods were a hell of a place to read.

And since he'd spent most of yesterday's deluge haunting the library in quest of what Dave (and Mr. Poe) would have called "quaint and curious volumes of forgotten lore," he had God's plenty of *that* to occupy him.

So he stared at the banks a moment longer, and the river between them a touch longer than that, quieted Tori with a tap of a finger, raised his staff on high—and, in the style of Charlton Heston, yelled, *"Behold!"*

No one heard—he hoped. The Oconee drank most of his voice and carried it away toward Lexington. And trees wrapped the rest in colored leaves and would not let go.

And with that, Aikin strode across the dam and into the woods.

He found it sooner than expected and could've kicked himself for not exploring such a landmark more thoroughly. But there it was: an ancient white oak that had been zapped decades ago by lightning, reducing it to a twist of knobby trunk and gnarled and broken limbs, from which the bark was still sloughing like a bad case of leprosy. Beside it, Siamese-twin maples made a V that framed the westering sun—but they only served to confirm what he already knew. This was it: the place from his dream by which a Straight Track lay.

He'd been here before, too. But he'd been so busy gawking at the tree itself, he'd not noticed the surrounding terrain.

Had he deigned to look lower, however, he'd surely have seen the signs Dave had reluctantly described on the jaunt down from Enotah County. Like the way nothing actually grew on a yard-wide stretch of ground, and leaves seemed undisturbed there—and oddly unmoldered; how ants and beetles turned aside as they approached it, and spiders spun no webs across its path. Briars grew along it too: not so thick as to draw notice, but enough to dissuade the unwary.

Aikin smiled as he crouched beside it. Tracks went everywhere, Dave had said; but in this World, at least, were unseen; nor did they follow its exact contours. He could not, for instance, pace this screwy trail for mile on mile unending. Rather, it would simply disappear at some point, as it passed through another World Wall. As far as he knew, which was as much as Dave had told him, the Track that ran through the Sullivans' river bottom and thence up the mountain behind their house was the longest stretch in North America where Tir-Nan-Og and the Lands of Men precisely coincided. This was shorter—had to be—and to prove it, Aikin shucked his pack, fumbled out a map, and noted how the Track's route, if extended, would carry it through a subdivision one way and into the concrete tangle of the bypass—with all its attendant steel—the other.

But here it lingered. Here it waited, all unknown. The Promised Land indeed. The road to wonder.

And then he could wait no longer.

A briar snagged his elbow as he eased his arm through that almost-invisible barrier of blackberry thorns and over the Track itself. Slowly he lowered his palm, tensing as it neared the surface as if he feared a shock, though Dave had said nothing would happen unless the Track were activated, which no mortal could accomplish. Or unless, as had been the case with one of Dave's grandsires, certain obscure natural conditions pertained, which Dave could not more specifically define.

. . . closer, and he found himself straining his eyes in quest of what he could *not* see, had *never* seen—and might not get to see, if Dave had told him true. "A glimmer of gold on the ground, yet above it and within it," Dave had said. "That's what a Track looks like when it's activated. It's kinda like dust in a shaft of sunlight," he'd added. "And seems like it gets thicker the more . . . magical the place you're near. Otherwise . . . watch for long strips of barren ground—and briars."

But Aikin saw no golden glimmer. Then again, he

didn't have Second Sight. Dave did. *His* eyes burned when they were near an activated Track. They burned in the presence of the substance of Faerie or the powers thereof. Magic came to Dave unasked. Was it, therefore, too much to expect that someone who wanted magic as desperately as he did be granted this one small boon?

. . . closer, and he almost touched it, then relented. Suppose the same thing happened to him as had happened to Dave and his brother? Suppose the Track held him bound, unable to escape?

Stupid, Daniels, he argued back. *No way folks don't walk over this all the time.*

And with that, he closed his eyes, took a deep breath—and laid his hand upon the Track.

Did a spark jump between his fingers and the earth as he closed those last few millimeters? Maybe. *Probably* it was a prickling of pine straw. And was the earth warmer there? Possibly again. But the sun also lay in long beams across the fallen leaves, so they could've been heated longer. And had the wind picked up, bringing the scent of strange flowers? Again, that was possible. But the wind had been gusting all day, and his hands were sticky with the sap of a dozen plants he'd collected in passing, some of them quite fragrant.

No, he just couldn't tell. Not this way. Reluctantly, he rose.

One final test remained, however, which he both longed for and dreaded. Steeling himself, he took a deep breath and stepped full upon the Track.

Nothing.

Merely the warmth of the sun on his shoulders.

Another breath, and he took a pace.

Again, nothing.

Another of each, and still no response.

Finally he took fifteen strides one way, then fifteen back the other. Nothing changed. No energy awoke beneath his feet, though they were bare, the better to feel such things. And no visions came to him; no gold glittered on the needles. Nothing altered at all.

But this had to be the place. *Had* to be.

Sparing one final glare for the blasted oak, he stepped off the Track. A briar snared his leg in passing, leaving straight red scratches across his calf. "Fuck you," he snapped. "I can't do shit on that Track beside you, but you can have a friggin' field day with me!"

The briars did not respond. Aikin retrieved his pack, found a place in surveying distance of both Track and oak, reactivated Tori, chose a book from his stash, and commenced to read.

It was not botany that occupied him, or Wildlife Management or Orienteering. Rather, it was every single book he had found in the library when he'd claimed a terminal and called up Ley Lines and Straight Tracks in the subject data base—all three of 'em. He'd chased 'em down anyway, and raided their bibliographies, and from them gleaned a couple more. And then by browsing the stacks to either side of *that* assembly, he'd finally accumulated a pile. *The View Over Atlantis* was one; *The Old Straight Track*—a new, annotated, edition—another. Probably he should have checked the periodical indices as well, and the folklore journals. And he would—tomorrow. But even the arcanely compromised could stare at CRTs only so long when there were actual pages to be read. It was, therefore, with a keen sense of anticipation that Aikin opened *The Old Straight Track*.

Most of an hour later, he closed it again. There was interesting stuff in there, no doubt; mostly about how a man named Watkins had noticed how sacred sites in England tended to line up with distinctive natural features and locales significant to prehistoric Britain. From them (so the annotations read) later, less pragmatic folk had hypothesized a system of lines carrying the "earth power" (whatever that was). But he found no mention of Faerie whatever, and no suggestion how this supposed earth power might be accessed.

The View Over Atlantis was no help either. From some promising references to the lines being used to direct magic, it lapsed into a discussion of how the Chinese geomancers had used the concepts of yin and yang represented in those same earth forces to reorder the landscape of their entire country—which was still cool, sort of. But *then* it had latched onto the mystic symbology of the proportions of the Great Pyramid— and that had quickly gone to mind-fuck bullshit. Aikin was not fond of math that did not pertain to the roll of percentile dice. That the Great Pyramid was in the geographic center of the world's land masses, and its height a certain percent of the distance to the sun and another to the diameter of the earth was interesting, if suspect, trivia. But mostly it smacked of people with too little to do.

Trouble was, those two books had been the most promising. The others were long shots at best. He scanned the topmost: John Gregory's *Giants in the Earth*. But it was so dull it set him first to yawning, then to nodding off. And then (as a growling stomach informed him, before the beeping of his watch did the same), it was time to go questing for dinner.

Reluctantly, he gathered up his books, notebooks, and the plastic bags of hastily labeled flora. It had grown cool with the approach of evening, and he put on his shirt before shouldering the pack. Shoes too: scruffy sneakers. Finally, he ejected Tori and chose another tape. Enya's "Exile" promptly melted into the woods, soft and plaintive. Aikin smiled at the music— he loved that song. A pause to slip on the headphones, and he started back to his cabin.

He did not hear the rustle of unseen leaves behind him, or the patter of oddly laid feet.

Interlude III:
When Duty Whispers Low

(Athens, Georgia—
Tuesday, October 27—afternoon)

David glanced one last time at the sheaf of faxes he'd picked up at Bel-Jean Copy Center moments before—the ones he'd received from Uncle Dale—and punched the number for long-distance information into the phone in the Anthro department lounge. This late, the place was empty. Fortunately.

"What city, please?" a far-too-perky voice queried promptly.

"Clayton, Georgia."

"Go ahead."

"I'd like a number for John Devlin. Could be unlisted, I guess," he added, inanely.

A staticky pause ensued, followed, electronically, by the number. David took a deep breath and punched it in, along with his PIN, wondering, as it began to ring, if this was too long a shot, if this was even the same guy who'd been David-the-Elder's friend in the weeks before his death, and was he going to sound like an utter dweeb when—*if*—anyone answered.

Someone did. Male. Youngish. Voice soft but clear; Southern accent edged with mountain twang. " 'Lo?"

"Uh, hello," David began, shifting his weight and fidgeting with a copy of Charles Hudson's *The Southeastern Indians* someone had left unattended. "Uh . . . could I speak to John Devlin, please?"

"You got 'im." The voice was neutral. Polite but a tad

70

impatient, as though the guy got lots of calls from strangers.

"Uh, well . . . you don't know me, but my name's David Sullivan. I'm sorry to bother you, but—"

"Oh shit, you're *him*!"

"What?" David blurted out before he could stop. "I mean—"

"I knew your uncle," Devlin replied. "You sound just like him."

"I . . . *do*?"

"Sorry," Devlin went on, with a chuckle. "You kinda caught me off guard. Your voice. Your name—same as his, and all."

"So you're the right John Devlin? The one my uncle talked about in his letters?"

"If he talked about any John Devlin, it was me."

David swallowed, trying to determine how to proceed now that the ice was broken. Devlin spared him the trouble. "You know, I was just *thinkin'* 'bout ol' Dave the other day," he confided. "I was workin' on one of my poems and had to check the dates on some stuff, and found a card your uncle—hard to think of him that way, 'cause he talked about you like you were his son or brother—sent me right before . . . what happened, and that made me realize that we were comin' up on the anniversary."

"It was last Saturday."

"Bummed you, didn't it? Sure as hell bummed *me*!"

David relaxed. This wasn't going so bad. Not bad at all, actually. "How'd you know him? You weren't in his unit—"

"Didn't have that pleasure," Devlin sighed. "I was out by then, snoopin' 'round lookin' for . . . answers, I guess you could call 'em. Happened into a bookstore one day, and saw this American guy with white-blond hair—the kind you'd notice, 'specially over there—prowlin' through the philosophy section. Something about the way he wore his body said 'Ranger'—which is what I was. Had on an Enotah County 'Possums sweatshirt, which told me he was from my neck of the woods. So him bein' a Ranger, a mountain boy, and probably literate, I figured I oughta speak. I did. We hit it off—and spent most of his free time for the next few weeks prowlin' around archaeological sites—book-stores—a bar or three. He told me a lot about you."

David had almost forgotten this was a two-way conversation, so caught up had he become. "Yeah, well, we were pretty close."

"Sounds like."

"Uh, like I said, I'm sorry to bug you . . . but I've been thinkin' about him a lot lately, with the anniversary, and all. And I got to wonderin' about . . . exactly how he died. I've seen the report, and all. But—I mean, I know *you* weren't there. But I don't know any of his friends from the unit. And I thought you might've heard something . . ."

"Hmmmm," Devlin grunted, sounding serious and a touch uncomfortable. "Can't help *much*, that's for sure. I heard about it from a street kid we knew, when he didn't show up for lunch one day. Dave had given him a baseball cap, I think. I got there just as they were—there's no good way to say it—pickin' up the pieces, but they wouldn't let me help. I tried to find out what I could, but they were real tight-ass about it."

"But it *was* a hand grenade?"

"Yep."

"One of ours?"

A pause. "Yep."

An echoing pause. "This is gonna sound funny, but please don't laugh 'cause it's really serious stuff to me. But . . . was there anything, you know, *weird* about it? Or do *you* have any idea who did it; if there was anything strange about him?"

"You really *are* a lot like him," Devlin mused. "But weird? I don't know. They let out that it was one of *them* with a stolen weapon; but from what I caught in

a bar where a bunch of his buds were hangin' out—
they didn't know me, see, and were drunk as skunks—
they figured it was one of their guys that thought that
ol' Dave was just too perfect."

"But nothing *really* strange?"

Devlin hesitated. David could hear his breath hiss.
"Like what?"

"Like . . . angels," David asked carefully. "I know
that sounds crazy, but—"

"God!" Devlin broke in. "There *was* something
about angels, as a matter of fact. Really weird, too, now
I think of it. See, these guys were talkin' 'bout that guy
they thought might've done it, and said that he'd really
flipped out since then—blew his brains out later, as a
matter of fact, which I guess is why there wasn't more
of an inquiry. But before all that, he'd apparently been
braggin' that—and I quote—'Ol' Sullivan may think
he's God Almighty, but *I'm* the one that's fuckin' an
angel.' End of quote."

"Well," David gulped, "that answers that, I guess."

"What?"

"About the angel. I was wonderin' if she was . . .
real."

"Was she?" Devlin sounded remarkably nonchalant—as though it was perfectly normal to discuss eso-
terica with strangers.

"I dunno," David hedged. "But I think I just found
out who she was. *What* she was, rather."

Another long pause from Devlin. "Well, David-the-
Younger, I suspect most folks would ask what you
meant by that, but knowin' who you're kin to, I'm probably smart not to. I've seen some things myself, and
ole Dave told me he'd seen some more, and you sound
like me when I'm tryin' not to talk about . . . certain
subjects."

David chuckled grimly. "Yeah, well, I don't think it'd
be cool to say more—'least not on the phone. And I

guess I'd better let you go. I got class in a couple minutes."

"And I've got a book to write. But if I can help, let me know. And if I think of anything, I'll let you know. You got a number?"

David told him.

"Okay, then," Devlin said, "you take care of yourself . . . and remember that your uncle was a good man. But you sound like a pretty good guy yourself, like you've got a lot of his . . . magic. And I mean that word, precisely."

". . . Thanks." David choked. "And thanks for talkin'."

"Carry on."

David hung up the phone.

And breathed a long, ragged sigh. He now had independent corroboration for his dream. For somehow he knew without a doubt that no way on earth was John Devlin a liar.

Chapter VI:
Trick or Treat?

(Jackson County, Georgia—
Wednesday, October 28—afternoon)

"Yeah, but are they *always* true?" David asked pointedly. He folded his arms, flopped against the doorjamb of his and Alec's study, and tried very hard *not* to glare.

"Far as I know," Alec muttered, not looking up from his desk, where as best David could tell, he was watching a Mandelbrot screen saver smooth out fractal curves of black and orange—appropriate, given it was nearly Halloween. Stupid, too, in view of the number of papers piling up in Alec's classes. He appeared to be severely preoccupied—but not with Geology 101, computer science, or art appreciation. *Or* with discussing the antics of a certain ulunsuti he'd refused to show pouch or pot of for the last four days.

"You know any time they weren't?" David persisted.

Silence. The screen enlarged a random rectangle, the contents of which it commenced to refine. One hall and two rooms away, a dirty dish shifted with a delicate "clink." The stereo was off, for a change.

More silence. Then, almost a growl: "My word not good enough?"

"What's *that* supposed to mean?"

Alec whipped around abruptly, face nigh as dark as his Nine Inch Nails T-shirt, eyes wild as his spiky hair. "You know fucking well!"

"I know that when you use the 'F' word you're pissed.

75

I'd *like* to know why, seein' how you're the one who wouldn't answer!"

"If you're so *fucking* smart," Alec hissed, "I wouldn't have to *fucking* remind you every *fucking* day that I *hate* talking about *fucking* magic, which is what the *fucking* rock is—and does. More to the *fucking* point, I hate *thinking* about how it works. I hate the fact that it can't decide if it's critter, stone, or veggie. And right now I'm *still* hating the fact that I let you and Aik talk me into using the *fucking* thing!"

David slammed his fist against the wall. The front door rattled. "Well *I* hate the fact that Uki told you to study it, and you're not doin' shit about it!"

"It scares me!"

"You're *supposed* to be scared of the unknown," David snorted. "You gonna be a scientist, you gotta regard stuff like this as a puzzle—a source of inspiration."

"Yeah, well, the rock's a little *too* puzzling."

"Maybe it *wouldn't* be if you'd even *try* to figure out how it works!" David shot back. "Like what its range is, or how much blood it takes for what reaction—stuff like that. Or," he added for effect, "how *accurate* its visions are."

Alec dived into the ensuing pause. "You've used it as much as I have, Mr. Anthropologist! Nothing's stopping *you* from studying it to your heart's content. I've already told you it works best when you just worry at it—but apparently that's not good enough. And it'd *help* if you'd talk about what it showed you—but of course that'd require you to actually be here."

"I'm here now!"

" 'Cause Liz ran you off."

"I didn't see her all weekend!"

"I don't think *seeing* her's what you missed."

David gaped incredulously. "Good God, McLean, I thought we worked that out years ago! I *love* Liz—but that doesn't mean I don't care about you!"

"Just not enough to actually *live* with me," Alec

sniffed. "*I'm* just supposed to baby-sit your stuff while you're out working your willie—"

"Jealous!"

"Damned right! I mean shit, man, do you have any *idea* what it's like to be buddies with somebody for practically your whole life, and share . . . *everything* with 'em, and then have 'em slam the door in your face and stick matches to the bruises!"

A deep breath. For calm. For friendship. Barely. "There're other women, Alec. The only one makin' you celibate's you!"

"And my goddamn fucking *memory*! You think I could be happy with a mortal woman when the first woman I ever made it with was from Faerie?"

"Won't know till you try, will you?"

Silence.

"Ten thousand single girls seven miles down the road, kid; and you're hung better'n I am."

Alec took a deep breath. "So what *did* you dream? I mean, just in case you actually feel like *telling* me."

"Some stuff about David-the-Elder. The day he died, and stuff."

"Not good enough."

David stomped a venturesome roach with a bare foot.

"You said, 'And stuff,' David," Alec sighed. "I know you won't flat out lie to me —but that doesn't mean you're telling all the truth. I think that little 'and stuff' hides a shitload of *something* that's made you a ring-tailed bitch the last few days. I think *that*'s why you've been sleeping over at Liz's: 'cause she won't bug you about this. You give me grief about being celibate, and not facing stuff that's making me unhappy, and all— and you're doing the same thing! You're as afraid to face . . . *something* as I am. I bet you're afraid to stay over here 'cause you're scared you'll talk in your sleep, or I'll invoke the Vow, or you'll . . . just break down."

Tears stung David's eyes. He blinked them away

without embarrassment. Alec's eyes were also gleaming. But at least that bond still existed. At least they were still—mostly—honest about emotions. It was one of the things that made their friendship special. "Got my number, don't you?" David managed at last.

"Sorry." A crooked smile lit Alec's face as he rose.

It required but one step into the tiny room for David to meet him halfway. "Me too," he whispered—and enfolded his roommate with a hearty hug.

"See why I hate that thing now?" Alec choked into David's shoulder. "Goddamn rock's got us so wired we can't even *talk* to each other."

"Love you, man," David replied simply. "There's just some heavy stuff goin' on I gotta work out solo."

"Download to me when you're done, okay?"

"Promise," David agreed—because it would lessen Alec's pain, and he *had* to do something to stop all this hurting. His Faery allies had proven unreliable. He dared not risk his best friend. And he *would* tell the truth—when he could.

Alec pushed him away, but not roughly.

David mussed his hair. "You okay?"

"I'll live," Alec conceded, nodding toward the front window, beyond which an avenue of pines paralleled Jefferson River Road. " 'Sides, one of the devils just drove up."

David barely had time to wipe his eyes on the hem of his black T-shirt before the first knock sounded. "Just a sec," he called, while Alec bolted for the john. Three steps brought him to the front door. A pause for breath, and he opened it. "Hi, Liz!" He tried very hard to look casual.

An eyebrow lifted knowingly above green eyes as his girlfriend slipped inside. A thrift store carpetbag weighted one slender arm, complicating the obligatory hug. He settled for a misaimed kiss. The westering sun, beaming down the hall from the living room, turned Liz's cap of feathery hair to copper flame and cast her

pointy features into molten gold. "Fox goddess?" David
mused aloud, nodding toward the mirror opposite the
door. "Or . . . who was that jackal-headed gal? You
know, the Egyptian?"

"*Huh?*" But then Liz found her reflection. "Oh, okay
. . . Good thing I know how you think."

"I *like* foxes!"

"I know."

" 'Specially vixens."

"Good for you."

"What're female jackals called, I wonder?"

"Ma'am," Liz informed him promptly. "The Egyptian's a guy, by the way."

"But could he play blues on a chain saw?"

Liz bared her teeth. "Your bedroom doing anything
useful?"

"Accumulating dust atop mountains of clutter, moving slowly toward entropy, and"—David wrinkled his
nose—"yep, Alec's socks are startin' to turn."

Liz sniffed in turn. "Your sneakers, more likely. *I*
know what a neatnik the A-Boy is."

David finally managed to shift his attention from her
face. She was wearing a black scoop-necked top like a
leotard, an embroidered Guatemalan vest, and cutoffs
over scarlet tights. "So, what's in the bag, wench?" he
wondered.

"The reason I asked about your bedroom."

"Go for it."

Liz paused to give him a more satisfactory smooch,
then pranced through the door across from the study
and shut it. Not for the first time did David question
the decision made when he and Alec had moved into
the tiny house two months back, to share one bedroom
and use the other for schoolwork, hobbies, etc.; so that
both would command equal space. Trouble was, he had
more *stuff*, but Alec had more clothes—which didn't
cook with the closets. Still, for those times Liz slept

over, there was always the foldout couch in the living room.

Alec reemerged just then, caught him staring into space, and waved a hand in front of his eyes. "You cool?"

"Have to be," David murmured. "Consider the alternative."

Alec pinched his butt.

"Go to the living room and sit facing the hall," Liz called through the flimsy door. *"Now!"*

David exchanged bemused shrugs with his roomie and complied, pausing only to snare a Dr Pepper from the kitchen.

"You set?" Liz yelled a few minutes later.

"Sitting, technically," Alec gave back, from the sofa. "But yeah."

"Close your eyes, and don't open 'em until I say."

David did, clamping a hand over Alec's as well, just to be sure. Alec elbowed him in the ribs. David pinched his nostrils shut.

"Ready!" David hollered.

Footsteps approached, more high-heel staccato than sneaker slap. "Okay!" Liz snickered from the near end of the hall. "Anytime!"

David slitted one eye open—then stretched both very wide indeed. *"Whoa!"* he yipped approvingly. "Eep!" Alec echoed.

Liz was totally transformed. She'd always been cute in a pixie sort of way, and had matured into a genuinely attractive woman who appealed to David even more because she didn't need makeup to look good, and had brows and lashes dark enough to show—which wasn't a given with redheads. She'd always had a great, if funky, sense of style. Now, however . . . Well, he suddenly found himself gawking at a petitely seductive figure that bore scant resemblance to his sweetie.

Black. That was his first impression. Black tank top (not the leotard) that left arms and an enticing arc of upper bosom bare; skintight black leather pants; calf-high black boots with mid-rise heels; hand-wide black belt set with a double row of silver dog-collar studs; black wig artfully teased into irregular curves and spikes.

But that could've been any townie girl (or boy, for that matter) out to show the world how weird they were. What narrowed the costume to specificity were the details: white powder hastily applied to arms, throat, and face; lips, brows, and lashes redrawn in stark red and black. And the clinchers: a four-inch silver and gray-cloisonné ankh depending from a silver chain to gleam between perky little breasts, and a delicately drawn spiral unwinding from the corner of one eye onto her cheek.

"Death," Alec gulped into the breathless silence. "You look like Death!"

"Exactly!" David cried, through a widening grin.

"Think this'll do for the 40 Watt's Halloween bash?" Liz giggled. "The theme *is* comics and cartoons."

"It will very definitely do," David assured her. " 'Cept that I'm not sure anybody'll recognize you unless they read *Sandman*. 'Course I won't be able to *match* it . . ."

"Wanta bet?" Liz countered wickedly.

"Gimme a hint?"

"Trust me."

"Not after *that*!"

"You don't like it?"

"I love it!"

"The makeup's a quickie, but I couldn't wait."

"You're not, by any chance, thinkin' of doing me as Dream, are you?" David inquired slyly. "So we'd be a set?"

A brow lifted once again. "Dream's tall and thin."

"—Like ol' Alec here?" David cuffed his roommate—and got punched back for his pains.

"Perhaps," Liz answered coyly. "I—" She paused,

head tilted. Listening. David caught it too. So, by his sudden tensing, did Alec.

A faint scratching at the door.

"Aikin," David sighed. "Didn't hear him drive up."

"Probably parked up by the road," Alec opined. "He does that when he wants to be 'specially sneaky."

More scratching.

"It's open!" David hollered.

No dark-haired forestry major stealthed in. The scratching intensified.

"Cat?" Alec suggested, rising.

"Could be," David acknowledged. "There's been one hangin' around."

Alec sniffed derisively and padded down the hall. The door squeaked when he opened it. "Oh *hell*!"

"What . . . ?"

"Uh . . . Dave," Alec urged through clenched teeth, "you better get your butt up here."

David grimaced sourly, but rose. "What—?" He peered around the door. "Holy shit!"

"What is it," Liz called from the living room.

"Your guess," David replied, as he stared at the fox-sized creature calmly grooming itself on the porch. "But unless I've gone brain-dead, I'd say it's an . . . enfield."

"*What?*" Liz joined them before he could explain.

It *was* an enfield, too: no other beast had the body of a fox and the talons of an eagle in lieu of front paws.

It was also a creature from Faerie.

David felt a delicate chill of mixed alarm and wonder thrill up his spine as he eased closer. His hand rattled the screen. The enfield peered up at him, dark eyes bright and wary, but *not* alarmed. Intelligence showed there, too, of a kind—like the Faery deer had displayed up on the mountain. Enfields *were* fairly bright, David knew: smarter than dogs, less than monkeys, and more sweet-tempered than either foxes or raptors—unless you pissed one off, in which case you'd better hope things were cool with your next of kin, 'cause eagle talons driven by canine muscle were mondo worse than plain old fox jambs.

The enfield sat back on its haunches, looking very heraldic, and licked a foreleg at the juncture of fur and feathers. It sniffed the air, then whistled.

"Polite little sucker," Alec whispered.

"And absolutely fearless," from Liz.

David pushed the screen open enough to squeeze through. The enfield regarded him expectantly as he eased into a crouch. "Hey . . . *boy?*" he crooned, "Oops, no! Sorry! Hey little lady, what 'cha doin' here? Long way from home, aren't 'cha?"

He was no more than a yard from it now, and caught its odor: cinnamon more than musk. It whistle-trilled: a soothing sound like a cat purring in a drafty house. Slowly, he extended his knuckles toward its black-pointed muzzle.

"You came to the right place, kid," he murmured. "Anybody else 'round here would've run, screamed, or shot you."

The enfield rose, stretched like a cat, and stepped daintily forward. It nosed his knuckles curiously, then licked them—and sauntered past him toward the door a dazed-faced Alec still held open.

Alec didn't move, though whether from wonder, fear, or conditioned politeness that said one did not slam a door in a visitor's face—even a four-legged drop-by from the dreaded Faerie—was unclear. And with the way unimpeded, the creature slipped past him into the house. By the time David recovered enough to follow, it had curled up on the sofa. He knelt on the floor beside it, careful lest it be disturbed. Liz joined him.

Alec claimed an armchair opposite. The enfield promptly raised its head, leapt off the couch, and pranced across the carpet to drape itself across his feet, chin propped contentedly upon one sneakered toe.

"Likes you," David smirked. He resisted the urge to pet it.

Alec rolled his eyes. "Great!" he grunted. "Just peachy."

"Pretty little critter," Liz noted.

"Yeah," Alec sighed. "But . . . what the hell's it *doing* here?"

"Adoring your feet, apparently. Must like the smell of Doctor Scholl's."

"Seriously."

David exhaled wearily "Yeah, well, that's kinda the question, isn't it? I mean, it's neat as hell to have a critter like this park in your living room. On the other hand, the implications are scary as shit."

"No *joke*?" Alec snorted. "Golly!"

"Okay," David began pointedly, "let's look at this logically. First of all, this thing's from Faerie: we all know that. Second, critters from there don't come here of their own free will; but since this one *is* here, we can only assume it got here by accident."

"Not necessarily," Liz countered. "Somebody could've brought it deliberately, or it could've come *with* someone but not by their choice."

"Yeah," David admitted. "You're right. I just don't like to think about things like that."

"The borders are sealed," Alec reminded them.

"Closed," David corrected. "*Sealed* means you *can't* pass through 'em; Lugh's gotta physically link himself to the land to do that, and it hurts like hell. *Closed* means he'll kick ass if he finds you there. He's supposed to have closed them after the war between him and Erenn. The Powersmiths told him to or they'd kick *his* ass."

"So Alec's little buddy came solo?"

A shrug. "Anyone here by Lugh's leave is bound to have sense enough not to bring something so obviously alien. Anyone *else* would have more on his mind than ornamental critters."

"Therefore . . ."

"Therefore, it *probably* came of its own will. And if that's the case, it could only have come by the Tracks—or straight through the World Walls. Normally, I'd go with the former, in spite of the fact that critters can't usually activate 'em. Only, they *can*, sometimes, when they're charged up with adrenaline—like Ailill was that time he was changed into a deer—"

"And you guys *saw* a Faery deer just last Saturday!" Liz exclaimed.

"—That almost had to have come through the World Walls," David finished. "Right. There's no Track near there, and the way it just sorta *was* and was gone again makes that the obvious choice."

"Not good," Alec muttered. "Not good at all."

"Not if it means something's up with the World Walls," David agreed. "Makin' 'em grow thin in places, and all. Only, I can't think of any reason that'd be happening that didn't already exist. I mean, iron or steel in this World can burn through in time, if they're in big enough hunks. But it takes forever in most places—longer than it takes the metal to turn to rust and blow away—*unless* there's already a weak place in the World Walls. Or unless the iron lies *very* near a Track for a long time—like happens up by my folks' place.

"Therefore, something *else* is messing up the World Walls."

"Or something entirely different's goin' on we haven't thought of."

"So, what do we do?" Alec wondered. And finally gave in the obvious temptation to scratch the enfield between the ears. Its eyes closed blissfully. It chirped.

"About what?"

"The critter, first off. I mean, we can't exactly walk

up to the World Walls and start laying plaster across the holes."

"Interesting idea, though," David chuckled. "Make a good painting for Myra. But seriously . . . I don't see any choice but to hang on to the little sucker. She seems well behaved, and *we* know what she is. But if we turn her out, God knows what'll happen. I mean, the *last* thing the folks in Faerie need is humans gettin' concrete proof the place exists—which we have."

Alec froze in mid-caress. "We *keep* it?"

Another shrug. "I'm open to suggestions. But for the time being . . . yeah. Maybe we can contact somebody in Faerie and ask them what to do."

Alec scowled. "And how do you propose to do this? As if I didn't know!"

"*Sorry!*" David grumbled. "Like I said, I'm open to suggestions."

Alec puffed his cheeks. "Well," he began, "presumably Ms. Field here's still in the substance of Faerie— we could find out with some iron, I guess—just a *touch*, Liz! And if she is, then Faerie'll start drawing on her sooner or later—it always does. And when that happens . . . she oughta find her way back by instinct."

David scratched his chin. "So you're sayin' we wait until she starts gettin' antsy, then—"

"Hightail it to the nearest Track and hope she gets on."

"And if she doesn't?"

"Who knows?"

"I—Oh, crap!"

Alec looked startled. "What?"

David grimaced irritably. "I think that really *is* Aikin. Scratching at the door, I mean."

"Christ," Liz cried. "We've gotta hide the evidence!"

"Where?" Alec whispered, gazing frantically around the room.

David leapt to his feet. "Anywhere—but do it fast. You know Aik: we don't answer, he'll try the back." He eyed the door to the rear stoop ominously, then the archway into the kitchen—which was a dead end. The hall was obviously out—which left the bedroom, since the study had no door. *If* Aikin didn't simply barge in.

More scratching.

"Bedroom!" David hissed. "Now! I'll stall."

—At which point the front door swung open and a familiar figure eased in. Alec bolted for the back, which was still out of Aikin's sight line, but the enfield dug in with both talons and would not let go—not so much from maliciousness, it seemed, as a simple desire to stay with him. "Ouch! Fuck! Get the hell off me . . . *beast!*" he yipped, fairly dancing a jig as the enfield hung on for dear life.

Aikin was there in an instant. "I'm not *on* you—yet," he drawled. And then saw what clutched Alec's leg— and what it did for forepaws. "Ohshit*wow*!" he blurted in a rush. "What's *that*?"

"Enfield," David choked resignedly.

Aikin shook his head. "Too lively for a gun."

"The gun was named for the critter!"

Aikin was on his knees by then, happily engaged in trying to disengage the enfield from Alec's jeans, which were already in tatters below one knee. Fortunately, he had a true empathy with wildlife, and though he had no qualms about killing animals for sport (and using as much of what he bagged as possible), he also genuinely liked them. Thus, he was competently gentle as he clutched the enfield with his right hand and carefully freed first one talon, then the other with the left, pausing as he did to examine them critically.

"Bit of endangered species research?" he asked a tad too nonchalantly. David wondered if he was going to accuse them of holding out on him—which, from pure force of habit, they almost had.

"Only one of its kind—in this World—I hope," David told him. "I think they're pretty common in Faerie.

And before you get the wrong idea: we've *not* been hidin' it. That little lady showed up not five minutes ago and was makin' herself perfectly at home until you arrived, at which point she latched onto Alec like a leech."

Aikin had not released the enfield, but neither did it seem inclined to resist his inspection. It licked his knuckles. He let it. "They always this friendly?"

David shrugged helplessly. "I've only met a couple."

Aikin was examining the claw/upper arm juncture. "Whoa! How many joints we *got* in this leg anyway?"

"What do you mean?"

"Foxes—which is what this gal mostly looks like—walk on their toes. Half of what we call leg is actually foot; their heels are inches above the ground. This one's . . . not like that. —Oh, and by the way, can I borrow your Warner Brothers video again? I wanta check some stuff on my costume."

Caught off guard by the non sequitur, David blinked. "The one of which you refused to speak last week?" he managed finally. "Or is this week's secret different?"

"Yes and no." Aikin had not stopped examining the enfield.

David could think of nothing useful to say. It had been an . . . eventful ten minutes.

Aikin rose with deliberate care. "Hold on to that a sec," he commanded, pointing to the beast. "No! Stay!"—When it made to follow him. "I wanta get some pictures."

"You *what*?" David screeched.

Aikin regarded him calmly. "I want to take its picture, preferably several. I'd *really* like to take her back to Whitehall with me, in fact; but that's probably out of the question—without Alec's leg goin' along, at any rate, which I doubt he's too keen on. But since I may never get another chance to observe a mythical beast this close . . . well, basically, you guys owe me."

David eyed him narrowly. "Only if you let Liz do the developing."

"I'll consider it," Aikin replied noncommittally—and stalked toward the door. He paused half-in, half-out. "Got a yardstick?"

Before anyone could reply, a rusty blur leapt from the floor where it had been lolling and streaked down the hall. And before even Aikin's reflexes could close the screen, the enfield had slipped between his legs and zipped outside. He spun around instantly, but already it had vanished. "Shit," he spat bitterly. "Damn."

David pushed past him onto the porch and frantically scanned the bushy lawn and the avenue of pines that paralleled the road. The enfield was nowhere to be seen. His friends joined him as he jogged to the highway and looked up and down, then made a quick tour of the perimeter of the small wooded lot.

Nothing.

Enfields were forest creatures, so his Faery friend Fionchadd had told him. And the unimproved acreage adjoining *Casa McLean y Sullivan* to the east was thoroughly wooded. A cow pasture lay beyond the fence at the edge of the backyard, and behind it were yet more trees.

"Feel like doin' some trackin'?" David asked Aikin between panting breaths, as he slowed by the tumbledown shed that passed for a garage.

Aikin's face was tight with disappointment. "Cammie's havin' me to dinner, and she'll have a shit-fit if I'm not dead on time. Plus, I've got a killer test tomorrow and have absolutely *gotta* study. 'Sides," he added, "I figured you'd be glad to see it go."

"I am—sort of," David admitted. "The trouble starts if anyone *else* sees it."

Aikin raised an eyebrow. "You ever stop to think how, out of all the houses on this road, it chose the only folks who *wouldn't* go ballistic?"

"We don't know that," Alec shot back. "It could've scratched at every door for miles."

"I don't think so," David countered slowly. "I think it knew *exactly* where to come."

"How so?" From Liz.

"They're mondo-good trackers, for one thing," David replied, "So Nuada says, anyway—which is why Lugh keeps so many of 'em around. But they're also psychic as hell—can track by scent, or residual body-heat—*or* by thought patterns, especially strong emotions, like, for instance, the desire to escape, or *not* be caught or found. Therefore, assuming this gal blundered here by accident, we're probably the only folks for miles who would have anything even vaguely familiar in our brain patterns: namely, our awareness of Faerie. I mean I know it's a stretch, but . . ."

"What's their range?" Liz broke in, pragmatically.

David shrugged. "No idea."

"So why'd it boogie off like that?"

Another shrug. "Maybe it didn't like Aikin's vibes, or something. I mean, would you like being poked and measured and prodded by Mr. Ranger, Sir-in-training?"

Aikin looked as though he were about to explode— from a variety of possible causes. "God, I hate this," he growled. "I mean, this is the neatest thing that's happened for . . . *years*—and for once, I really *cannot* hang around. I really do have to grab that video and fly."

Alec rummaged through the neatly ranked boxes in the bookcase beside the TV and produced the appropriate box. "Kill the wabbit," he said deadpan.

Aikin snatched it. "Magic helmet," he cried, with what sounded suspiciously like forced glee—and leapt off the porch.

"Carry on," David called, as his friend jogged toward the black Chevy S-10 that had replaced his Nova at high school graduation. "And if you see the critter again, hang *on to* it."

"Oh yes," Aikin nodded, as he climbed into the cab. "You can bet on *that!*"

Chapter VII:
House Guest

(Athens, Georgia—
Thursday, October 29—late afternoon)

"The first ninety percent of a project takes the first ninety percent of the time," Aikin had read in the science library men's room. *"The remaining ten percent takes the other ninety."*

He was stuck in the second batch. Midterms were long since over, he *still* hadn't finished his plant collection—and now trees were shedding their leaves right and left, less-hardly stock was wilting in earnest, and he was supposed to submit *green* specimens. *What I get for taking botany* fall *quarter,* he grumbled silently, as he squatted on a nature trail below the be-herbed bank that loomed above the wooded floodplain between the Phoenix and the river. The building's roof was barely visible from where he crouched, so he pointedly didn't look. Better to pretend this was virgin forest—like that he'd glimpsed in his dream of Faerie.

Faerie . . .

No! He'd gnawed *that* bone too long already—since Dave had started sporting a certain odd ring four summers back, in fact. Of course, it had been no big deal—at first. But then silence had piled atop weirdness, and cryptic reference on puzzling act, until what had begun as confused frustration had ended in outright rage. Not that his friends had actually *liked* excluding him, Dave had hastened to add, no more than he'd liked being on the receiving end. Nor, in all honesty, would he have acted any different had he been in their Reeboks. Still, it had hurt—a lot.

But his long drought of deprivation seemed to be ending in a monsoon. First the white deer, then Dave's increased willingness to talk about other Worlds, followed by the aborted scrying and the dream. Never mind the Track less than half a mile from his cabin, which was as close to his base as the one at the Sullivans' farm was to Dave's. And then yesterday's business with the enfield.

Trouble was, he could live without Faerie when it was remote. But when it was suddenly all over the place—*that* was different. Ignorance had given way to knowledge, finally. But what he *wanted*, to put him on a par with his friends, was experience. He did *not*, however, need the annoyance of trying to achieve it now!

Not with the demon academia starting to demand more than lip service sacrifice.

So here he was in the soggy woods (at least it was warm, though more rain was in the forecast) trying very hard to scare up the several genera he had no examples of yet, when it was the last thing he really wanted to do. Idly, he sifted the leaves beside the trail. Nothing new. Then again, why should there be? And why bother with dead leaves anyway? What he needed was live growth: specifically, jack-in-the-pulpit and Sagittarius. Which were more likely to grow close to water than on a shaded bank eighty yards inshore.

He had just straightened with the intent of acting on that brilliant insight, when the telltale rattle-rustle of leaves atop the bank signaled the presence of four-legged company. Squirrel, probably, perhaps a chipmunk, though it was early in the afternoon for either to be really active, the hours after dawn and preceding sunset being best—if one were hunting. Hunting squirrels, that is; nobody bothered with chippies.

Rustle, rattle, rustle . . .

He cocked his head, victim, as usual, of surfeit of

curiosity. *Too big for a squirrel.* He craned his neck, searching the tangled greenery. *Rabbit . . . ?*

More rustling.

Wrong rhythm for a bunny, and likely bigger yet. Which narrowed the options to cat, dog (domestic type, one each), 'coon, or an atypically diurnal 'possum.

A shrug, and he turned away. Only there it was again, louder and closer, both. He spun back around, backed up a pace to survey the bank, saw nothing, and had started to beat feet again, when he caught a flash of movement: rat-sized, but tan with black stripes.

It *had* been a chipmunk.

Losin' it, Daniels. Sounded bigger.

At which point the chipmunk erupted from whatever shelter had proved untenable, and launched itself down the slope, across the trail, and into the knee-high grass between the bank and the river—followed, to his amazement, by a rust-toned blur that could only be a fox, bushy tail and black-tipped ears barely visible as it flashed less than three yards from his feet. "Son of a bitch!" he cried—and dashed after.

Though foxes were fairly common in Georgia, he'd never encountered one so close to the Phoenix, so in that alone it bore scrutiny. It was a fast little sucker, too, by the way the grass rippled in its wake—which ended abruptly in a muddled swirl of motion through which rose the thrash/grunt-swish/grunt-growl of an unequal struggle, punctuated by the strangled chirp of a chipmunk *in extremis*.

And since he was in excellent shape (mostly from jogging, though he also pumped iron now and then), Aikin was not even slightly winded when, ten feet from the patch of gyrating grass, he shifted his noisy plunge to silent stealth.

Nothing yet, though the grass still swayed and shifted in a way that wasn't natural, and he could hear a grinding sound and—he thought—the crunch-snap of tiny bones breaking. He winced, then caught himself and scowled. What were chipmunks *for*, in the grand, cold scheme of things, but to be eaten by predators? And people gave *hunters* grief? Ha! Better to be shot dead unexpectedly in your prime, than be slowly chomped alive, or succumb to hunger and disease in old age.

Disease . . . God, suppose the fox had rabies? Many wild carnivores in Georgia did. And this one *was* behaving a tad oddly simply by being about in the middle of the day. On the other hand, there was a climbable tree two yards to the right . . .

Another step, and by craning his neck he finally glimpsed his quarry—sitting calmly on its haunches with its jaws working vigorously as it choked down its kill. It was facing away from him, but he glimpsed a striped tail and one leg dangling from its jaws. And when it raised a forepaw to scratch its chin, Aikin's mouth dropped open.

Not a paw! A *talon*! This was no fox; it was a bloody *enfield*! In fact, now he looked at it, it could very well be the same impossible beast he'd examined yesterday at Dave's.

It *had* run off, after all. And Dave had said something about Faerie exerting a draw on anything from there that entered another World. And where was the nearest way back home? The Track that ran through the woods across the river!

So what did he do now? He hadn't brought his camera—*again*—but he was damned if he was gonna let the critter escape without investigation. Well, he could check for tracks, for one thing, and maybe get some plaster casts. Possibly there'd be scat, too, from which he could gain a sense of diet. And, of course, he could simply observe: see how an alien predator adapted to a (presumably) new environment.

Only . . . the alien predator had also noticed *him*, indeed had swiveled gracefully around and was ambling

his way, utterly nonchalant, utterly unconcerned—
and very unalien and un–predator-like indeed. In fact,
it was acting a great deal like a country-reared house
cat: wanting to be petted one moment, hunting live
game in the woods the next.

It had approached to within two yards now, and he
eased down before it, extending a hand as he had yesterday, trying *not* to think about scientific investigation. "Hey, girl," he whispered. "What's happenin'—
'sides hunting? So, are you tame, or what? You some
Faery boy's pet? Some AWOL heraldic toy?"

The enfield blinked and crept closer yet, its body
slung low above the ground as though it were stalk-
ing—then lunged straight at him, veering aside at the
last possible instant to dart onto the trail, where it
promptly stopped again and looked around implor-
ingly.

He followed. Could not resist—first because the critter was interesting in its own right; second, because he
might never see one again if he *didn't* keep an eye on
it. And finally, because it was from Faerie, and every
moment he was exposed to any aspect of that place
was bliss.

Ten feet away, and it was moving again—dammit!
He followed doggedly as the enfield calmly pranced
along the trail, toward the cabin, and, not incidentally,
the dam. So which way would it turn there, if at all?
Right, which would bring it between the cabin and the
Phoenix? Or left, across the river, to the Track?

It chose the latter, and Aikin had to hustle to keep
up, as his quarry leapt atop broken chunks of mill foun-
dations he was forced to climb over or go around. By
the time he'd conquered the confusion of concrete
blocks (they'd always reminded him of that scene in
Highlander where Sean Connery and Clancy Brown
destroyed a pele-tower with swordplay), the beast was
licking its talons in the center of the span.

Strangest thing for a thousand miles, and there you

sit like a knot on a log. God, I hope my roomies aren't watchin'!

Ten feet to his furry goal, and the enfield rose and trotted ahead, exactly like Aikin's old sheltie, Maybeline, did when she wanted him to follow.

He did. Nor was he surprised when, upon hopping off the barrier's end, the creature took the straightest route to the lightning-blasted oak and the bifurcated maple—which was directly through a laurel hell. Aikin lost sight of her there, and briefly feared she had vanished into Faerie without permitting that final glimpse he so desperately desired. Shoot, even if he caught her in the act of vanishing, that'd be cool enough: the proof he needed that she truly was from another World.

But when he finally made it around the troublesome clump of shrubbery, there she was: calmly combing her tail through her claws right beside the strip of suspect ground. She looked up at him curiously, blinked the dark eyes that flanked her sharp, black-tipped nose, trill-whistled once—and stepped onto the Track.

"Shit!" Aikin spat, before he could stop himself—or contrive a more appropriate exclamation of wonder. He hopped back reflexively—which brought him up solid against the oak. And stared wide-eyed, as what seconds before had been merely a stretch of ground carpeted with dead leaves on which nothing grew, suddenly began to glow, as though a layer of dust suspended just above its surface had caught fire and was burning to golden embers. And even as he watched, that light spread from the enfield's feet several yards either way along the Track.

The animal trilled coyly.

"Tryin' to lead me astray, huh?" Aikin muttered, as he recovered enough to ease closer, aware at some level that maybe the *beast* did have an agenda, and perhaps he ought to beware.

On the other hand, if they were as psychic as Dave had said, maybe it had simply picked up on his own desire and was acting accordingly. In which case . . .

Another trill.

Closer yet, and the briars scraped against his jeans—whereupon he closed his eyes and took the fateful step.

And this time, even through rubber soles, he felt something—not unpleasant, as he had feared; merely a subtle tingle, like a low-level electric shock without the pain. In fact, now he analyzed it, a soothing flow of energy was creeping up his legs, easing every tired muscle and strained sinew in its wake.

The enfield trilled again, and trotted off—west. Aikin hesitated but an instant, then took a deep breath and followed. *Only ten paces,* he told himself. *More than that . . . you shouldn't.*

Two paces, and nothing had changed, save that it was like walking on springy turf barefoot; it was that invigorating. Oh, and there was an indefinable sweetness in the air: a draught of spring on the eve of winter. Two more steps, and that breeze grew stronger—and didn't that hickory over to his right show more leaves than it ought, and greener? Five more paces, and the trees were in full leaf; some were species he'd never seen before; and the briars, which had been thin and wilted as an old man's hair, were suddenly grown *much* thicker, in diameter and number both, and were starting to loop about themselves like living Celtic knotwork.

And then he saw the green-and-orange bird that lit upon a particularly heavy whorl of briar to nip at a small bright fruit that was patently *not* a blackberry—and shivered, though with delight or fear was unclear. He *recognized* that bird! Carolina parakeet, it was, extinct in *his* World a hundred years!

He *had* to get his camera.

Fortunately, the enfield seemed disinclined to continue, had in fact flopped down in the middle of the Track four yards farther on, and was sniffing at turf that showed green grass, where ten paces east it had sported only dead leaves.

"Don't move!" he told the bird, as he turned and strode back down the Track. —And felt a jolt of genuine fear when he didn't immediately spot the blasted oak. Four paces brought it into view, however (he wasn't sure exactly how, as the trees right next to it had worn leaves an instant before), and five more put him beside it.

On dead leaves, flanked by halfhearted briars.

Yet the Track still glowed beneath his sneakers. And seemed to glow more brightly when a scrabbling among the leaves proved to be the enfield returning.

"Can't live without me, huh?" he told it—and stepped back into his own World. The beast angled across to follow—which pleased him mightily. But just as it ducked beneath a spray of intervening briars, a stray sprig snared its ear.

It yipped in startlement and thrashed its head—which drove the briar deeper.

Aikin needed no further prompting. Before intellect had time to argue reflexes out of so impulsive a decision, he leapt the short distance between himself and the Track, and in one smooth, firm move, seized the creature's shoulders, fully expecting an armful of teeth for his pains. Instead, it whimpered.

"It's okay, girl," he told it, resecuring his hold with one hand while the other gently disentangled the briar from the long, black-tufted ear. It growled and flinched—which tore the briar free and produced a thin smear of blood barely visible amid its fur. It did not try to escape, however, and Aikin did not release it. "You really must belong to somebody," he murmured, stroking its back. "Or else Faery critters are decorative but dumb."

It licked his hand.

Impulsively, he picked it up, tucking it into the cradle of his arms like the oversize cat it felt like (courtesy of looser joints than those of the fox it more closely resembled), and rose. The Track dimmed to nothing behind him. A moment later, he was marching across the dam, and shortly after that, had found the trail that wound up the bluff above the nature trail to his cabin.

"Roomies oughta be in class," he informed it. And would be leaving on a weekend field trip midday tomorrow, he added to himself. So the question was, could he hide his odd charge from prying eyes for the next eighteen hours?

At which point he found himself confronting the foundation of his home-away-from-home. The cabin—one of several built as housing for Forestry majors, this most recently—was set on a steep slope in such a way that the front was level with a skimpy yard-cum-parking area barely big enough to accommodate four vehicles; while the rear, which sported a porch, soared out into the open air on posts that screened a sort of service patio beneath. A concrete retaining wall backed it, *and*, on one end, a ten-foot-square basement, outside which a previous occupant had conveniently stored a number of white fiberglass cages of the type one used to take Fluffy or FooFoo to the vet.

"Well, you ain't Fluffy or FooFoo," Aikin told the complacent enfield. "But I bet one of these'll do."

He found a beagle-sized one, popped the latch on the metal door, and made to thrust the beast inside.

As it neared the chrome steel bars, however, Aikin felt it stiffen within his grip, then start to struggle. It began to hiss and cry. He caught the faintest hint of the stench of burning hair.

"Oops, cold iron," he sighed. "Well, forget *that*! But I tell you what: I'll give you something better—but you'll have to be quiet, okay?"

The enfield licked his chin.

"Why do I think you understand me? And not just my thoughts either!"

Another lick.

It was all predicated on no one being upstairs, of course—as he eased from under the porch to peer up the slope to the east. The coast was clear: no vehicles lurked before the cabin save his own. Other than the small risk of someone arriving just at the wrong time, or seeing him from one of the other cabins, he was home free. Taking a deep breath, he scrambled up the slope, turned left at the top, and (after trying the knob, which would mean someone *was* home), unlocked the door—which required some creative juggling of hands, keys, and critter.

Fortunately, the basement key hung on a nail just inside the entrance, and he was able to retrieve it without going in. An instant later, he assailed the basement door. The lock resisted briefly, and he feared someone had changed it. But then it clicked and the door swung open. The room beyond had a concrete floor, cinder block walls, and shelves along two sides on which an odd lot of outdoorsy gear was piled. Aikin closed the door behind him, strode to the middle of the room, and slowly eased the enfield down. It rubbed against his leg. "You oughta be okay in here," he told it. "Just stay away from anything that feels like iron or steel. I'm gonna go see what I can find to feed you, but don't *you* say a word! No way in hell I could explain something like you!"

And with that, he backed toward the door. The enfield took a tentative step in his wake, then elected not to follow.

"Take care, kid," he called softly. "Dinner's on the way, and then I'm gonna get my camera and my tape measure and my yardstick, and *we* are gonna party!"

Chapter VIII:
Spirits in the Night

(Athens, Georgia—
Friday, October 30—sunset)

"Could've been worse," Alec smirked, bent kissing-close to David's ear to make himself heard above the thunder of rock and roll that was well-nigh deafening even two blocks from ground zero and *inside* the cab of Liz's Ranger. "It *could've* been Keebler."

David rolled his eyes, then squinted through the windshield at their black-clad designated driver, who had just disembarked and was surveying Hancock Street like a townie-girl grim reaper searching for lab-lackeys to scythe. He sighed dramatically, checked the rearview mirror to confirm that his pointed rubber ears were on straight, and adjusted the fake-fur vest that accented his bare torso. "I don't know about this . . ."

Alec paused with his hand on the door handle and grinned at him through white pancake around black-ringed eyes beneath a silver-shot wig akin to Liz's: Dream, from *Sandman*; brother to Liz's Death from the same graphic novel. A lull in the music made speaking viable. "How so?"

"Well, it makes us a mixed visual metaphor, for one thing."

"What you get for trusting women."

"Just 'cause *you're* tall and slim . . ."

"Just 'cause *you're* short, blond, snub-nosed, and muscular—and have no chest hair to speak of."

"Nobody'll know who I am."

" 'Course they will! Folks read *Elfquest* 'round here. Aik says they sell *lots* of 'em over at Comics and Music."

Liz gestured like manic semaphore, then mouthed an impatient,"You coming?"

Alec hit the street.

David followed. The late-day breeze flowed cool across his skin—more skin than he preferred to display in public, as a point of fact; Liz wasn't the only one flashing cleavage, though his was mostly evident when he sat. "That's how they're drawn," she'd explained. "But I guess cloth doesn't stretch the same as leather."

Still, all things considered, she'd done a bang-up job. The fur vest, she'd cut down from a tawny thrift store coat; the flared leather pants that hung perilously low across his hipbones and lower yet fore and aft, she'd faked from painter's canvas and Masada thongs. The peacock feather on the quasi sporran-codpiece had come from his landlord's flock, and the pointy-toed boots were courtesy of Myra's chums in the Society for Creative Anachronism. The short curved sword was plywood and foamcore, per a new city ordinance that forbade public display of weapons that could be taken for real; but the thick white-blond hair, part of which was bound up in a topknot, was his own. All in all, he really did look the part of Cutter, the chief of the Wolf-riders from *Elfquest*.

"I just hope we can get *in*!" Alec grumbled, as they joined Liz on the sidewalk.

"That's the point of comin' early," David countered cheerfully. "And see and be seen, of course. Speakin' of which," he added to Liz, "any sign of Hunterman?"

"S'posed to meet us here at sunset."

David scanned the slit of sky visible between the Athens Post Office and Franklin Financial. The sun was conveniently revealed there, so close to the horizon, he expected to see rooftops smolder.

"I'd give him five minutes," Alec opined.

"Three." From Liz.

David was glad he'd left his watch at home. *He* was in the mood for some serious living for the moment. Some major-league kick-ass partying-down.

And for forgetting.

It'd been a bitch-kitty couple of days. A bitch-kitty week, in fact, what with the ongoing grief of classes, plus Alec's whining, plus trying to thread a romance with Liz through her duties as a resident assistant in Reed Hall—never mind that song and dance with the enfield back on Wednesday and the blowup with Aikin the Saturday before.

And absolutely never mind his most persistent demon: that troubling revelation about David-the-Elder, which was a freshly tined pitchfork prodding his psyche. *Just when you think you can trust folks,* he told himself, for the millionth time that week, *they show you their asshole side.*

The sun tapped the horizon. Shadows went as sharp-edged and ominous as David's frustration had lately been. As if to voice that tension, the air awoke with the strident opening fanfare from "Ride of the Valkyries."

David jumped about a foot straight up. Dream's mouth dropped open; Death's eyes narrowed suspiciously. The music was blaring from the waist-high azalea hedge that separated City Hall from the sidewalk, just below the infamous double-barreled cannon.

Louder, that music shrieked, and at the precise moment the first busty soprano should have begun bellowing, an unlikely figure leapt from behind the bushes and mounted the landmark's muzzle. David's fast call was of a shortish male cased from thigh to chin in a tube of duct-taped and silver-sprayed cardboard that was surely supposed to be armor but in fact resembled a garbage can; an outsize horned helmet silhouetted against a lavender sky; and a stubby cross-hilted sword swung aloft. Whereupon the figure struck a martial pose and yelled, at the top of its lungs, "Kill the wabbit!"

And vaulted down to join them, pausing in transit to reach into the hedge and switch off the boombox stashed there.

"Magic helmet!" David laughed, thwacking the headgear with his sword. "Jesus, man; that's *wonderful*

Aikin raised his own bogus weapon in warning. "Watch it!" he warned, with a fiendish grin—and swung.

David blocked reflexively, and for a moment Elmer Fudd's Wagnerian hero from "What's Opera, Doc?" faced off against an elf-chief from an alternative comic book. Blows were struck. Thrusts were met and parried. And then Elmer got past Cutter's guard and stabbed (none too gently, for a wooden sword) his stomach, just as Cutter smacked Elmer's inverted-wok-with-cow-horns chime-ringing hard.

"Stir-fried brains," Alec-Dream observed, deadpan, as both toppled.

"More work for me," Liz-Death sighed. "I wonder who I should carry off first."

"The elf," Aikin volunteered instantly, between throes. "That way I can groove on the music longer."

Alec checked his watch and motioned downhill, toward the ten-block heart of downtown Athens. "C'mon, folks," he cried, flinging his black cape out dramatically. "Sandman says it's time to party!"

"Where'd Liz go?" Alec yelled five minutes later, from where he and David jostled with a couple hundred fellow revelers on College Avenue, from which traffic had been barred for the night. Voices rumbled and roared and rose now and then to a primal shriek. The music was louder still.

"Must've seen a soul she wanted to collect in Barnett's," David shouted back. His gaze drifted from the brightly lit window wall to his right, back to the street—where a possibly female Garfield was dancing with a probably white Don King, while a gleeful Lorena Bobbitt (complete with plastic butcher knife and appropriate, if oversize, severed appendage) tried to break in—all to the music of Shaken, Not Stirred's third frantically incomprehensible number exploding from the portable bandstand at the juncture of College and Broad.

Yep, he thought, Halloween was definitely cooking with gas. Actually, it was Halloween *Eve*, but since the thirty-first abutted a Sunday, and bars closed early then (never mind the pagan overtones of this most ancient of holidays, which were best kept safely distanced, the Religious Right insisted), the downtown merchants and club owners had designated Friday for the "official" observance, and had most of the neighboring streets plugged with bandstands to prove it. Of course there'd be celebrating on Saturday too; no proper Athenian ever missed a chance to party. But the big ones with prizes were all tonight.

Like the Cartoon-and-Comics bash at the 40 Watt.

"Who's playing, anyway?" Alec wondered. "I forgot."

"Mrs. Atkins and The Woggles," David shot back. Aikin, intent on Shaken, was oblivious.

"Who's opening?"

"Who knows?"

"Best we be at it, then," Alec said. "Here comes Ms. Death."

"Treat?" Liz prompted, tossing each of them a Hershey bar.

"More like tricks, in *that* garb," Alec giggled. He snared Elmer by an ear, and the mismatched foursome got moving.

"Cammie couldn't come?" Liz asked Aikin offhand, as they careened around the corner onto Clayton Street.

Aikin scowled minutely and muttered a terse, "Moving," but David caught a trace of relief in his expression—which didn't quite fit. In fact, now he thought of it, Aik had been acting odd all day: breathlessly impatient on the phone when they'd worked out the evening's logistics, as though he'd been interrupted in the middle of something both strenuous and important—like sex (though if Mr. Forestry and his study wench had started pollinating, it was news to him)—then almost giddily up when he'd surprised them a few minutes back; and then antsy as an echidna on speed while they'd waited for Liz just now. None of which were like calm, quiet, terminally secretive Mighty Hunter Daniels. But maybe Aik had his own demons.

"Watch it!" someone slurred from behind, forcing David to skip sideways or be collected by a staggering fat man dressed, coincidentally, as Satan.

"Ego te exorciso . . ." David called back promptly.

"Nice buns, elf!" someone else—female—hooted approvingly, as he recovered.

Liz growled.

Alec and Aikin grinned.

"You know," David told them, "I could get into this. Maybe I'll wear these to class."

Liz slapped the pertinent location. "Don't you *dare!*"

David tickled her.

And the four of them moved on—but not in silence.

By resisting the snares of the tempting blues thudding up from D.T.'s Downunder, and the half-priced costumes at The Junkman's Daughter's Brother, they won through to Lumpkin Street. Another band was blaring from Frijoleros halfway down, all at odds with the upscale quasi pub subtlety of the Globe on the nearer corner, which had contented itself with artfully carved jack-o'-lanterns in each of its deep-set windows.

They angled across Lumpkin and Clayton on the fly (avoiding Jeff-from-Barnett's dressed as Elvis, a hooker in corset and fishnet hose, and the third generic flasher they'd been underwhelmed by in a block), to pause for breath beneath the Georgia Theater's marquee, where the classic horror film *Freaks* had been playing non-stop all day, accompanied by hourly beer specials. An overpriced parking lot came next. And then they saw the line down Washington Street to the 40 Watt. All block and a half of it.

Aikin groaned resoundingly.

"Oh cheer up, Fuddsy," Alec chided. "It'll be *three* blocks in ten minutes."

"Kill the wabbel!" Aikin snarled, with feeling.

David barely heard him; he was staring across the street at a tall young man in mime makeup and terrorist fatigues, juggling bright plastic hand grenades.

"Two Low-brows an' a Coke," Alec announced three hours later, as he squeezed between David and Liz. He whisked his cloak aside to reveal a cola and a pair of draft beers—which would've raised eyebrows back home, not the least because all three of the partakers were underage. Still, even well–brought-up mountain kids could access fake IDs—especially when two of them studio-sat for a well-known graphic artist, and the other was a world-class hacker.

Like Liz, the fourth member of their tribe was not partaking; first because he didn't drink in public, and second, because he was dancing like a fool. David watched him from where they were scrunched up at a table beside the dance floor. Mighty Hunter Fudd's feet had gone manic one beat back, and were now well-nigh invisible, as the band segued into something that allowed him to jig. Actually, one could jig to lots of stuff, David knew. And buckdance too. Too bad the Madonna wannabe who partnered him kept stopping to adjust her cones.

As if playing to Aikin alone, the Woggles were giving it *their* best shot as well. Red-haired Manfred "Professor" Jones was screaming like a happy banshee; Tim "Timmy Tom-Tom" Terelli pounded the drums like a shaman at a puberty rite; while Martin "Zorko" Brooks and Patrick "Buzz Bomb" O'Connor swapped riffs on guitar and bass. The piece was called "Mad Dog 22."

Though "Mad Man" might have been more appropriate, if one took their cues from Aik.

The music grew louder and faster yet. Feeling reckless, David chugged his beer and dragged Liz onto the floor. Alec downed his too, and joined them.

Five more songs, another brew apiece—and a very sweaty David Sullivan had to admit he was both bushed and buzzed.

"Where's Fuddsy?" he gasped, as he flopped against the wall beside Liz, who, having stood this one out because she didn't like the song, was comparing costume notes with one of the girls on her hall. A very *pretty* girl, David couldn't help but notice, in well-done Prince Valiant drag that showed a shocking amount of ample bosom. She regarded him frankly, if a tad glass-eyed; her gaze sagging from his face, past his chest, to his belly, and lower—where it lingered. "Nice . . . feather," she giggled.

David grinned.

The girl leered back.

Liz glowered. "I'll lend you the pattern," she snapped, and turned to David. *"What?"* she demanded, brows lifted pointedly.

"I said, 'where's Aikin?' More to the point, where's Alec? Aik can take care of himself. Mr. Sandman's had a few."

"So've you."

David managed a crooked smile. "It happens."

"McLean's walkin' his lizard," someone offered helpfully from David's left. A glance that way put him eye to beak with Scrooge McDuck, though Goofy would've been a better choice, as the guy was over six feet tall. David squinted at him, trying to place the voice behind the fake-fur and plastic. "Gil?" he ventured.

"Possibly," McDuck quacked cryptically, and waddled away.

David stood on tiptoes (cursing yet again that he was only five-seven—Aikin alone of his buds was shorter), and surveyed the thick-packed crowd.

The Woggles had proclaimed a break, and canned music was the order of the night (the obligatory REM), which meant it was time to refill drinks, attend to bodily functions, reconnect with strayed companions, and toss one's cookies at need.

Aikin, however, seemed disinclined to pursue any of those options. In fact, with or without sword and magic helmet, he was nowhere in sight.

"Prob'ly sneaked off," David allowed eventually.

"Be just like him," Liz agreed, easing her arm around him so that her hand rested on his hip, her fingers inside the waistband.

"He's a big boy, though. He's not been drinkin' and he's got his own wheels."

"Acting funny, though."

David scowled at her, wishing he was not so buzzed. "How so?"

A shrug. "I dunno. Just funny. Wired—distracted. Something like that."

David shrugged in turn and returned his attention to the dance floor. The band had picked up their instruments again, after a very short break indeed, and was laying down a fine opening riff for what promised to be an *amazingly* fast number. He peered down at his half-finished Löwenbräu. "Think I'll sit this 'un out," he said. And surveyed the dancers again.

And well-nigh dropped his cup.

"Shit!" he hissed.

No one heard—apparently. But he also hoped no one *saw* the tall, dark-haired woman who had just melted from the mob on the opposite side of the darkened room. If she was wearing an actual *costume*, it didn't register; though he got an impression of layers of gray, green, and black. And if that costume represented anyone from cartoons or comics, it mattered even less.

What he *did* notice was her face: white as a moon among stars, but in a way that suggested natural pallor; features as elegantly chiseled as a celebrity model's; and waist-length black hair that flowed like spun night around her. Her brows were dark and arching, her eyes scarcely paler, and slanted exotically.

His eyes were burning like fire, and not from smoke or tears. For, incredible as it seemed, the woman was one of the Sidhe!

"Three's the charm," he muttered so softly no one heard. "Deer, enfield, and this. Something's *gotta* be goin' on."

But what? Well, Faerie was evidently slopping out all over, for one thing; and traditional day for such occurrences notwithstanding, it seemed *very* unlikely that he'd hear not a peep from there for two years, then encounter the denizens of that place thrice in less than a week. In fact, this lady was a day early, if she wanted to observe true Samhain.

So what *was* she doing here? More to the point, was she doing *anything* besides enjoying herself? And was there anything more than coincidence to the fact that three of the dozen or so mortals in the country who could recognize what she was happened to be in this same room?

Or—troubling thought—were there *more* than a dozen? Did other mortals likewise know of Faerie? Like that John Devlin guy, maybe? He'd certainly seemed to know *something*! Unfortunately, Nuada, who was his principal contact among the Sidhe, had refused to tell, and he hadn't thought to ask Fionchadd until the Faery youth was out of the loop and back home with his mom's Powersmith kin across an impassable sea. But if something *was* stirring up traffic between the Worlds, how widespread was it? He knew of three recent incursions himself, but that didn't mean there weren't others. But was Faerie *really* leaking, or was that mere paranoia?

And what did he do about it?

If anything.

He didn't *need* this, dammit! Juggling school and money and friendships and *relationships* and work-study and career plans was complex enough without Faerie muddying the waters. Never mind his simmering little vendetta against the Morrigu, that so far had amounted to no more than unfocused anger, but on which he was determined to make good.

Still, if he had a *serious* death wish, he supposed he could con a pocketknife off somebody (AWOL Aikin surely had one), and hold the lady at bay with cold iron until she gave him the straight scoop—*assuming* she still wore the substance of Faerie, which wasn't necessarily the case; nor wise, given the amount of ferrous metal about.

But even he wasn't fool enough to snatch someone off the dance floor in the middle of a crowded club. After this song . . . Well, he'd watch her carefully, *then* decide.

Besides, if he didn't stop staring at her, his eyes were gonna burn right through his skull.

—At which point the woman spun around. And with the distraction of that too-beautiful face removed, he dragged his gaze away, feigning nonchalance with a sip of beer.

"Liz—" he began. But she was at the bar having her cup refilled. Alec was—apparently—still peeing.

And Aikin . . . ?

He rose on tiptoes again. Still no Mighty Hunter. But as his gaze swept the crowd, he got a second jolt.

Another one!

Another Faery woman had just squeezed through the entrance. She wasn't as flash as the first one, granted, was clad in jeans and a tie-dyed T-shirt, in fact, and could almost have been an attractive Indian, Hawaiian, or Oriental. But there was no mistaking the burning in his eyes. The effect was not as strong as with the other woman, however: possibly a function of differing degrees of glamour, he supposed. Or—

"Shit!" he gasped; for someone had jostled the new arrival into one of the steel I beams that braced a wall. He held his breath, expecting a pained reaction—but there was none. Well, that settled one thing, then: the newcomer was *definitely* wearing the substance of the Mortal World; no way she could have endured that contact otherwise. Which perhaps explained why his eyes weren't tingling as much—and also meant she would be less likely to do anything untoward, since changing to human clay reduced one's capacity for magic.

But again, what did he do?

Watch, for the moment. Watch . . . and wait.

Fortunately, the second woman seemed as bent on dancing as the first. Not bothering to select a partner, she pranced straight onto the floor. And had not gone five paces—her slender body was already swaying with the beat—when she froze. Her head whipped around in David's direction; her eyes narrowed dramatically. He first thought she'd spotted him, and tried to merge with the wall. But by following her line of sight, he realized that she was staring at her more exotically clad countrywoman. For almost five seconds she stood there, then puffed her cheeks, scowled like an irate spinster, spun on her heel—and marched straight back the way she had come. Before David could react, she had vanished through the outside door.

"Too bad," a male voice sighed beside him. David started, having completely forgotten he was in a room full of people, many of whom were friends, and more at least vague acquaintances. After puzzling his way past a film of blue greasepaint, he recognized the jumpsuit-clad speaker as a guy named Mark, who'd lived next door in Milledge Hall the year before, and with whom he'd since shared a couple of anthropology classes. He was a security guard at the main library.

"Huh?" David mumbled, to cover.

"That girl who just left. Guess she didn't like the crowd."

"Or undercover smurfs," David countered, trying to be witty and casual, though his heart clearly wasn't in it.

A shrug. "Prob'ly not her style anyway."

"You *know* her?"

Another shrug. "Seen her around the library some; mostly late at night, which is slightly odd for a woman. Had to run her out once."

"Anything . . . special about her?"

"Like what?"

"Never mind."

"So what's the big deal, then?"

"Nothing, really. She just . . . reminds me of somebody."

Mark grimaced thoughtfully. "Could be a grad student, if that helps. Maybe history, or something. Usually when I see her she's reading history books."

"So why isn't the 'Watt her style?"

"I dunno. Maybe just 'cause she looks so serious and intense all the time..Preoccupied, you know. Not the partying type."

David nodded curtly, tacitly rendering the conversation just one more sound bite. "Catch you later," Mark grunted, and ambled away.

"Who was that?" Liz asked, over his shoulder, having just that moment returned. She handed him a cup of water and kept one for herself.

"Used to live next to me in the dorm."

"Think you oughta check on Mr. Dream?"

"I suppose," David replied, and pushed through the crowd toward the men's room.

He met Alec coming out as he was going in, and spun around to pace him. "Jesus Christ," he snapped. "What were you *doin'* in there? Transcribing *Origin of Species* in piss on the floor?"

Alec bared his teeth in a snarly grin. "It was *A Brief*

History of Time, and I had to wait for the guy ahead of me to finish *Paradise Lost.* And we used the wall."

Together they worked their way toward where Liz had managed to co-opt a table. "So why aren't you guys—" Alec began. And broke off in mid-sentence. His hand shot out and grabbed David's biceps so fiercely David skidded and almost toppled backward. Alec had frozen in his tracks. The grip tightened into genuine pain.

"Shit fire, McLean! What—?"

"It's *her!*" Alec gasped softly, though David heard him even above the deafening rendition of "Wild Man" that was rattling the walls and setting the floor to quaking.

"Who . . . ?" But David already knew.

Alec dipped his head toward the white-faced woman in gray, green, and black, the blatantly exotic Faery woman whose very presence had apparently prompted her fellow de Danaan to leave.

"Eva! It's Eva!"

David squinted through a drift of cigarette smoke that further confounded the already uncertain light. "No way!"

"Well, it's her goddamned *sister* then!"

"Did she *have* one?"

"I dunno."

David clamped his free hand on Alec's wrist—noting as he did that his friend was trembling. Alec's grip on *his* arm was actually making his fingers go numb. "Cool it," he hissed. "Eva's dead. You saw her die!"

"And we both know the Sidhe don't stay dead!"

"Yeah, but resurrection involves startin' over from scratch, from the womb . . . It could take years."

"*Usually* involves!" Alec corrected vehemently. "If they're strong enough, their spirits can build new bodies almost instantly. It just hurts like hell."

"Was Eva that strong?"

Alec was still staring at the woman, his eyes

squeezed to tearful slits. "Maybe not," he gritted.

—And wrenched free of David and fled.

"I'm sorry," Alec choked two minutes later. "I really am sorry, guys, but I just can't go back in there!"

Stripped to a black tank top, boots, and jeans, he was slumped on the knee-high brick rim of a planter in the building-sized minipark a block up the street from the 'Watt, with his head in his hands and his elbows on his knees. Dream's wig was a blot of silver-shot blackness amid the dying flowers behind him. David and Liz flanked him, David with an arm across his shoulders.

"Don't you think you're kinda overreacting?" David murmured. "I mean, *think* about it, man. No way it could've been Eva. And you said yourself it didn't *really* look like her."

"No, but it reminded me of her like a kick in the guts can remind you there's a half-ton animal attached to that horseshoe you just found. Or— Never mind," he finished sloppily. "I'm not makin' any sense."

"You've just had a few too many," David chuckled sympathetically. " 'Course I have too . . ."

Alec slapped a hand on David's knee, where it rested, heavy and unnerved. "If I go back, she'll be in there, Dave. And that'll remind me too much of . . . all that. And I just can't *deal* with that!"

"So don't look at her!" Liz snorted.

David scowled at her across Alec's head, wondering why someone who was usually the soul of diplomacy had decided to play bitch-queen now. Of course, she hadn't *seen* those two women, either. Maybe that was it: the fact that he hadn't reported them *instantly* . . .

"I can't *help* but look!" Alec protested.

"Okay," David sighed. "No big deal."

"It's just too hard, man."

"Have some water," Liz offered guiltily, having brought her cup along. Alec took it and swallowed sloppily. He poured the remainder over his head. "Thanks," he mumbled. "Hey, thanks to both you guys."

David could only nod helplessly. Alec was right: seeing the woman again *would* do more harm than good; though the sooner he came to terms with his lost love, the better for all concerned. On the other hand, he'd all but decided to confront her himself, before this crisis had derailed him. Now, though—well, he frankly wasn't sure he had the balls.

"Oh shit!" Alec gulped, slapping his hand over his mouth as he twisted around—and was violently sick into the planter. David held him until he stopped heaving, and used a corner of Dream's cloak to wipe his face. Liz produced a second cup of water.

"You gonna be okay?" David asked seriously, as he steadied his roomie. "I mean, Jesus, what happened? It hit you all at once?"

"Guess so," Alec mumbled. "But Dave?"

"Yeah."

"Take me home."

David hesitated the briefest instant. Then, "Sure. Like I said, it's no big deal. We got what we came for— mostly."

"You think he'll be all right by himself?" Liz whispered.

—Not softly enough, evidently, for Alec stiffened. "You're not stayin' *home*?"

A longer hesitation, as David and Liz exchanged resigned glances. He'd hoped to find Aikin and have him nursemaid Alec while he spent the night at Liz's. But maybe that wasn't such a good idea—especially since Aik hadn't resurfaced. And looking at Alec's sudden pallor, his set jaw and wild, worried eyes, he knew that tonight friendship had to come first.

"Yeah," he said gently, urging Alec to his feet. "I can do that. C'mon, man, let's go."

"I hate 'er," Alec slurred, as he let himself be steered

along. "I hate 'er 'cause I love 'er! And I gotta find out if she loves me."

"Alec—"

"They've got 'er," Alec interrupted. "I know they have. I *know*!"

"Sure," David agreed. "Here, watch your step."

Alec froze in place, and was therefore well-nigh immovable. "I've gotta find 'er, Dave," he wailed. "I've *got* to!"

"Fine," David told him, a little shortly. "So what d' you say you start lookin' at home?"

"Home . . ." Alec repeated dully.

"Yeah, man, home. You can start lookin' tomorrow."

"Home," Alec said again. "Don't let me be alone tonight, Dave."

A deep, uncertain breath. "I won't, man, I promise." Then, above his nodding head: "Uh, Liz, can you help me here?"

"Home," Alec mumbled, as his friends urged him along. "Home, home, home . . ."

"Home," David echoed. "Yeah, right, let's get you home."

"Gotta find 'er!" Alec screamed at the stars. "Gotta *find* 'er!"

And Death could only glare at Dream and wish for dawn.

Chapter IX:
On Track

(Athens, Georgia—
Friday, October 30—night)

The last light on Milledge Avenue flicked from red to green and Aikin stomped the gas. The S-10's tires chirped obligingly, but with rather less conviction and far harsher tones than a certain *other* something chirped—when it didn't whistle or trill. He grinned in anticipation, and cranked the radio up loud. WUOG-FM had just replaced Michelle Malone's "Has Anybody Seen My Monster?" (transparent homage to Halloween), with the Cranberries' "Zombie"—which was more his speed.

And speed was of the essence, as midnight approached. Why it *had* to be then, he wasn't sure, save that it was one of the "between" times, and, more to the point, the particular "between" time when he was least likely to be observed. Roomies tended to be about at dusk and dawn, and he had to play boy-student at noon. Last night's witching hour had simply been *too* soon—he'd still been checking out the enfield then, never mind the study session already locked in with Cammie, who was sufficiently insecure about whatever was evolving between the two of them to be tolerant of temporal caprice. But tonight, Whitehall Forest would for all intents be deserted. Tonight was Aikin's own. Probably just as well, too—for even Mighty Hunters were skittish about *certain* things on genuine Halloween.

119

Sighing, he shifted his hands on the wheel and relaxed into the backrest, noting absently how the scanty suburb past where Milledge Avenue ducked beneath the bypass to become Whitehall Road had lapsed into pastures under starlit skies. Actually, he corrected, there was mostly sky glow from Athens, the heart of which lay two miles back; but a few of the first magnitude sparklers were visible anyway—and, now he looked, a ghosting of clouds like the shadow of Alec's Dream cloak. More prosaic by far were the barns and service buildings of the Agricultural Research Stations that claimed most of the open land to either side. Ahead lay woods—and research of another kind.

He wondered if they'd missed him yet: that trio of excellent friends he'd not so much abandoned as discreetly disengaged from back at the 'Watt. Hopefully they were still boogying till they dropped. *Probably* Dave (the sharpest) had discovered that he'd been dancing like a fiend one minute and was gone the next. *Likely* they'd be pissed, but eventually forgive him— again. Trouble was, while he loved music, the louder and live-er the better, he loathed crowds and the press of humanity, especially mobs as unrestrained as the 40 Watt crew had been. It was just too hard to hang on to your *self*, dammit; he could always feel his edges starting to blur, as though people had magnetic fields that tugged at his personality, and too many would fragment him utterly.

Perhaps that explained the attraction of Faerie: not so much the sheer wonder of the place (though Dave had observed that anyone as curious as Aikin was *had* to be part cat), as because that land was lightly populated (so Dave had also said), with many inhabitants of less-than-human size. Solitude should therefore be more accessible there. And with immortality to spend, there would never be any cause to hurry; so that a guy might actually have time to think and observe and learn and enjoy and . . . just *be*! Shoot, on the ride back down here from home Dave had recounted the tale of a Sidhe lord who'd planted an acorn and not moved from that spot while the tree grew, flourished, died, and withered away. And one of Dave's Faery friends—Fionchadd was his name—had once coupled with a woman for a week and never lost his erection. Shape-changing had been involved too, from both participants, and at least one sex shift as well. ("Eternity Outlasts Prudery," was a popular quote among the more pragmatic Sidhe.)

And speaking of staying power, Whitehall had ended but the Cranberries hadn't.

Aikin paused for the stop sign where his road teed into another. The coast clear, he goosed the gas again and roared across the highway into what looked like a private driveway flanking a tree-studded lawn. The brick Victorian mansion on the right had been a gift, with the adjoining woods, to the Forestry School. He saluted it by killing his lights, thinking (as he always did) how lucky the facility manager who lived there was, and how evocative those turrets and towers were this time of year, especially when cut out against such wild skies as had prevailed earlier in the week. Now it loomed above half-bare trees, guardian to what was in some ways a land as remote to the rank and file as Faerie was to him.

A metal-pipe gate blocked further progress, and he halted by a check-post while he fumbled above the visor for his key-card. That located, he inserted it, heard the mechanism click, and watched as multihundred pounds of steel slowly retracted along a fence.

He was through in a flash and into the woods—pines, mostly, the foliage broken here and there by lab buildings, side roads, and a sign pointing toward the deer pens. Once he jolted over railroad tracks. And then he was home.

Not bothering to lock the pickup, he jogged to the darkened cabin and zipped inside. Twin alcoves faced each other across a common room–kitchen that ran straight across to the deck. He took the left, then turned sharp right into the rearmost of the two bedrooms that flanked that side's bath.

Elmer Fudd's helmet, he flung on the unmade bed, along with the plywood sword. The cardboard armor he unseamed from nave to chaps with one well-placed yank, but the borrowed chain mail beneath (which had been pretty pointless, given how little of it had been visible) took longer, forcing him to bend double and shake to shuck out of it—and at that it claimed his shirt and a selection of hair. The fringed moccasins puddled on the floor, but he hesitated at his sweatpants, since they were decent warm-weather nightwear, finally exchanging them for his usual cammos, a black sweatshirt, and a multipocketed vest. He also chose duck shoes over Reeboks and added a hat—a nondescript floppy thing Dave kept threatening to burn. Then, shouldering the knapsack he'd packed before leaving for the 'Watt, he slipped back outside, locked the door, and went in search of magic.

The enfield was asleep where he'd left it: curled atop a pile of towels in the legless remains of a molded fiberglass chair. The cardboard box filled with kitty litter he'd found on one of the shelves did not seem to have been used, but neither were there suspicious odors, merely the pervasive scent of cinnamon. The food— half a pound of hamburger and a can of tuna—had all been eaten, however, and the water bowl was down. The creature had not moved, though, and for a moment he feared it was dead.

"Hey, Ms. Field," he called softly. "Wake up!"

It stirred groggily, and Aikin realized two things. First, it probably *wasn't* nocturnal, or it would've been prowling around antsily by now. And second, though most even vaguely wild animals slept with hair triggers and woke like a shot, this one seemed as slow to get going as a frat boy on Sunday morning.

"Hey, girl, c'mon," he urged again, crouching and slapping his thighs encouragingly.

The enfield rose stiffly, yawned hugely, and sauntered out of the chair. Its talons rasped on the rough concrete floor, its rear claws clicked counterpoint.

But instead of strolling into Aikin's welcoming grasp, it twisted past him and pranced directly to the door, as though it read his intentions perfectly and was dispensing with unnecessary formalities. "Bitch!" he grunted good-naturedly, and followed.

One thing about enfields, he discovered a moment later—or about this one, anyway—was that they sure could make a beeline when they wanted to. Though this gal had seemed more than willing to choose the crooked road when he'd followed her around yesterday, tonight she forsook trails, paths—everything—in favor of a straight shot to the near side of the dam. That this burst of single-mindedness required him to slide on his butt down a kudzu-covered bank, leap a water-filled ditch at the bottom, slog through a patch of poison ivy too large to circumnavigate, and finally jump ten feet to the old mill road, did not seem to concern her. It was as though the beast were saying, "All right, kid, let's see how much you *really* want this thing."

Trouble was, Aikin had not yet determined for certain what this thing *was*.

But then why so much effort to do this at midnight?

And it wouldn't matter anyway, if he lost sight of the blessed beast.

It was already halfway across the dam, and he'd barely worked his way through the ruined mill. And though he'd been there at night countless times before, something about *this* night—the way the moon played games with colors and shadows, washing out red, giving everything a cast or edge of blue, while the rising autumn breeze first dulled, then amplified the cries of insects and the rolling rush of water—cast a pall of strangeness across the mundane world, rendering it as glamorous as any dream of Faerie.

And in that context, the creature calmly strolling across a diminishing, dead-straight line of white-gold concrete above a glittering blackness that might be river or the star-studded emptiness of an inverted sky, seemed completely unremarkable.

The moon had transfigured the night; the enfield, in a sense, had restored normalcy.

And Aikin had gained the dam.

As soon as his feet touched that yard-wide surface, his guide was off again. He followed at a dangerous trot. The dam was like one of those bridges in the myths, he thought: like the sword edge one must run along to win the princess, or the spear points Cuchulain had dashed across to impress his troops.

Faster, and the world whipped by: black and gold, indigo and violet; the river loud below his feet; the wind whistling past his ears. And, louder, the click of dry twigs on the opposite shore.

He had almost caught up with the beast now, and leapt from the end of the dam scant seconds behind it—to see it scamper straight into the laurel hell halfway up the bank. He followed doggedly, navigating by the steady rhythm of mismatched feet upon the ground.

And then he pushed through a screen of waxy leaves and found himself beside the blasted oak and bifurcated maple—beyond which the enfield sat patiently beside what even the gloom revealed to be a stretch of ground without growth. At which point it occurred to him again that perhaps he should distrust all of this. That it was unwise to follow a mythical beast onto a magical road at a dubious time of the year. That some agency beyond his own unruly emotions might be influencing the animal: tempting him with his heart's desire in order to claim him utterly.

Only that didn't make sense. God knew he'd puzzled

at that enough over the last day or so to last him a lifetime.

No, as best *he* could figure, the critter had emerged here the day he'd found the Track, sensed his obsession with Faerie and probably his friendship with Alec and Dave as well, along with his intention of visiting them—and followed him (preceded him, actually) to their place, possibly from simple curiosity.

And then, once it had found them, it had picked up all kinds of mixed intentions toward it, become alarmed—and fled. Only it had also sensed *his* interest, maybe—which was basically positive—and hung around where he was. And once it knew what *he* wanted, why . . . the rest made perfect sense.

Besides, he hadn't *known* about this place until the ulunsuti had revealed it, and that had surely been in response to his frustration at the failure of Dave and Alec's scrying. And since the jewel was from the Cherokee Overworld, not Faerie at all, what possible connection could there be between a suspiciously helpful enfield and a hunk of quasi crystal from the head of a serpent two Worlds away?

None that made any sense to him!

Besides, he'd only go a little way, a counted number of strides, and then backtrack. And if the critter returned with him, fine, and if not . . . well, it had to go home sometime, but at least he'd have joined the select brotherhood of those who had walked the roads between the Worlds.

All of which assumed the enfield activated the damned thing—which, obsessed with a sudden fit of grooming as it was, it seemed disinclined to do.

"Don't want your mom to see you scruffy, huh?" he told it.

It paused in mid talon lick and blinked at him. A pause for a yawn, and it rose, carefully twisted through the briars, and leapt onto the Track.

Aikin gasped. The effect had been impressive

enough the previous time he'd seen it—and that by
light of day, which tended to wash out other forms of
illumination.

Now, however, the Track glowed like a ten-yard strip
of sand, each grain of which was a perfect sphere of
golden neon. Not quite solid, yet certainly less tenuous
than air, that surface was; and the haze of light seemed
at once to lie on it, like yellow fog eight inches deep,
and within it, like rocks that displayed natural fluores-
cence. The enfield was practically up to its chest in the
stuff—and walking westward. To the east, the glow was
already fading, even as more brightness awoke in the
creature's path.

Get on now or lose 'em both! he told himself. And
with that, he took a deep breath and stepped into the
light.

The shock was stronger than previously: that invigorating tingle that pooled around his feet like water
through leaky boots. Perhaps that strengthening was a
function of the time, he thought, or of the date. Dave
said things of Power tended to grow stronger as they
approached certain auspicious occasions—like "between" times or cross-quarter days such as Halloween:
those days that lay midway between the solstices and
the equinoxes. Well, it *was* Halloween now, given that
it was just a trace past midnight. But the true traditional Samhain when all the World Walls were supposed to open wide was still twenty-four hours off.

Meantime, he had a critter to keep up with.

It had moved on again, and was barely visible as a
dark blot against the yellow haze. Another deep breath,
and he strode toward it, careful to count his paces.

"One, two, three, four, five . . ."

On *three* things began to change. The glow of the
Track grew . . . shallower, yet at the same time spread
to either side, and commenced to curve upward maybe
two yards out, as though defining the bottom arc of an
enormous tube or tunnel.

The forest was still beside him, though: the familiar Georgia woods—only they were becoming less familiar with each step, the trees rapidly regaining their leaves and growing subtly larger and more impressive, while undergrowth (mostly ferns) waxed lusher and wilder and more luxurious. He suddenly wished that he could see the stars, but all he could make out when he gazed skyward was a filigree of branches far above, that gave the impression of the vaults of some vast cosmic cathedral with a nave as long as the way between the Worlds.

". . . nineteen, twenty, twenty-one . . ." he counted. Twenty-one: seven times three: luck multiplied by itself and added to itself to create another lucky number. (*What I get for reading that Atlantis book.*) Twenty-one strides; maybe this was a good place to stop.

The enfield obviously had other plans; indeed, was almost out of sight.

Aikin hesitated, then noted how *very* thick and alive the whorling briars waist-high around him looked, and was off again.

". . . forty-seven, forty-eight, forty-nine . . ."

Forty-nine: seven times seven: another lucky number, especially as four plus nine was thirteen, which reduced to four, which was another significant numeral.

He had almost caught up with his guide now—and suddenly felt a need to rest. Perhaps that was the Track playing games with him: making him feel good, when in fact it was sustaining him with his own stolen vitality—which had just run out. Whereupon a troubling thought struck him. The Tracks bent time and warped space, he'd been told. So, was he dealing with perceived time or actual time here? Was his sudden fatigue due to his having walked for hours, when it seemed but forty-nine paces? Would—troubling thought for sure—he step off the Track at the end of this experiment to discover that what he had experienced as minutes had in fact been days—weeks—years, even—in the world beyond the Tracks, and that he had not only missed the deadline for his plant collection, but finals, his graduation, and for all he knew, the Second Coming as well. A sudden chill raced across his body. Maybe this *was* a good time to retreat. He'd already pressed his luck twice, once by assaying the Track at all, again by daring it this far. Perhaps he should do like the folks in *Flatliners* and stretch the limits (of clinical death in their case, of strides along a magical road in his) a few degrees at a time. Yeah, best he corral the critter and head for home.

Sighing, he scanned the way ahead—but caught no sign of the beast, no telltale tufted ears and black-tipped tail.

Great!

But did he *really* have anything to fear? Shoot, he'd simply turn around right here, count forty-nine steps—and hope that put him even with a blasted oak, instead of that lad there, that looked far too much like a silver-barked sequoia.

He had just resettled his backpack (Why had he brought so much stuff, he wondered. *"Be prepared,"* his Eagle Scout aspect replied) when he caught what could only be low-pitched voices.

He stared around wildly, but saw only the glow of the Track, and the looming trunks of trees to either side, their roots screened by the waist-high loops of briars that seemed to pulse rhythmically, as though their swirls and spirals carried not sap but blood. Their thorns were forbidding too: silver as daggers and as flat, as long as his hand, with tips that glittered like needles and channels in their broader sides like some swords had, to let the blood run down.

Nowhere to go, then, but back along the Track, back to the safety of the real world.

Or perhaps he should stand his ground. He'd wanted Faerie, after all, and though wandering around after magical critters on Straight Tracks was certainly exciting enough by most folks' standards, they were not, technically, Tir-Nan-Og. And if he'd lost a bit of nerve about going all the way to the actual Faery kingdom . . . well, at least some of its inhabitants seemed on their way to meet him! Or—he shuddered—maybe inhabitants of *somewhere else*. Perhaps someplace where sturdy Generation X-ers were considered delicacies.

So what should he do?

Stay where you are until you see who it is, he decided. *And if they look hostile, head for the hills and hope you don't lose count while running.*

And then it made no difference anyway, because They-of-the-Voices were in sight.

The first thing Aikin saw was spears: long slender poles bobbing along above the Track haze, which seemed to be waist deep there. He still could not make out individual words, but somehow he *did* get a sense of the emotions that rode behind them: distress, mostly; sadness, despair; and a strong thread of anger, as though they who trod the Track were not pleased to be doing so.

And then he realized that what he had taken for spears were not weapons at all, but simply yard-long poles from which globes of yellow-white light floated like miniature suns, linked to the staves by silver chains. Banners flew from some, but they were ragged, their colors washed-out and faded.

At which point something occurred to Aikin, which should've occurred far earlier, had he not been so caught up in wonder.

The tips of those staves were roughly level with the top of his head (as best he could tell—they were still thirty or forty yards off). Which meant that whoever carried them couldn't be much taller than his waist.

Which proved to be the case, when, an instant later,

the haze thinned about the vanguard of that company, to reveal a very strange sight indeed.

Dave had told him about the Sidhe: the Tuatha de Danaan—the Seelie Court: the old gods of Ireland; how they were man-sized or a tad taller, slender, and far, far more beautiful; and how every garment and jewel and bit of armor they wore was a thing of wonder. But there were lesser denizens of Faerie as well, beings of less-refined nature and lofty stature. The lesser fey, Dave called them, adding that he'd never met one, only glimpsed them now and then; and that the greater Sidhe seemed to hold them in low regard, rather as men considered other primates.

Lesser fey . . .

Well, none of that score-odd company would have risen above the bottom of his rib cage, and most were shorter. Men and women both, they were, but not beautiful as the Sidhe were said to be. Rather, these beings ranged from plain to downright ugly, that judgment derived mostly from their rough, wrinkled skin and a lack of regularity among their features: close-set eyes or receding chins or crooked noses or too-long upper lips. There was no outright grotesquery, merely a pervasive homeliness, which impression was borne out by their clothes: archaic in cut, ranging from sleeveless belted tunics made from squares of cloth pieced together, through doublets and hose and long gowns, to kilts, plaids, and full-sleeved white shirts— all rendered in heavy, loose-woven fabrics dyed in faded colors. Not a few of those garments were torn and mended, and one or two of that number went unshod.

They were also encumbered, mostly with carpetbags or larger cases, and one pair of women sat the seat of a small wagon pulled by goat-sized horses with leopard-spotted coats. Indeed, the beasts looked far happier, cleaner, and better kept and fed than their more human compatriots.

Which was not difficult, for the company looked very unhappy indeed. Not a squinty eye glittered with joy, not a downcast mouth curved with even a tentative smile.

They look like refugees, Aikin realized, as he stood his ground, dumbfounded. *They look like they've just fled home with whatever they could carry.*

The leader—a sturdy man in a gray-green checked tunic worn above stone-colored leggings and bare feet—froze in place just then, and stared at Aikin quizzically: not precisely in shock, but perhaps caught off guard. He stiffened abruptly, and his fist curled on the hilt of a dagger the length of Aikin's hand. Eyes black as a mouse's narrowed in a seamed face above a blunt nose. He ran a hand through shoulder-length hair the color of shadows in an old farmhouse.

And then he shouted.

Aikin couldn't understand a word—so much for what Dave had said about Faery communication being automatic. His response was to stand straighter, take a deep breath, and lift an eyebrow quizzically.

"Slo-wer," he said in English. *"Mas despacio"* he added in Spanish—and immediately felt like a fool.

Someone flung something dark at him. It splashed against his leg. The smell of spoiled fruit pervaded the air, so cloyingly sweet it clogged his nostrils.

"I'm not your enemy," he tried again, easing aside to permit the party to pass.

"Mortal man," someone growled from back in the ranks—and Aikin *did* understand that. "Far from home, ain't he? He goes any farther, he'll know how we feel, to lose the place he came from past regainin'."

"Shush, Gargyn," a female voice rasped. "He c'n hear you!"

"Don't give a rotten gourd if he do," that voice gave back. "His World's destroyin' our'n, 'tis only fair if our'n gets him back."

"I'm *not* your enemy," Aikin repeated, backing even

closer to the marge, and wondering if he really should
bolt, and if so, how accurate those knives were if
thrown, and how sharp. Maybe they were even like
elfshot, and would strike him down where he stood. He
wondered what happened to those who died upon the
Tracks. Dave had never told him. Perhaps he'd never
wondered. Or didn't know.

The leader glanced behind him apprehensively, and
Aikin got the sense he was worried about something,
almost as though he feared pursuit.

"Tell you what," Aikin said. "You folks pass, I'll follow, and get off where I'm supposed to."

"Like he c'n tell!" someone giggled.

The leader snapped something sharp in that incomprehensible language, and started off again. The small
wagon's axles squeaked ominously as they commenced
to roll.

At which point Aikin felt something brush against
his calves, and looked down to see the enfield peering
at him from between his legs, apparently having
sneaked around the refugees through the briars.

He was *not* prepared for the party's reaction.

There was a communal intake of breath, a simulta-
neous harsh, angry hiss. A murmur of indignation and
the sound of fumblings—and then the air was thick
with thrown objects, some of which glittered disturbingly.

Aikin raised his hand to shield his face, and felt his
forearms sting with countless tiny prickles, somewhere
between thorns and broken glass. Someone raised
what really was a spear. The point glittered balefully.

The enfield uttered a trill of alarm—and bolted.

But she did not run down the Track, neither toward
the company and past them, or back the way Aikin
and she had come.

Instead, she leapt through a gap in the briar wall he
had not noted before, and disappeared.

"*Wait!*" Aikin yelled, fearing to lose even that shaky

ally, in the face of obvious hostility. And with that he spun around and plunged after.

Something bright swished by his ear. Something sharp—a briar, probably—tore at his thigh as he leapt through the gap in the thorns. And then everything *changed*.

There was no mutter of indignant voices, no clatter of thrown objects upon dry ground. The quality of light had altered, losing the pervasive glow of the Tracks. Come to think of it, so had the terrain. There were no sky-tall trees now—no trees at all, in fact—merely high, rolling moorland and blasted heath beneath twilight skies.

A backward glance showed no horde of waist-high refugees, either—and no Straight Track for them to trek upon. He scrambled back there—and found nothing. Nothing save a thinning of the moss, where it lay behind sparse-spun whorls of briar.

But the Tracks had been *activated*! The wee folk had to have been going *somewhere*!

Well, they certainly weren't activated now. Probably, this was more of that supposed temporal dislocation: the speed of bodies upon the Tracks much faster than the speed by which they would be perceived by an observer. A flash in the eye, the activated Track would have been, to someone where Aikin stood. A shooting star of magic along something even more arcane.

Maybe.

But speaking of things arcane, nowhere in any direction was there any sign of the enfield: the enfield upon which he relied to reaccess the Tracks: the Tracks he must follow to get back home.

A drop of cold scraped his cheek, and he raised a finger to touch that icy runnel: a single drop of rain.

Clouds scudded through skies grown ominous and gloomy.

Apruptly, fear clenched Aikin's heart in fists of iron.

Before he could stop himself, he was crying.

But what else could a mortal man *do*? He was lost in an unknown country beside an invisible road, neither of whose laws he remotely understood.

Chapter X:
Rude Awakening

(Jackson County, Georgia—
Saturday, October 31—morning)

A mime in urban cammos was hunting rabbits with green plastic hand grenades, lobbing them off two-dimensional cliffs at human-sized bunnies that, with a stark-naked Alec McLean, danced to rock and roll. Explosions kept time to the beat and sent up blood-colored fireworks with each burst. Someone—probably that white-faced Faery woman at the base of a mesa that suddenly looked a lot like the buildings on Clayton Street—was going to very high-tech town on a complex keyboard-synthesizer thing. It sounded like King Crimson or Emerson, Lake, and Palmer, the way she'd sample some random noise, then drag it out to a tortuous dissolution, extracting melody along the way. Just now she seemed to have sampled a doorbell, because there was certainly a protracted, jingly ringing, repeated at intervals.

On the fourth repetition, David came groggily awake. "Fuck," he grunted. "Fuck you, tel'phone!"

He considered letting the answering machine do its thing—or yelling at Alec to assume that errand. Only, the machine wasn't picking up until the sixth ring, and he didn't think he could listen to its insistent angst that long. Plus, the nightstand that held the damned thing was closer to his bed than his roomie's—and Alec *had* had a world-class awful night, until he'd abdicated. David knew: he'd nursed him through two gut-wracking,

135

guilt-tripping hours. If he heard a slurred, "Gotta find 'er, man; gotta *find* 'er," one more time, he was gonna shoot somebody. Probably Alec himself. That'd put him out of both their miseries.

Rrrriiinnnnggggg!

"Fuck," David growled again, and fumbled an arm from under the cover, to send his fingers stumbling over the nightstand like an overweight, drunken tarantula. He missed twice, though he found the wet washcloth he'd bathed Alec's face with, and the water glass he'd finally managed to empty into him, in the name of brotherly affection.

Rrrriiinnnnnggggg!

"Fuck brotherly affection"—as he finally got the receiver off the cradle, dragged it to his ear, then retracted both beneath sheets that seemed to cover only his upper half.

" 'Lo . . . ?" he mumbled, making a point to sound even sleepier than he was.

"This David?" a hoarse female voice wondered. The slight country twang sounded familiar, but mind-fogged as he was, he couldn't place it.

"Yeah," he managed, through a yawn.

"Uh, well . . . this is Cammie," the caller continued uncertainly. "You know: Aikin's . . . friend, and—well, I was kinda wondering if he spent the night at your place last night."

David scratched his side. "Not unless he sneaked in after I crashed." Then, more alertly, having noticed the nervous edge on the young woman's voice, "I mean, he did the Halloween thing with us last night, but he split early. Like, one minute he was there, and the next, he'd just . . . disappeared."

"He does that," Cammie replied. "But . . . like, I'm moving, see, and he was supposed to help me haul some stuff in his truck this mornin', only he didn't show, and he's always real punctual, and I keep gettin' his machine, so I figured maybe he'd unplugged his phone or something. But then I remembered he'd said something about partyin' with you guys, only I wasn't *sure* if you guys were pickin' him up, or if he was gonna drive, so I thought if he *had* gone with you, he'd have stayed over at your place—I mean, I *knew* it was a long shot . . ."

"Yeah," David grunted, because he'd only caught about half of what he'd heard. He shifted to a more comfortable sprawl. The sheets promptly oozed to the floor. A glimpse at his watch (nestled inside Cutter's vest on the floor) showed that it was late morning—and *far* later than he wanted it to be. The sun was shining in the unshaded window with a vengeance, its cheery yellow beams narrowly missing Alec's face. *His* sheets had barely shifted since David tucked him in. The guy looked too damned peaceful. "Yeah," he repeated, inanely.

"No, but see," Cammie went on breathlessly, "I called one of my friends out at Whitehall to see if his truck was there and then call me back, so she did, and she said it *was*, but then my friend went over there and knocked, and nobody answered, so she looked in his window and saw his costume and stuff just thrown around his room like he took it off in a hurry. And—"

"So he's prob'ly out collectin' leaves or something . . ."

"Not if he was gonna help me move that stuff! You're his buddy, you know what a time nut he is: he's *never* late. If he even *thinks* he's gonna be, he calls."

"So you thought maybe he'd got real drunk or something, and we'd stopped by his place on the way back and dropped off his truck . . ."

A troubled pause. "Yeah, I guess I kinda thought something like that—but I'm kinda worried now. See—well, this is gonna sound *really* crazy, but . . . he's been, like, real preoccupied the last couple of days, and I know he keeps a journal—he tapes it while he's drivin', and then transcribes it on his PC. But anyway, this friend of mine had loaned him a bunch of lecture tapes, so while she was over there, she saw some tapes and a player in his truck and thought they might be hers, and she needed 'em back, and the truck was unlocked, so she just reached in and got 'em. Only she stuck one in, you know, to see if she'd got the right one. And she backed it up a little, and it was Aik workin' on his journal . . . and the part she caught—just the tail end—was him sayin', 'It's Halloween eve, and I'm goin' to town with some friends, and then I'm gonna let the enfield out, and *really* party.' "

David sat bolt upright. "*Enfield*? You're sure the word was *enfield*?"

Cammie's control was weakening. "That's . . . some kinda *gun*, isn't it, and I think Aik's got one, so I got scared, and all. I mean, he's been actin' *real* strange lately, and . . ."

David was on his feet, abruptly all attention. "It's cool—I think. Not what *you* think, anyway. But—Oh crap, I guess I'd better get over there."

"Want me to meet you? I mean, if something's *happened* . . ."

"Nothing has," David assured her firmly, adding a silent, *I hope,* before continuing. "I think I know what he meant, and if I'm right—"

"He's not gonna . . . *shoot* himself, or anything, is he?"

"No," David said with conviction. "Look, this is something . . . secret between him and me; something we've . . . been workin' on that I can't tell you about. So just hang tight, and I'll go over to his place and check things out. Did your friend take that tape?"

"She, uh, kinda freaked and thought it might be . . . evidence, or something. It's where she left it. She didn't even lock the truck."

David couldn't stifle a grim chuckle.

"It's *not* funny!"

"Yeah, well, sometimes you gotta laugh to keep from cryin'."

"So you really think Aik's okay?"

"I think so."

"So where is he?"

A pause. "I think he's gone walkabout in the . . . woods."

The ensuing hesitation suggested that Cammie was unconvinced. "Know anybody with a truck?" she laughed almost hysterically.

"Not that's available right now," David replied with a heartiness he didn't feel, and hung up.

Alec was still cutting uppercase Zs when David looked in on him eight minutes later. In spite of an odd sense of urgency that was already toasting him around the edges (his middle remained very soggy indeed), he'd forced himself to stay cool long enough to make a pot of real coffee, chug a cup, and leave the rest for his roommate, along with a note—in the unlikely event Alec rejoined the living before he returned. He hoped the guy appreciated what he and Liz had done. Lugging a barely conscious comic-hero around wasn't fun. Nor was undressing one who'd tossed 'em all down his front, nor supporting one in the shower in hopes of getting him sufficiently clean and sober to put to bed. Any *one* of those things would have been tolerable, but the cumulative effect . . . well, that kinda got to a guy— 'specially when he'd been more than a little buzzed himself.

No rest for the weary, he sighed, and turned away. Giving his hastily scribbled note a "Stay there!" swat to affix it to the front door, he puffed his cheeks, eased outside—and headed for the battered '66 Mustang he'd long ago nicknamed The Mustang-of-Death.

He wished he hadn't called it that now. He'd already had too much dying.

* * *

Unfortunately, Whitehall was clear across town from *Casa McLean y Sullivan*, which was effectively in the country. And double-unfortunately, there was no quick way there. The bypass curved so far around that it took as long as cutting straight through town, with its only real advantage being a lack of stoplights—which was illusionary time-saving at best. David chose that route, however, because, with fewer distractions, it was easier to think.

He didn't *need* this, dammit! He had his own demons to quell, and they didn't include buds going psycho right and left. Shoot, it was like Alec and Aikin were suddenly two different people, with Aik manic as hell one minute and morose the next, and Alec's ongoing mooning over Eva suddenly maxed way past overload.

So what had changed? What had made two normally rational guys go stark raving bonkers? For that matter, when had all these changes occurred? When was their last, relatively speaking, normal day? Well, he'd been antsy about the anniversary of David-the-Elder's death, but had managed to keep that more or less under control—until the dream. Aikin had been—overtly—fine until they'd seen the deer. And Alec—

It was the ulunsuti! It had to be! Everything pointed to that failed scrying last Saturday. Certainly his own nagging grief had resurfaced then, with the dream he'd had after the attempted divination. The A-Men had conked out then, too—and been strangely reticent thereafter. But if his own dream—vision, whatever—of David-the-Elder's death had been a function of the ulunsuti, was there any reason his buds couldn't have had *similar* dreams?

"It works best if you worry at it," Alec had said over and over. And on that day, the anniversary of David-the-Elder's death, he'd certainly been . . . not so much worried, as preoccupied—which was much the same thing.

And what had Alec been worrying about? Eva—of

course. And what had pushed his buttons again last night? Someone who looked like her!

Almost he turned around at that, for a coldness gripped his gut so strongly he well-nigh spewed his coffee. But no, Alec, at least, was okay. Ten minutes ago he'd been flat on his back in bed, dead to the world. Soon as he got back from this little errand, though, they'd have a talk, and he'd invoke the Vow, and they'd have a tiff, but all this secret angst would come out, and things'd be cool again. He'd have to spill his own guts too, of course, but that was the price one paid.

So what was gnawing Aikin? What, last Saturday, would have been his hidden obsession? *Faerie!* Specifically, his desire to experience that otherness first-hand.

But suppose the enfield had shown up again, as was perfectly possible. And suppose Aik had found it—again, quite reasonable, given how the critter had warmed to him—and suppose he'd tried to get it to show him how to *access* that place . . .

Yeah, that was it! Had to be . . .

Or maybe the little dweeb really was collecting leaves.

He floored the accelerator.

It was twenty minutes to Whitehall from *Casa McLean y Sullivan*. Five of those had elapsed before David's revelation. He made the remaining fifteen in ten.

Happily, the gate was open when he arrived, so he didn't have to either explain himself or park the car and run the remaining two miles to the cabin.

Even better, there was no one about. He'd been afraid Cammie had missed his request that she not drop by, and there was no telling *what* might be up with whichever neighbor had conducted that initial survey. And while Cammie's nameless friend might be spying from one of the nearby cabins, *that* he could handle. If affairs lay as he suspected, he'd not be around long anyway.

Still, his drive had given him time to work out a rough battle plan, and the coffee was finally kicking in enough to jump-start his logic, so that he was at once wired to the hilt and strangely calm when he ground to a halt in Aikin's yard.

A quick check of the windows proved that Cammie had been right about the costume: it was scattered around the room—floor and bed both, the latter evidently not slept in. David tried the front door, but it was locked and he had no key. Aikin's pickup wasn't, however, and he quickly found the suspect tape and confirmed the quote about the enfield. He thought of listening to more, since the key to this whole affair was almost certainly squirreled away in there, but one more thing needed checking first. Aik had said he would take *the* enfield. That implied he had it at his beck and call. Probably he wouldn't have stashed it in his room (nor was there any sign of that), but there were a number of other places he could think of right off that might do.

Scowling, he made his way down the still-muddy slope beside the cabin to its lower level. Yep, there they were: the fiberglass cages he'd remembered from his last visit. All were empty, but by the time he was in a position to inspect them, he'd also seen the open basement door—and the footprints: two sets of muddy sneaker treads that, by their small size, were surely Aikin's, one going in, one going out across the concrete porch. The second set was also more widely spaced, as though his friend had been in a hurry. And when David followed them, he found the third.

It had rained like hell Monday and Tuesday, and sprinkled again briefly Friday afternoon. There was, therefore, plenty of damp earth around—certainly enough to show the tracks of a four-footed beast that had obviously jumped off the porch and headed south toward the river. A beast with the hind paws of a fox and the forepaws of an eagle. Aikin's prints ran beside them and sometimes on top.

David paced them.

Aikin might have been called Mighty Hunter, but David was no slouch himself. And one of the many wood skills David-the-Elder had taught him was how to follow a trail. And if that trail was made by a guy in a hurry and a mythical beast with distinctive footsies, why, that was even easier. Besides, he quickly realized, the route was absolutely dead straight. He lost it briefly, when he was forced to skirt a patch of poison ivy, but found it again with no trouble: both sets of tracks (newly muddied) heading onto the dam—which had but one exit. And sure enough, more prints showed on the other side, angling directly into the woods.

A moment later, David found the Track.

He should've known!

Tracks went everywhere, though they didn't coincide with this World all that often. But it had never occurred to him that one might run near Athens. On the other hand, an enfield had obviously entered the Lands of Men somehow; and if he'd bothered to listen to his own arguments a few days back, he'd have known they weren't coming through the World Walls. Plus, those two Faery women he'd seen at the 'Watt last night had to have come from somewhere, and now, he thought, he knew where.

A Straight Track four miles from Athens. And more to the point, less than half a mile from the cabin of the one person in the whole town who would most appreciate that fact—and just possibly be reckless enough or frustrated enough to get on it.

Especially if it was activated.

He examined the ground thereabouts. Sure enough, the enfield's prints showed clear in a sandy patch near the obligatory veil of briars. Aik's were there too: facing the Track. Or more accurately, were there, and then *weren't*; as though he'd simply disappeared. A check twenty feet either way along that strip of barren ground showed no sign anyone had stepped off again.

He stared one last time at the enfield's spoor, and straightened, willing the Sight to come, as it sometimes would. But all he got was an intensification of that itchy tingle the presence of magic always evoked.

So what now? Aik had obviously followed an enfield onto the Tracks, probably the previous midnight, if David knew his buddy. *He* had no means of accessing them any more than Aik had—without the enfield.

But there *was* a way he could locate the guy pronto.

Right. He'd just call up old hung-over Mister Dream and get him to drag his not-so-fuzzy butt over here with the ulunsuti. They'd do a scrying—close to the Tracks would be best—and that'd determine their next course of action. He already had an idea what that would have to be, but didn't want to think about it—mostly because there was bound to be a row.

But if Aik had got on the Tracks at midnight, and it was pushing noon now . . . well, that was an awfully long time for simple adventuring. And while David trusted his friend's resourcefulness—and his theoretical knowledge of things arcane as well—there was just too much risk when one stayed too long in Faerie.

And the longer Aikin stayed, the worse that risk would be.

All at once he was running.

The trouble with magic, David grumbled five minutes later, was that you couldn't talk about it to just anyone. *Or* in front of just anyone. That was why he'd resisted pounding on cabin doors back at Whitehall, and instead was calling from a pay phone in a shed by the gate. Happily, no one was about to inquire what a suspiciously long-haired nonmajor was doing hanging around the Forestry School's Holy of Holies. And certainly not one so wired he was dancing from foot to foot.

He was getting the flip side of his own telephone, too: having to suffer through all six rings. Which probably meant that Alec was still zoned—and *might* mean that he was going to sleep through the whole thing, message included. In which case he'd have to call Liz and get *her* to roust his roomie—which he didn't want to do, because then he'd have to explain everything all over again, which would take time he might not have. Plus, Liz would certainly want to be present for anything that happened, and while he knew logically that she could take care of herself in arcane situations, he'd become protective lately, and wanted to spare her as much of *that* as he could.

Only it didn't matter anyway, because *she* was the one who picked up between ring number five and six. He could tell by the way her voice quivered when she answered that something wasn't right.

"Liz, it's me. What the hell're you *doin'* over there?"

"Alec," she shot back breathlessly. "He's . . . gone."

"Gone?"

"He left you a note saying he'd gone onto the Tracks, and he's not here."

David slumped against the wall; his empty stomach turned a long slow cartwheel. "Oh Christ, no!" Then: "You're sure? He was sound asleep when I left less than an hour ago."

"Well, he's not in the house, the yard, or up and down the road; I've looked. I was writing you a note in case we missed each other, and then I was gonna come looking for you. What's up over there?"

"Aikin's gone too!"

A pause, then, "You're kidding!"

" 'Fraid not. He evidently caught up with that enfield again and followed it to a Track I just found and—"

"Wandered right on out of the World," Liz sighed. "Why am I not surprised?"

"Right—so I was callin' to get Alec to bring the ulunsuti, so we could use it to locate him. I couldn't think of anything else—"

"It probably *is* the only thing . . . but there's a problem with that."

"What? You know where he hides it, so you can bring it, and we can use it to look for both of 'em. And—"

"It's not that simple, David; if you'll just listen!"

"What?"

"It's *gone*! The ulunsuti's gone! I came over with some hair of the dog for you bad boys, and let myself in, figuring I'd surprise you—brunch in bed, and that kind of thing. But when I got in, there was *smoke* coming from the bathroom, so I checked, and there was a little fire dying out in the tub—and stuff around it to indicate Alec had made a World gate. So I kinda panicked—'specially since you were gone too. But then I found your note—it had fallen off the door; I don't think Alec had seen it—and the one Alec had left as well."

"Why didn't you think he'd seen mine?"

" 'Cause I don't think he'd gate off somewhere while something was going on with one of his friends."

"I dunno, Liz, you saw him last night. He was pretty fried over the Eva thing. Maybe he just woke up and couldn't stand wondering about her any longer. You know how that's been eatin' him. I think seein' those Faery women last night put him over the top."

"*I* didn't see 'em."

"Which is *not* our problem."

Another pause. "Still want me to come over?"

"I guess you better. But read me Alec's note first, okay?"

"Sure. He did it on the computer," she added. The rattle of paper ensued, then:

11:17 AM
Dave,

*Thanks for looking out for me last night. I hope
you're not too pissed, 'cause you're probably
gonna be a lot more pissed when you find out
what I've done now. If I'm lucky, I'll have finished
my little quest and be back before you can do
anything about it, anyway—which I guess ren-
ders this note redundant, unless something's
gone wrong. Oh well! I'm not gonna tell you more
'cause I know you well enough to know you'd find
some way to come after me, and this is my battle.
You've probably figured out by now that I've
taken the ulunsuti and gone "tracking"—and
that's as much as you need to know. If you're
reading this, I've succeeded, at least as far as getting where I wanted. If I'm telling you this, I've
succeeded all the way. And if someone else is telling you this, God knows what's happened, but
you probably ought to plan a wake. But either
way, I figured we were both better off if I wasn't
sitting around beating my meat. I didn't tell you
about this, 'cause I knew you'd either try to talk
me out of it, or try to come along, and it's not your
battle; it really isn't.*
So take care, bro, and . . . pax.
*(P.S. You must have my hangover, 'cause my
head's clear as a bell.)*
(P.P.S. Thanks for making coffee.)

Alec

"Well," David groaned, pounding the clapboard wall
beside him. "That's just *great*."

"Yeah," Liz sighed. "So what do we do?"

"I don't know," David replied flatly. "I just don't
know. I can't think straight right now."

"Are *you* okay?"

"More or less. Why?"

"Just wondered. I don't need to lose you too."

"Thanks."

"Know what *I* think we should do?"

"I'm . . . open to suggestions."

"Okay, then. We need to get both our friends back, right? And they've both done things that were really stupid. But Alec at least *sort* of knows what he's up against, and he's got magical whatsits to protect him, if he bothers to use 'em. Aikin doesn't, and he's been gone longer. He's on his own and probably in over his head, since he's not back yet. So we deal with Aikin first, and then look for Alec. Besides, Alec *might* be back any minute."

"So might Aikin."

"Yeah," Liz said, "but we can't be certain, can we? So hang tight, I'm on my way."

Chapter XI:
Off Track

(Near a Straight Track—no time—dusk)

Okay, Daniels, get your act together, Aikin told himself. *You wanted this; now deal with it! You're an Eagle Scout! You did Outward Bound . . .*

Only . . . Outward Bound didn't exactly prepare you for being dumped into another *World*. And there was no merit badge, last time he checked, for Straight Track Manipulation or Faery Realm Survival.

If he even *was* in Faerie. That was an interesting question, too: Was this murky, misty country part of Tir-Nan-Og at all?—or one of the pocket universes that lay beside the Tracks?—or some other place entirely? Another locale on good old terra firma, maybe? In which case he was still in deep shit, but one escapable by phones and credit cards—assuming, of course, this was also his own *time*, which, given the fact that it'd been a shade past midnight when he'd left Whitehall and it was now something resembling twilight, was definitely *not* a given.

No! He wouldn't think about that—dared not! First things first—and first had to be figuring out what sort of land he'd blundered into. And with that, he wiped rain (he hoped it was *only* rain now; no way he wanted to meet the Lords of Faerie crying) off his cheek, cleaned his glasses, and took stock of his surroundings.

Well . . . the drizzly, twilight landscape *looked* a very great deal like Scotland, and he knew how Scotland looked, because he'd spent part of one summer there

with his mom, who was a globe-trotting archaeologist.
Actually, it looked like the *highlands* of Scotland; had
the same desolate rolling hills with hints of higher ones
beyond; the same scruffy, low-grown vegetation—
gorse and heather and who knew what. There was also
the same pervasive dampness, as if rain lay always in
wait, even when it wasn't actually falling, or fog lurked
just *beyond*, eager to assert itself and fill up the hollows
with weirdness. The foliage around his ankles was wet
even now, and from more than the fading drizzle; the
moss below it felt squishy. To his right, a runnel of
water tinkled between banks that were even parts
rocks and heather.

And there was the looming sky: wild and storm-
tossed like something from a Romantic painting, showing but the faintest tinge of sunset fire along the backs
of clouds that roiled and tore and shifted like a movie
on fast-forward. It was a sky at once awesome and
grim: dark and brooding, with flashes of silver among
the layers that spoke of unseen lightning. And yet, so
quickly did those cumuli roll and tumble that an instant later the drizzle vanished and stars winked
through rents to his right, taunting him with a brightness borne of clean air far from the Lands of Men. It
was frustrating, too, for those distant suns were revealed too patchily to resolve into any patterns that
might possibly provide some sense of location.

But then a vast sheet of cloud straight overhead tore
asunder, as though it had read his wish and acted on
command, and he saw a great many stars indeed. His
astronomy merit badge was no help at all, though, because every one was strange. Certainly, the sky *he*
knew never held five sparklies in a straight line, each
as bright as Sirius and equally spaced. No way they
could be planets, either, because not a week gone by
he'd pointed out Jupiter, Saturn, and Mars to Cammie—and they couldn't possibly have shifted to so pre-

cise an alignment in the interim—nor added two accomplices.

"I'm in another World," he told the wind—which was picking up even as the moor—heath—desolation—whatever it was—grew darker yet. "I'm in a fucking other *universe!*"

Alone—so far as he knew, since the enfield had gone AWOL—and with no agenda in place to ensure survival. Oh, he had food in his backpack, a change of clothes, matches, and a couple of plastic garbage bags that would help when it came to shelter. But he'd never given much thought to what he'd do if he actually *got* to Faerie. His assumption had always been that he'd get the lay of the land, sightsee a bit, then make a beeline to Lugh's palace and rely on name-dropping—David, Alec, or Liz (or Fionchadd or Nuada, if he was brave)—to get him by. And of course the Faery folk would be so amazed at his arrival and so bound by the laws of hospitality, they'd show him a good time and send him on his way, and he'd be satisfied.

He had *not* counted on being alone on a cold, wet, windy moor with true night quickly drawing nigh.

Fortunately, he *felt* just fine—his earlier fatigue having vanished—so he supposed first priority ought to be getting a bearing on his location. And since he was presently standing at the foot of a long steep ridge which lay to what, in his own World, would have been the north (assuming directions hadn't twisted around along with time when he abandoned the Track), the reasonable solution was to climb it, so as to command a wider range of landscape.

That decided, he resettled his pack, took a deep breath (the air tasted wonderful here, though it smelled faintly of decay) and set off up the hill, wading through calf-high heather. The only sounds were the hiss of his breathing, the rasp of foliage against his cammos, the faint slop/suck/squish of the saturated moss, and the pervasive moan of the wind.

Abruptly, he was longing for music. David had often accused him of requiring a sound track for his life, wondering why someone who craved solitude as much as he did needed to have U2 or Enya or Tori Amos along for the ride. But now he really *did* need them— or somebody—and found himself wondering what would be most appropriate for this climb. Something dark, of course, but with drive; and definitely with a Celtic twinge, since this place had a strong air of the Isles. The theme to *Far and Away*, perhaps? Only that was a little too light to complement the wild sky. And then he had it: from *The Last of the Mohicans*—the part that orchestrated the battle on the mountainside. That scene had been filmed near his old home turf— over in North Carolina (doubling for the too-commercialized Catskills)—and the rolling, relentless grind of what was either fiddle or hurdy-gurdy was perfect. He tried to imagine it, as he trudged along: the repetitive melody slowly swelling in volume and acquiring dark undertones of bass that seemed to evoke the infrasound of the very earth itself, both rising to merge in a burst of brass.

He tried to whistle it, but his thread of tune sounded frail and thin in the rising wind. Scowling, he contented himself with regarding the height above, and soldiered grimly on, noting that his legs were getting sore, and his fatigues were soaked to the knees. It was colder, too: as though summer and winter battled in the air. In fact, there were actual hot and cold spots, like ones found in bodies of water, only these were all around him.

And as he continued on, more land came into view, and he noted that many of the surrounding summits were studded with standing stones: singly, or in pairs, groups, or circles. They looked familiar, too—conceptually—and he recalled how, on a trip to Ireland, he'd scrambled atop the lone menhir that crowned a hill in Connemara National Park and quartered the compass with his gaze without seeing one obvious token of modern man.

And then he reached the ridgeline—and felt at once exalted and dismayed.

It was a hell of a view, that was for sure: a country as wild and full of latent magic as any he could imagine, for all that every element it contained was sufficiently mundane to exist in his own World.

But it went on *forever*! Saving the megaliths, there was no sign of man at all! No lights—not so much as a campfire. *Nothing!*

So what did he do now? Good sense said go back down the ridge, locate the Straight Track, and see if he could contrive some way to activate it. Shoot, if he was lucky, the enfield would return; and if he was *very* lucky, the beast might even sense his need and trigger the Track itself.

But before he did any of that, he'd check out the view one last time, to imprint it indelibly on the romantic part of his soul. So it was, then, that he began a slow circuit of the ridgetop, surveying every quadrant in turn. And so it was, too, that a flash lightning to the possible-east revealed something he'd missed before, that now stuck out in stark relief as sheeted brightness lit the clouds there.

It was a tower—or the ruins of one. Nothing big, and certainly not as imposing or *other*-looking as Lugh's place in Tir-Nan-Og. But it *did* offer two tokens of hope: human-type life *had* lived here once, and shelter was available—which he would need if the storm that had exposed the tower moved closer. Already he'd felt new darts of rain against his cheeks—and he had no desire to be caught outside by a downpour on these moors.

And since the tower was a surety, whereas cooperation from the Track was not, he directed his steps to the former.

—And had barely gone five paces when a new realization brought him up short. The tower lay in what he'd assumed was the east, and was mostly visible when cut out against the lightning. Yet so quickly were those dark clouds moving, that the sky there had cleared already and a steadier light shone forth: that of a heavy, yellow moon, newly risen. "Hey, man!" he called to it, for he had been observing good old Luna since he was kid, and knew its movements and phases. Only . . . *this* moon was full! No big deal, in the abstract; it happened every twenty-eight days. But the moon was supposed to be full in his World *tomorrow* night; and his practiced gaze was discerning enough to note even one day's change, and this was *definitely* a full moon. Which, if there was any analogy between his World and this (which was a pretty big if, given that the stars were all wrong) meant he had somehow gained over eighteen hours and was out on the moors on Halloween night! And while Halloween was his favorite holiday back in Georgia, he was not at all certain he wanted to confront it here, without the veneer of plastic and neon to enforce disbelief.

Halloween felt *real* here. This was a place where the dead *could* rise, where witches could ply the air on broomsticks, where all the dark things of earth could walk the land and have their way. Aikin suddenly wished, very hard, that he was a fundamentalist business major with an IQ of about 95 and the imagination of a turnip.

No, forget turnips: folks had used big ones hollowed out to hold candles back in the old country. They'd been precursors of jack-o'-lanterns.

Which was only making him more wired, and getting him no closer to the ragged black spike of tower.

But he was far less than halfway down the ridge on that side when a gust of wind swept off the heights and caught him, plastering his shirt to his arms and whipping his hat right off. The wind howled ominously, and a glance behind showed the storm moving in that way.

But then the wind dropped abruptly, to reveal *other* sounds that had hidden in it: the distant, clear shriek of a hunting horn—and, slightly closer, the belling of countless hounds.

Aikin had been hunting all his life and had sampled almost every variation, from rising in the wee hours to stalk the woods alone, through wading through briars listening to dogs cry as they flushed a rabbit, to riding red-clad on horseback as hounds coursed across Virginia meadows. Yet something about *this* horn chilled him to the very depths of his soul. It had sounded as though whoever winded it was crazed with anger, and the belling of the hounds spoke of both hunger and insanity.

And then he recalled who was most likely to be out hunting on Halloween night, especially in Celtic countries—or their Faery analogues.

Many names they called the leader of that host, familiar from countless novels and gaming manuals: Cernunnos and Herne were but two of the more popular ones. But it could also be The Devil's Dandy Dogs, or the Gabriel Brachets, or the Slough, or the Cwn Annwyn. And another name there was too, both more vague and more descriptive, and that was simply the Wild Hunt.

Aikin did not want to know what quarry such a . . . being might be seeking on these soggy, empty moors. But he doubted the Huntsman and his fellows (if any) would be content with voles or mice. All at once he remembered what he'd told David last weekend up on Lookout Rock: that at the end of seven years the queen of the Fairies paid a tithe to hell. That's what the mortal knight in "Tam Lin" had told his paramour. But now he recalled the rest, how the knight "so fair and full of flesh" feared that tithe would be himself.

And with that in his mind, and the screech of the horn and the belling of hounds far too close behind him, Aikin started running.

Chapter XII:
The Woman in the Woods

*(Whitehall Forest—Athens, Georgia—
Saturday, October 31—noonish)*

"Stop that!" David snarled at his stomach, which
had not so much growled as caterwauled. He slapped
it for emphasis and tried to recall the last solid food
he'd eaten. Popcorn at the 'Watt didn't count, nor did
the Hershey bar Liz had given him before that—which
left cold pizza at home last night.

Scowling, he checked his watch, then stared at
Whitehall Mansion, across the road from which he'd
just phoned Liz. God *damn* it, why couldn't that girl
have given him time to talk her out of coming over? If
she was bringing the ulunsuti, that was one thing; he
could *use* the oracular stone—to find two buddies gone
AWOL among the Worlds. But if she was simply in-
tending to hang around . . . well, how much help could
she be?

No, that wasn't fair. Liz was as smart as he was,
strong for her size, moderately psychic, able to scry
and had her act together common-sense–wise far better than Alec, for all that both he and Aikin had larger
data bases. The bottom line was that he wanted to protect her.

Except that was a lie too. What he *really* wanted was
to hide from her, because if she found out that whatever visions had motivated two of his buddies to hit
the Tracks had originated in the ulunsuti, no way she'd
not ask if he'd had one too. And he'd either have to

fib—which he didn't want to do—or tell the truth, which could easily lead him to confess his desire for vengeance against that traitorous bitch of a Daoine Sidhe called the Morrigu. And if he admitted *that*, he'd *never* be able to act on it unilaterally, because Liz would behave exactly as he was acting now.

So what was the difference between her fooling with dangerous matters and him doing the same? Alec and Aikin were like cherished brothers, and he loved them dearly and deep; Liz likewise loved him—but *her* love was something that transcended Worlds and lives. He didn't deserve it, either, not as big a jerk as he often was. But he'd be a damned fool to reject it.

So in the meantime, what did he do? Well, his protesting tummy suggested that a run to the nearest fast-food place wouldn't be out of line. If he hurried, he could make it to the McDonald's out on Gaines School Road before Liz arrived.

On the other hand, Aikin would be better served if he searched for clues back at the cabin. There were the tapes, for one thing, that contained notes for his journal. He was bound to find something there. That was the *right* thing to do, too; his stomach would, therefore, have to wait.

It was with that decision in place (but still under appeal from his gut) that he abandoned the pay phone by the gate and returned to the Mustang. He had just thumped down inside, when he caught movement in the rearview mirror.

And since Whitehall was a place where folks tended to ask hangers-around their business, he was instantly wary—especially when the vehicle proved to be white with red-and-black markings: the University of Georgia Motor Pool's corporate livery. He resisted an urge to slump down and pretend to be invisible in favor of at least *looking* like he knew what he was doing. Besides, he knew some folks at Whitehall, and most of them knew Aikin, so he only had to do a bit of name-dropping and he'd be in the clear.

At least that was his line of reasoning, until the car—a late-model Taurus—passed from his mirror and into his actual line of sight.

"Christ!" he gasped—and immediately sat bolt upright. His eyes were burning like fire—as they did in the presence of Faery magic!

At which point he noted two things. First, when viewed directly, with his own natural eyes, both car and driver seemed to shift and waver, as though they were not quite substantial. Second, by squinting a bit, and sort of looking at the road sideways, he discovered that what appeared to be an automobile with driver was in fact a horse and rider. Specifically, a white horse astride which sat a slender, dark-haired woman in flowing robes of gray, green, and black.

And as best he could tell from her clothing—and her profile when he briefly glimpsed it—it was the same woman he had seen at the 40 Watt last night: the exotic-looking lady whose presence had prompted her late-arriving countrywoman to leave.

He wondered if she was *also* wearing the substance of the Lands of Men, so as to accommodate cold iron, with which Man's World abounded. Probably so: that was one reason the Sidhe—in which company this woman clearly was numbered—put on mortal form. The other was more complex, but boiled down to the fact that it decreased the pull of one's home World. You wore the stuff of the Lands of Men if you were planning to hang around there awhile—and didn't expect to do much magic.

And since the horse/car job was evidently a simple glamour, and casting a glamour was certainly easier than co-opting genuine wheels . . . Well, it made sense to him, anyway. As for the car being UGA Motor Pool, why, that was simplicity itself: driving one of their vehicles meant you were on official business; therefore,

no one noticed you; therefore, no one gave you grief—
especially if that business took you to restricted-access
Whitehall Forest.

But what would a Faery woman *want* in Whitehall
Forest?

A Straight Track, for one thing! One that had already
claimed his buddy Aikin.

All of this reasoning had patterned itself in David's
mind more or less instantly, thus the woman had
barely had time to urge her insubstantial steed past the
gate (*iron* gate, of which the creature seemed wary,
hinting that it had been called there from Faerie) before David had hatched a plan to follow.

The Mustang was too conspicuous, of course, and it
would take some real doing to shadow the Faery and
not appear to, given the leisurely pace she was affect-
ing. However . . .

David rifled through the clutter in his backseat,
eventually unearthed his gym bag, sorted hastily
through it until he located some shorts that were only
slightly ripe, swapped them for his jeans in the car,
transferred certain essentials to a red nylon fanny
pack, skinned off his T-shirt and tucked it into his
waistband—and started jogging. If he timed it right, he
could *just* keep up with the horse (which mostly
looked like a horse now, perhaps because that was
what he expected to see). And if he showed signs of
catching up, he could always walk a spell and pretend
to wheeze; and if the quarry pulled ahead—well, he
was still a damned fine runner. And if Liz caught up
with him while they were in transit, it wouldn't hurt
her to jog a little too.

Fortunately, no black Ford Ranger idled up behind
him during the whole two-mile trek. Equally fortunate,
he jogged a lot, and had excellent wind and good stamina, so was not even breathing hard when the woman
urged the horse down a dirt road that split off an eighth
of a mile shy of Aikin's cabin. He promptly lost sight

of her and nearly panicked, until he recalled where the Straight Track lay.

The rest was both simple and hard. Simple, because he now knew beyond reasonable doubt where the Faery was heading—and hard, because he had to keep up with her without attracting notice.

The worst part was the dam, because it was a fairly long dam, and it wasn't far from its southern terminus to where the Track hid in the woods; yet he had to wait for his quarry to cross completely before venturing upon it himself. He could already hear the horse's hooves on the concrete, and knew, had he had any doubt before, that no mortal equine passed there. No way a regular old dobbin would walk across a yard-wide wall bracketed by running water.

If he could have swum the river quickly, he would have, but as it was, he had no choice but to simply brazen it out and trot across the dam as though he knew what he was doing. He was an art major out looking for autumn leaves for a project, if she confronted him.

Yeah, sure! If he could see through Faery glamour, no way she'd not be able to see through human lies.

He timed it exactly right.

And thanks to years of Aikin's bitching about noise in the woods, his quarry still hadn't noticed him as she reined the horse to a halt beside the Track and dismounted. Scarcely daring to breathe, he eased up behind the blasted oak he'd noted earlier and peered around it.

And almost cried out, as his eyes caught fire.

He shut them instantly, and tried not to claw at them; aware on some level that they were only reacting to the use of magic—Power, the Sidhe called it—but concerned all the same. God knew he'd heard plenty of tales of folks who spied on Faeries being struck blind—and just because the woman hadn't noted his pursuit didn't mean she was unaware of it.

But already the pain had faded a tad, and he was unable to resist a second peek.

At least the Faery wasn't facing his way—but something was definitely happening to her, something difficult to describe or understand. Clearly, she was . . . *changing*—yet that wasn't quite the right word, because her form itself did not alter. More, it was as if she'd caught fire from the ground and invisible flames were working their way upward through her flesh, every cell in turn flaring to brilliance, then subsiding into something . . . *different*. Refined rather. And then he knew. The woman was replacing the coarse clay of the Lands of Men with the more rarefied stuff of Faerie.

And any second she'd climb back on that horse and set its hooves upon the still-quiescent Track—and he'd lose her.

Taking a deep breath, he unfolded a certain something he'd withdrawn from his fanny pouch when he'd hopped off the end of the dam, gripped it firmly in his right hand—and leapt toward her.

Two steps it took in spite of that, and the Faery spun around on the second, but by then he had piled into her, knocked her to the ground, and laid hold of her in such a way she could not free herself without damage, while holding his Gerber knife perilously near her throat.

"You're too pretty for a rapist," she said calmly. But her eyes were wild and furious.

David started and nearly lost his grip. "I'm not," he blurted out, before he could stop himself.

"So what *are* you—besides a fool?"

"I think you know!"

"I think you should tell me. Actually, I think you should get off me, *then* tell me, and then—perhaps—I will not seek justice."

David's eyes narrowed, but he did not move the knife, though he felt the woman tense, as though she was preparing to fling him away. Or turn him into a toad, though he wasn't sure the Sidhe could do that to mortals. "In whose court?" he gasped at last. "The one in Athens . . . or the one in Tir-Nan-Og?"

The Faery blinked blankly. "Tir-*what*?"

"Look," David growled, feeling at once very silly and perilously close to panic, "what're you doin' here?"

"I *was* riding my horse. I thought I might collect some wildflowers."

"It's illegal to pick flowers out here," David countered sweetly. "Five minutes ago that horse looked a whole lot like a Ford Taurus; and most horses I know would *die* before they'd amble casually across a dam like that one back there!"

The woman smiled cryptically. "You have *very* good eyes then . . . and you seem to attract a certain sort of trouble."

"What's that supposed to mean?"

"Remove that . . . object from my throat and I might tell you."

"The knife? Or the *iron*?"

"The . . . iron!"

David eased the blade away a fraction. "Don't try to escape," he hissed. "I absolutely don't want to hurt you, but I've gotta have some answers."

"Three's the usual number," the Faery chuckled grimly. "Or would you rather have three wishes?"

"I know what two of 'em would be right off," David replied. "I'd have to think about the other."

"And what might these boons be?"

"You gonna grant 'em?"

"Do you really think I can?"

"I think I'm tired of playin' games! Now what the hell's goin' on? Since we've effectively established *what* you are, who are you, and what're you doin' here?"

"I told you! Everything I said is the literal truth."

"Well then," David gritted, "since you're so fond of

the truth, maybe you could explain what you were doin' in the 40 Watt last night."

"Dancing."

"What about that other woman?"

"Which other woman? There were very many."

"You know which other woman!"

"I know I'm running out of patience!"

David swallowed hard. "Aikin Daniels," he snapped. "Does that name mean anything to you?"

"I have heard it in . . . certain quarters."

"Have you seen him in the last, say, thirteen hours—*human* time?"

"No."

The knife moved closer—to no obvious effect.

"Would you get off me now?"

David didn't move. "What about Alec McLean?"

"What about him?"

"You seen him in . . . the last day?"

"At the club last night, for an instant. He did not look happy."

David exhaled wearily and rolled off the woman. She did not move, but sat up in place and brushed at her sleeves, where leaves had stuck to them.

"So *are* you from Faerie?" David asked.

"It would seem that you think so."

"Goddamn it!" David spat, jumping to his feet. "God-*dammit*! I don't *need* this, lady! I've got a problem that involves that piece of Track there; you know how to work 'em; and I'd *appreciate* it if you'd just . . . cooperate!"

"So you assume that if you bully me, I will be delighted to do your bidding? Well, think again—*David Sullivan*!"

"I'm . . . sorry," David mumbled softly, not meeting her eyes. "Sometimes you don't have much choice—or don't think you do. Sometimes you gotta take a wrong action over none."

"So what do you want from me?"

"You can start by tellin' me what's goin' on in Faerie. Why're so many of you guys suddenly turnin' up here?"

"The Borders are closed," the woman replied. "One would be a fool to defy he who ordered traffic between the two suspended. No one from *there* dares venture here, and no one from here who finds his way there will be allowed to return. Which *you* should think on long and hard." And which, David noted, was not an answer.

"*You're* here."

"Perhaps I am a fool."

"Would this fool have a name, then? Or would you rather I just *called* you that?"

"Of course I do!" the woman flared. "But I certainly will not give it to you! Now tell me what you want and let me be about my business. Nothing good ever comes of your kind trafficking with mine—as you well know!"

"No," a third voice broke in from behind them, "it doesn't."

David twisted around—and with a mix of relief and dire concern saw that it was Liz, dressed in full woodsman's kit, easing out from behind the blasted oak.

"You heard that, did you?" he asked, with his best helpless grin.

"Sure did."

"How much?"

"Started with 'he did not look happy.' "

"So you know?"

Liz nodded. "I take it this is the lady you saw at the 'Watt?"

"One of 'em. The one that freaked Alec." David turned back to the Faery. "You still haven't told me why that other woman left when she saw you."

"And you have not told me why you have come here."

David puffed his cheeks. "I'm probably takin' a

chance with this," he sighed. "But . . . I'm lookin' for two of my buddies."

The woman's lips grew thin. "And you think they are upon the Trod?"

"If that's what you call it. At least one of 'em is, I'm almost sure."

"Tell me, then!"

David did, as sketchily as he could, beginning with Aikin, who was their more immediate concern.

The Faery scowled darkly when he paused for breath—but, he was relieved to see, not at him.

"So *are* the World Walls leakin'?" he asked abruptly.

"They might be," the woman hissed. "It is not for me to say."

David was on the verge of a scathing retort, when the Faery rose. "I will make a bargain with you," she announced. "Since it is because of a creature of Faerie that your friend has passed this way, it is for Faerie to find him. But I will do that thing only if you will promise to ask no more questions about my activities here."

"Not even your name?"

"Especially not that!"

"Nor what you're doin' in mortal substance, hauntin' rock and roll clubs, and pretendin' to drive Ford Tauruses?"

"Not them either."

"You said 'friend,' " Liz broke in. "What about Alec?"

"You have not *told* me about Alec."

"You haven't given me a chance," David shot back—and laid out that tale as well.

"How do you know he is on the Tracks?" the woman inquired when he had finished.

"He . . . didn't actually *say* he was on the Tracks," David admitted, gaze fixed hard on the Faery. "He said he'd 'gone Tracking.' "

"And," Liz put in, "he went wherever he did from Athens—and how many Tracks can there be near here?"

"Many," the Faery retorted. "But only one that our kind could access from your World."

David took a deep breath. "How 'bout if he went straight through the World Walls?"

"*Mortals* cannot pass through the World Walls!"

"Not by our own power," David countered. "We can. . . . That is, Alec can. He has something . . . magical that lets him."

The woman's eyes narrowed. "And what might this something be?"

David shook his head. "I don't think I oughta tell you. And if you know as much as you hint, you know anyway. But if you'll help us find him—and Aikin, of course; you probably need to find him first—if we *do* find him, I'll ask him to show you."

"You are a very great deal of trouble, human," the woman snorted.

"I'm also very curious," David snapped. "And I promised not to ask you any questions—and believe me, I've got a boodle, like, why you were in our World when the borders are supposed to be closed. Or—"

"Enough!" the woman growled. "I have said I will seek your friend. If I must, I will search for this other as well—*when* I have concluded the first."

"He's been gone longer," Liz added helpfully.

"But time runs oddly on the Tracks around here," the woman gave back. "Yet if what you related is true, he cannot have gone far. I should be able to determine *that* very quickly."

"We're going with you, of course," Liz said into the ensuing pause. She stepped smartly forward and wrapped an arm around David. He patted the hand that curved around his waist—and nodded agreement.

The Faery glared at him. "I would prefer that you did not, but it seems pointless to argue. Very well, come—or stay."

And with that, she caught the horse's reins with one hand, and strode toward the Track.

David was there in a flash, grabbing her arm as she made to step upon it. "I'm not that big a fool," he snorted. "You could be on that thing and gone!"

"I do not break my word," the woman spat icily. And stomped down on that strip of barren ground.

The Track flared to brilliant, shimmering life. David gasped. It had been a long time since he'd seen a Track activated, a very long time indeed. His wonderlust flamed strong within him, like a leaf catching fire from a coal. Taking a deep breath, he followed the Faery— still gripping her arm—and, with Liz bringing up the rear, came full upon the Track. Its light promptly lapped up around him, and with it came that subtle flow of invigorating energy he'd almost forgotten. He breathed a happy sigh.

And released the woman's arm. "Sorry," he told her, with a lopsided grin. "I just kinda felt like I had to."

The Faery raised an eyebrow, then turned and surveyed the Track, where it arrowed toward the west. Immediately, she stiffened, then squatted down and extended her hands over the glowing, shifting surface. Almost David thought he saw images form there, but it made his eyes burn even worse and he had no choice but to look away.

For a long moment the woman remained motionless, then rose. Her face was grim. "Your friend indeed came here," she said. "I have sensed both his presence and that of a female enfield. But he is beyond help," she continued, her voice falling to a whisper. "For the Wild Hunt has also passed this way, and more recently— and if the Hunt is on his trail, he is doomed. Even I dare go no farther."

David could only stare dully at the ground and shake his head. "No," he said at last, grateful for the comfort of Liz's hand in his own. "*You* can stay here if you want, but I got him into this, I've gotta get him out."

Chapter XIII:
Over the Hills and Far Away

(The Straight Tracks—no time—night)

He had seen them now—and wished, most fervently, that he had not.

Caught in the open when the first mounted figure crested the ridge behind him, with the ruined spike of tower that was his goal still nearly half a mile distant, Aikin had found no choice but to fling himself flat where he stood and try to hide—in a particularly dense patch of gorse on the tower side of the car-wide stream he'd leapt scant seconds before. The foliage had obligingly frothed over him, providing a prickly screen—at least from visual surveillance by *ordinary* hunters. Fortunately, he was clad, in part, in camouflage. And fortunately, too, the fact that he'd crossed a body of water would give most things tracking him by scent pause—if that scent was not already obscured by the layer of mud, moss, and heather sheddings that begrimed the front of his body. Now if he could just keep quiet and still, he might have a chance—only that could be a problem, given how cold and wet the ground he sprawled upon was. In spite of himself, he shivered. But he shivered worse when he peered through the scanty twigwork at the dozen-odd figures silhouetted against the writhing sky.

Black was the ruling image: black man-shapes astride black horses atop a ridge of black-shadowed earth. Black spears stabbed the heavens there, and black banners snapped and worried around the nervous wind. One figure was taller than the others—or closer, or both—and that one alone wore a helm— Aikin *hoped* it was a helm—crowned with the rack of an impressive stag.

Abruptly, the eastern clouds ripped asunder and gave the moon free rein to play—and play it did, across those figures a quarter mile away. Yet even at that range Aikin caught the gleam of metal on armor and shields and weaponry—and once, he was certain, on what should have been eyes.

The moon showed other eyes, too: living ones, smaller, more closely set, and eddying about the horses' legs like paired embers of hellish red in a blot of knee-high smoke. *Hounds,* he knew. A hunting pack. But neither Host nor hounds poured down the slope to pursue him, though the pack was nosing the very spot where he'd lingered.

Aikin wanted very badly to bolt, but managed to hold his peace, to watch and wait, with his chin resting on one hand, while, beneath a foot-high bank before him, a pool of calm water shone like a blued-steel mirror, choked off by debris from the swifter flood.

So what were those guys gonna do?

"Shit!" he hissed into his hand. Something had moved not a yard beyond his nose. For an instant he thought it was the dratted enfield returning at the worst possible time, but then he realized that it was something in the water itself—a reflection, perhaps. Only it didn't exactly look like one, and as he continued to stare at that dark water, the movements upon it—or within it, it was hard to tell which—stabilized into images: all too familiar ones.

It was the Hunt—no longer atop the ridge. But how had they come so close so fast, to be reflected here? Except, wait—He raised his head just enough to scan the horizon. Yep, there they were, right where he'd left them, still not giving chase. And then one of those shapes shaded its eyes, and he saw that gesture continued in the water, and *knew*. There was something magic about this silent pool: he had wondered what the Hunt was about, and the water had shown him— still was, when he stared at it again.

And this time he saw the horned Huntsman as from no more than a few yards' distance: a tall dark shape beneath a voluminous cloak that might have been fabric or fur or feathers, and which billowed about him in frantic tatters as though he had ripped clouds from that thunderous sky and made of them a garment that had no other goal but to flee back to the heavens once more. He could see that one's head better, too, but still wasn't sure if the rack was grown from the Huntsman's flesh, or part of his regalia; for those antlers issued from elaborate bosses set on either side of an intricate silver cap helm, the long ear- and nose-pieces of which obscured the man's face, save for his sweeping black mustache—and his eyes.

—His eyes: a deep-set glitter in the darkness beneath the embossed browridges, that scanned slowly back and forth as he surveyed the valley in which Aikin sheltered. Slowly . . . slowly—and then, abruptly, he jerked his whole head around. Aikin flinched reflexively and tensed all over again, but then the Huntsman raised a complexly shaped and figured horn to his lips and blew a note like lightning striking a winded trumpet, and with a grunt from his mount (a black horse in black bardings) and a rustle of armor and jingle of mail, he and his Host swept back across the ridge.

—Out of sight to Aikin's mortal eyes, but not to the pond. It was like watching a video there, complete with Dolby sound, only a zillion times scarier. He wondered, suddenly, if the Hunt knew it was being observed by possible quarry—or cared. For maybe a minute that company rode across the moors, until one of the hounds belled loudly, and the Hunt veered in a direction Aikin *thought* might be toward the place he'd entered this World, and all at once he caught movement in the bushes directly in its path.

For the second time since he had hidden, he mistook that frantically leaping form for the enfield, for it was roughly the beast's size and color. But when it burst out on a stretch of open ground, Aikin discovered it was a person.

Sort of a person, he amended, for the figure was less than waist-high. By its size and wizened features, its bare feet, and the patched and ragged clothes (rusty breeches and a sleeveless patchwork tunic belted with golden links), he surmised it was one of the band of small folk he'd encountered what was probably less than a quarter hour ago. He wondered too if the figure might not have come in search of him—to confound his torment with further slings and arrows, or help him return whence he'd come.

But the Hunt was on that small form now; dogs—black dogs with flame-red eyes—coursing ahead of the pounding hooves like some black and evil tide. Aikin held his breath as the lead hound, which alone of that company wore a collar and alone had crimson ears, drew ahead of the pack and closed in for the kill. He could practically hear its jaws snapping, the thudding of its feet, the eager whoosh of its breath.

And then the little man uttered an indignant cry, and spun around to face it. The dog skidded to a halt, and they met eye to eye—at the man's level (like him meeting a horse, Aikin concluded inanely)—and for a moment the Faery looked as though he was about to lash out with his fists. Instead, he simply stood glaring: weak, helpless, and defeated, a refugee who had not reached whatever haven had been his dream.

With his thumb and little finger, the man sketched a sign across his torso, and closed his eyes. The dogs, which had gathered around panting, moved. In an instant they had knocked him to the ground and pinned him to it with huge hairy paws. A few nudged him with sharp-toothed muzzles, and one ripped his tunic open with a swipe of claws, exposing a chest matted with ruddy hair. A vast dark shadow fell upon him, and Aikin's point of view shifted to that of someone gazing down on the trembling half man from horseback height. A spear descended from the horned figure to his left, its point probing toward the helpless Faery.

Closer and closer, and Aikin couldn't watch, yet had to; thus his eyes were wide open when that glittering icy point tapped the center of the Faery's exposed chest. A dull thump, and blood sprang forth, at that lightest of touches; yet the Huntsman did not drive that weapon home, but simply left it in place, while blood pooled around it: a scarlet lake in the valley of the little man's sternum. The Faery tried to push it away, of course, with both hands around the shaft, but the strength seemed to have left his limbs, and Aikin could only stare wide-eyed as, empowered by its own weight and a sharpness that transcended sharp, that point pierced muscle and bone and found the wee one's heart.

The Faery cried out once, a word that almost had to mean "No!" and with that his eyes popped open, only to go dull and unfocused. A swirl of white vapor rose from a wound that was far too small to have cost a life, and drifted toward the sky. The Huntsman had apparently been awaiting that, too, and withdrew the spear from the flaccid body—to stab it through that cloud of mist and nothing, and suck it in.

"Another soul for my hungry cauldron," he told the rider beside him. And the Huntsman set spurs to sides and once again was moving.

Aikin's gorge rose at what he'd witnessed. Those guys had *murdered* somebody, dammit: someone small and helpless and afraid. And he tasted bile all over again when he realized that the Hunt had turned back his way. As best he could tell, it had covered at least half a mile in pursuit of the little man—which put it close to three-quarters of one from him. The tower was less than that up the next slope. If he could reach it ahead of them, maybe he could hide—locate a defensible position—*anything* to buy time.

Reluctantly, he tore his gaze away from the black pool, glanced at the rise beyond it, saw its summit still clear—and thrust himself to his feet to run as hard as he could in the opposite direction.

It was the longest run of his life, that headlong rush up the open slope—or so he thought. The air that had earlier tasted so thick and sweet seemed now insufficiently dense to sustain life, and ripped into his lungs like new-forged flames, leaving pain in lieu of sustenance. And the scrubby vegetation, that seconds before had seemed entirely *too* short, when he cowered beneath it, abruptly seemed too tall, and impeded his every step, so that to run through it was like running through mud (or one of those nightmares in which you can never run fast enough, but the nameless *it* can make all speed), and every leaf and twig tore at him and slowed him, so that he had to lift his knees strenuously high or else be utterly entangled. His heart was laboring, too, thudding along like the beat of the music back at the 'Watt. And a trio of fine clear pains had awakened in both overstressed thighs and one side.

But the cover was lower now, and more rocks showed as he approached the height. Yet just as he began to slow, his shaky peace was shattered by another winding of the horn. In spite of himself, he spun around, and saw that which made his blood run cold: black figures on black horses pursuing black dogs down a slope only slightly less stygian. It was true then, what he'd feared: The little man had been merely a diversion—an appetizer before the main course—which was clearly him.

Well, he'd give 'em a fight, he would. And he'd meet 'em on his own ground: Lord of this tower, if only for five minutes. (He had no doubt it was deserted, for he wasn't fifty yards away now and no one had hailed him through empty windows or gaping doors, or from what he could see through a rent in the side, was probably a missing roof.) No sirree, he wouldn't die as a helpless serf, a cowering mini man.

And with that, he redoubled his efforts.

Forty yards, and his legs were going numb with fatigue.

. . . Thirty and he could barely move them (and wondered where all the strength and stamina that were his vanity in the Lands of Men had gone).

. . . Twenty, and the blackness of the tower revealed a darker blackness that was surely a doorway.

. . . Ten, and his other side caught fire from the first, giving him twin stitches. He gasped, but stumbled onward, was vaguely aware of an archway looming before him, then over him, then as a blackness behind, as he tumbled to his knees on moss-covered cobblestones.

Breathless, giddy, he stayed there, panting, sweating, trying to still his heart, while striving even harder to contrive some means of staving off the Hunt. Maybe he could reason with him—it—them—whatever. But the lives of sentients obviously did not concern them, and Dave had likewise hinted that most denizens of Faerie tended to regard humans as little more than gifted vermin.

But if he was going to act from a position of strength, he'd damned well better be at it! Which meant, first off, that he needed to set himself at a higher level than his adversaries. Already he was probing the darkness, seeking stairs, a ladder—anything that would raise him above the Huntman's head.

Instead, he saw two bright lights, close-set among the shadows beside a shattered ramp—and nearly cried out, thinking the hounds already upon him.

Only . . . the hounds had red eye-shine and this did not—at which point whatever it was vented a low-pitched whistle-trill, stepped into what passed for light, and stood revealed as the troublesome enfield.

If a creature could look alarmed, that one did, for every muscle in its body trembled, and every hair was erect, with a species of anticipatory fear he'd never observed in an animal. The belling of the hounds was growing louder, too; and with each attenuated howl, its ears flared and flicked, while it wrinkled its dainty nose to taste the breezes.

"Death rides on 'em, kid," he told it dully. "Mine, if not yours."

The enfield blinked at him, tilted its head as though considering his remark, and trotted warily across the broken flagstones to where he sprawled on all fours, too tired to rise.

The horn blared again, closer yet, and the enfield started. It was shaking even worse, Aikin noted, as was he. And if the beasts of Faerie feared the Hunt, what hope had a mortal boy?

The Hunt was still approaching, too, as a glance over his shoulder revealed. The vanguard of hounds had reached the place he'd hidden and were nosing about there; it was only a matter of time now, surely, until they found his spoor.

Yet the pack seemed confounded, with several of its number questing north and south. Stupid—for surely he'd been visible when they breasted the rise. Surely those who drove the pack had seen him. But perhaps that didn't matter; perhaps it was watching the hounds that pleasured the Hunt, not the quarry, even when sighted. Perhaps it *was* the quest and not the kill.

Perhaps pigs farted Frank Zappa tunes in Bob Jones University whorehouses.

The enfield barked sharply—a new sound for it, and so loud he feared the hounds would hear and hasten the inevitable. He glared at it, startled and angry—this was, after all, its fault; had it not leapt from the trail, he'd not have been prompted to pursue it. To his sur-

prise, it glared back—and bared its teeth, black eyes
wide and glittering. A low growl issued from its throat
and he was certain it was about to attack. *Can't trust
a canine,* he grumbled to himself. *Not when the chips
are down.*

But the growl wasn't for him, he saw in an instant.
For without him noticing it, one of the hounds had
made its way to his sanctum. His heart flip-flopped
when he got a good look at it: far larger than he'd expected—hundred forty-fifty pounds easy—and effectively blocking the exit. Moonlight slashed across its
coat, but did not reflect off hide or hair, as though the
beast's very substance drank it down as it would soon
enough drink his life. He scrambled backward—tried
to—but as he moved, so did the enfield. It shot across
the cobbles faster than he could have believed, and just
as the hound opened its mouth to bell forth the alarm
that would bring the whole Hunt down upon him, vulpine fangs found its throat. The dog vented a rattling
gasp, followed by a whimper of pain—and collapsed,
blood pulsing from savaged arteries. It steamed in the
clammy air, smelling less like blood than hot metal.

Not until its legs had stopped twitching, however, did
the enfield release its hold. But there was something
odd about the way it was looking at him now: grinning
in its foxy way, so that he could see the darkness that
stained its fangs, the matted wetness around its mouth.
A strange light woke in its eyes that reminded him too
much of intelligence. And then, with a low growl, it
sprang again—at *him!*

"Shit!" he spat—and tried to knock it away, even as
he scrambled to evade it, caught an elbow on an uneven paving stone, and tumbled sideways, to slam hard
into the floor.

Somehow the enfield twisted around his awkward
blow, and leapt straight toward his face. He raised his
free arm to block—and screamed, as pain flooded his
wrist. Vision became a blur of varying shades of dark-

ness sparked with red; sound was scrapes and rattles, harsh breathing and strangled curses. The stench of blood thickened the air.

Abruptly the enfield released his arm—it had brought blood but done no real damage, so far as he could tell—and retreated. He kicked at it savagely, only to hear it whimper; its rage returned to calm. Indeed, it was blinking wide eyes at him, and as he tried to determine what to do next, it rubbed against his legs, then sat down, and calmly licked the blood from its muzzle.

Blood . . .

His blood, at least in part, for his forearm was red with the stuff.

But he had no thought to spare for that, for the enfield was acting odder than ever. In fact, it seemed to be . . . growing, expanding in all directions, as its proportions blurred and shifted. Its head was larger, but the ears were shrinking. Its tail had lost both mass and hair, and was now scarcely a nubbin. Far more skin showed than fur all over, and what hair was present was darkening. The hind legs changed articulation; forelegs gained meaty arms where had been thin-scaled talons.

It was becoming human! The enfield, crouched still on all fours in front of him, was turning into a man!

In fact, he realized, as it twisted onto its side, it was turning into . . .

Into *him*!

There on the shattered flagstones of that abandoned tower, the enfield had become his identical twin! Naked, for certain, but—minus assorted scars and snippets—definitely all Aikin.

"What?" he cried in alarm, as his twin rose unsteadily to its feet. It looked frightened—(Did *he* look that scared?)—and more frightened yet, when the horn sounded closer yet and a tide of yips and barks rolled up from the adjoining valley. A glance that way showed the dogs halfway to the tower, with the Hunt but a short way behind.

"What . . . ?" Aikin asked again, but his twin shook its head and pointed to its mouth, then shook its head once more.

"Can't talk?" Aikin whispered harshly. "But why . . . ?"

In reply, his alter self dashed to the dead hound's body, thrust a hand into the blood at the torn throat, and brought it to its lips, then pointed at him, and repeated the charade.

"You want me to do that?" Aikin managed. "Why? There's no time for games!"

Not hardly: in less than a minute the hounds would arrive.

And there was nowhere to hide! Not now.

His twin looked truly desperate, and was repeating its pantomine ever more frantically.

"Fuck it," Aikin sighed finally. "What've I got to lose?" And with that he scrambled toward the body, knelt beside it, and crammed three fingers into the neck wound. Not pausing to think what he did, nor give himself time to dread, he closed his eyes and stuck the fingers into his mouth.

The blood tasted awful—and then he didn't taste it at all, as pain seized him and doubled him over where he crouched, while his blood took fire, his bones dissolved, and his muscles, his organs—his very *brain* were torn asunder. It was like being drunker than he'd ever been and more hung over, all at once, with a five-hour cudgeling thrown in. His senses had all gone wild, were showing him sensations he'd never suspected, and denying him familiar ones. He could no longer kneel, but had to lie flat, to stretch his paws along the floor—

—paws?

He had *paws*?

Black paws that reflected no moonlight.

He had become a hound!

He was also damned uncomfortable, because heavy wet things were encumbering him in unlikely places. *Clothes,* something more distant than it ought to be provided. *Things to be escaped from,* another aspect advised.

He did, struggling out of the restricting fabric like a moth from a cocoon. Other hands were on him then, helping him: that boy that looked like him, covering his own nakedness with borrowed disguise.

And then a rattle of claws against the bare stone of the hill outside signaled the arrival of the pack. A hound peered in, sniffed uncertainly, and opened its mouth.

And as that first thunderous "yo-yo-yo . . . !" roared into the cold night air, Aikin-That-Was-*Not*-Aikin bolted. Aikin-Who-Was-The-Hound watched in amazement as his own body deftly leapt the corpse of the dead dog and fled into the open air.

"Yo-yo-yo!" the hound cried again, but by that time Not-Aikin was running.

But to Real-Aikin's surprise, the Hunt did not give chase. Rather, the pack waited, sides heaving, tongues lolling, nostrils tasting the air, as though they knew this quarry was worth a long pursuit, and sport was better continued than curtailed. After all, how often did Himself get to hunt mortal men on the fringe of Faerie?

Himself . . . ? Real-Aikin wondered where that term had come from. But as he sought an answer, something else captured him unawares, and he too found himself moving. Instinct, something told his human aspect: animal reflex reacting to its conditioning and taking charge. And perhaps he ought to let it; certainly it wouldn't do for Himself to suspect anything.

Before Aikin knew it, he was belling: sending deep, clear notes into the cold, wild air. The hound nearest him—a bitch nearly into season, his nose informed him—stared at him, startled, but he dashed in beside her. And then quickly lost himself amid the swirl and jostle of the others.

No one was chasing the boy . . . yet. Himself did not want them to. And already the boy—who was very fast for one of his kind—was a good way off and still running, angling south toward the circle of low stones that crowned the next hill down. Probably Himself would let him get almost there and wind the horn again.

Or maybe sooner . . .

It *was* sooner; for with one smooth, inexorable motion, the antlered man towering above him raised his horn to his lips and blew.

And what a note: what a perfect sound to set a hound's blood pumping and his heart to racing, and the taste of boy-blood-to-be washing across his tongue as he tasted the storm-laden air. A cold drizzle began to fall in earnest, cooling his fur, but his blood was hot and eager for the kill.

And kill he would, as first the hound to his left, and then the one to his right set off down the hill toward that frightened boy. Aikin-That-Was went with them, and the faster he moved and the closer he got, the more Hound-That-Is took over.

Aikin-That-Was was terrified. Hound-That-Is rather liked it. For Hound-That-Is truly *was* a very mighty Hunter.

Chapter XIV:
Sight for Sore Eyes

(The Straight Tracks—no time)

"I got him into this; I've gotta get him out."

And that was the bottom line, wasn't it? In and out. Yin and yang. Black and white.

It was noon, David noted dully. And that was a *between* time—and sure enough, here he was: hung up between. It was true Halloween now, and that marked the gate between the light half of the year and the dark; between summer and winter—between life and death. He was in the woods, but surrounded, just out of sight, by town. The trees hereabouts were rooted in the red clay and rich loam of middle Georgia, but his feet stood on a glowing strip of sod that was born of some other place, some other time, probably even some other chemistry and physics. And Liz was gripping his right hand, with her human flesh and bone— the slender body he had loved, and the brilliant mind that no one had fully tasted; while before him, dressed in robes of gray, green, and black, no longer looking even vaguely mortal, stood the nameless Faery woman who had— perhaps—pronounced Aikin Daniels's doom.

"The Wild Hunt," Liz breathed—and all that betweenness collapsed into a clot of cold hard dread that threatened to freeze David's soul. "I have to go," he told her. "You know I have no choice."

"And you know I don't either," she echoed, with a grim smile.

David exhaled wearily. For a moment he forgot the

Faery woman, forgot everything as he gazed upon his lady. *God, but he didn't deserve a woman like this . . .*
"That's probably just as well," he sighed at last, with a frivolity he didn't feel and doubted she believed. "Given the luck I've had lately, I'd *better* keep you where I can see you. All I need's to chase down Aik and Alec and find out *you've* gone haring off to an Otherworld. I—"

The Faery woman's horse stamped impatiently. David shrugged to conclude what didn't *need* conclusion, then stared at the beast, wondering if its impatient exhalation really had contained tiny flames. Liz patted its nose.

The Faery woman had remained silent since her pronouncement about the Hunt, but her mouth had gone hard, her brow wrinkled, as though she wrestled with some difficult decision. Eventually she exhaled deeply, and when she spoke, her voice held no trace of human slang, syntax, or accent, was fully that of someone born and bred in a World where language was among the highest arts. "I would not have it repeated," she intoned, with the formality of one taking vows, "—in Tir-Nan-Og or Erenn or Annwyn, either—that one of my ancient lineage showed herself less valiant than a pair of new-grown mortals. Yet when haste is truly needed, human feet are slow."

And with that, she closed her eyes and drew herself up very straight, her jaw set, her whole tall body as tense as a soldier facing certain death—like those at the end of *Gallipoli*.

"God *damn*," David gasped abruptly—for his eyes were burning and tingling more violently than the use of Power had ever prompted. He clamped them shut— had no choice—and the burning of tears was cool compared to the flames the Sight had woken there. "Goddamn!" he gulped again, and Liz drew him close, folding him in her arms as pain made him shudder shamelessly. He wondered dimly why *she* wasn't affected: she'd certainly seen the Faery woman as clearly as he—and the horse and the glowing Track.

But he alone had the Sight, and maybe that made the difference. Or perhaps the woman was exacting her price for his earlier assault—he'd never yet met a denizen of Faerie who'd let a mortal best him unscathed. Even his friends there kept score, and would remind him of even the tiniest slights long after he'd forgotten them. Immortals had long memories. Immortals could wait forever.

But he had his own pride, his own curiosity. And so it was that he fought through pain and tears and watched blearily but defiantly as the Faery woman *changed*. One moment she wore the face he knew, the next she showed many features at once, most of them female, most—but not all of them—human. She stabilized briefly in a particularly striking shape, as though she had settled on it—and David started, for there was something familiar about that visage. But before he could drag the memories from beneath his veil of pain, that entire *form* vanished, replaced with a larger, four-legged one: a huge black horse.

David swallowed hard, blinking back tears as the burning subsided to a tingle. He wiped them on the back of his hand. Liz passed him a bandanna, which he lavishly applied.

Those who watch what they should not, pay for that watching, came a thought into his mind—which, while alarming in its own right, was still better than watching equine lips shape human phrases. The white horse whickered, as though reminding them it was still present.

Woman on stallion; man on mare, came that thought again. *Thus is balance maintained.*

"Whitey here's a boy," Liz observed, with a trace of disappointment. "Looks like you get to ride your shape-shifting friend." David blinked at her, puzzled by the hard edge in her voice, and saw resigned disapproval darken her emerald eyes. "I'd rather ride with you," she grumbled. "But this isn't the time to argue."

I could shift you all, came the mare-woman's thought, unbidden.

"We're fine," David growled. "Let's travel." He clamped Liz in one long, strong embrace, and gave her a leg up on the white, which, he noted, sported reins but no saddle. Fortunately Liz was a first-class rider, with no qualms about riding bareback.

He, on the other hand, was wearing skimpy running shorts and nothing else save a fanny pack, socks, sneakers—and a T-shirt, when he fished it from his waistband and snugged it on. Nor had he been on a horse in over a year. Blister time for sure, he concluded warily, as he reached for the black mare's mane with one hand and her shoulder with the other.

And froze.

That pain-blurred glimpse of the shape-shifting was still playing through his mind, as wonders of that sort tended to do; and while he'd been dealing with mundane logistics, part of him had been worrying at those images like a tongue probing a popcorn husk lodged between two teeth. *Something* hadn't been quite right: one of those half-seen faces had struck a familiar chord, sending recognition chiming through his mind—without the name and history that ought to accompany it.

And then he *did* recall—and his hands slid off the mare. He wasn't *certain*—had observed those features for but the briefest instant when they'd seemed poised to stabilize into finality—but it seemed to him—*seemed,* he acknowledged—that the woman had almost chosen the face of the Morrigu.

The Morrigu . . .

The Crow of Battles. The Reveler Among the Slain. The woman—if that term applied to such a being—who gloried in death when women's ancient role was to bring forth life. Who, in the guise of an angel, had worked David-the-Elder's doom.

The woman upon whom he had sworn to be avenged.

Gritting his teeth so hard he feared they would splinter, he grabbed the mane again, and climbed upon what could well be his enemy.

Chapter XV:
Blood on the Tracks

(The Straight Tracks—no place, no time)

Fear smelled good. Then again, *everything* smelled good, Aikin-That-Was concluded—smelled interesting, anyway—when one was a hound. Funny how he'd never noticed that rich flood of odors before, or suspected their absence. It was like being born blind then suddenly being gifted with sight at a fireworks display; like regaining one's hearing amidst a symphony. And he could scarce contain his wonder, as he leapt along with his pack-mates. Faery men—horse—dog: each had a distinctive overodor; but beneath it, each individual smelled different, in a way he could note once and remember, as an earlier self had catalogued faces. And those scents spoke of other things too: of food eaten, and the condition of bodies; of the sweat of exertion on the Lords of the Hunt; their frequency of bathing; and their choice of metal armor, leather trappings, garments, and perfume.

But he smelled land too: earth of varying compositions and degrees of dampness; and the plants that grew upon it, each element of which likewise gave forth its own odor.

And over everything, like the wash of black-gray that was the sky, or the drones of a bagpipe or hurdy-gurdy, lay the scent of magic and the scent of fear.

Magic was hard to define, save that it was strong, clear, pure, and growing closer; and that some part of him identified it with what another aspect would have called gold or yellow. But fear—ah, what sweetness! What strength! What richness! And that fear at once sprang up from the earth where footsteps had fallen upon it, and floated on the air like a breeze presaging thunder, from he who fled ahead.

Aikin-That-Was could see the quarry now; had loped his way near the head of the pack and no longer gazed upon gorse and horses' hooves and the aft ends of other hounds. But something shifted in his brain at that, for there was a familiarity with that staggering form that went beyond his knowledge of Himself or those who rode their heavy horses with him, always a little way back, watching, observing, but nevertheless poised for the kill. They chased a boy, that was clear: young, dark-haired, healthy as few mortal men he seemed to recall hunting were anymore. He was making good speed, too: had covered nearly a mile, with the pack in steady but leisurely pursuit. There was no hurry, though; for the lad, though quick for his kind, would tire eventually and falter. The Hunt would not. His pack-mates would not. And then the smell of fear would give way to the taste of blood, which though not so ethereal was far more satisfying.

No! another part of the hound protested. *That's my blood you're thinking about! The one you chase is . . .* me!

It was all very confusing, because when Aikin-That-Was thought about things like that, others came with it, and he remembered he was not one of the Wild Hunt's pack at all, but a terrified young human lost past redemption in a World not his own. And when he recalled that, his senses overloaded and his reflexes tangled up and he faltered at his running, and the other hounds glared at him accusingly—which so far those who drove the Hunt had not noticed. It was like he imagined LSD would be, though he'd never tried that stuff. Or some of those mind-fucks Carlos Casteneda had dared at the urging of Don Juan. Two realities at once. Two sets of memories. Two sets of instincts. Those that watched and analyzed were his; those that drove the body, the hound's. But the hound was in control—had to be, to function—and Aikin-That-Was had not the strength to prevent it. As it was, maintaining his sense of self was like trying to talk at a rock concert, with the decibels pounding at his reason and drowning his words and dulling his thoughts and thudding up through his very flesh, so that it was easier simply to run with the flow and *be*.

Besides, it was *fun* to smell the fear.

He had no idea how long he'd run, only that they'd gone down at least one slope and up another, that he was near the head of the pack, and that the ground beneath him shook with the hooves behind him. The horn had not winded lately, however; and the Host rode silently, not speaking, not singing, lost, it seemed, in their thoughts, or the hunt itself, or dreams of glory and dripping gore.

In the process of dodging a rock outcrop, the bitch ahead of him turned aside, which afforded the best glimpse yet of a long stony slope; an odd-clad boy halfway up; and a crown of standing stones at the top, athwart a strip of golden light that smelled strongly of magic. He *thought* it was gold, anyway, but there was an oddness about it, as though it only registered when viewed obliquely. Part of him yipped with joy, and a disturbing word formed in a mind that both understood and denied: *home*!

Abruptly he stumbled, his forelegs having briefly recalled they ought to be arms—that he ought not to go on all fours.

The dog behind promptly collided with him, and red rage washed away sentience, and he whipped around and snarled. But then the bulk of the pack swept by, and gold-shod hooves pounded perilously close, and he ran again—toward the boy-who-was-not, toward the magic. Toward home.

They were on the Track now, and the smell of magic was strong in his nostrils; and the feel of it was like cold liquid fire against his feet, feeding him energy, feeding him force, feeding him drive—setting every sense to tingling, twisting each perception to sharper focus.

The boy had almost stopped, could barely plod along, there in the shadow of the standing stones. He was cornered, afraid, and knew he gazed on death. It showed in his scent, part of him knew; and it showed on his face, another acknowledged. *Die!* one aspect gloated. *Run!* the other countered wildly.

But the boy merely turned and limped into the circle of megaliths where the yellow-gold magic finally welcomed him. He stepped on it, but didn't seem to notice, though Aikin-That-Was felt it flare beneath his feet, and saw the magic brighten. Wide that boy's eyes were, and fearful, but bravely he stood: legs braced, chest thrown out, and a weapon—an edge of what his nose told him was the dreaded steel—flared like flame in his hand. It would be hot if it touched him, for the fires of the Worlds' first making never slept in iron or its kindred alloys. But Himself would not let it come near—and if it did, he could endure it: the pain a balance to the joy of the hunt.

Dimly he noted the rest of the pack fanning out to either side to encircle the stone-crowned hilltop. Dimly, too, he sensed the Hunt moving to range their mounts behind. Himself alone remained on the Track, pacing his stallion solemnly forward, as though he had all the time in the World. Hooves clopped loudly against bare rock as he ambled along, with the golden stuff of magic swirling and eddying around his horse's legs well past its hocks. Aikin-That-Was smelled pleasure and brazen armor and boiled wyvern-leather, and with it, anticipation—and the faintest underwhiff of confusion. One hand dropped from the reins to the spear beneath his arm, then paused, while the other sought the horn. He lifted it, then paused again, pulled his mustache (*What good were teeth that small?*) and said one word, softly, slowly, and very very clearly, even in the wind.

Aikin-That-Was didn't know that word by its sound, but the hound recognized it sure enough, and that one word was "kill."

The pack lunged forward. He lunged with it—saw black-furred bodies leap across naked stone like a tide of hot, quick shadows, teeth flashing like polished stars against the nothingness of night-toned hair.

The quarry's fear exploded as they attacked, and the scent well-nigh clogged Aikin-That-Was's nostrils, so rich it was. And then the dog to his left leapt forward, and the one to his right followed suit, and one hurled himself skyward from behind the lad to fall full upon his shoulders. The boy staggered, then sprawled. The narrow flame of iron flew from his hand to skitter across the granite. It brushed a bitch. She twisted around it. The wind stank of burning hair.

A cry broke the night: free of language yet full of fear, its sharpness abruptly strangled, as a strong scent of blood filled the air.

Aikin-That-Was fell into blackness, like being far-gone on a drunk. There was no way to stop the hound now, its instincts were too strong, were undergoing too much stimulation. Vaguely he felt it shouldering aside its fellows; distantly he knew it had reached his alter self. And for all that, he still knew far too clearly when it somehow gained the boy's throat and drove its canines home.

He tasted blood, and the joy was overpowering. But then a sound split the sky, as though the very clouds were shrieking. He jerked his head up, jaws dripping gore, to see Himself slowly dismount and walk forward, spear clutched like life in his hand.

The boy was dead—or dying, had lived but instants with his throat torn open. "Get away," the Huntsman spat, eyes flashing like the gathering lightning, mustache black as the hovering storm. Aikin-That-Was still didn't recognize the language, but he grasped the meaning well enough and withdrew, risking a snarl at being deprived at such a moment.

Himself glared at him—too long, perhaps—then kicked a malingering bitch aside, to stand beside the lifeless body. Grimly he crouched down and fingered the boy's clothing, his shoes, the pack that had weighted his back. A finger brushed the metal buckle at his waist, and he hissed and yanked it back as though burned, then laughed a cold, dull chuckle.

"Will you drink this one's soul?" someone called behind him—a woman, giddy to the point of insanity, afire with the madness of the hunt. She, he understood.

"It would not mix well with those I have already tasted tonight," the Huntsman sighed in the same tongue. "But if you would have some token, may I offer this?" And with that, he took the fallen knife delicately by its plastic handle, and deftly sliced off the dead boy's ear. He held it aloft, grinning wickedly, then paused, as though deciding whether to present it to the hounds or the wild-haired woman whose face was a mask of hungry anticipation, her hair red as the blood just shed. "Give me!" she yelled, and flung out her hand.

Himself grinned—and tossed it to her. She skewered it on a dagger: a thing like ice and needles, that had appeared in her hand as if by magic.

"And the body?" someone else called.

"The Track will devour it soon enough," Himself replied, swinging up on his vast horse again. "Now let us ride, for surely the night will grant us other quarry."

And with that, the Huntsman whirled away, with the rest of the shadowy Host in his wake. The pack *followed* for a change, as though being denied their quarry had robbed them of their strength.

Aikin-That-Was found himself alone—standing

amid sweet-scented magic in the center of a circle of
standing stones, staring through canine eyes at his own
torn and bloody corpse.

And with that, the hound was swept aside. Aikin
reached out to touch his other self—but it was still a
black-haired paw that moved. He wanted to weep, but
no tears could he call from his eyes. His cry of anguish
was a whimpered yip.

Things could get no worse. Far from home he had
already been, and terrified; but now his one tenuous
means of returning lay dead before him, and he could
not even mourn in his own body. Hunter he had been,
then hunted, and after that hunter again. But what was
he now besides lost and frightened and trapped? Left
alone with the dead on the day the dead were said to
rise.

But the boy was *not* rising, was simply sprawled
across the stones with his throat torn out.

Only . . . hadn't the eyes been open when Aikin had
last dared glimpse them? And hadn't the fingers of the
nearer hand been curled? And surely the mouth had
been bent in a rictus of pain . . .

Yet the eyes were closed now, the fingers extended,
the lips ever so faintly curved.

And then, faint but clear, came the slow liquid hiss
of labored breath.

He jumped back reflexively—and saw the chest
shudder, then slowly rise. A choke, then another, and
the eyelids fluttered.

He stepped forward again, then froze, for the horn
had sounded, calling the pack across the moors, or
sending it on ahead. But his human aspect was ascen-
dant now, and had been more intent on soft human
breathing close by than gold and ivory horns winded
afar. And the echoes were diminishing.

Another breath—another—and the boy opened
eyes that were bright with fear and agony, and somehow scrambled up on his elbow. The wound in his neck

pulsed, and bright blood fountained. Fear redoubled in those eyes, and before Aikin could react, the boy raised his free fingers to his throat and set them to the wound where the blood ran out most eagerly. He grunted, as though that effort cost him pain on top of what already had to be agony; his jaw clamped tight as a steel trap. But then red ran down his arm—and with one smooth motion, the boy swung the ensanguined hand away from his neck and toward his doppelgänger.

Aikin shrank back, but the hound had scented blood again and reawakened, and before he could stop himself, he leapt forward and licked that limb.

And for the second time in less than an hour, Aikin's world turned over.

His body was aflame—no, was freezing like ice—no, was exploding. It stretched here, shifted there, contracted other places. Cold washed certain parts, heat others. Colors grew stronger, as sounds and scents and tastes receded. And then, with one final twist that wrung forth a cry that was both canine howl and young man's scream, he once again was human.

—Sprawled naked on rock the color of death, with a circle of gray stones around him like lurking vultures. The sky had gone entirely black, and the wind was howling. Rain, that had been sporadic mist, suddenly fell in torrents like a hail of tiny knives.

From somewhere a sharper pain lanced into his forearm. He flinched, even as he jerked his head around to see the boy gnawing away at his wrist: teeth not designed for such duty ripping and tearing at flesh that had not expected it. "Shit!" he spat, and tried to wrench free—from pain and image both. No one should see *himself* from without this way, and certainly not trying to devour his own body. Yet in spite of his disgust, he closed his eyes and accepted, gritting his teeth as his other self ground those dull little incisors home.

He screamed once—couldn't help it—as agony shot both ways up his limb when the boy's teeth broke skin and muscle and finally found a vein.

And released him.

Aikin was glad he didn't have to feel the change that warped his clothed twin's body. He looked away, where a day before he'd have sworn many oaths he would've watched the transformation through or died. But he'd been too close to death now, and knew it too well, with its cousins fear and pain. A long time he waited, as the groaning snaps of muscles stretching and bones reshaping and joints realigning mixed with the roar of the soaking rain.

Only when they ended in a long soft sigh, did he look around again.

To see his old friend/nemesis/problem/research subject/quasi pet the enfield struggling out of a pile of torn and thoroughly soaked clothing.

It whistled at him and grinned. He whistled back—tried to. It pranced up to him and licked his wounded arm—which already seemed to be healed. He scratched its head through its sodden fur. It trilled. A troubling thought struck him, and he reached down to probe its neck with shaking fingers that found no injury. There *was* something odd about it, however, though it took a moment to determine what. The beast was missing an ear.

"Wonder if the other one changed back," he giggled punchily, as he made his unsteady way upright. The Track was gone—almost; the merest hint of glimmer pooled about his wet, bare, and very cold feet. He danced there in place, hugging himself, and wished for hot food and dry clothes and a roaring fire.

Instead, he had cold and rain and blasted moors, a magical animal, and a circle of standing stones, amidst which he stood naked as a newborn god.

He had barely located his glasses and commenced to untangle his clothing when the worst sound in the world assailed his ears: the pounding of distant hooves that could only mean the Hunt was returning.

Chapter XVI:
Reunion

(The Straight Tracks—no time)

Magic . . .

Though it had been part of his life for over four years now, David had forgotten what magic was truly like.

Once it had been an abstract: a concept desired, yet as remote as traveling through time or to other planets; real in a sense that it was part of his cultural heritage, and—in books, films, and games—an exotic ornament to his everyday life, but not *really* real. But then it had *become* real, and with it had come wonder beyond belief, joy beyond expressing—and fear, trouble, and pain in easily equal portions. Nothing in his daily life had ever threatened his existence as his adventures in Faerie had. Nor had he ever had to fight simply to survive up in Enotah County, or make snap decisions that determined the fates of everyone he remotely loved while at UGA.

Faerie—and the magic that was its lifeblood—had forced those experiences upon him, and had thus come to be distrusted, its capricious incursions into his life events to be avoided. And the *fact* that it complicated his life had, over the last two years, when it had grown increasingly removed, made it a topic to be shunned, so that eventually his *perception* of it had superseded the fact.

But the fact was back again, in spades; and in spite of himself, he couldn't restrain the joy—the *energy*— he felt as he rode a jet black Faery steed, that was also a mysterious woman, bareback down a golden Straight Track. Liz rode with him, on the white stallion; sometimes alongside, sometimes—when the briars that braced the Track whorled close or the Road itself narrowed—behind. They spoke little, lost, as both of them seemed to be, in thought—and the rebirth of wonder.

It'd been an odd journey, that was for sure. Time had at once compressed and expanded, so that he had no idea how long they'd been trotting along. He'd noted the usual sequence of effects, of course: how they'd seemed to pass among the woods of the Lands of Men, until those woods gradually *changed*, becoming richer, denser, more lavish—more primeval: transfigured by magic into what he could only term a forest archetype.

It'd all *been* woods, too: not once had they traversed other "places" or marched into lands, that by some fundamental . . . *oddness* were blatantly not their own.

Still, Aikin had gone this way, the Faery woman had assured them before her *change*, and they had no choice but to trust her if they would recover their friend. But surely even fleet-footed Mighty Hunter Daniels could not have come so far, not as curious as he was. Shoot, the first time he glimpsed anything even vaguely outré, he'd have been at it like a shot, notebook, ruler, and camera firmly in hand.

That image prompted David to vent a grim chuckle. It would've been his reaction too, a few years back. In fact, Aik reminded him of how he'd been the first time he'd come face-to-face with Faerie, unaware of its dangers. Though almost exactly the same age as his forester friend, he suddenly felt eons older.

So did his bod. For however energizing treading a Track might be, he was astride a horse when he hadn't ridden in a while; that horse held a probable grudge toward him; and his legs were paying the price. Already twinges were shooting up the muscles inside his thighs, where they stretched in unaccustomed ways to accom-

modate the mare's impressive girth. Never mind the
friction all that bouncing and sliding produced, which,
lubed by sweat both equine and human, would play
merry hell on sensitive skin.

"This is a pain in the ass," he growled to an alto-
gether calmer Liz—and meant it.

Liz snickered back—probably because she knew it
was expected. He loved her for that, too, and for not
pushing, for letting him fight his own battle. And the
really great thing was that if the chips were down, she
would fight for him, beside him—or against him, if
need be—to the death.

He hoped it didn't come to that.

Abruptly, the horse-woman slowed to an amble. David yipped softly: startled. There being no action he
could take to locate his friend beyond trusting a possibly untrustworthy beast, he'd lost himself in reverie.
But now, apparently, something had altered. The mare
ducked her head—once, twice—and whickered.
There, came her thought into his mind—for the first
time since they'd left the Lands of Men. *If you strain
your eyes, you can see.*

David promptly leaned forward over the horse's
shoulders to stare along the Track. The thick, dark briars, which had been head-high, so that their journey
was like prowling the aisles of a wrought-iron ware-
house in New Orleans after dark, now faded into a
vagueness of whorling, lit by silvery gold. The sky was
not to be contemplated—it rarely was on the Tracks,
though it never held stars. And the Track itself was a
narrowing point of haze.

But something moved in the distance: something
that rose above the golden light and bobbed along away
from them. Something that might be a shorter-than-
average but pleasantly muscular young man. "Aikin,"
David breathed—to himself, Liz, and the mare: all
three. And also, perhaps, to the Track.

It is, the horse-woman acknowledged.

"So what are you waitin' for?" he demanded harshly.

To see if anything else *rides this way. Your friend may appear within quick reach, but as you well know, distances on the Tracks are deceiving.*

—As David discovered when they were once more moving. For the figure ahead grew no closer, yet the longer they rode, the slower he seemed to progress, as though he were mired in molasses or reduced to videotape run in slow motion.

The landscape, by contrast, was shifting rapidly. With every step, the briars diminished in size and complexity of looping, and fell farther back from the sides of the Track, so that Liz could ride beside him constantly, her pretty, pointy features wary and intent. And as the briars receded, landscape was revealed: trees, like sequoias but with bark like silver fur, then a stretch of desert that lasted no more than five breaths. And then, all at once, the briars shrank to a near-invisible tangle, like hair-thin barbed wire left to rust for ages.

—And David found himself surrounded by rolling moor. He glanced at Liz, whose eyes had widened with wonder, then could not resist checking behind—where the moor continued unabated, marked only by a suddenly dull streak of Track. It was faded up ahead, too, and it took a moment to realize that was because it was raining. They had ridden into a cold, misty clamminess, and as they proceeded along at what some part of him knew was *not* a pace a man could maintain, the mist became drizzle, became what was well-nigh a thunderstorm.

They'd lost sight of Aikin, too, though that was because they rode uphill, and the Track, though it ran arrow straight, nevertheless followed the contours of that World, and Aikin had gone down the other side.

All at once dark shapes loomed out of the downpour. David first thought them a circle of impossibly tall, black-clad men. But then he rode close enough to tell even through the slashing veils of water and a faceful of sodden blond hair, that they traversed a circle of standing stones atop a high round hill. And when they'd passed through that circle and started down the opposite slope, they once again saw Aikin.

He was much closer—no more than a hundred yards—and this near, even with the rain and the glimmer of the Track that presently had much the look of gold-lit steam, they could likewise see the distinctive shape of an enfield loping ahead of him, its supple, fox-like body arching out of the yellow fog, then lost within it once more.

But why was Aik running? He'd been jogging when they first sighted him, and hadn't looked back once in the interim. And in spite of the rain, surely he could see *something*—or hear them, for the horses' hooves had certainly rung loud when they'd passed through the circle of stones.

But if anything, Aik seemed more frightened. For the first time David kicked his mount in the flanks. "Hurry!" he snapped, "don't lose him!"

It is not us he fears, came that voiceless reply.

"Screw this!" David spat, and shouted:

"Aikin!" His cry rang harsh in the stormy night— but the rain and the mist and the cold seemed to force it back down his throat, or drown it, as though beneath a soggy blanket.

"Aikin!" he yelled again. "Goddamn it, Aik, it's *us*! Dave and Liz! Slow the fuck *down* . . . Mighty Hunter!"

And with that the dark shape scampering ahead did slow—and turned, as though frozen with despair, to face them. Lightning flashed obligingly—the first since they'd come there—and showed a face David knew: wide cheekbones, pointy chin, (hatless) dark hair a smudge of points across his brow.

And all at once, though the horse had seemed to move no faster, they were upon him.

David dismounted before the mare had truly

halted—and spoiled the reunion by touching down in a strip of mud and slipping, to sprawl flat on his back in rich, earth-scented ooze. His first clear view of his friend was as a shape cut out against a circle of driving rain, while walls of some nameless knee-high flower-herb-weed rose around his head and to one side a black horse looked blithely on. Aikin grabbed him under the shoulders as he scrambled up—and clamped him in a *very* thorough embrace.

"Forgot you don't like huggin' guys, huh?" David laughed giddily into his buddy's ear

"I don't," Aikin muttered back—and hugged him harder. "But it's better'n bein' scared shitless on some weird-ass moor."

Liz had joined them by then, within reach, but not intruding. David drew her in, and for a moment the three of them stood there, arms locked around each other's shoulders, heads so close that even in the rain they could feel the others' breath.

"So," Aikin gasped shakily. "Am I bein' rescued, or are you guys lost, or what?"

"The first," David replied. "I *hope*." He raised his head abruptly, for it had just occurred to him that the tenuous agreement with the Faery woman had not been well-defined, and now that they'd found their friend, she was free of obligation. Yet she still stood there, on the Track, beside the white stallion, maybe two paces off. And then he remembered something he'd been trying very hard not to recall, which was why the Faery had feared to join them in the first place.

"The Wild Hunt," David blurted, before he could stop himself.

Aikin—across whose shoulders his arm still lay—stiffened and met his eyes with a gaze at once resigned, hopeless, and grim. "I thought you were him," he mumbled. "I heard your horses and thought you were him comin' back."

David gaped incredulously. "You've *met* him?"

Aikin took a deep breath. "You could say that."

"And *lived*?"

"I guess I'd have to say yes *and* no."

"Jesus Christ!" David gasped. "How?"

Aikin slapped him on the back. "How 'bout if we talk about that later? Say back at your place, assumin' . . . Oh shit!"

"What?"

"The enfield! It was here and now it's gone again." Aikin looked around, puzzled. "It saved my life—twice."

There is a first time for everything, then, the horse-woman snorted. *But if you desire to return to your own Land—which I especially recommend tonight, with Himself out Riding—I would be glad and more than glad to see that accomplished.*

"You'll get no argument from me," Aikin admitted.

Good, said the horse-woman promptly. *It is not wise to argue with folk from Faerie—when one walks its Borders so blatantly, in defiance of Lugh's ban.*

"What ban?" From Aikin.

That the Borders 'twixt the two be closed; that those from other Worlds found here not be suffered to leave.

"So you're breaking the law?" Liz wondered.

Perhaps. But here we are still on the fringe.

David puffed his cheeks. "I hate to be a dweeb," he began, "and I know I owe you about a dozen favors . . . but talkin' in my head is *really* distracting. So do you think you could, like, go back to bein' a woman, and . . . do something about this blessed rain?"

I could easily accomplish the former, but I prefer wet hide to wet hair. As for the latter, it is not for one such as I to command someone else's sky.

David cocked his head and lifted a dark brow hopefully.

You might want to close your eyes, came that "voice" again. *You did not seem to enjoy it . . . last time.*

David grimaced sourly but looked away, using gentle

pressure on his companions' shoulders to urge their acquiescence. To his surprise, Aikin didn't resist at all.

"Gosh, MH," he chided. "You mean you don't *want* to watch someone do magic?"

"I've had enough shape-shifting," Aikin muttered, and fell silent, gazing out at the sodden moors. The rain had grown softer, its steadily falling sheets now less like well-soaked whips than soggy feathers. David stared at the ground, at the puddles of dark water filling the low places there. One lay right at his feet and he found his gaze drawn to it, even us he heard the Faery woman gasp and a series of odd sounds commence, their edges dulled by the hiss of the rain. He resisted the urge to turn around, to confirm what his earlier glimpse of the *change* had suggested: that this woman, in some aspect, was the very likeness of the Morrigu, if not the lady herself. Only . . . he'd be a fool to do that now; probably was, anyway, to even think suchlike, if the Sidhe read thoughts as easily as he suspected.

David, therefore, kept his gaze firmly focused on the pool between his sneakers. His body shielded it, so that it was like a black mirror, but as he peered at it, wondering what was happening behind him, he caught movement there. He blinked in mild alarm, but hunched over, intent on that odd new occurrence—and felt his eyes tingle as they did in the presence of magic: gently, though, not the agony that had assailed him when the woman had shape-shifted earlier. And even as he watched, that movement became a wavering figure which resolved into the very image of the mare. David flinched reflexively, but there was no pain as he watched the horse flow and shift, become a woman/many women/all women, then subside into the form he recognized from the woods at Whitehall. And for the briefest of instants before that shape resolved, he was certain he gazed on the Morrigu. His breath hissed sharply and he tensed but held his peace.

"I am finished," came a woman's voice at his back.

David turned hesitantly—and saw exactly the same woman he'd seen earlier, save that her face and hair were soaked. But *not* her clothes, he noted—not yet—wrought, as they apparently were, of glamour. Aikin had turned with him, and David heard his buddy's breath catch, and recalled that Aik had never, to his knowledge, seen a woman from Faerie. A pretty woman was still a pretty woman, and Aik liked pretty women.

David nudged him in the ribs and cleared his throat. Aikin covered a preposterous grin with a cough. "Where's McLean?" he asked unexpectedly. "I thought he usually tagged along on these little outings."

David gave him the short form of his roommate's disappearance.

"Which I guess makes it my fault," Aikin sighed when he had finished. "Hey, but wait; when did you say he AWOLed?"

"Cammie reported you missing this morning—October 31. I hit your place 'round eleven, and called Liz before noon. He cut out somewhere in there."

"Twelve hours, basically," Aikin mused. "I've been gone twelve hours in our World—only it felt more like twenty minutes here." He glanced at the Faery woman. "Uh, pleased to meet you, by the way," he added. "And thanks for helpin' these guys find me. And . . . Well, I hate to ask this, but . . ."

"I have already decided to escort you back to your World," the Faery finished for him.

"What about Alec?" Liz reminded them. "We've still gotta find him—and if *he's* on the Tracks, and *we're* on the Tracks . . . well, it just makes sense to look for him while we're here."

"The Tracks are a vast country," the Faery observed icily. "You speak of them as though they all touched each other, but while all ultimately connect, those your friend has assayed could be as remote from this as . . . I-85 is from the M-1 in Britain or the German autobahn."

David frowned. "You know a *lot* about our World."

"It is to my advantage, and the advantage of Faerie, to know these things. Do not your own people say, 'Know thy enemy?' Do you yourself not know Lord Nuada, who makes a special study of the affairs of men?"

"You know Nuada?"

"All in Faerie know Nuada Airgetlam."

"Alec," Liz reminded them again, looking pointedly at the Faery, "it seems to me that you're evading that issue. I mean just 'cause Alec *might* be on a Track that's remote from this one, doesn't mean he *is*."

The woman glared at her.

David studied the Faery thoughtfully, still wildly uncertain whether he could trust her, but equally fearful of screwing any chance they might have of rescuing—if that was the proper term for one who might or might not be in danger—his best friend.

"—Besides," Liz persisted, "what would it *hurt* to just check the Tracks and *see* if you can find him? I mean, we're not asking you to take us to him, if there's some reason you can't. It *was* his stupidity that got him here, or wherever. But it's our obligation to try to get him back—or don't you understand about friends? If you've been in our World any time at all, you *have* to understand about friends."

"I understand all too well," the woman growled. "And I understand loyalty too!"

David lifted an eyebrow expectantly.

"Very well," the woman sighed, "but hear what I say and pay heed. I will seek your friend upon the Tracks. But I tell you plain, I fear that if he *is* here, the Hunt will target him next, for his very alienness will proclaim his presence like drums and trumpets. And if you are too close, the Hunt will seek you—*us*—as well." She paused, then went on. "And this too, I will tell you: I will have to be very careful indeed, for *any* Power set

·upon the Track when the Hunt rides will attract his notice. Would you risk this? Would you have me call the Wild Hunt to you?"

"We've risked as much before," David noted grimly. "I'd risk twice as much again." And fell silent.

"Even if you *don't* do it," Liz added, "I will—or try to. You're not the only one here who can search for him, you're only the one who can do it most easily. But I can work magic too—sort of. I don't make a big deal out of it, and I don't like to do it, but . . . I can scry."

"I will do it!" the woman repeated. "I have said as much, and I will be as good as my word. But I thought it my duty to warn you."

"Fine," David grunted, noting absently that the rain had moved off and that the sky was marginally lighter. A star glimmered through a rent in the heavy clouds. He wiped his hair out of his face and waited.

"I will need something that belonged to him," the woman told them. "A part of him would be better—hair, perhaps."

"You didn't to find Aikin," Liz observed, while she searched her pockets.

"Only his footprints beside the Track," the woman retorted. "Only air he had breathed."

Having no pockets in his running shorts, David searched his fanny pack—and was very surprised to find nothing that had belonged to his roomie. He had scads of stuff at home, of course, and a bunch in his wallet. But when he'd strapped on the pack he'd only transferred his license, car keys, and cash, not the photos or other small mementos.

"Aik?" David prompted, exasperated.

"Nada."

David grimaced sourly. "You'd think as much as we borrow stuff, and all, there'd be something."

Aikin shrugged helplessly. "Evidently not."

David stared at him perplexedly, as though he might catch something his buddy had missed. But no, those were definitely Aik's clothes: sweatshirt, vest, cammo fatigues . . . "Those the pants you were wearin' when we went huntin'?" he asked suddenly.

Aikin nodded. " 'Fraid so."

"The ones you got blood all over?"

Another nod. "We got blood all over everything."

"You washed 'em since then?"

"Of course—but the blood didn't all come out. Not that you could tell just now."

David gnawed his lip. "Then they're the ones Alec wiped his hand on!"

"Huh?"

"You remember! He nicked himself when he sliced into the deer, and you said something snotty, and he wiped his hand on your leg!"

"But it was just a smear, and I've washed 'em, and now they're wet again."

"It would be enough," the Faery broke in. "Blood holds one's most fundamental essence. Very little would be sufficient."

Aikin regarded her dubiously. "Do I gotta take 'em off?"

The woman flashed him a wicked smile. "I would not *object* if you removed them, but a touch should suffice. Only show me where."

"I don't *know* where," Aikin mumbled back, and David suspected that if the light were better, he'd see that his friend was blushing. "I think it was on my thigh. My left thigh."

"Never mind." the woman said, and knelt before him. Without further ado, she ran her hands over the designated limb, starting with the knee and working up. David grinned at Aikin over the woman's head. Liz glowered.

The hand froze midway up the leg. "Do not move. This won't hurt, but do not distract me." And with that she closed her eyes and laid her other hand flat on the ground, where the Track still glimmered faintly. It immediately pulsed like silent lightning. and David saw that brightness flash outward along its length, like the flow of electrons along a power line. The air went tense. His eyes burned. He shut them at once—then turned his gaze back to the ground, to the pool where he'd watched the change, wondering, all at once, if he could see Alec there.

He certainly saw something—but not his roommate. Rather, he beheld a complex lattice of straight lines superimposed upon the black, along which a point of light raced faster than his eye could follow, like Alec's computer creating, then solving, a maze. But instead of reaching a terminus, the light slowed, then stopped—as another light flared to life a short way ahead of it. The woman's light promptly switched directions and fled back the way it had come. The other light followed doggedly, but far more slowly.

The woman gasped, then jerked her hand from the ground as if burned. Aikin grunted and knocked the other away. "Sorry," he mumbled instantly, slapping at his leg, from which steam—or smoke—was rising. "Sorry, but that hurt!"

"Sorry I am too," the woman echoed, as she rose shakily to her feet. David braced her, for she seemed on the verge of fainting. "Sorry, I am," she repeated. "For I bear doubly ill tidings. First, he who shed that blood is not on the Tracks, or surely I would have sensed him."

"Not on the Tracks?" David groaned. "Then where the hell is he?"

"I do not know," the woman gasped, with a tremor in her voice. "But something *else* most certainly is, and is coming this way very quickly."

Chapter XVII:
Childe Alec to the
Dark Tower Came

(An uncertain place—no time)

Behind gleamed the white tile walls of a bathroom in Jackson County, Georgia: before him a black tower loomed in a nameless land: a cutout of jet against a silver sky.

Likewise at his back, someone was rapping on the front doorjamb—but someone more beguiling beckoned beyond heavy oak portals ahead: unheard, unseen.

The image still swam in Alec's inner eye: the focus he'd tried to hold firm while he ignited certain herbs in the tub and drizzled certain others atop the ensuing flames, then primed the ulunsuti lavishly with his own blood (the slice in his left palm still throbbed unmercifully), and, when the fire blazed high, thrust the oracular stone within and watched the gate between Worlds arise: a borderless shimmer of *otherness* where a wall and window had been. He'd not conjured the tower, though, but the face of a beautiful dark-haired woman: wing-browed and ivory-cheeked, slender but nigh as tall as he, dressed gypsy-hippie style, and with a dimple in her right cheek when she smiled.

More knocks rattled the screen door. *This was it, then.* Holding his breath, he twisted awkwardly around, reached back through the gate, and snatched the ulunsuti from where it glowed and sparked within

the fading fire that was still scorching iron-stained por-
celain a World away. The image faded instantly, struck
from his mind by the double trauma of hot quasi stone
against injured flesh. The air of two Worlds thickened
with the stench of hair crisping on his fingers.

Another round of knocks vanished with a hiss like a
TV switching channels—and the gate dissolved.

The pain promptly pushed past overload. With a
flinch, he dropped the ulunsuti. A sparkle fountained
up where it hit: gray-silver and glittering, as though a
billion antique mirrors had been ground to dust and
spread across the land. "Shit!" he spat, having almost
damaged his only means of returning—his only means
of rescuing Eva, of quelling the principal demon that
had haunted him for nigh on four years now.

He bit his lip, lest further curses disturb the thin dry
air. Already he was sweating—though that could've
been from nerves or pain as easily as heat, which was
as pervasive as a desert's. Dropping to a wary squat, he
retrieved the crystal with his undamaged hand and
fumbled it into a backpack, where it joined certain sup-
plies. That accomplished, he wiped the other on his
jeans and dared a look at it. Logic promised one thing,
experience another; but experience won, and showed
neither an inch-long gash at the base of his thumb, nor
burn blisters across his palm; merely a pale white line
centering a splotch of red: the mirror image of the
ulunsuti.

The dust was still stirring, too, and found its way into
his nostrils, prompting a sneeze. It smelled like glass
and silver, like stale memories flaked away so that only
impressions remained to prickle inside his head.

As he rose, his good hand brushed the hilt of the
sword thrust through his belt—not that he knew how
to use it, of course, beyond the bare minimum of
blocks and parries David had tried to teach him. Not
that it mattered anyway, for the sword was mostly a
prop their artist friend Myra had acquired at Scarboro

Faire and presented to David on whim. David had real swords, real *Faery* swords in fact, but he'd dared not appropriate one of them. Something told him not to: something that said a weapon conferred with honor, belonging to someone honorable, should not be used for covert activities, nor to rescue someone who perhaps had no honor at all.

So why had he brought the damned thing?

As a comfort, foremost, he supposed; he wasn't fool enough to roam Otherworlds without some kind of protection, some minimal intimidation factor. And because it was three feet of solid steel—and if there was anything Faeries feared, it was ferrous metal.

Impulsively, he yanked it out and flourished it—spinning in place to slash at the air where the gate had stood—then felt foolish and lowered it again, but did not sheathe it. Better to take stock of his environment—such as it was.

He stood upon an endless flat plain, though it could as easily have been the bottom of a vast sphere, for there was no obvious horizon and the sky was the same color as the gray-silver sand he bestrode, save that it seemed somewhat brighter. —Certainly bright enough to reveal a single shattered stump of black and blasted tower rising like defiance an indeterminate distance before him: the tower from his dream. Nothing living moved in that landscape, but a steady wind hissed and whispered and raised strangely shaped dust devils from the plain. Between him and his goal was emptiness, save a smattering of slender man-high stones that rose like angular fingers probing their way up from underground. *Best give them a wide berth,* he concluded, though the direct route to the tower ran among them.

From habit, he checked his watch, but the LCDs showed nothing useful; the numbers flickered faster than he could focus one instant, froze in place at some incomprehensible time the next. *Not good.* He'd hoped to have this over quickly. In and out had been the plan:

gate through to Eva's prison, grab her, then gate back. Less than five minutes max, and most of that spent building another fire to raise that second gate. *Assuming* Eva cooperated. Assuming she hadn't lied when she'd told him as she lay dying in Dale Sullivan's yard that while she'd only pretended to love him initially, she'd discovered at last that she loved him clear and true.

As, he thought, he still loved her.

He hadn't counted on arriving *outside* the tower, though, and wondered why that had occurred. Perhaps because the stone didn't always respond to what you *thought* you were asking; perhaps because he'd assumed he'd been thinking of Eva when the stronger image in his mind, being more recent, was of the tower itself.

But he'd come this far, no way he'd go back now; not when there was no obvious threat.

And so he strode toward his goal, skirting the first of the faceted stones by a healthy distance, yet near enough to determine that they were columns of fractured obsidian. *Sharper than the finest steel weapons,* he reminded himself. Something against which he dared not let himself fall.

But while he was squinting at the next one, his gaze drifted away from the tower: and when he looked back again, it was far, far closer.

In fact, it filled a quarter of the perceived vertical height of the sky—near enough to show fissures and a shattered crown and deeper darknesses along its shaft that might be windows and doors. There was an organic feel about it too: as though it had not been drawn by architects and made of blocks set one by one, but had been spun up from the liquid stuff of the underearth itself into a shape like a vast tree trunk wrought of frozen obsidian wrapped with ropy lava.

Another few steps, and it was suddenly *much* nearer. He was still tracing the broken dragon's teeth of its battered battlements when they attacked.

Fortunately, he heard them first: the jingling hiss of the crystal sand as they rose from underneath it, the glassy pingy rattle of their armor as they scurried forward.

They were man-shaped but knee-high, slender even in their armor, but with longer fingers and wider feet than any of human kind. Mostly he saw scales: armor— he *hoped*—gray-silver and vitreous, as though each dime-sized plate had been flaked from obsidian and set into silver leather from throat to biceps to thighs. Or maybe that was their *flesh*! Maybe those weren't helms at all: those knobbed and spiked affairs that covered their heads to cheekbone level, revealing only wide mouths with pointed teeth and the glitter of feral red eyes. Maybe those odd excrescences at shoulder and elbow and knees weren't armor either, but outgrowths of vitreous bone.

But those were *definitely* swords those warriors— perhaps a dozen of them—were wielding as they rushed to encircle him from ten yards out. Swords with a thousand razor-sharp edges of flaked obsidian primed to slice to the bone, to pare meat away before he even felt it.

Alec's brain went numb. Reality tunneled. Those guys really were out to hurt him, quite possibly to kill him thoroughly dead. There'd be no second chances with these lads, not like swapping broomstick blows with Aik or David. And they were small and quick and surely had amazing reflexes, and by the look of them were used to killing things, and were clearly playing for keeps.

And he was standing there as if frozen, as though waiting for someone to change the channel, or call foul or hold, or roll more dice. And while reality suddenly seemed remote and distant and dreamlike, the first time one of those swords bit into his body it would suddenly be very real indeed—and too late.

None of which Alec even knew that he thought, so quickly did it flash through his mind before fight-or-flight took over.

He was taller—a giant to them—and was wearing thick clothing and carrying a sword of steel. He had height and reach . . .

Screaming for no more reason than tension release, he leapt into the air and dashed toward the tower.

The two warriors who blocked his path on that side hesitated—likely because they'd not expected him to move at all, and certainly not so abruptly. *Probably not used to fighting someone as big as me,* he thought, and slashed out at the nearer.

The man jumped back, dropping his shorter weapon as he flipped backward, landed badly, and sprawled. The follow-through caught his mate, and Alec heard a chirp of pain and the tinkle of shattering glass as his blade smashed into the little being's side. He wasn't sure if it bit, and secretly hoped it hadn't, but the momentum alone was sufficient to sweep the fellow off his feet and hurl him into the next two warriors down. They collapsed into a pile—and strident, angry voices from behind rose into a howl that made every hair on his body prickle to full alert.

He ran—had somehow made an opening, and used it. Steps whispered across the sand in his wake: scurry, hiss-hiss, scrape. The air smelled like red-hot glass. Faster, he pounded, but two were closing in to the right, big feet skimming across the sand. Faster yet, and he knew he'd been a fool to turn his back on armed warriors, no matter how diminutive. Any second one of those glassy swords would stab into his back—or slash his knees or ankles and hamstring him.

Suddenly, he could stand the stress no longer and pivoted around on one foot, aided by the slippery sand. The sword arched out—and caught the closest pursuer across the chest. Blood scribed a counterarc in the air, but Alec felt sick enough to vomit—and before he could stop himself yelled, "Go away, goddammit! I don't wanta hurt you!"

The one he'd struck staggered backward, showing an unprotected throat. His fellows to either side caught him as he toppled. "They did not tell us we would face the Death of Iron," one cried.

"Then stay the hell away!" Alec gasped breathlessly. "Neither of us wants to die."

"They said to guard the tower," another voice muttered. "They did not say we had to succeed."

And with a hiss like a serpent slithering over paper, the men slid their feet into the sand, ran a few steps, and slipped back into the earth, leaving a splatter of broken scales where the injured one had stood—and a chain of wet red cogwheels: the only color in all that gray land.

Alec swallowed hard and wiped his sweating brow, then turned and jogged onward—to the tower.

That was too easy, he told himself, as that titanic black mass loomed closer with each step. *Way too easy.*

It had to be a trick.

Or did it? The little guys *had* seemed disgruntled—stuck with a rotten post, they'd implied. And even without that, wasn't the mere fact that Eva's incarceration depended on a preposterously unlikely set of conditions more than sufficient to ensure her continued captivity? How many mortals had she even met, after all—unless she'd gone a-whoring in the Lands of Men, as was also possible. But even so, how many would've loved her? None, by her own admission—which was probably true; otherwise Lugh would've been aware of it. No, he'd been clever, the High King of Tir-Nan-Og had: too honorable to base Eva's release upon an impossibility, he'd also known that only one mortal man loved her—a person, safely based in another World he was loath to leave, and unaware that Eva's release hinged on him.

But Lugh hadn't counted on the ulunsuti. Not because he was stupid, Alec bet, but because he was simply unused to thinking that other races might possess means to access Faerie on their own, that there might be magic free in the Lands of Men that had no part of Tir-Nan-Og.

This was it then: walk in, take the girl, and boogie—and they'd all be satisfied.

Or maybe not, for part of Alec knew that he had no idea *what* would happen once Eva was free. Would she still love him? Would he find that he no longer loved her? Would she be willing to hide out in Athens, or would she urge him to come to Faerie? Would her release open a whole new box of difficulties for himself and his friends, or free him to get on with his life?

He didn't know.

And he had no better notion when he found himself facing the first of a sprawling tide of low half circle steps that angled up to the tower's door. Not until he'd gained the top did he see the guards.

They stepped from hidden alcoves to either side of the deep fissure there: two of them, and they made Alec shiver in a way that the sand-skimming wee folk had not.

These were man-sized.

Man-shaped too—in part.

Equal parts, in fact: sleek-muscled in the way of Faerie men, and handsome.

—That's how *half* their bodies were: the right side of the one to his left, and the opposing portion of the other.

The remaining halves were more hideous than anything he'd ever seen, with only the proper number of limbs, digits, and orifices to mark them as even vaguely human. *Those* parts resembled warped tree branches left to rot, and overgrown with moss and fungus. Bark-rough brows abutted Faery-smooth ones on their faces; lips like knife-torn gashes merged with softly curved ones. Red squinty eyes followed his movements quickly, even as wide green ones did more slowly. It was as if two beings—a warrior of the Sidhe and some troll or orc or goblin—had been cleft in twain from crown to crotch and rejoined with the matching half of the other.

At least they were clothed—in porcelained mail corselets and cap helms of dark green metal that gave some unity to their disparate sides.

Each also held a naked sword crossways before him.

Still giddy from his adrenaline high, Alec swallowed but held his ground, though sweat that had nothing to do with heat broke out across his wire-taut body. So far the guards had offered no more than passive threat—and bluster had stood him in good stead just now. So what did he have to lose by seeking parley first?

"I don't wanta fight," he called hoarsely.

"Then you are wise, for you would surely not emerge the victor," the guard to his left replied, in a voice both clear and rough.

"This is an iron sword," Alec continued. "I guess I oughta warn you."

"We can see that it is," the other guard responded gravely.

"Think you could let me by?"

"Do you love she who dwells within?"

A curt nod. "I do."

"Yet you will not fight for her . . ."

"I can't love her if I'm dead."

A delicate brow kinked upward; a misshapen one slammed down in the adjoining head.

It struck Alec then that these guards seemed to relish their post as little as their smaller analogues. So maybe he could bluff his way through here as well. "Well," he began slyly, "it seems to me that the lady in there's not the only one who's under a fairly major curse; like maybe you guys are on somebody's list too:

maybe you're stuck here 'cause of some screwy condition the same as Eva is."

Two sets of mismatched eyes sought each other.

"We cannot speak of it," one muttered.

"So what's the deal, then?" Alec asked, wondering why he was going along with this screwed-up fairy tale. On the other hand, he wasn't making the rules or setting the agenda.

The guards neither put up their swords nor moved away from the door, but finally the right-hand one spoke, and it seemed as though the distorted part moved his lips more freely.

"We were not always as you see us," that one began. "Elf and troll we were, and alike from side to side. We were also friends, for though of different kindred we learned to look beyond each other's skins and see that our souls bore one likeness. We grew up together on the fringes of Tir-Nan-Og where the Daoine Sidhe come but infrequently and do not tarry long. Neither of us had brothers or sisters; we only had each other. As I said, we were friends."

"And eventually," the other continued, "we became lovers. Such things are not censured in Faerie, and no one objected, until a woman from the court at Tir-Nan-Og chanced our way while hunting. I met her—my elven-self did. She looked at me and fell in love—or lust. I repulsed her, not because she was a woman, and certainly not because she was not fair, but because it seemed she would claim for free that closeness which is too precious to be casually conferred. She did not take kindly to my rebuff, yet went her way. But then a day later, she saw me and my friend . . . together, and could not contain herself. She cursed us, and with a sword one of her fellows carried, smote us in twain—and rejoined us, saying that we two should at once be together and apart forever, so that if we kissed each other or held each other, we would only grasp ourselves."

"We appealed to Lugh," the first went on, "but he was fighting his great battle, and his daughter held his high seat. She it was who sat in judgment—and upheld her sister's curse."

"But leavened it with hope," the other put in. "And set us here as guards."

"Who are commanded to let no one pass," the mirror twin concluded.

"Fine," Alec sighed, "I don't suppose there's any chance *I* could release you, is there? And maybe get off that way?"

Two heads shook. "We cannot say."

"But is it possible—theoretically? Can't you at least level with me that far?"

The two glanced at each other then nodded. "It . . . is."

And with that, they surged forward, swords gleaming bright in unmatched right hands.

Alec stumbled back, found the top step too quickly—and fell, the treads' edges stabbing hard into his thighs, hips, and shoulders. Fortunately, he didn't hit his head, and managed to struggle up on one elbow before the right-hand guard was upon him. He kicked, missed, then kicked again—and caught a woody shin with his left bootheel. The guard grunted, but continued on. Alec barely got his blade up to block as two other swords flashed down.

But slowly . . . so slowly. Certainly not with the lightning reflexes and razor dexterity he expected of Faery warriors. He knocked the first away with ease, and thrust aside the second in its wake, so that it rang against the steps.

Somehow he scrambled to his feet, halfway down the flight, and met them again, head-on, blade weaving inexpertly before him.

The left one charged, then brought his blade around. Out of nowhere, David's lessons surfaced, and Alec blocked it. The air thrummed with the belling of steel against . . . some other metal—and smelled of hot metal, too; for the Faery blade was glowing faintly where Alec's sword had connected.

And then the other moved forward, but more slowly than his fellow. In fact, he was limping. Alec swung at the unshielded elven side.

—And hit! Against all hope, he struck home. The guard screamed as metal seared across his unarmored forearm.

And two yards to his right, his other half flinched.

So that was it! Pain to either part affected the whole. These really *were* two bifurcate beings—which probably explained why they were so slow and clumsy: their limbs had to coordinate two sets of reflexes, two sets of instincts, two levels of training, even.

So what were they doing as guards?

Providing intimidation, Alec decided—and aimed another blow at the injured one, who'd found his own blade obstructed by his companion's wildly flailing arm.

This time Alec struck no glancing blow to the wrist, but hit full in the body of the Faery half—which grunted from impact, or pain, as porcelained links broke and splintered mail scattered. When Alec yanked his blade free, blood stained it. Both halves of that one's face went white. Steam issued from a bubbling rent in the mail.

The *other* cried out—and dropped his sword.

And Alec was suddenly facing one odd-looking warrior who was weaponless, and a mirror twin who was not.

Except that right brain drove left-side muscles, and left drove right, and there seemed to be some bond between like halves that transcended attachment. Therefore, the part that drove the remaining sword was attached to a remote body, which, though weaponless, was fully functional.

Alec leapt sideways, and struck again—*not* at the

preposterous thing with the weapon, but at the exposed right side of its woody twin.

And twisted his stroke at the last second, to catch it just below his fungied knee.

The blade sliced clean through, and the guard collapsed where he stood. The air smelled of burning wood. Already injured, the other likewise toppled.

Alec dropped back, frankly astonished.

Yet they lived! All four pieces did.

"It was thought," one panted, "that divided as we were, we would fight as two warriors yet die as four; that it would take a blow to each part of us to claim the whole. But that reckoned on Faery warriors, not on a human who commands the dreaded iron."

"With the dreaded iron," the other voice continued, "one blow can wound both portions of whichever body it strikes."

"And blows strong enough to cleave our skulls would likewise cleave our entire bodies—"

"—Freeing you to rejoin your original halves before you died?" Alec finished.

"You have guessed the rest of our riddle," the topmost guard affirmed.

"You have only to see it done to free us," the bottom added. "Rejoined, we can muster sufficient will to fight the iron infection."

Still mostly running on instinct, Alec raised his sword to follow that suggestion; but then his eyes narrow suspiciously. "You won't fight *me* again, will you?"

"We have done our duty," the upper one answered. "But hurry, for if any of our four parts dies, all are doomed."

Alec swallowed hard. "You'll have to sit up," he managed, reaching to help the topmost to an unsteady seat on the next step down. That one immediately tore off his helm, closed his eyes, and thrust his head far forward.

"I'm not sure about this," Alec admitted frankly. "I'm

not conditioned to split the skulls of folks I've just talked to. And . . . what if I miss?"

"Simply aim for the juncture of our two halves," that one murmured.

"Think of it as splitting firewood," came a slow weak chuckle from the other.

"But . . ."

"Act! *Now!*"

Alec did. As soon as the impulse came, he swung his sword behind his back two-handed; then arched it up and over, to bring it down hard where thick gold-copper hair met what looked like moldy moss.

He struck true. The sword dug in—and continued down through the guard's body until it struck the mail hauberk, whereupon he wrenched it free.

He couldn't watch the rest, as the body split asunder and odd sounds began to issue from the portions he couldn't see, while hands tore frantically at armor. "Here," he gritted, when he could no longer resist a peek, and ran the swordpoint down the front of the mail coat from throat to leg slit. The gleaming links parted easily. He didn't look at what lay inside.

The blow to the second guard went quickly. Instinct was driving now, and instinct told him it was unwise to question what he did.

Nor did he look at the aftermath of his messy operation, merely stood breathing heavily, leaning against his sword, whose point rested atop a stone step (where it was slowly sinking in). Abruptly, reality spun, and he sat down with a thump, a wave of nausea playing tag with a strong urge to go unconscious. He bent over and stuck his head between his knees, fumbling at his canteen. Found, he drank a long draught of what no longer tasted precisely like Georgia well water. When he seemed unlikely to faint, he rose again. And pointedly did not look at four odd shapes groping for each other across the steps.

"Sorry, guys," he gasped. "If you need me, I'll do

what I can; otherwise . . ." Hearing no reply, he pushed through the tower door.

And entered emptiness: charred, twisted emptiness.

Obviously a fire had raged here once, flaring up from a hearth in the center of the floor to lick the ceiling with sufficient heat to set the gold and silver ornaments there a-dripping, or running in lumpy pools down the black glass walls. Soot—actual *soot*—drifted down from distant vaulted heights, disturbed by the breeze that wafted in from the blasted plain. Dust motes danced with each other: black carbon and some unknown substance of mirror-silver.

Up.

He had to go up!

Fortunately, there was a ramp: a long wedge of stone set flush against the wall and spiraling upward into darkness.

He jogged that way, hoping there were no more surprises, and wishing he'd thought to *ask* if there were. None appeared, anyway, and his hardest task became keeping his footing on a slope made slick with layers of soot interspersed with dust-fine glass. Once he slipped, but somehow he made it to a long opening in the ceiling of the entrance chamber and passed through.

The next level was similar to the one below but less ravaged by fire, though a long rent showed in one wall, and the whole area around another window had fallen away. Shreds of singed tapestries lay close against scorched walls, and not all the shards of bright-colored glass upon the floor were melted.

The ramp continued.

Five times Alec passed through ceilings as he continued his arduous trek, through air that grew hotter by the instant, and thicker with the dust of ages.

Yet each level's furnishings were in better repair— and its walls more problematical, as though something had shaken the keep down from above, even as flame broke free to wash it from below.

Abruptly, there were no more floors. Rather, he stood in a chamber no wider than his outstretched arms (less sword), and not much longer. The wall to the right was so broken it resembled thick glass filigree, but the one to the left was solid.

Ahead lay a door: thick boards of what looked like solid oak, joined by dense strapwork of dark metal.

Alec touched the sword to a spot of naked wood.

Smoke erupted.

He thought of leaving it there—but that might catch it on fire, which was *not* the plan. Not when Eva presumably lay beyond. And then it occurred to him that he hadn't yet actually knocked—and did.

"Come in, oh Mortal who loves me," a soft, tired, but achingly familiar female voice answered.

Chapter XVIII:
Walls

(The Straight Tracks—no time)

"I don't understand," Aikin gasped, his words barely audible between the thundering thumps of the black mare's hooves against whatever presently lay beneath the golden glimmer of the Track. "I only *took* forty-nine steps!"

"Don't ask me!" David shot back, his voice gone wobbly as he was forced to yell to make himself heard—and that with Aikin (who couldn't ride) pressed hard against his back, arms clamped around him panic-tight. At least the mare-that-was-also-a-woman wasn't giving them attitude right now. In fact, she was running very smoothly indeed—for a horse. David couldn't help but recall all those stories about Faery steeds whose riders never fell off, and hoped this was one. A fall was *not* a comforting notion—not with nothing but vicious-looking briars to either side. Certainly not with the Wild Hunt on their Track if not—so far—their trail.

Yeah, anything that made a Faery woman shape-shift in order to flee in near–blind panic wasn't something he wanted to tangle with. Never mind poor Aikin. He'd *seen* Aik's face when she'd named their pursuer, seen it go just about as white as snow. And that was as much information as he needed.

But Aik wanted to know more—about everything, apparently, never mind their circumstances, or the one he'd just escaped—and so they were yelling in each other's ears and faces, and had been, for at least five minutes. Liz had it lucky: a mount to herself and no overcurious would-be forester to give her grief. At least conversation kept his mind off his tortured sitter.

For a while.

"Forty-nine paces," Aikin repeated. "I counted, so I could go back that many."

It would not have succeeded, the Faery's thought came into David's mind, though she was obviously addressing his corider. *Not once you had entered another World. It is like gears meshing with one another: as long as you stay on the same gear—the same Track from the same World—you are secure. You can watch other gears go by, and if you are careful, you can step off the rim and onto a spoke of* your *wheel, and be home. But once you venture onto* another *gear, you are in trouble; because that gear may not be the same size; and may spin past* your *gear at a different rate. Do you see?*

"Sort of," Aikin muttered. "Kinda."

David dared a glance to the right, to where Liz rode close beside. He smiled grimly. She smiled back. "You catch that?" he shouted.

She shook her head jerkily. "Too complex for me," she called back, risking a glance over her shoulder.

David resisted the temptation to follow her example. He'd just as soon *not* know what was back there—if anything was.

"How much longer?" he yelled again—at the horse.

You do not need to shout to address me, the Faery gave back. *Thoughts are only masked by other thoughts.*

"Sorry."

Too long, I fear—to answer your question. We must . . . go all the way around the gear on which we found your friend.

"God, this is confusing," Aikin growled. "If they're *Straight* Tracks, how can they also be cogwheels? And if you're on the rim of one, there shouldn't be a problem finding your own spoke."

Ah, but the Tracks are not precisely the rims of gears or their teeth, the horse-woman replied. *They are more like the place where two gears meet: the point of tangency. In fact, some say there are no Tracks, merely points in space, but that we see that point at all times simultaneously, which gives it the illusion of length. And, of course, anything that spins produces inertia—the tendency to continue in a straight line . . . And of course the Tracks are straight . . .*

"Never mind," Aikin groaned. "Sounds too much like math."

It is an idea of my own, the woman replied. *Based on readings I did in your World. I—*

She broke off abruptly, and David felt a wash of panic slap against the walls of his mind. Aik must have felt it too, because he tensed. He heard Liz bite off a cry of pain.

He comes!

The black mare gathered herself and ran faster. The white stallion followed. The pounding of their hooves acquired a more-urgent cadence; their breaths roared through two sets of teeth. Sweat splattered David's face—or spittle. It was all he could do to maintain his hold on the reins and still try to accommodate Aikin, who clutched him grimly. "Shit," Aikin gasped. "God damn."

David started to reply, but the words froze in his throat as a sound found his ear: the brazen bellow of a hunting horn echoing up the Track from behind.

Close.

Too close.

He had to look.

A deep breath, and he glanced backward, past the wildly whipping darkness of Aikin's hair, to the gold-lit tube of the Track. He saw nothing at first—but his eyes burned abruptly the way they did only in the pres-

ence of Power used profligately and close by. And
somehow, he could *see*: black shapes cut out against
the gold—five—ten—a *dozen* riders on horses, with
cloaks billowing like storm clouds and armor flashing
in disturbing dark colors he wasn't certain he should
be able to see, as though his vision had skewed toward
ultraviolet—which perhaps, with the Sight, it had. The
lead rider wore stag's antlers—metal helm, beast's
head, or grown from his own flesh and bone, he
couldn't tell, nor wanted to. He only knew he was afraid
as he'd never been afraid; as though that one image
had sparked something primal and instinctive, like the
fear of snakes or spiders.

He shut his eyes, unable to watch longer, yet unable
to resist. And when the tension of not knowing grew
too great, and he opened them again, the Hunt was
closer. And this time the horn brought with it the baying and yapping and belling of hounds. He could see
them now, where before the Track glow had hidden
them: a tide of black that flowed before the horses:
black ears and black backs and black tails; lolling
tongues and flashing red eyes and white teeth that
looked like deadly foam on the crests of canine waves,
as their leaps brought them above the Track.

"This is . . . *bad*, David," Liz shouted.

David tore his gaze away from their pursuit to meet
his lady's. They touched glances in lieu of hands. It was
enough. Comfort sparked across the few yards between
them: comfort and concern.

The Lands of Men, the Faery told them, her unheard
voice nevertheless carrying a breathless quality. *If we
can reach the Lands of Men anywhere, perhaps he
will not follow us there.*

"But there's only that one entrance, isn't there?" David cried.

*If we can get close enough, we can go straight
through the World Walls themselves. It is not a thing
I would desire; it will be unpleasant; and I cannot*

say where—or when—we would emerge, but it is better than what awaits us on the tip of the Huntsman's spear.

"Who *is* he?" Aikin broke in. "Or . . . what?"

He was here when the Tuatha de Danaan came, the horse-woman answered. *He met us when we arrived, and he fought with our greatest warriors—Lugh and Nuada and Bres and Angus Og and Finvarra and Bobh Derg. No one proved victorious. Finally, he gave us the land uncontested, but would not relinquish the Tracks—nor, one night a year, any lands that lie upon them. Then he rides.*

"So he's not Faery?"

As the folk of Faerie are to mortal men, so he is to Faery folk. Sometimes he wears our seeming and our substance, but not always. Mostly he is wildness, and death without regret, and chaos unrestrained. He is darkness without light, night without morning, wounds without healing, blood that will never clot. Your ancestors drew him in caves: horned and skinned and huge-phallused. And tonight, of all nights, he is king.

"And those who ride with him?"

Fools, idiots, the young without wisdom, the eternally insane.

"But if we can make it through the World Walls—"

We may survive! Now hush, for I must seek a certain . . . something.

David had no choice but to comply. Anything that would improve their chances he'd certainly go along with—even if it thrust him back into his own thoughts, into the isolation of his private, fear-born hell.

At least he had Aikin with him, another human presence warm at his back, strong arms locked around him: solid, tangible muscle and blood and bone. Liz rode alone, and that was almost more than he could bear. How *she* stood it, he didn't know. Perhaps she was stronger than he; he'd long suspected as much, in fact.

Alec let troubles tie him in knots and then went ballistic and overreacted. Himself—he let angst build to critical mass, only to have it explode into grim, determined—and, too often, wrong—action. Aik watched and festered and plotted, then did the unexpected. Liz simply let obstacles wash over her, regarded them coolly, had her say, and moved on.

God, but he wished he was riding with her now!

"My fault," Aikin whispered—yet he heard.

"No more than mine," David called back. "If we'd been straight with you, like we should've—"

The horn cut him off again—close, so close, behind. The horse stumbled—misstepped, perhaps—or tripped. And David realized to his horror that the vanguard of the hounds were at the mare's heels. He glimpsed one toothy maw, saw Aikin's eyes go crazy-wide, then shut abruptly. Pain tore into his ankle. A downward glance showed a hound falling back with a scrap of what he prayed was only shoe leather in its teeth.

Hold for your life! From the horse-woman.

David did, hoping Aikin had also heard that command—likely he had, for his grip, if possible, grew tighter. Tight enough, maybe, to crack ribs.

And then the mare simply leapt, as though to clear a hurdle—and somehow, impossibly, in the middle of that leap, turned left in midair. David caught a flash of a solid wall of briars heading straight toward him, and flinched, as pain with a thousand edges thrust itself in his face. "Liz . . . !" he screamed.

And then the world turned over . . . his stomach and inner ears tied each other into complex knots . . . cold and hot strobed across his flesh—*bitter* cold.

He opened his eyes.

And didn't close them again nearly fast enough to miss what no one *should* see: an endless *nothingness* in which nothing moved yet everything did. The only way he could describe it was as an infinitely large TV tuned to a nonexistent channel, save in three dimensions, and with himself a single pixel in the center. Scan lines zipped in every direction, yet nothing changed.

"Where . . . ?" he tried to ask, but no sound answered.

No *air* . . . ?

Or simply no *time*?

We are within the World Walls, the Faery replied. *I sensed a weakening in them and chose to risk it, though it is a place of madness. Guard your thoughts and try to think of nothing, for only the insane can preserve their minds here intact.*

"The Hunt . . . ?"

If we are lucky, he has passed us. But he will return!

"So . . ."

This will buy us time. I hope *it will give me a chance to look for . . .* Yes! *Beyond luck, I have found it!*

"What?"

Silence—but the mare was moving. Even with his eyes closed, David felt reality blur. Yet even as he braced himself for . . . whatever she was about, he heard a horn. Pixels danced behind his lids, vibrating in harmony with that sound. Not-color became pervasive noise.

Now! the Faery cried.

—And leapt again.

Everything *changed* once more. For a timeless instant smells had colors, sounds had tastes, textures had scents, colors became breezes one could feel.

And then it ebbed away into a nothingness even more profound then heretofore—

—And reality came rushing back: grimy walls and exhaust fumes and, in the distance, music—*electric* music: rock and roll.

"Oh my God!" David heard Liz gasp, her voice a mix

of awe and relief: the sweetest sound in the world.

Aikin's iron grip relaxed the merest bit. David dragged in a long breath and opened his eyes. "Athens! Jesus Christ, we're back in *Athens*!"

"No joke," Aikin breathed and released his hold, the horse, for the nonce, having gone still.

"Did we escape him—it—whatever?" From Liz.

I hope so, but I fear not, the horse-woman replied. *What I most fear is that we have made him angry. And if you anger one such as he, nothing will stop him, not the Tracks, not the World Walls, nothing! My hope is that he will not find the proper* when *to reach us here.*

"When . . . is it, anyway?" David panted.

Aikin wiggled behind him, presumably to check the sky. "Shit!" he spat. "Can't tell for the sky glow. Only . . . that music: it's InYerFace—I think. Sounds like 'em, anyway. Or Donkey. Might be Gavin's 'Fridge or the Lotus Eaters."

David suppressed a nervous giggle that was dangerously close to hysteria.

"Those folks were all 'sposed to be playin' on Halloween," Aikin explained. "That means this probably *is* our Athens, our Halloween, and our year."

David's eyes had finally adjusted to a stationary reality, albeit a dimly lit one. The dirty bricks of an alley limited vision to either side, but ahead lay a strip of sidewalk, with, beyond it, a line of pavement down which a Toyota crept at speculative idle. With no urging from him, the mare paced toward the light. It clarified into a blank, gray-enameled wall, but a familiar sign showed to the right as they emerged: the one for Jackson Street Books. And if this was Jackson, then a block to the left was Clayton, and one block down it was College Avenue, the heart of downtown. More to the point, if this was Halloween, there'd be folks everywhere. Surely the Hunt wouldn't follow them into a crowd.

Perhaps not, the Faery observed. *But madness runs free in the Lands of Men tonight. That may attract him. For who would notice him here?*

"I don't care," Liz inserted unexpectedly. "If we *have* to face him, I'd rather it was on our ground than his."

"Right," David agreed, and urged the mare forward. An instant later, they squinted into the glare of artificial light. Before he knew it, they had reached the corner of Jackson and Clayton. And blessedly, away to the right dark shapes capered around a Dumpster someone had torched, while a voice shrieked drunkenly, "How 'bout them dawgs?"—only to be drowned out when whatever band was playing closest found a few more clicks on the amp dial and blanked out the air with white noise.

Without the slightest prompting, the horse ambled toward those dancing figures and that thunderous roar. Madness, David thought grimly, loomed ahead. And a worse kind of madness quite possibly rode behind.

And then whoever was singing one block over gave up on lyrics and began to scream.

Or perhaps that was the baying of unseen hounds.

Chapter XIX:
Awakening

(Aife's tower—an uncertain place—no time)

Time stopped for Alec.

Surely it had—no way else his entire perception could have narrowed to the sentence he'd just heard pronounced, whose cadences still vibrated in the hot dusty air before that ancient oak door at the top of a shattered tower in . . . *nowhere*.

"Come in, oh Mortal who loves me . . ."

Eva's voice.

Eva's!

He could almost *see* her words: see the mirror-silver dust motes bunch and disperse in response to those tones. Certainly he *felt* them—as a soothing smoothness in his ears, but likewise as agencies that set his body to warring with itself. Part of him—that which had desired this reunion so long the impulse itself had become a force to be reckoned with—relaxed, knowing all he had to do was push through that door and he and Eva would be together again.

But another aspect went tense and nervous, as the abstract and hypothetical became imminent and real. Any instant mystery would resolve into truth, and he'd learn whether she still loved him, and maybe discover the same about himself. He felt like a soldier on the eve of his first battle. Would he fight or run away? Would he survive or become a statistic? The single certainty was that life would never be the same.

For a long breathless moment he stood frozen, one

hand on the hilt of the sword with which he'd prodded
the door, the other hovering upon the pouch that contained the ulunsuti. There was still time. It was perfectly possible to build a fire, imagine the house in
Jackson County, and gate back home.

To square one.

—Where the beast of not knowing would haunt him
for the rest of his life. He'd faced warriors scant
minutes before. What could he fear from a woman?

That she'd lie to him?

That he'd misread her feelings or his own?

That what he'd taken for love was merely lust?

That . . .

"Stop it, you fool!" he growled aloud, and thrust
through the door.

And dream became reality.

If the room beyond was not *precisely* the one he'd
seen in his vision, it was only because he was viewing
it from another angle. There were the same cracked
and fissured walls circling a chamber maybe ten yards
across, the same organic arches rising to a vaulted ceiling easily as tall, from which stones had fallen, revealing patches of darkness or the silvery no-color that was
the sky. The floor was also the same: flagstones strewn
with threadbare furs and worn hides of beasts that did
not exist in the Lands of Men. Halfway around the
right-hand wall, a low platform supported a bed strewn
with more furs and a profusion of silk and velvet pil-
lows in colors like faded jewels, while festoons of tat-
tered crimson comprised a canopy from the center of
the vault to the headboard.

Directly opposite, a window narrow as his shoulders
and twice his height looked on nothingness. And before it, wedged into an inset seat like a luminescent
shadow, sat Eva: dark-haired, pale, and beautiful; in a
long white gown of simple cut that left her shoulders
bare.

She rose as he entered, and strode forward: slowly,

almost stately in her measured tread. And it came to him that he'd only seen her in mortal disguise—she'd favored gypsy-style togs—and once in the armor of Lugh's guard, which reduced male and female to one likeness and showed how similar were the faces of both sexes among the Sidhe.

This was no gypsy, however, and no woman in warrior drag.

This was a *queen*. Deposed, yes, and in exile, shorn of the trappings of her royalty, but a queen nonetheless. Not Eva of the earth, but Aife of the Daoine Sidhe.

Alec felt the rags of his hero persona slip to the floor as the vision before him made him realize only too clearly how unlike he and Aife were: she of Faery nobility, an immortal, able to work magic, betray princes, and precipitate wars and trials and deadly vengeance; while he was simply Alec McLean: barely a junior in college, averagely tall, averagely handsome, above averagely bright, but so were all his friends, so it didn't matter. And no great genius when it came to the social graces; no master at doing the right thing at the right time. Certainly no champion at wooing Faery ladies.

What could she possibly see in him?

What indeed?

Swallowing hard, he squared his shoulders and advanced to meet her. His steps rang loud on the floor, and he felt more awkward than ever; still didn't know whether to rush to embrace her or hold back and let her come to him (which would reveal where *her* head was regarding this reunion); whether to fall on the floor at her feet, or run screaming out the door.

For her part, she continued as before, but with a sad smile that brightened shyly as she drew near, so that her stature seemed to shrink and the glamour of stateliness to dim as she halted the reach of their extended hands away.

And suddenly, she was no more than a woman. Not

quite as tall as he, but slim; beautiful, but no more than he'd seen at UGA.

"Alec McLean," she whispered. "My Alec."

"Uh, yeah," he managed, inanely. "And if I wanted to sound *really* dumb, I'd do like Luke Skywalker and say, 'I'm here to rescue you.'"

"Aren't you?"

He blushed. "I guess. Uh, I mean, yeah—yes—I am. I mean—well, it sounds kinda stupid to *say* it."

"Have I changed that much?" she chuckled. "Or have you?"

Alec stared at the floor. It was impossible to think while looking at her, impossible to compose his thoughts while gazing at those dark blue eyes. Impossible not to recall what had passed between them, what lay hidden beneath her clothes and stirred to life under his.

"You haven't," he began shakily. "That is, you're the same but . . . different . . . I mean . . . oh hell!" he blurted finally, and closed his eyes. Calm fingers found his trembling ones and drew him toward the low seat that followed the curve of the wall beside the window.

"Many are the things I have pondered," Aife murmured, as she sank down beside him—not *too* close, he was both relieved and perplexed to note. "And foremost among them is that which has passed 'twixt you and me and brought me to this state."

Alec started to speak, but she silenced him with a finger against his lips. "You wonder if I love you," she said. "And you wonder if you love *me* or the memory you have kept so faithfully. You wonder how you can ever fit loving one such as I into the World you know, or whether you are brave enough to dwell in mine."

"Yeah," Alec sighed. "You got it."

"You also wonder how it is that I am alive and in my own right body, when you saw me die."

Another nod. "Right again."

"That at least, is simple enough to explain, as the

others are not," she said. "I truly died when you saw me die—that is, my body became inviable as a housing for my soul, for the agony washing through my physical self was more than my *other* self could bear, and so my soul dissolved the Silver Cord and fled. That which remained became merely so much matter; yet that which was *me* persisted. I could then have willed my soul into a child new-quickened in some Faery woman's womb, and grown up with full cognizance of who I had been. Or I could have exerted my will and gathered substance and become my former self in a matter of days. Neither would free me from Lugh's justice, only the Death of Iron. My choice was thus to serve my sentence at once or wait. I chose the former, for by then I knew that I *did* love you, that I *had* been a traitor to my king, and that it was my duty to surrender myself to justice—which I did. The rest is as I related when you came to me in a dream a few days ago: that since I feigned love to betray a mortal man and a Faery king, only *true* love would be the key to my release."

"That's . . . what I thought," Alec acknowledged weakly, with a sick feeling in his gut—for something had changed. When first they'd met they had shared a bond of loneliness—his of finding himself odd man out with David and Liz, hers of being a foreigner (how foreign he'd not suspected) in an alien land. She'd been exotic, but had seemed to enjoy his company, and had laughed and joked and shared naïvetés with him.

But at least they'd been equals—so it seemed.

Now, however, a barrier had risen where he'd expected none, and he could no longer love her as Eva: another human, another same-aged friend. For *Aife* was his superior—in wisdom; knowledge, power, and actual (if not apparent) age. And it frightened him past knowing.

"You're . . . not how I remember," he mumbled bleakly, feeling the weight of every word as it left his tongue, as though each were a shovelful of earth cast into his grave, shutting his corpse off from light.

Eva smiled and patted his hand. "Yet you came."

Alec tried to smile back. He wondered if he'd hurt her, or if she was secretly relieved. He wondered if he even believed what he'd just said.

"So what does this mean?" he asked finally. "I came to rescue you, and I thought I was the . . . mortal man who loved you, and I *do* love you—sort of . . . and I *want* to love you like I used to love you; only . . . now I'm not sure about things, 'cept that I just want the best for you 'cause—this is gonna sound stupid— you're a good person, I think. But . . . well, hell. *Can* I still rescue you? Or does the . . . truth change every- thing?"

"Truth," she echoed softly. "In *truth*, you loved me because I loved you—or seemed to. No one else did at that time, and the cold part of me saw that and knew you were ripe for manipulation, and so I did. But I like- wise sensed the love you kept for your friend, and how he had hurt you, and how you hated yourself for hating him for loving another, and I could not help but love you for that. And to speak *more* truth: you loved me when you came here, and that is enough to win my release."

"So, you're free to go?"

Aife remained where she was. "Yes," she smiled. "But there is no hurry. Fast or slow, it is the same to Lugh, now that you are here."

"My friends—"

"Time passes differently here than there, you should know that." She touched his hand.

A thrill pulsed through him that had nothing to do with intellect. Her fingers traced the length of his thigh. He closed his eyes and shuddered. His face felt hot.

"So you *do* love me," she whispered. "In a way."

"Of . . . c-course I do," he stammered, not looking at her. "I'm only human, and you're a beautiful, beautiful lady . . ."

"But . . . ?"

"But I don't *really* love you. And to do . . . *that*, I have to *really* love you. I have to trust you. You have to be an equal—and you can't be."

"Did you love me before?"

"Something . . . else was thinking then."

Aife laughed. The fingers stroked higher, farther in . . . Closer. Alec swallowed again. His groin tightened in spite of himself. God, it felt so good, and it had been so long, and he'd wanted it so badly, and it ought to be the same because the bodies would be the same . . .

But the minds wouldn't.

There was *more* honesty between them, which should bring them closer—yet it didn't.

"Love me," Eva murmured.

"I shouldn't. I—"

"You have nothing to fear," she said before he could finish. "I am your perfect lover, the only woman with whom you can let go completely, without guilt or fear. I know your body, and so you have no need to be shy. You have known mine, and so no new mysteries await you there. You were clumsy before, but you have had years in which to recall and refine and perfect your desire."

"I . . ." Alec tried again. But her hand slid inside his shirt.

"Oh hell," he gasped. "Why not?"

Cold awakened him.

God, he was cold too!

—All over!

Wind blew chill across his shoulders—his thighs, the small of his back, his feet and buttocks. He rolled onto his side, drew himself in a tight ball, one arm clasped around his knees while the other fumbled for the furs to tug over him—and for Aife to draw her into one last guilty embrace.

He found neither.

Only more cold, and a harsh-edged wetness some dim part of him identified as grass.

Grass? When before there had been soft furs and prickly velvets and Aife's skin.

. . . Aife's skin. Over and over, he'd stroked and kissed and caressed Aife's silky skin.

So where was she now?

And why was he so cold, when Aife's odd prison land was desert-hot, and her body warm, and the ardor that had suddenly inflamed him hotter than the hottest fire?

Perhaps those things had simply moved.

He uncoiled a fraction, and stretched farther, noting that whatever he lay on was cold and rough.

Like the ground.

An eye popped open.

"Oh, God, *no!*" he groaned into cool night air, as goose bumps marched across his limbs. His stomach turned giddy cartwheels, but his brain went totally numb.

He was squinting at a date: 1961. That date was carved on a slab of lichened granite as gray as the walls of Aife's tower.

But *not* a tower: a tombstone.

Others showed beyond it: arches of gray in a greater darkness that spoke of night.

Night in the Lands of Men.

In a graveyard on a cold hillside.

Alone.

Abruptly, he sat up, hugging himself, rubbing his bare arms and shoulders as he shuddered uncontrollably. He bowed his head, not caring if anyone saw him, naked as he was and somewhere he probably ought not to be after dark. Tears blurred the landscape into an abstract vision of gray and black, with only the dull yellow glow of the starless sky to give color.

—But no hope. He gazed on the color of hopelessness.

It had happened again! He'd given his love to a Faery woman and she'd used him: taken him for all he had, soul and body too, and abandoned him. "God, I must have 'easy fuck' written all over me," he spat. "I must have a screw slot a foot long in my back."

He pounded the tombstone with a fist. Pounded till it hurt. Blood glazed his knuckles.

"Why?" he screamed at the sky. "What the fuck did I ever do to *you*? What's so fucking wrong with wanting somebody to love you?"

His voice died away into sobs, and he curled up again on the ground, arms wrapped around himself as though his own flesh was his only comfort.

"Shit," he grunted, when tears would no longer flow. And with the sound of his voice came the realization that whatever agony rent his soul, a casual passerby would only see some weirdo doing something kinky on a grave. They wouldn't know that he felt as dead as one of the local residents—inside.

He sat up again and wiped his eyes, blinking at the landscape, at the sky glow that said he was near a city. "So where am I?" he asked the tombstone, peering shakily around, even as more chills wracked him. Twisting about, he made a slow assessment of the environs. As he did, his gaze brushed something he hadn't noted before, there in the lee of the tombstone: a pile of fabric, a pair of sturdy boots.

His clothes.

He almost wept, as his life became one small element simpler. Pawing through them, he found underwear and jeans and pulled them on. He felt for his pockets automatically, and located his wallet, his checkbook, his keys. (Why would someone take such things to Faerie he remembered wondering, when he'd put them there. *You think they've got teller machines in Tir-Nan-Og? Think someone's gonna ask for your ID?*)

And then that coldness that had only barely relaxed

its grip on his heart clamped down again with full, vicious force.

Where was the ulunsuti?

He'd fished it out of his pack during a lull in their lovemaking and shown it to her, then placed it atop his clothes beside Aife's bed (even in the heat of passion, he was neat) . . .

And here was the sword, and the frigging *pack* . . .

He emptied the latter—to no effect.

Desperate, then, he sprang to his feet, slapping at his pockets, though sense told him that was stupid. His boots then? He checked them.

Nothing—of course.

Recklessly—panicked—he sorted through the rest of his clothing and found no oracular stone. Somehow he finished dressing, then knelt and patted the earth around where he'd lain, slowly, methodically, lest his writhings have knocked it away.

No luck. He knew in a way he could not explain that the ulunsuti—the jewel from the head of the great uktena, that a shaman in another World had given him in trust—was gone.

Biting back another frustrated shout, he flopped against the tombstone, hands thrust so deeply into his pockets that he half expected to feel startled devils protesting his invading nails.

He touched paper. Fresh, crisp paper, that his fingers knew without knowing was not that of the Lands of Men.

Holding his breath, he withdrew his hand.

The paper was folded twice, sealed with wax, and utterly wrinkle-free. The seal smelled like Aife's skin. Still barely breathing, he fumbled it open.

The whorling alphabet was none he knew, and the language could not possibly have been English—the balance of long words to short was wrong, and there were too many diacritical marks. Yet he could read it:

It is only fitting that one who has caused so much grief should give pleasure in return.
I begin to see what Aife saw in you.

And that was all. No name. No thank you. No apology.

And no Aife!

Somehow that got through to him: Aife in the third person.

That had not been her!

Then who had it been, that had lured him to a pocket universe, lied to him, seduced him, stolen—apparently—the ulunsuti, and sent him here in one final bitter flourish: a naked wannabe-knight on a cold hillside?

Not Aife!

Which both gave him hope and filled him with new despair, for now it was all to do over. All that dreaming and dreading and anticipation and hope and fear, all that psyching had been in vain.

Not Aife.

"Fucking shit!" Alec growled at the night—and rose from the tombstone.

And as he did, the wind shifted and brought with it the sound of music.

Loud music.

Rock and roll played with conviction outdoors.

It came from beyond the curve in the road at the bottom of the hill. Squaring his shoulders, he started that way, and had not gone far at all before he beheld a familiar landmark.

A pyramid it was, made of marble or granite, and roughly a yard on a side. Trinkets lay about it: gauds and baubles, feathers, bright stones, and the paraphernalia of kitsch.

He recognized it, though, had made pilgrimage to it like countless other freshmen seeking the graves of dead rock heroes.

He didn't need to see the name graven there. No other tombstone was like that one, nor situated so. It was the grave of Ricky Wilson, once of the B-52's.

He was in Oconee Hills Cemetery.

In Athens.

And by the full moon glimmering dimly in the gray-gold sky, and the music that sounded louder even as he made his slow grim way along, it was likely Halloween night.

True Halloween.

When the dead were said to rise.

Alec hoped they did. Maybe they could give him some pointers on how it felt to be alive.

Chapter XX:
True Hallows

(Athens, Georgia—
Saturday, October 31—night)

It looked like a Dance of Death: one of those medieval woodcuts wrought by guilt-laden Germans, in which a phalanx of skeletal, decaying, and/or demonic creatures perpetrated unspeakable torments on not-always-so-innocent peasants, all illuminated by raging bonfires. Yeah, that's how the revelry down Clayton Street *looked*, even if the flaming Dumpster was neither medieval nor city-approved. The rest, however, was spot on: people of all ages, roaming sidewalk and street alike, capering with wild abandon—in cloaks and wigs, spandex, sheets, and towels—and the pillage of a thousand thrift store raids. It was the whole world in microcosm—the whole lunatic *fringe,* anyway—with traditional ghosts, witches, and vampires ranged against their Generation-X analogues: rock stars, movie icons, and cultural celebs, with a healthy dose of off-color libido thrown in. As for cackling demons . . . well, easily a dozen bands, in clubs and street alike, tortured the very air with electric cacophony.

Trouble was, it could well become the real thing, if the Hunt broke through the World Walls as the Faery woman feared. David found himself straining his hearing in quest of far direr and more ancient sounds than howling guitars and gibbering synthesizers.

Instead, he heard someone yell, "Hey, look at Roy and Dale!"—and found himself blushing furiously,

246

given that he was wearing jogging shorts, sneaks, and a T-shirt, not rawhide, a stetson, and jeans. Of course, he *was* astride a handsome jet black mare with a wild-eyed guy in cammos hanging on behind, and a sharp-looking redheaded wench pacing a white stallion alongside—but horses weren't costumes, quite, even if they did earn more stares as they clop-clopped around the corner toward the heart of the Dance. A city cop stared too, eyes going hard and narrow before he puffed his cheeks and strode toward them, ticket book in hand. Just as he was about to speak, the horse-woman wheeled around and galloped back up Jackson the way they'd come. Not until they'd turned left onto Washington did she slow. Liz's mount clattered to a halt beside her. Two blocks from ground zero, the street was essentially deserted.

Get down, the Faery ordered. *I am too conspicuous.*

"But . . ."

Down!

David scowled, but Liz was already climbing off the white with graceful expertise. Aikin slid down with a muffled "oof" and a scratch of gravel that meant he'd stumbled. David dismounted slowly—and could barely stand when he reached the ground. His thighs and calves were cramping into knots, never mind the raw patches lining them, that made him wish for a barrel-sized ice cube to wrap his legs around. Aikin braced him as he staggered, and then that unheard voice found his mind:

Hurry! In here!

David glanced around and saw the mare duck into the shadowed recess between two buildings across the street from the Georgian Hotel. He followed stiffly, with Aikin's aid. Liz was still staring at the stallion.

He can care for himself, the horse-woman said. *Now hurry!*

Liz shrugged and joined them, twining her hand with David's as they entered that blot of darkness. David didn't watch the transformation this time—mostly for fear of what he might see, though to give their erstwhile mount credit, she'd provided admirable aid in situations not rightly her concern. As it was, the air pulsed briefly with energy, while the sound of skin and muscle stretching and joints realigning somehow overrode the roar of music. A swishing followed, then a long relieved sigh. "I infinitely prefer this shape," came a woman's lilting murmur.

David could resist no longer. A sideways glance showed the same figure he'd seen thrice before, save that the black, gray, and green robe-dress-thing had been exchanged for baggy black pants, a thigh-length khaki tunic, and a silvery vest. Glamour, probably; clothes didn't change when you shifted shape.

"I can cast a glamour on you, if you like," the woman offered. "I could give you . . . costumes."

"Thanks but no thanks." Aikin muttered. "I've had enough shape-changing lately, even bogus type."

"Yeah," Liz echoed, "unless you can make us invisible to the Hunt."

The woman shook her head. "Nothing can do that. Our only hope is to survive the night. He will not pursue past dawn."

"Or in a crowd?"

"That might slow him or force him to change his methods; it will not stop him."

"So what do we do?" Aikin persisted. "We can't get home without bummin' rides, and if we do, we're isolated—but the clubs close at midnight . . ."

"At which point we crash in my dorm room," Liz broke in. "Or in Myra's studio. Whichever."

"And in the meantime, hang out in the crowd as long as we can: safety in numbers, and all?" Aikin wondered.

"Sounds like a plan," David acknowledged, then paused and regarded the Faery. "I'm not tryin' to be rude or anything, but . . . you don't have to hang around any longer. You've fulfilled as much of the deal as we can reasonably expect. 'Course you're *welcome* to stay," he added.

"I am as safe here as in Faerie, for the nonce," the woman replied. "And I am curious to see how events . . . resolve."

"Well, whatever happens," Aikin growled, "we'd best not get caught in here."

"No," David agreed—and froze. A sound had sliced through the duller rumble of music: a familiar sound, sharp as broken glass, deep as a sword wound in unprotected flesh.

The horn.

—From the darkness behind them!

"Run!" David yelled, tugging Liz along as he sprint-limped toward the sidewalk. Behind them, the baying of hounds and the flapping of cloaks joined that eerie winding—and soon enough, the thudding of hooves on something hard to describe that shifted abruptly to a sharper clatter on pavement. A glance dared over his shoulder showed something he'd as soon not have seen: a slit of gray/gold light where the blank wall at the end of the recess had been, through which a tide of darkness poured, that resolved into black hounds, black horses, and black-armored riders with eyes of fire and gore.

In spite of his raw and cramping legs, David ran. He heard Liz stifle a scream, Aikin not suppress a curse— and words in an unintelligible tongue from the Faery. He wished he had time to puzzle her out: why she'd thrown in with them when she could surely have escaped some other way, why she seemed to have no Power in this place which was neither hers nor the realm of the Hunt . . .

The clamor diminished as they reached the sidewalk and pounded left up Washington toward civilization. The horn squalled again, but muffled; and the noises of pursuit went muddled and unclear. David sensed that the Hunt was mustering itself in the gloom: re-grouping for one final race to the kill.

"Faster," he panted. "Fast as you can."

A bank flashed by to the left; City Hall loomed ahead on the right. They turned left down College, toward where the Allhallows madness maelstromed most thickly.

Faster, and the sounds of pursuit diminished—or were drowned by guitars and drums from the street band at College and Clayton. Closer, and David had to slow, though every sense was on red alert. Closer . . . People began to brush past; he caught snatches of conversation, the scent of beer and whiskey riding the breeze . . .

Closer—and rounding the corner from Clayton they came: careening full tilt straight toward them, having circled the block to cut them off.

"Shit!" David groaned, as he dashed into the barricaded street. The Hunt was between them and the heart of the crowd.

Somehow they made the other side, angling back uphill past the parking garage where the Palace Theater had been. Not so many people there, but a bunch of clubs farther down. If they could get to one . . . the Atomic Cafe, say . . .

As they made one last push before the corner, David glimpsed their reflections in the plate glass windows of the unleased space on the garage's ground floor. They looked harried if intact, but behind came . . . *not* horses and riders and hounds, but a seething clot of night, like black fog or dirty steam. *So even the Wild Hunt fears to be seen* too *clearly in the Lands of Men,* David noted.

As if that made any difference.

And by then they'd gained the corner and whipped around it. Half a block now, and they'd make the Atomic, and please God let there not be a cover, and let no one's ID get questioned.

A quarter block, and the darkness gained the corner behind.

Not much farther—but the gloom was arching around beside them—which meant it could have caught them had it desired.

—Beside them . . . and *past* them, in part.

Too late David grasped their plan.

They were being herded.

Herded toward where yet another alley gaped.

And they had no choice: brick walls one way; shadowy darkness the other, through which lights flared, revelers showed as silhouettes, and music went oddly muffled.

And which they dared not enter.

"Do something!" Liz snapped at the Faery.

"I cannot. He is an older power than I, and greater. And this night is his."

And then Aikin stumbled on a curb, and the Hunt closed in.

An instant later, so did the walls. And this alley, David knew from his freshman prowling days, had no exit.

Just three walls—three *blank* walls, save for a door at one side (locked, presumably), dirty pavement, a bad smell, muffled music, a muddy sky . . . and an end plugged by the Hunt, which, as it passed the throat of the alley, regained more-tangible form. Eyes first: red eyes; then heads of hounds and horses, and more knowing eyes under waving hair and helms . . .

A black horse paced forward, slowly, deliberately. The black-armored man astride it was antlered and carried a spear, and his cloak billowed, though there was no wind. Another man flanked him to the right but back a way, face blunt and grim, auburn hair wildly limed. Bare-chested he was, his torso showing an intricacy of swirling blue tattoos. He was also barefoot, and his loose trousers were red-and-black checked. He carried a thick-bladed sword.

To the left . . .

David swallowed hard as he gazed on that figure; for however awful the Huntsman was, with his relentless blackness, there was still some sense of thought behind his eyes.

This woman was madness incarnate—white-skinned, red-haired madness; that hair flying wild around her head in tangled masses that at times seemed to resolve into serpents—or battle flags—or gore-soaked limbs. Her arms were bare, and her night-colored gown was slit to her belly. By her perfect features, by the angle of her jaw, cheekbones, and chin, she was clearly one of the Sidhe.

Gone mad.

For blood patterned her arms and breast, as though she'd smeared it there like a child working designs in fingerpaint. Her hands were ensanguined to the wrists, and her lips leaked gore. When her gaze, which darted everywhere like a fly above a corpse, finally lit on David, she laughed.

Gibbered, rather say.

Whether there was sense to those utterances or not, they conjured images of vast battlefields strewn with corpses of every race and nation: chain mail and plate, bare skin and armored, elaborate uniforms and non-descript fatigues. Swords and shields, knives and axes and maces; blades straight or curved, single edged or bi or tri; rifles and mortars and tanks. Banners of silk and linen and hemp, bright-dyed or faded. And everywhere severed limbs and smashed skulls and piles of steaming viscera, over which dark birds whirled and speculated, and atop which more than one lit to feast. And surely one of those birds had the same eyes as the crazy woman; surely one of those slain was the very likeness of David-the-Elder.

Somehow David tore his gaze away. Liz's fingers tightened in his hand, as she drew close against him. A stronger hand clamped hard upon his shoulder. "This is a crock," Aikin muttered.

"Kill them! Split their skulls, shatter their bones!" the red-haired woman shrieked, kicking her horse forward. "Show me their hearts where they beat in their chests! Carve the blood eagle thrice and let it fly. Float their brains in cups of blood, with their eyeballs as ornaments!"

"I will do what I will!" the Huntsman snapped—and moved closer.

David backed up. His companions did the same. One step, two, and they were halfway down the alley. Four yards separated them from the Hunt, then three. The Huntsman lowered his spear, pointing it first at David, then at Liz, then at Aikin, where it paused. "No one eludes me," that dark figure spat, with a grim laugh. "Yet had you but kept your earlier shape you would have been safe; for I hunt no one twice *in the same body*."

The tip wavered. No more than a yard separated it from Aikin's chest. But just when David feared to see it thrust home, it moved again, to where the Faery woman stood at Liz's right.

Another step, and the spear tapped her breast above her heart.

The woman never flinched. "You would not dare!" she hissed.

"I hunt whom and what I please when it pleases me," the Huntsman replied. "And though I know that you are other than you seem, still, I own no one master: human, god, nor Faery."

"Not even the sister of one who travels with you?" the woman shot back, gazing at the gibbering Huntress, who was leaning over her mount's head like a gargoyle atop a charnel house.

David's breath caught, not only at the challenge, which hinted both at hope and betrayal, but because the gesture had brought the madwoman's face into range of the alley's sole illumination. And somehow that single dim bulb washed the blood from her lips, cheeks, and chin, and showed her features whole: the features, he realized with sick despair, of the Morrigu.

Which confused him more than ever, for their Faery companion had also worn those features—he thought. At which point something began to nag at him: something that would probably have been clear had not panic overridden it.

—Panic, and the words of the Huntsman, when, after a pause during which the spear point did not waver, he shook his head and spoke:

"Kinship will not save you, not when you walk the Tracks *this* night unguarded. For have you not heard that this night is mine?"

"Not even if by so doing you incur not only Lugh's wrath, but that of the Queen of Ys?" a new female voice cried, from behind them. *"I stand with the mortals and their . . . friend."*

David jumped half out of his skin, then twisted around—to see, stepping from the alley's single door, another Faery woman. The very one, surely, whom he'd spotted the previous night at the 40 Watt: the *second* one, whom his friend Mark claimed to have seen in the library. Now, though dressed in student togs—a white silk shirt above black jeans—she stood revealed as some great lady among the Daoine Sidhe.

But what was all that about the Queen of Ys?

Who *was* the Queen of Ys?

The Huntsman paused, as though considering. Then: "The Queen of *Ys*, you say?"

"Aye!"

"You are not her."

"I am her daughter!"

"Rigantana?"

"Aye!"

"What difference does it make?" the tattooed man snapped, as he ambled up beside his leader. The ends of his mustache showed a disturbing shade of red.

"The *difference*," Rigantana said coolly, "is that these fine hounds that seethe about your mounts would not exist had the House of Ys not bred them."

"Which is no reason to let these mortals live—nor two chattering Faery bitches!"

Rigantana glared at Mr. Tattoo for a long moment, as though regarding a spider she would grind into the dirt, then turned back to the Huntsman. (God, she was a cool one, David decided—or insane.) "There *was* a promise," she observed.

The Huntsman's eyes narrowed beneath his horned helm. The spear remained where it was: inches from the Faery woman's breast. "There was," he growled eventually.

"*What* promise?" the gibbering woman shouted. "I have not seen *near* enough blood tonight, and these are merely mortals!"

"Not all of them," the Huntsman snarled back, threatening her with his free hand. "And as for the promise . . . When your kind came to this World I resisted them, and then I fought them. The Realms of Faerie sent champions, whom I defeated. Only Ys sent gifts instead: hounds which never tired and could track forever. I swore then that I would never use that pack against those who presented them: that I would never hunt anyone of Ys's royal house, or under that kindred's protection."

"Which protection I hereby confer upon these three humans and . . . one other," Rigantana said clearly. She smiled, a little smugly, but her eyes were grim.

Abruptly the spear ripped skyward, leaving an afterimage like backward lightning. David cried out, fearing to see the Faery woman's body crumple, awash with blood.

Instead, she stepped back—intact.

For a long moment the Huntsman regarded them. "The Tracks are mine!" he gritted. "Walk them at your peril!"

"You defy me?" From Rigantana.

"Quarry who fear are better than quarry caught unaware," the Huntsman replied. "But tonight . . . they are free of me."

"Fool!" the tattooed man spat. "You—"

The Huntsman smashed him in the chest with the butt of the spear. He went pale and fell silent, eyes wide and dazed. A trickle of red oozed from the corner of his mouth.

"No . . . blood?" the gibbering woman whined, like a pouting child.

"No blood . . . *here*," the Hunt told her, and spun his horse around.

And then, like a thundercloud evaporating, they were gone.

David gaped incredulously, heart pounding, legs scarcely able to support him.

"Shit!" Aikin breathed beside him, releasing his shoulder. David turned to give Liz a desperate hug, only to see both Faery women striding toward the alley's open end. The air crackled with unresolved tension. David released Liz and followed them as quickly as he could, but his raw thighs made it hard to walk and were cramping worse than ever, so that the women had reached the sidewalk before he caught up with them. "Wait!" he panted.

Rigantana froze, then turned to look at him. Her face was stern and impatient, as though her next word would be "Well?"

David had just opened his mouth—though he had no idea which of the zillion questions crowding down to his tongue from his brain would jostle to the forefront—when Liz grabbed his arm. "Look!" she cried. "Is that—?"

"Alec!" David finished for her, as he followed her gaze up the street to the right. "Jesus Christ, it's *Alec*!"

"Looks like hell, too," Aikin noted.

"God, you're right!" David agreed. And sore legs notwithstanding, was elbowing his way through a thickening clump of revelers that had flooded the street during their standoff with the Hunt—in anticipation, evidently, of the band setting up at the next corner down.

"Alec!" David yelled again, as he drew nearer. But already he knew something was wrong. Oh, his roomie looked okay—intact, anyway—though he likewise resembled a refugee from a week-long trek in the woods (save for the sword he was clutching); but he was also weaving along like someone half-awake, and his eyes were wide and staring, as though he were drunk, stoned—or dazed.

A deft pair of sidesteps to clear a generic ghost and a giant bunny, and David was sliding an arm around his best friend. "Oh, man . . . what the hell's wrong?"

"Cold hillside," Alec mumbled—and collapsed against David's chest. It took a moment to realize that his buddy was crying: sobbing his heart out into his shoulder. David didn't resist—not with so much heart-wrenching angst evident in Alec's action. An instant later, Liz and Aikin joined them, with, more distantly, Rigantana and the nameless other. David looked up desperately. "Get him something to drink," he begged the party in general, and was grateful to see the nameless one nod, then vanish into the crowd.

"C'mon, man, sit down," David urged, as Alec showed sign of regaining control. "C'mon, let's go"—he looked around—"over there: the bus stop. We can talk there, but there's still people around—and something tells me we *need* people around."

"I'm sorry," Alec choked dully. "I did something really dumb."

"You're not alone," Aikin echoed under his breath.

"So what're you guys doin' here?" Alec managed a minute later, when he'd slumped down beneath the canopy of the ornate new shelter that served City Hall. "I tried to call home, but no one was there, so I figured I'd see who was around . . . And here you were . . ."

"Whoa," David inserted. "You're gettin' outta order

here. Last we knew you'd zapped into Faerie. Obviously you're back—or didn't make it. Equally obviously something's happened. So maybe you'd better 'fess up, given that *we're* all safe now."

"From what?" Alec asked, sounding marginally more coherent.

"All in good time," Liz said. "You first."

Alec nodded, and in fits and starts, with many pauses during which he seemed embarrassed about certain details, laid out the whole tale of what he called his fool's errand. His friends listened without interruption, as did Rigantana. But David found himself watching her as much as his roommate. *Something* was bugging her: something very troubling indeed, by the way her jaw had grown tense and her brow was furrowing more deeply every second. And then, when Alec was relating how he'd awakened in Oconee Hills with his clothes and gear but no ulunsuti, she obviously could restrain herself no longer.

"That woman . . ." Rigantana gritted. "She who lay with you, who stole the oracular stone: she was my *mother*!" She spat out the last word, as though it disgusted her. David was startled at her vehemence.

"Oh, God!" Alec moaned. "*Shit.*"

"I . . . sense another story impending," David sighed. "As best I can figure, there's one down and three to go—plus whatever's up with whatsername."

"Where'd she go, anyway?" Aikin wondered, rising on tiptoes to scan the mob.

"For something to drink—I hope. But she must've gone to Atlanta to get it."

"I'd as soon not wait," Rigantana said. "And I do owe some explanation—though obviously you've figured out part of it already."

"Sit," David said. She did.

"Hear, then," Rigantana began, and with that phrase the grad student persona vanished utterly, for all her mundane attire. "As I have said," she continued, "my name is Rigantana, and I am of Faerie. I know that you have visited that realm and know somewhat about it. You therefore know of the various Realms: Tir-Nan-Og, Annwyn, Erenn . . ."

"Right," David acknowledged, nodding. Aikin was leaning forward attentively.

"Then you also know that there are other realms which touch the ones you know, and of these the greatest is Ys, which in Faerie can only be reached through Annwyn—one cannot sail there direct from Tir-Nan-Og. My mother, Rhiannon, is queen of Ys; and of her I will speak more in a moment. For now, be it known that one unique aspect of Ys is that it overlaps the Lands of Men underwater, for which reason my mother tends to restrict her Otherworldly visits to a land that touches Ys beyond a different set of World Walls than those which veil it from the Lands of Men— a place not unlike this, save that it contains more . . . magic."

"Like our World touches Faerie and Galunlati," David inserted, "but Faerie and Galunlati don't touch each other?"

"Exactly."

"So what's the deal with the ulunsuti?" Alec broke in "And what's your mother doing here? Why'd she play that stupid game?"

"You will not like the answer."

"Didn't figure I would."

Rigantana gnawed her lip. "I suppose I have spilled enough secrets already, what harm can a few more do? Very well, the situation is this: You mortal folk can use iron with no harm to yourselves, and you use it in profligate amounts. And you mortals know that too much iron in one place for too long can weaken the World Walls—even burn holes into the substance of Faerie, or actually burn Faerie. Such incursions were already a source of tension in Tir-Nan-Og, though less so in other realms, especially my mother's. But of late there has come to be gating directly through the World Walls: gating performed by you and your friends through the agency of the ulunsuti and certain scales. Now, I am certain you held no ill will toward Faerie when you made these gates, and we ourselves could not have predicted the effect they would have—but it now seems that any gate between Worlds made by the ulunsuti does irreparable damage to the World Walls. Indeed, those 'twixt here and Tir-Nan-Og have become dangerously weak, so that the lesser fey, at least, feel—and are—threatened."

"Like those little guys I met on the Track!" Aikin blurted out. "Oh, I haven't told you 'bout that, have I? They looked like refugees. And they said something 'bout our World destroyin' theirs."

"They *were* refugees," Rigantana acknowledged. "And your world *is* destroying theirs, in places. And since you speak of the small folk, you should know that Lugh, great king though he is, has never given them much notice—certainly not as much as my mother bestows upon them. Thus, increasing numbers of them have lately been claiming sanctuary in Ys, it being the Faery realm most remote from the Lands of Men. This was acceptable—for a time. But Ys is small, and my mother no longer has room for so many newcomers. She therefore came to Tir-Nan-Og at Lughnasadh to petition Lugh, first, to pay more heed to the needs of what small fey remain; secondly, to address the problem of mortal encroachment directly; and, finally, to try to learn more about the nature of those troublesome gates.

"And now," she went on after a pause, "she seems to have taken matters into her own hands."

"What makes you think that?" David asked.

Rigantana scowled. "By reading between the words of what your friend has told us, I must assume that my mother—who is a good ruler as far as her folk are concerned, though not at all fond of your kind—must have tricked Alec McLean into venturing onto the Tracks with the gating stone, for the sole purpose of relieving him of that object."

"But *why*?" Alec protested. "All she had to do was explain all this, and I'd have stopped letting anyone use it. Shoot, I'd have been *glad* to do that."

"Save that I think my mother has other plans for it," Rigantana countered. "I suspect—*suspect*, mind you—that she intends to use the stone to construct a gate of her own, from Ys into that other World that overlaps it, on which she has become fixated. I think she hopes to resettle the refugees from Tir-Nan-Og there."

Liz's eyes narrowed suspiciously. "So why are you telling us this? You being her daughter, and all?"

"Because I do not agree with her," Rigantana snorted. "My mother and I have never gotten along. That is why I have never returned to her court from Lugh's, where I was fostered. Indeed, I regard him as a second father—a second parent, rather, for I never knew my sire."

"And why the college student act?" David inquired. "I mean, while you're spillin' the beans, and all."

"I am in Lugh's service," Rigantana answered, with a smile. "More precisely, I am in *Nuada's* service. I have been in your World, in your substance, for nearly six months, doing what your kind call . . . 'damage control.' Specifically, I have been charged with manipulating physical written or visual evidence that might lead mortal men to suspect that Faerie—or any other World—exists."

"What kind of evidence?" From Aikin.

"Newspapers, microfilm archives, videotapes—though there are mercifully few of those. Suchlike as that."

"Which explains the library!" David gasped. "They've got the master copies of loads of stuff there."

"The Georgia Newspaper Project!" Liz added. "God, you're right!"

"Which is why I chose to base myself in Athens," Rigantana said, "that, and the fact that this town, more than most, has retained its magic—and another fact as well."

"What?"

"Why, that *you* were here, David Sullivan: you and your troublesome friends. A third of the mortals in this part of the World who have been to other Worlds live in this town or are friends with those who do. But *you* are the nexus, David. You are the one around whom all revolves."

"But I don't *want* it to!" David protested. "It's neat enough in its own way, but it's only complicated my life! I never get to *enjoy* it!"

"Still, you needed to be watched—so I have. In my persona as Tana, I have."

David rolled his eyes at Liz. She shrugged, then glanced sideways. *"Finally!"* she grumbled. " 'Bout time."

David followed her gaze, and saw the other Faery woman approaching, and could have kicked himself for not asking Rigantana about her—not that they'd really had time.

"So where'd you go for this?" Liz demanded fearlessly, when the woman passed around a cardboard tray of what looked and fizzed like Cokes. "Bogart?"

"I do not *travel* with mortal money," the woman retorted. "There are also such things as lines, and I did not feel inclined to advance myself with Power. It is harder than you think to use it in this World—and there was no true emergency, since Alec McLean was not like to die."

David took the tray and offered Alec a Coke. He gulped it ravenously; David chose another and drank it more slowly. The nameless woman was staring hard at Rigantana. Rigantana matched that stare, and David got an odd sense of rivals trying to glare each other down. "Greetings to you, Lady Rigantana," the nameless one said at last, her voice cold as frost. "My companions owe you much, as do I: I whose part it is to collect, not bestow."

Rigantana smiled back, but it was not mirth that curved her lips. "And greetings to you . . . Lady Morrigu."

Morrigu! The word curved around David's heart like a squeezing hand. Before he could stop to think, he was moving.

"Morrigu!" he hissed. "I thought so!"

And with that, he grabbed the sword Alec had set beside him, and leapt toward the Mistress of Battles.

Chapter XXI:
Deceptions and Inceptions

(Athens, Georgia—
Saturday, October 31—night)

"No, David!" Alec, Liz, and Aikin yelled as one, their voices slamming against the decorative brick walls of the bus stop more loudly than the band tuning up down the street. David felt Aikin's strong arms lock around his chest and biceps, even as Alec grabbed his wrist and Liz pried the sword hilt from his fingers.

"Leave me the fuck *alone!*" he shouted, rationality having dissolved all in a second, as a week's worth of suspicions proved true with the naming of their mysterious companion as the Morrigu.

"David!" From Liz.

"Cool it, Dave, just cool it!" Aikin echoed.

"She killed my uncle," David growled. "She *killed* him!"

But already he was resisting those restraining hands less vehemently. Anger had flashed and gone in three seconds: anger he hadn't known he possessed so fiercely. Anger forced to overload by the stress of the last few hours.

"Okay," he grunted, and let Liz secure the weapon. He shrugged out of Aikin's grip, but still stood glaring at the Morrigu. "I'll let her defend herself, and then I'll— Oh, just fuck it!"

For her part, the Morrigu seemed easily as furious as David, but her rage manifested exactly the opposite way: in dead, icy calm; in a carriage that could have withstood glaciers; in a set of mouth that would have given Hitler pause; and in eyes that flashed a fire that could melt titanium.

"Well," she said at last, glaring at Rigantana, "since this face no longer serves me, I suppose I should resume my own."

And with that, heat like flame erupted in David's eyes. He shut them instantly, heard Aikin mumble a strangled, "damn!" but didn't open them again until his companions' breathing steadied.

And this time he knew her features: the Morrigu: Lugh's mistress of battles, she who oversaw all conflicts involving Tir-Nan-Og or its denizens. A tall red-haired queen of the Sidhe, she was; robed in crimson velvet, around the cuffs and hem of which marched an endless file of crows worked in black beads and faceted hematites. "Now," she demanded, "what is this about?"

"You *know* what it's about," David shot back, feeling that anger spark again. "You have to! You were there."

"Suppose I was *not*," the Morrigu replied placidly, but with a sting of acid in her words. "Suppose, as they say in your land, I am innocent until proven guilty. What then are your charges?"

"You killed my uncle—David-the-Elder. Not you directly, but you were with the guy who did it. You seduced him—probably—and to impress you, he started flashin' 'round this grenade—he was a soldier, see— and then you got him stoned on hashish, and he . . . pulled the pin and threw it—at my uncle."

"Christ!" Alec breathed behind him. "Now I see. It was in your dream, wasn't it?"

The Morrigu's eyes narrowed, as did Liz's. "*What* dream? What are you speaking of, boy? I have bedded many mortals, and some of them have been soldiers, but none were fond of hashish." A pause, then: "Where was this supposed to have been accomplished?"

David shrugged. "The Middle East. Lebanon—Syria.

Maybe Iraq or Libya or Tunisia. They wouldn't tell us for sure. It was screwy."

"I have not seen the Levant since before you were born," the Morrigu informed him.

"So *you* say!"

"I will place my hand on that Iron blade there and swear, if you like—if that is required to prove my honesty."

David shook his head. "Pain's nothing for someone like you. It wouldn't prove anything."

"Though you've trusted my honor before?"

"That *was* before!"

"Very well, let me look in your mind and see what it is that has made you think this thing."

"Like hell!" David flared. "No tellin' what'd happen if you did that!"

"Perhaps I already have!"

"Okay, David," Liz put in. "You know what you're talking about, but the rest of us have no idea. So how 'bout you tell us? You're not gonna get anywhere just yelling."

David puffed his cheeks and scowled. "Oh, fuck it! Might as well, I guess."

And with that, he related the tale of the vision the ulunsuti had given him on Lookout Rock. And as he spoke the details came rushing back as clearly as if he'd witnessed those events scant seconds before. Almost he couldn't finish, almost those recollections became too much for him. By the time he concluded, he was sweating. He drank deep of his Coke, noting absently that his hands were shaking. Liz eased around to massage his shoulders.

Throughout his narrative, the Morrigu had held her peace, though he suspected she was prowling around in his mind, perhaps in quest of lies, perhaps merely seeking clarification of some point he'd missed, some spin or impression it hadn't occurred to him to relate, or language made impossible to reveal. Her face had remained impassive, though her jaw had tensed once or twice.

Finally, she took a long, slow breath. "It was not me," she whispered; and her tones bore the ring of ritual. "It was almost certainly my . . . sister Neman."

"The . . . one who rode with the Hunt?" Liz ventured.

The Morrigu shook her head. "That was another of . . . us."

"Macha!" David blurted suddenly. "Of course."

Liz looked at him askance. No one else spoke at all, though Rigantana raised an eyebrow in delicate amusement. "I begin to see why Nuada regards you so highly," she observed.

" 'Cause I remember my folklore?" David shot back. "Big deal."

"Yeah," Alec grunted. "I avoid that stuff like the plague."

David glared at him, then looked back at the Morrigu and took a deep breath. "It's rude to talk about people in front of them," he said. "It'd be best if the lady explained it herself. 'Sides, I might be wrong."

It was the Morrigu's turn to lift a brow. "Courtesy becomes you more than ire," she informed him. "But you are correct . . . mostly. There are three of us. Sisters is the most convenient term, but we are closer than that. Three at one birth, and so alike in our bodies, minds, and thoughts that we were literally one. The Babd, they began to call us, for none could distinguish us. Sometimes we could not distinguish ourselves, and perhaps that is what drove two of us mad. Or perhaps I am also mad, in a different way, and do not know it. Of the three, I am the Morrigu—a title, actually; I never give my name. I am also the most conventionally sane—and the role I have claimed for myself is that of encouraging heroes. It is my joy to take raw clay—mortal men, even, like yourselves—and shape it into something more. Sometimes men—

or women—fail and are cast aside. Sometimes I succeed beyond my dreams. Sometimes—"

"You were doing that on the Tracks, weren't you?" Liz broke in. "You were testing David, to see what he'd do if he faced the Hunt. Even when you made us run, you were watching him."

The Morrigu smiled faintly. "Yet the threat was real, and my shame at being less brave than a mortal was real. And my fear of the Hunt was real as well."

No one responded.

"But to continue my tale," the Morrigu went on, "my two sisters are called Macha and Neman. Macha you met—if that word is appropriate—a few moments ago. She is the least sane of us, the one who glories in death and destruction for its own sake, without regret or guilt. Mostly she rides with the Hunt now; but wherever there is battle—violence—disaster—there will she be, for she is the reveler among the slain."

"I know," David breathed. "I . . . saw."

The Morrigu nodded. "So mad is she that she cannot confine her madness. It leaks from her like foul water from a sieve, and though I love her as my sister, I detest the things she does."

"And Neman?" David prompted.

"Neman is a trickster. She has no honor, only a craving for amusement. Most often this consists of inciting confusion among the ranks, so that men fight against their own comrades—"

"Friendly fire," Aikin blurted out. "She's the goddess of friendly fire!"

The Morrigu cocked her head. "Essentially that is true, though she is no goddess, no more than any of the Sidhe."

"That asshole who killed my uncle thought she was!" David retorted. "He called her an angel."

Again the Morrigu nodded. "It was reasonable for one such as he to think as much, for what other term do such poor ignorant fools have for immortal beings

whose beauty surpasses their own? No, do not inter-
rupt"—when David would have protested—"you *were*
correct, in a way."

"How?"

"Since those men who meet her most often think of
her as a goddess, they often call her one—and she en-
joys that adoration. Sometimes she even takes that
'form' and pretends to be a deity of whatever folk invoke her. And for those without manifesting gods—like
most folk in your World these days, such as that man
in the Levant—she might well claim to be an angel."

And with that she fell silent. David felt her eyes on
him, burning with resentment and accusation. "Now
do you see?" she concluded.

David nodded numbly. "I see that I accused you
falsely, and I'm sorry—but that doesn't really *change*
things! I mean, David-the-Elder's still dead! One of
your sisters still screwed around and got him killed,
and that's just impossible to forgive. I don't know what
I can do about it, unless *you* can take me to wherever
she is and let me kill her with iron, but—"

"Uh-uh," Aikin inserted. "You don't wanta do that,
man; you just think you do. It'd feel good for about five
minutes and then you'd hate yourself for the rest of
your life. I mean, *think*, man: that guy who killed your
uncle, he didn't like him, so he offed him: pull the pin,
throw the bomb, bang! You're pissed at Neman. So
you—"

"Yeah, I get it," David growled. "And you're right. But
it still hurts, guys. It hurts so goddamned *much*!"

"I know," Aikin acknowledged. "But I've seen more
death than any of you folks, even if it's mostly animals,
and as of today, I've been on both sides of a hunt. And
while I still believe that killing's part of nature, killin'
like *you're* talkin' about's not a thing you even want to
think about doin'."

David fell silent. They were right, dammit. He didn't
like it, but they were. Killing anyone—anything sapi-

ent—was not a thing a man could do and still call himself civilized—or sane. Certainly not when done for vengeance's sake. He stared across the street, where someone had set another Dumpster alight, to where music thundered like the drums of hell. To where the Dance of Death had swept closer down Washington Street . . .

"Oh shit!" Alec exclaimed abruptly, pounding his knees with his fists. "I just remembered something!"

"Like what?" From Aikin.

"Like the ulunsuti! See, if Rigantana's right, and her mom stole it . . . well, gee, I mean she doesn't know what to *do* with it. She doesn't know how it works!"

"She will find out," Rigantana shot back instantly. "Objects of power are her special study."

"Yeah, well, it's not from her World, though," Alec retorted. "It's from a World at two removes from Faerie, so who knows what'll happen if she tries to use it? Sure, she knew enough to send me a false dream through it, but that doesn't mean she knows everything. Like, the worst thing is that four times a year you have to feed it the blood of a large animal or it'll go mad. I don't know what that *means*, exactly, and I don't want to, but I don't wanta even think what'd happen if that occurred in Faerie, or the time differential screwed it up, or if it reacted some weird way to Faery blood or the blood of Faery animals, or—"

"Not good," Rigantana broke in, sounding very human again. "And unfortunately, I have no idea what my mother knows about it, only that she has almost certainly been watching you with her arts, so that whatever she attempts is *probably* safe, as far as she's concerned."

"Great," Alec groaned. "Just peachy."

"I didn't think you *liked* it," Aikin observed. "I guess you don't have to worry now!"

"Only about Uki," Alec shot back. "Only that a shaman in another World gave it to me and could be really pissed if something bad happened 'cause I was stupid. Only about the Worlds," he added. "Like if gating from here to Tir-Nan-Og fucks up the World Walls, who knows what'll happen when folks start zapping between Ys and wherever. And is it gonna be, like, a permanent gate, or what?"

"Sounds like we need to get it back," David sighed. "I don't even want to think about what's involved in tryin' to do that, but it sounds like what we oughta do."

"And we generally screw up if we *don't* do what we oughta do," Liz agreed.

"Fuck," said Alec. "Fuck, fuck, fuck—but you're right."

Rigantana had not spoken for several moments, but was looking more troubled by the instant, and even the Morrigu's face was tense with concern. "This is probably a moot discussion," Rigantana said at last. "The stone is surely out of reach."

David looked up sharply. "How do you know?"

"Because if I were my mother, as soon as I procured it, I would have taken it to the coast, where ships wait to sail the Tracks for Annwyn, as they can do only at certain times of year, of which this is one. Barring that, I would have sent it there in haste."

"If I knew Rhiannon," the Morrigu mused, "she only *sent* it ahead. Do not forget what night this is: Lugh and the court of Tir-Nan-Og ride the Tracks tonight— and need not fear even the Hunt, for it will not attack so many. Usually they ride to the sea on this day, to meet those who have made the crossing, and to bid farewell to those who depart for Erenn and Annwyn. And Rhiannon loves ceremony, and likewise loves to ride; and it is years and years since she has joined the Rade in Tir-Nan-Og, save perhaps at Lughnasadh just past."

"And if she *does* ride with Lugh," Rigantana cried, "perhaps we can meet them and enlist *Lugh's* aid."

"Whoa!" Alec said. "What makes you think Lugh's gonna listen to *us*?"

"Sovereignty is a fluid thing," Rigantana replied. "Lugh rules Tir-Nan-Og, but he is likewise concerned for the Lands of Men that underlie it, for all of Faerie depends on your World for its shape—its very existence. In that sense, he may look upon you as one of his subjects who has been wronged. Certainly you know how important honor is to him. If you were to meet him, and demand redress for a wrong—the theft of the ulunsuti—he might listen. Perhaps he would even set things right, for I doubt my mother has told him of her intentions regarding that stone. It would be most unlike her."

David exhaled sharply. "And if I asked *him* for vengeance against Neman, what would he do?"

"Pay blood price, most likely."

"No," the Morrigu countered, "he would not. She is not his subject, nor does she dwell in Tir-Nan-Og."

"Where is she, then?" David snapped, as a surge of irrational anger took flame again. He fought it down.

"She is in Annwyn," the Morrigu told him flatly. "She is almost beyond *my* reach there; certainly she is beyond yours."

"You owe me," David spat. "You goddamn owe me!"

"I cannot give you a mortal's life," the Morrigu shot back. "Nor can Lugh, nor Nuada, nor Arawn, nor Finvarra, nor Rhiannon, nor Manannan mac Lir. Your kinsman's soul is beyond our reach."

"I want justice."

Rigantana eyed him sharply. "Justice? Or what your kind call closure?"

David blinked at her. "What do you mean?"

"He is gone beyond recall," Rigantana said. "Never more will he walk the Lands of Men in the body once he wore. Yet what pains you most, I think, is that not only do you miss him, but you never held a proper parting. He left and you thought to see him again, but he did not return, and there are things yet unsaid between you. You were not . . . finished with him."

"I'll *never* be finished."

"No," the Morrigu acknowledged in turn. "And as I said, I cannot give you a mortal's life . . . but if you are brave, perhaps I *can* give you that last meeting."

David blinked at her through a veil of tears. Did he dare believe her? Did he dare *not*? *Something* survived death, he knew; his friend Calvin had journeyed to the Ghostcountry a couple of years back, to placate the shade of his own father and rescue a boy whose own grief had sent him there. But himself and David-the-Elder . . . ? Was it possible?

"H-how?" he whispered at last.

"The Crimson Road," the Morrigu replied. "That is as much as you need to know . . . for now."

"But what about the ulunsuti?" Alec asked quietly. "What about catching the Rade?"

"If we seek one," the Morrigu announced, "we seek the other."

Chapter XXII:
Raid on a Rade

(Athens, Georgia—
Saturday, October 31—near midnight)

"We *could* reach Faerie directly through the World Walls," the Morrigu told the company at large. "It would then be simple to locate the Track the Rade will follow. Yet given that we also seek whomever Rhiannon has entrusted with the oracular stone, who surely have ridden ahead, we had best take the Track from here instead—and breaking the World Walls hereabouts so soon after they have been breached twice would not be prudent."

Unfortunately, the nearest Track was at Whitehall Forest. Equally inconvenient was the fact that David's car was stranded beside Aikin's at the latter's cabin, as was Liz's. Alec's was back at *Casa McLean y Sullivan* in Jackson County. Bumming a ride from a friend would have required *finding* someone, then awkward explanations they had no time for, and finally, a capacious vehicle, since there were now six of them, none of whom seemed inclined to remain behind.

In the end, Aikin produced some cash and called a cab.

The taxi dropped them off at the cabin.

"I'm glad that's over," growled the Morrigu, who still wore the substance of Faerie. "I could have borne the heat of Iron but little longer."

David lifted an eyebrow. "So why didn't you *change*?"

"Because it is unpleasant," she snapped. "Because it consumes Power in profligate amounts—and because . . . I am tired."

"I didn't know you folks *got* tired."

"Different things weary us than you," Rigantana supplied, "but we tire."

At which point the cab's taillights vanished around a curve, leaving them alone in Aikin's yard.

Five minutes later they stood beside the Track.

And a moment after that, six white riderless horses came galloping down its golden surface, only to halt at the last possible instant beside the blasted oak and the bifurcated maple.

David's legs still hadn't forgiven him for their last go-round with horses when he once again found himself riding bareback down a Straight Track.

Time moved curiously. Mostly they rode through a tunnel of arm-thick whorling briars colored luminous blue and gold like a Maxfield Parrish painting. For a long time—or perhaps no time at all—no one spoke. Reality seemed to merge with dream. Possibly it was a healing dream, too, for stress and strain melted from mortal faces, and the two Faery ladies withdrew into their own ponderings. At some point Alec noticed that his clothes were clean, Aikin that his were dry, David that his raw-rubbed thighs no longer pained him, and Liz that her jeans bore the softness and sheen of silk.

"So," David began abruptly—and Alec half expected to hear the tinkling of the silence as it was broken. "So," he ventured again, addressing the Morrigu, who, as befitted her rank, rode at the head of the file, " 'scuse me for bein' nosy, but . . . what in the world were you doin' in the 40 Watt last night?"

Alec grinned, having been wondering the very same thing—what part of him wasn't *avoiding* wondering about certain things.

The Morrigu continued on at the quick yet stately

pace she'd established, nor did she look back when, after a thoughtful pause, she spoke.

"I have been in Erenn since Beltaine," she said. "I spent the bright season with Finvarra, the High King there, seeking to repair what rifts remain after the war he waged against Lugh for the youth, Fionchadd. That accomplished, I set sail for Tir-Nan-Og, intent on meeting Lugh's host at the coast, when their Samhain Riding takes them there. But the Tracks and the Seas between the Realms have been calmer this season than is their wont, and so we arrived a day early—yesterday, by your reckoning. Not having had occasion to roam freely in Tir-Nan-Og—or the Lands of Men beneath it—for some time, I chose to take the slow path back to Lugh's stronghold. As I made my way north, it occurred to me that my route took me past that part of the Lands of Men in which certain troublesome young mortals of my acquaintance dwell, on whom I ought to spy; and with that in mind, I left the Track near this odd, magical, mortal city, of which I had heard so much. Once in your World, it was simple to seek you out, so strong has the taint of Faerie lodged upon you. But what I did *not* realize is how much revelry your kind engage in on Samhain. And the closer to the madness I ventured—it was not unlike a battle frenzy—the more I began to hear music."

She paused, as if listening to unheard singing.

"Music . . . ah, music! Many are the things mortal men have writ about the Sidhe, and many are the errors they have stated, but one item about which they have *not* lied is the fondness we hold for music—even your sort of music: loud, raw, discordant, but full of emotion and energy and drive. And naturally, like all in Faerie, I love to dance, so I dared the place you saw me."

"But why the disguise?" David wondered.

"I did not want you to recognize me. I feared it would alarm you. Thus, I changed substance and englamoured myself as well, though perhaps I should have appeared as fully human. Yet I knew that your Sight would warn you anyway, and perhaps by appearing in Faery form, I could add wonder to your World, at a time it seems to need it."

"But why did Rigantana leave when she saw you?"

"Perhaps you should ask her."

Rigantana shrugged. "I wanted to experience that place and time as mortals do—and when I saw another Faery there, it destroyed any chance of that. Perhaps, too, I feared the Morrigu would acknowledge me—and I did not want to be accosted by anyone as blatantly exotic as she. I feared it would—what is the term?— blow my cover."

"The college student/damage control thing?"

"Yes."

"It would seem, though," the Morrigu mused after a thoughtful pause, "that we have not been the only ones visiting."

Another shrug from Rigantana. "Was that a question?"

"If you so choose."

"Would you rather I spoke to you or all this company?"

"Ignorance among them does more harm than knowledge."

"What do *you* know?"

"About what?"

"Politics—to start with."

The Morrigu's brow furrowed. "That Rhiannon's land was awash with lesser fey fleeing the encroachment of the Mortal World on Tir-Nan-Og. That she had come here to petition Lugh for aid and to stem that flow. But I had no notion of that queen's desperation, for we have met but seldom, and none of us save Arawn know her well."

Rigantana nodded grimly. "Desperate indeed, and

more so than I had thought, if her bedding of this mortal lad be proof."

The Morrigu nodded in turn. "Are there *other* things I should know? I lingered but briefly at the haven, and the folk there fear me too much to speak freely—as these young folk do not."

"We don't know any better," Aikin broke in, sounding a little giddy.

Rigantana silenced him with a glare. "As to news . . . most of it would bore our companions past enduring, and it is rude to be boring on a Rade. Except"—she paused thoughtfully, poised once again between Faery lady and mortal grad student—"except that perhaps there *is* something new that would interest both you and Master McLean."

Alec's ears pricked up at the mention of his name. Usually it was David who was the focus of activities involving Faerie. It had never occurred to him that the lords and ladies of that place might actually be aware of *his* existence.

"It involves the traitoress Aife," Rigantana went on. "She whose shape my mother stole in order to rob Alec of the ulunsuti."

"What *about* her?" Alec demanded, surprising himself with the harshness of his tone. *That* wasn't *her in the tower,* he kept telling himself. *There's still a chance something might come of her and me . . .*

"It may not be pleasant to hear, but the truth seldom is, whether in the Lands of Men or Faerie. And the truth is that there has been a shift in Lugh's policy toward Aife—more precisely, toward what punishment would befit her most. What is the last you knew?" she continued, to the Morrigu.

"That she had resumed her living shape soon after her death, submitted herself for justice, and been confined in a World near the Lands of Fire. I believe there was a tower."

"So it was when you departed," Rigantana acknowledged, "but the tower now stands empty—my mother had her own business there not a day gone by. Aife has been given another punishment, but Lugh will not reveal what it is, though it seems to please him, by which I assume it bears an ironic cast."

"But—" Alec began, frustrated, since *real* news of Aife seemed as remote as ever.

"Hold!" the Morrigu interrupted sharply. "We approach a crossroads. Those we seek will soon be arriving there."

Alec held his peace—had no choice. And then it didn't matter because the Morrigu's steed was suddenly galloping, and the others behind it, and though he'd ridden but seldom before, and rode without saddle or bridle now, somehow he kept his seat; neither jolted nor otherwise shaken. It totally unnerved him, too, and the closest description he could contrive was that it was like watching one of the chases in the *Star Wars* films: eyes saw movement, body felt none—but balance compensated anyway.

Abruptly the horse slowed—and the briars diminished to reveal what looked a great deal like a pine forest such as infested mundane Georgia. Or perhaps they *were* in mundane Georgia, though the air smelled suspiciously fresh and clean.

And then Alec heard a distant jingling-tinkle as of a thousand crystal bells, and saw a file of gold-toned lights winking among the trunks and branches to his right. In spite of himself, he strained forward. He'd seen the Sidhe riding before, of course, but never at night, and never on one of their "official" Rades. Only David had seen that. "Wow!" Aikin breathed beside him, which was as good a response as any.

"I agree," David said, glancing back, his face full of joyful anticipation Alec had seen far too rarely of late. And then the first rider cleared the trees and entered the open place before them.

Alec didn't recognize the man—no reason he

should; he knew maybe ten people from Tir-Nan-Og
well enough to have any sense of them as individuals.
This guy, however, *was* impressive. For a start, his
horse was blinding white—almost transparent yet almost silver—and he also *wore* white, though not the
armor Nuada favored (and this fellow had *two* good
arms, bare to the shoulders save for a pair of silver
bracelets); rather, he sported a simple tabard belted at
the waist and hanging fore and aft, to expose his bare
legs and feet to the hip. He was young, too, and beardless (but most Sidhe looked young, and few affected
whiskers), and his hair was as white as his garment.
Albino, Alec assumed, until the Faery glanced toward
them and Alec glimpsed his emerald eyes.

The youth frowned, but paced his horse into the precise center of what Alec now saw was the intersection
of the golden Track they'd been following with another,
which the host of the High King of Tir-Nan-Og trod.
"Hear me, all who ride the Tracks," the Faery cried.
"Hear me, and know that for this time I bear no name
but Light, and Light it is that leaves the World for six-
moons' span this night. This do I proclaim from this
crossroads, and all crossings we meet on our journey.
This do I proclaim in the name of Lugh Samildinach,
High King of Tir-Nan-Og, of whom only Night, Death,
and Eternity are greater Kings."

"And this do we hear and acknowledge," the Morrigu
called back.

The youth—Light—stared at her fixedly, then
shrugged and seemed to relax a tad, as the rest of the
host crowded up behind.

First came a phalanx of Lugh's knights, silver-
armored under white velvet surcoats blazoned with his
device: a golden sun-in-splendor. Behind them showed
faces Alec knew. Oisin was the first he recognized: the
ancient mortal granted immortality too late to save
him from old age and the blindness that turned his
eyes to silver. He it was who was Lugh's seer. Next he

noted Nuada: blond, gilt-haired, and handsomely grim in his silver scale armor that contrasted deliberately with the silver hand that was part of him.

And Lugh: dressed in white like the others, but—for the first time Alec had ever seen him so—bare-chested, the sweeps of his black mustache almost fouling his arching collarbones; black hair unbound and flowing past his shoulders. In fact, when Alec got a better look, he wore only a loincloth. Doubtless there was some obscure symbology there, but before he could puzzle one out, he saw the woman who rode beside Lugh—and did a double take; for, eschewing her elaborate white gown and gold-lined cloak, she was the image of Rigantana, who flanked the Morrigu at the head of their own party. Sisters they looked, even twins, though this lady, by her crown, was surely the troublesome Rhiannon.

Which meant—

Alec swallowed hard, as rage awoke within him. That woman sitting there so placidly had sent him false visions, led him into another World, lied to him, deceived him, stolen from him—and bedded him in disguise! He owed her a thousand insults, a thousand demands for justice.

David evidently sensed his anger, too, and divined his thoughts. "Easy, man," he murmured. "This isn't our game; go with the flow."

Light turned to face them, slender and straight on his white horse. "Who is it that meets Lugh's riding? Know you not that two hosts alone may travel the Tracks tonight; and the more Seelie of them is here?"

"Yet we *are* here," the Morrigu countered steadily, pacing her horse a step nearer her challenger. "We ride not by choice nor in defiance, but from necessity—and as for that other of whom you spoke: he should not trouble us."

Lugh's eyes narrowed as he urged his mount to the fore. He looked, Alec thought, exceedingly pissed.

Rhiannon (if that's who she was) simply looked mondo uneasy—save when her gaze fell on Rigantana, when she looked as though she could spit swords.

Lugh had reached the head of the line by then, and eased his mount between two of his vanguard. His gaze swept the Morrigu and her company imperiously, yet his words were mild:

"We were wondering where you were, Lady," he said. "You also seem to have acquired a retinue I do not recall you possessing—of which I am not certain I approve, given that I ordered the Borders closed 'twixt my realm and the Lands of Men."

"Sometimes one must disregard one's lord," the Morrigu replied stiffly. "If there is punishment due, I will bear it, but first you should hear my errand."

"Ride with us then," Lugh invited. "Such is your right, and for tonight, I extend that grace to your companions—though of course the Lady Rigantana does not need it."

Rigantana inclined her head solemnly.

"So," Lugh persisted, "will you join us?"

"No," the Morrigu told him flatly, with not so much as a single shake of her head. "Tonight I have other business, myself and these mortals here."

"And what might that business be?" Nuada wondered.

"The most important is to ask the High King if he knows of a traitor in his midst."

Lugh's black brows lifted as one. "And who might this traitor be?"

"Her name is Rhiannon, and she is queen, for this time, in Ys."

Rhiannon's response was to stare coldly at the Morrigu—though once, Alec was certain, her gaze flicked back to him, and a secret, spiteful smile curved her lips.

"These are hard charges for one queen to make of another," Lugh observed. "Yet you are one I trust; and it seems we may not proceed unless I hear you out."

"The way of my statement is this," the Morrigu began, and set out a brief, detailed account of Alec's aborted rescue of the false Aife. Alec wondered how she'd learned so much, given that she'd been absent when he'd told his tale. Probably directly from Rigantana's mind, he decided. *Hopefully.*

Lugh heard her quietly, but his face grew darker by the moment. "Lady Rhiannon," he snapped when she had finished, "would you join me?"

Rhiannon scowled, but did as commanded. Alec noticed that the guards suddenly looked much more vigilant and intense. A pair rode past Light and turned, effectively blocking further progress down the Track. Two others moved to close off the Track Alec's company rode, where it continued beyond the crossroads, while yet another set flanked Rigantana and the Morrigu. Clearly they were taking no chances in what might well be an explosive situation.

"Well, Lady," Lugh said, when Rhiannon sat beside him, gazing not at him, but at some unseen vista beyond any of their heads, "you have heard these accusations, and while the courtesy due a guest and fellow monarch forbids wresting the truth from your thoughts, courtesy likewise forbids you to lie to one who this last quarter has been your host."

Rhiannon did not reply.

"Silence is no answer," Rigantana called. "I know you mean well, but you have dishonored our House without seeking the honorable solution which was available to you."

"And what might that be?" Rhiannon sneered. "Assuming that I chose any solution at all."

"You could have *asked*!" Rigantana shot back. "Instead, you sent false dreams to this mortal and tortured him as surely as if you have set hot knives against his flesh."

"Do you *have* this object?" Lugh demanded, dark

eyes flashing. "Did you commit this treachery of which you are accused?"

"Did you *ever* have this object," Nuada added pointedly.

"She did," another voice broke in: high and wavery like that of an old man. Alec had to strain to make out the words, but knew that they came from the old blind man, Oisin, who was Lugh's seer. "The past is free for all to gaze upon who have the art," Oisin went on, "and though I cannot always see what I would when I choose to turn my inner eye there, yet it has shown me this lad asleep in a certain tower, and a woman beside him, who one moment wears the face of Aife and the next that of the Queen of Ys. I have seen her rise in the latter shape and steal the oracular stone. And in spite of her concern for the World Walls, I have seen her rip them asunder and leave the lad in his own World, naked on a cold hillside."

"Oisin never lies," Nuada said. "All in Faerie know that."

"He is a mortal," Rhiannon challenged promptly. "Mortals do naught *but* lie."

"So do Faeries," Alec spat, unable to control himself. "You sure as hell lied to *me*, you bitch!"

Lugh cocked a brow as though in amusement, then frowned again—at Rhiannon. "We may not search your mind, Lady, but there are those here who could certainly search your body, and my knights can search your mount and retinue and possessions. Therefore, I ask again: do you have this thing?"

"I do not," Rhiannon answered tautly.

"Then she has already sent it to the coast," Rigantana groaned. "We have ridden away from it."

Lugh studied Rhiannon perplexedly. "I *thought* your escort was smaller than when you arrived. Obviously they have taken this thing and fled, but my knights are faster than yours, and will overtake them."

"They'd better," Alec inserted edgily. "Or they could be in trouble."

"How so, young wizard?" From Lugh.

"Don't call me that!" Alec grumbled, more rudely than he'd intended. "But what I meant was that it has to be treated a particular way—like, if you don't feed it the blood of a large animal every so often, it'll go mad."

Lugh looked sharply at Rhiannon. "Did you know this?"

Rhiannon's response was to glare at Alec as though he were more loathsome than a slug.

Alec matched her glare. "I *would* have given it to you," he said quietly. "Lent it, anyway. I don't like doing that kind of thing, but if our folks are causing problems in Faerie, it's our job to try to set 'em straight. Obviously we can't do much, but we *could've* stopped using the ulunsuti to make gates, and we—that is, I— would've tried to help with the refugee thing."

Lugh regarded him steadily. "For good or ill, you have been wronged by a guest in my land; the onus of compensation, therefore, falls on me. My knights will surely recover this talisman, but if they do not, do you seek further redress?"

Alec shook his head. But then a thought occurred to him—rash perhaps, but what did he have to lose? "Aife," he whispered. "If she's not in her tower, where is she?"

Lugh nodded solemnly. "It is what I thought you would ask, and the answer is this: Aife is kin to the Queen of Ys—which explains her likeness to Rhiannon and Rigantana—and likewise to one of the Morrigu's favorite disguises. But since I did not entirely trust Rhiannon's intentions—for well you know what has befallen when other Faery rulers have challenged my judgments—I thought it best that Aife be moved to a place closer to hand, for which reason I changed her into an enfield, such as those I keep about my court—

in which guise, I am sorry to say, she escaped a few days past."

"And let me guess," David broke in. "She found her way onto the Tracks and got off in Athens."

"She was probably searching for you, Alec McLean," Oisin added.

"Probably," Nuada agreed. "I think she truly *did* love you—and though the beast-mind would have prevailed, still, it could not obscure strong feelings. She would have sensed your presence as soon as she came into your World, and more clearly in the mind of your friend Aikin. Then—"

Alec wasn't listening. "But . . . where is she *now*?" he blurted out.

"On the Tracks," Aikin sighed. "I found her out at Whitehall and followed her onto the Tracks and then lost her."

"She disappeared right after we found Aik," Liz explained. "I noticed her, but wasn't paying *attention* to her. I mean, a *lot* was going on."

Alec blinked at him stupidly. "But why would she do that? If—if she . . . loves *me*, why would she fool around with *you*?"

"Perhaps because she knew you disliked magic and would not deal with it willingly," Nuada ventured. "She therefore lured someone onto the Tracks she thought you—or your friends—would pursue. Probably she intended to bring you all to Tir-Nan-Og, where explanations would have been courtesy, if not necessity."

"Except that she bolted when she saw the little guys," Aikin broke in. "That was real fear, wasn't it? Animal mind overruling human?"

"Yes," Nuada acknowledged. "And it is ironic that that, of all Worlds, was the one you entered, for there alone could such shape-shifting as she wrought be accomplished. Something to do with the water, I think: manifesting desire, or some such."

Aikin eyed him narrowly. "How'd you know about all that?"

Nuada smiled. "You were thinking very loudly indeed."

"So Aife still walks the Tracks?" Lugh asked at last.

"Minus an ear, I'm afraid," Aikin admitted. "My fault."

"Her choice," Oisin corrected.

"All of which gives me an idea," Lugh announced, "assuming we can locate this . . . beast."

"Is it one like this?" one of the guards asked from where he blocked the continuation of the Morrigu's Track.

Alec started, and had to peer between the Faery women to see, trotting calmly from beneath the guards' horses, a familiar tawny form—looking for all the world like a smug, almost cartoony fox, save for the eagle talons that replaced what should have been vulpine forepaws, and the fact that it was missing an ear. It paused there, facing Light in the center of the crossroads, then peered first at Lugh, then at Alec—where, after a plaintive whistling trill, its gaze rested.

"Convenient," Lugh mused. "Perhaps she too saw her desire in the waters of that World and followed the Tracks to find it." And with that, he swung down from his horse and stepped to the center of the crossroads, where he knelt before the enfield. "At least it will be simple here, in this place of Power," he muttered—and laid both hands on the creature's head. Alec saw David tense, and felt a tightening of the air as some unseen force was brought to bear. Brightness smote his eyes; he blinked away tears, and when he could see again, Lugh's hand rested on a large orange house cat. The King of Tir-Nan-Og scooped it up with one hand, stroked it reflectively, then marched straight between the Morrigu and Rigantana.

It took Alec a moment to realize that *he* was the intended target, and then Lugh was handing the cat up to him. He had no choice but to accept it. An instant later it was purring in his arms. At which point a troubling suspicion awoke.

"Oh . . . no . . . !" he choked, shaking his head. "Uh uh. I'm not gonna be your jailer! I mean, with all due respect, I *hate* magic, and the last thing I need's one more magical whatsis to worry about. Shoot, look what happened the last time someone from another World gave me something."

Lugh's eyes twinkled mischievously as he pointedly backed away.

"No, wait—your honor! You can't be serious about this—aren't you the one who's concerned about damage control in our World? So the last thing you oughta want's one more piece of magic loose there!"

"It will not be loose," Lugh laughed, continuing his retreat. "In fact, I imagine it will be difficult for you to loose yourself *from* it. And since you despise magic, you are the best possible guardian for something magical—because you will not be tempted to use it. Finally, being in your service is fitting punishment for Aife's treachery, since it was *you* among all mortals whom she most wronged."

"But—"

"My decision has been made. We have other errands tonight, or do you forget that it was *you* who lately gated through the World Walls—which damaged my land. I do not have to overlook that!"

Alec swallowed hard. Would it *really* be that bad? He *liked* cats—sort of. Even one-eared ones.

"Two other things," Lugh added, as he climbed back on his stallion. "I have given her the substance of your World to relieve her of the draw of Faerie and so that she need not go constantly in dread of Iron. But she will briefly resume her enfield shape at dusk and dawn."

"Now you tell me!" Alec growled, even as he found himself stroking the cat's fur.

"Serving you may reduce her sentence, however," Lugh confided. "It will likewise hasten her return to human form—which surely you desire."

"But when . . . ?"

"When I so choose!" Lugh gave back, abruptly imperious again.

"Never mind," Alec grunted. "I'll deal with it."

"Indeed you will!" Lugh retorted with a disturbing chuckle. "Now we must continue the Rade." He surveyed the Morrigu's company. "I have granted all present the right to ride with us. Do you accept or stay? You first, David Sullivan."

David took a deep breath, and Alec suddenly felt very sorry for him. God knew Dave had been holding a lot back, not the least the impatience he must be feeling at this delay in his own ambiguous quest. "I . . . have another errand," David sighed. "I'm sorry."

"And you, Alec McLean: Do you ride with your friend or with the company who leave anon to retrieve your property?"

Another choice, Alec thought. Another damned choice, and he had no idea which was correct. The ulunsuti was his, and it had been his own stubborn silent folly that had lost it. But Dave was his truest friend and had borne far heavier burdens longer, unspoken for the most part, and unavenged.

"I go with David," Alec breathed finally.

"Liz Hughes?"

"With David, of course."

"And you, Aikin Daniels, who were so eager to visit my realm? What would *you* do?"

Aikin gnawed his lip, and Alec guessed that he was having a devil of a time choosing between logic and emotion, between loyalties—between one quest and another.

"You hesitate," Lugh said a little gruffly. "Is it so hard to see what is in your heart?"

"I . . . oughta go with Dave," Aikin admitted, his

voice very soft. "He's my friend and I owe it to him. But"—he paused and grinned at David—"sorry, man; but all my life I've wanted to ride with the Faeries."

Lugh nodded gravely. "I see in you a true love of Faerie such as few mortals possess anymore. But I have another quest for you, if you are brave."

Aikin's eyes were bright. "Yeah?"

"Someone needs to return the ulunsuti to young Mc-Lean when my knights retrieve it. If you like, you may ride with those I send to secure it."

"That'd be . . . great," Aikin whispered.

"There is one condition, however."

"What?"

"You will be unable to speak of what transpires there to any not here present."

Alec had to suppress a giggle at the irony, given how pissed Aik had been about *their* enforced silences. An exchange of glances with David and Liz showed that they'd been thinking the same.

"You will also need a swifter steed," Lugh concluded. "My squire will lend you his—then go! Rigantana, you may join them if you wish."

Aikin started to dismount, but Alec was already fumbling at his waist for the sword he'd been lugging around since he'd begun his own quest. "Hang on a sec," he called frantically.

Aikin twisted around, blinking in surprise.

"I don't know what good this'll do," Alec mumbled. "But it can't hurt."

"Iron is still Iron!" Nuada observed. "And however dull that blade may be, it has tasted Faery blood!"

Aikin accepted the weapon with a foolish smirk and a sketchy bow, uttered an embarrassed "Hey, thanks, man!" then slid off his faithful mare and strode to where a fair-haired youth was waiting beside an elegant but muscular stallion whose coat, if possible, was even whiter than that of the one he'd been riding. It also had a saddle and stirrups—which was a relief. The

Faery gave him a quick leg up, and Aikin tried not to appear too full of himself as he guided his new mount to where the six knights who had guarded the wings of the crossroads were regrouping at their juncture. They made room for him and Rigantana in their midst, and, as one, touched heel to flank and sped away.

Alec watched them go. The cat purred. He stroked its fur. He was, he realized, grinning.

"And now let us proceed!" Lugh cried, as new warriors rode up to replace those who had departed—warriors who, Alec noted, crowded close around a hard-jawed Rhiannon.

And then the host was moving, slowly, solemnly, as though they had all the time in the world: a long file of warriors and princes, lords and ladies, heralds and craftsmen and seers; all dressed in white and riding mounts that were not all horses, and bearing weapons that were not all swords or spears or daggers. Light rode with them, both the human personification, and that which every fragment of metal about them reflected.

And then the Rade had passed.

—Leaving a grim-faced David Sullivan to continue north, in the company of his best friend, his lady, a dangerous Faery queen—and a cat that was also an enfield and a woman.

Chapter XXIII:
Stags and Stones

(The Straight Tracks—no time)

The last thing Aikin expected while galloping full tilt along a Straight Track with a troop of Faery knights and the daughter of a Faery queen, all on a desperate race to recover an oracular stone, was boredom. Yet bored he was.

Though they indisputably rode a Track (he could tell by the unvarying line of gold that flashed beneath the hooves of the four horses that sped at a shocking pace before him), the rest of the landscape could as easily have been the south Georgia pine barrens he'd seen far too often on forays to Florida: mile on mile of dead-straight, dead-level, unrelieved boredom. Oh, he'd spent a few minutes trying to puzzle out the construction of the armor on the knight just ahead. But though his mount's gait held the eerie smoothness of all the steeds of Faerie, it was still bouncy and uneven to someone accustomed to cars, so that he could never quite focus on the details that intrigued him, never mind the intricacies of workmanship. Horses, it seemed, had no vertical hold—which he needed. In the end he gave up and rode—bored.

That galled him, too, because the *image* he'd had of riding with the Faeries was of seeing neat things and asking all kinds of questions about the Worlds and the Tracks and the folk thereof—questions it had surely not occurred to Dave to ask, never mind Alec or Liz.

But here he was in the equivalent of a candy store—

with no one to wait on him, all the goodies out of reach inside glass jars—and no money to spend in the bargain.

And he'd have been even more bored, had it not been for the pain: stretched muscles, *cramping* muscles, and abrasion, all three.

What I get for never taking riding lessons, he told himself, as he tried to shift to a more comfortable seat on a saddle obviously made for someone configured differently—narrower of foot, for one thing: he'd barely been able to get his eight-and-a-halfs in the stirrups when he'd hooked up with this batch of grim faced dudes bent on catching Rhiannon's bad boys, and by the time they were in transit, it was too late to complain.

He hoped he had skin on his legs when they got there—or pants, for that matter. Or even legs. He was afraid to look down, lest his cammos be smoking where they rubbed against saddle leather and horsehide both.

"Fuck this!" he muttered—and tried, yet again, to reseat himself. His right thigh promptly cramped. "Ouch! Damn! Hell!" he added, for emphasis.

He was trying to massage the over-stressed muscle loose, when the Track widened and one of those who rode in his wake galloped up to pace him. A sideways glance showed Rigantana.

"It would seem," she called, with a very-human grin—"that your . . . 'contact patch' is giving you grief."

Aikin rolled his eyes and tried to choose between venting his rapidly accumulating spleen (thereby sounding like a wimpy mortal and disgracing himself before a *very* pretty woman); suffering in silence (which, while more macho, might have long-term repercussions if he was doing something wrong that could be remedied and he didn't change it before incurring actual damage); and simply admitting meekly that he hurt like a son of a bitch and requesting advice.

"Yeah, well, I don't have radial ply legs," he grumbled at last.

"It hurt me too, when I learned," Rigantana told him breathlessly.

"You didn't do it by magic?"

"You cannot learn everything that way!" she laughed back. "One must learn any art or skill the . . . slow way first. Even then, it often takes more effort to effect a task with Power than with muscle or mind alone."

"But what about—?" he began, but had to abandon the conversation when the leader of their company sharply increased his pace, forcing the rest of the troop to do likewise or be left behind.

Aikin's stallion stretched out with the rest, and he concentrated on retaining his seat. Every muscle from his waist down promptly protested, and even his arms grew sore from gripping the reins so tightly. Rigantana fell back, but he was certain he heard her chuckle—and, therefore, scowled. And then he could do nothing but simply hang on while air howled past his face and whistled around the earpieces of his glasses, and the pine barrens became a blue-black blur.

Faster yet—and his right foot jolted from its stirrup. He kicked for it desperately as he nearly fell—found it—lost it again, and by reflex as much as volition yanked on the reins. His mount slowed immediately.

A knight flashed by, then another. The first glared at him, the second guffawed with open derision. Rigantana too surged past—and a clear voice reached back from the head of the line: "This is no good! If we could catch those we seek, we must have swifter steeds."

"Oh hell!" Aikin groaned, not caring who heard, and dropped the reins as their pace relaxed.

"—Or swifter riders," someone else told their captain, gazing at Aikin pointedly.

"Speed is still speed, and for everything there is a limit," the captain countered. "The boy slowed us no more than that dainty lady of yours."

Aikin's gaze sought automatically for the horse in question, and saw a beautiful mare, sides heaving violently and sweat—actual sweat—lathering her pearly white coat. Even Faerie, it seemed, had its earthy side.

"Were it not for the lad, we could shape-shift into fleeter forms," someone else flared.

"And would you shift Snow Spark as well? If so, you are stronger than I!"

"We could leave them . . ."

The captain snorted. "You know who rides the Tracks tonight! You would do well to find two hairs and a bone when you returned."

"Then what?"

The captain scratched his chin, eyes narrow beneath his silver half helm. "There is a World near here where we could both find faster mounts and leave our own to forage. And Himself is unlikely to go there."

"What World?"

"My father's. He discovered it while on a Rade, and Lugh granted it to him if he would explore it, share whatever he found there with the rest of Tir-Nan-Og, and let it serve as a way station for travelers on the Track."

"And what has he found?"

"Beasts we can ride. Swift beasts. Beasts bred not to tire."

And then they were riding again.

Yet little time had passed at all when the captain swung his stallion sharp right and off the Track. To Aikin, it looked as though he simply swerved between two pines and disappeared. But then his own mount followed suit—and the instant its legs cleared the Track, reality changed. He saw the pines flash by, glimpsed a fallen third lying between them. His horse leapt. He held on for dear life—

—And touched down in a meadow.

Maybe a mile wide, it was, and brightly lit, though not by any obvious sun, in contrast to the twilight of the Tracks. A forest of immense trees—conifers, they appeared, possibly sequoias—surrounded that meadow, and beyond it mountains lifted bare jagged peaks to the skies. Aikin got a sense of wildness, of a World untouched by either man or magic.

—Until he glimpsed the tower that rose above the trees in a slender fountain of pure white stone, its summit a filigree of arches that shouted to the soft warm wind that Power had wrought that thing.

And then he saw what shared the meadow, and forgot all else.

Deer.

Cervids, rather, for it was not proper to call these beasts that raised attentive but unconcerned heads above the knee-high grass deer any more than it was proper to apply that term to a moose. Deer implied delicacy and furtiveness and wary grace, coupled with odd starts and spontaneous bursts of leaping speed. It did not imply majesty. It did not imply shoulders higher than his head and palmate racks easily four yards wide.

"I'll be a son of a bitch!" he gasped, as he followed the captain toward the nearest: an impressive stag a hundred paces distant. "That's a goddamned Irish elk!"

"Is that what your folk call them?" Rigantana wondered, as she joined him.

"Well, I'm *supposed* to call 'em *Megaloceros giganteus*—that's the scientific name. But yeah, you got it."

The captain stared at him. "You have a *name* for them?"

"They're from our World—or their kinfolks are. *Were*, rather," he corrected. "They're extinct now. The last ones died in the Crimea ten thousand years ago."

"But not before some came here," the captain mused.

Something occurred to Aikin then, which made him slightly sick with fear—and giddy with wonder and awe. "We're . . . not gonna *ride* these guys, are we?"

The captain eyed him askance. "We must, if we are to fulfill Lugh's command. They are bred to ride and are swifter than horses."

"But those racks . . . Won't they get tangled up? I mean, the Tracks are awfully narrow . . ."

"They have not so far," the captain retorted, as he leapt down from his stallion.

"We have no saddles for these," someone called.

"Do you *need* one?"

Aikin, who followed close in the captain's wake, eyed the elk dubiously. "I . . . think *I* do."

The captain whirled on him, eyes aflame with irritation. "You were a fool to have come with us, and we were fools to have brought you!"

"But he is here," another countered—and reached into his saddlebag. He fumbled there for a moment, then produced a square of red fabric the size of a handkerchief, and two smaller ones. These he passed to Aikin. "When you mount, slip the larger inside your thighs and wrap the smaller about your hands. They will stick to anything unless you will it otherwise."

"They had better," the captain grumbled, "for we have wasted much time already." And with that he whistled a certain tone, and eight of the largest elk obediently trotted forward, to stand in a semicircle before the Faery knights. Aikin felt a thrill such as he had never known: not so much from magic-reared beasts confronting his mundane self, however, as from the old order facing the new. He was staring straight at the Pleistocene: at something none of his classmates nor learned professors would ever get to witness.

But he had no time to glory in that realization, for already the knights were mounting. The captain had claimed the largest, and Aikin suddenly found himself alone save for one other rider—facing a beast whose back was higher than his head—and he was a good six inches shorter than any male present; shorter, even, than Rigantana.

But just as he was trying to contrive something involving the three red squares, unexpectedly strong arms grabbed him from behind, swept him into the air, and the next thing he knew he was seated. He had barely sense enough to stuff the larger square beneath him and wrap the others around the hands he slapped on the juncture of neck and shoulder—and they were off again.

And if the last ride had been fast, this was faster.

One moment they were careening over the meadow; the next they were leaping what looked on one side like a fence, and as they crossed it like a fallen tree; and then they were back on the Tracks—moving faster than Aikin ever dared imagine an animal could move at any sustained clip.

Probably it was just as well the elks had such huge antlers, he decided, because they blocked much of the view ahead. And they cut off the wind as well, like the cowling on a motorcycle, so that he was actually less buffeted than before.

And then the wonder of it all caught up with him, and for a long time he simply rode, reveling in the knowledge that while many of his friends had ridden horses, he was unique among mortal men in having bestridden an Irish elk. So taken was he with this notion, in fact, that he was actually disappointed when the company slowed as they approached a fork in the Track. No, not a fork, he discovered when they reached it: a narrow X-intersection where another Track angled into theirs from the left.

The captain called a rest and all halted. To Aikin's surprise, none of the elks' racks struck another, which—given there was close to a hundred linear feet of nerveless bone sweeping around a close-grown space—was pretty amazing. He watched curiously as the captain dismounted and examined both arms of the V ahead. The man was scowling when he returned.

"Rhiannon's troop, without a doubt," he announced. "They came up the Track that joins this—a dozen of them, or I'm a babe. But here they split, and half went left and half right."

"Why?" someone wondered.

"Because my mother is no fool," Rigantana snorted. "She knew there might be pursuit, and so she sought to confound us."

"Still, they are not far ahead," the captain observed, "for we have made up a great deal of time. Yet it is obvious we must divide our strength, and that may not be good, for already Rhiannon's host outnumbers ours."

"Three and three?" a blond knight suggested. "And a . . . guest goes with each?"

"Perhaps," the captain grunted. "But we know who else rides the Tracks tonight, and something tells me he is near."

"You are under my protection," Rigantana noted.

"But you cannot protect two groups," a red-haired fellow retorted.

"And both these routes lead where we would go," the captain concluded. "One way is long, one short, but we do not know which band has the oracular stone—nor which one *He* will follow."

"If he does."

"He will."

"So Rigantana's host should be larger and take the longer path," the lone female knight suggested, "since it will be at risk longer."

"And the lad?"

Anger flared in Aikin at that. *Lad indeed!* He was tired of being talked about as though he wasn't present, tired of being treated as so much baggage. Tired—

"Oh shit," he blurted out all at once. "I've got an idea!"

Seven sets of eyes turned toward him. Most were less than friendly.

"You guys are afraid of the Hunt, right?" he blundered on breathlessly. "Well, he's already hunted me tonight—twice, in fact. And he said himself he never hunts a quarry more than once in his own skin."

The captain's eyes narrowed. "So you do not have to ride with Rigantana?"

"I . . . guess not."

"But you cannot ride alone! The short Track leads where we would go without trouble. But what would you do if you were first to locate our quarry? Would you confront Rhiannon's knights alone?"

Aikin shrugged. "Never thought of that," he admitted dully.

The captain gnawed his lip. "I will ride with you," he said at last. "I have more Power than any among our host save Rigantana, and likely more than Rhiannon's knights as well. This way we cover both options, and both parties have protection."

"*You* will have none," someone observed.

"I will have the fastest mount, the shortest road, and the sharpest sword," the captain shot back. "And something tells me the 'lad' is less a fool than we supposed."

Silence, followed by mumbled assent.

"Luck," Rigantana cried, as she moved into the vanguard of the host to the right.

"Luck," Aikin called back, as he followed the captain onto the remaining Track.

Thank God, Aikin thought, there were no more pines. Yet swamps full of gold-toned cypress hung with spun-silver Spanish moss through which the Track ran on a sort of nebulous causeway were little better to look at, and less comforting to contemplate—especially when he discovered he could often see the gleam of water beneath the Track that passed steadily beneath the elk's cloven hooves.

"Eellar," the captain declared at some point, his voice clear for all the whipping wind. "My name is Eellar."

"Aikin," Aikin yelled back. "Aikin Daniels."

"You are brave for a mortal."

"Maybe," Aikin hedged. "Or maybe I'm just really dumb."

"Sometimes it is hard to judge the two," the Faery knight acknowledged. "I feel rather foolish myself, just now. This is my first command: the first Rade in which I have ridden vanguard. Nothing was supposed to occur."

"Maybe nothing will," Aikin told him.

Eellar glanced over his shoulder. "Something already has," he groaned.

Aikin shuddered for no reason, but then he *did* have reason, for in spite of their pace, the wind had shifted around behind them and had bound other sounds within its own: the pounding of hooves and the baying of hounds, and the bray of a hunting horn whose notes could chill the bone.

And when Aikin finally dared look around, he could see them.

The Wild Hunt: hard on their heels.

"Ride!" Eellar spat. "Ride, for your life, if not mine!"

But for the first time their mounts failed them. Forests they had managed easily, but the swamp growth had grown thicker as they progressed, and tendrils of not-quite Spanish moss hung everywhere like glittering curtains dewed with silver and pearls. They were strong as metal too, apparently; for they caught at the elks' antlers as the pine branches on the last stretch of Track had not—and not only caught, they dragged, slowing their headlong rush. Aikin saw Eellar draw his sword and slash about him, cutting at the parasitic plants. Droplets of wet red fire flashed into the gloomy air. Aikin preferred *not* to think of them as blood.

And the Hunt, unencumbered by monstrous antlers, came thundering on.

—Yet it did not actually catch them, though it obviously could have. Instead, Aikin got the odd sense it was holding back.

Sound wasn't, however: the pounding of hooves, the rasping of canine breath—and now, above all, the wild shrill laughter of a woman who was obviously insane. Aikin wanted badly to plug his ears so as to shut out that last, yet dared not move his hands from his steed's shoulders. And so those tones reached him and played with his mind, and all at once the swamp was no longer void of animate life; all at once skulls rose from the water: skulls wearing helms of antique design he vaguely associated with the Spanish explorers who'd tried to build outposts on the coast of mundane Georgia. They didn't move, but they watched: eye sockets black and . . . hungry.

And then something sang past his ear, so close he felt pain crease the lobe. "Shit!" he yipped. Then, "Oh fuck!"—as he saw the crimson-fletched shaft that had buried itself in the juncture of Eellar's neck and shoulder an inch to the right of the spine, and precisely in the one place bare flesh showed between cuirass and cap helm.

The Faery captain promptly slumped forward: conscious still—Aikin hoped—but obviously fading. And then he toppled from his mount and tumbled to the side of the Track: a jumble of silver mail and white velvet buried half in glimmering golden light, half in stinking slime-gray mud.

Eellar's elk danced to a halt a dozen yards farther on, its antlers effectively blocking the width of the Track. Aikin's mount stumbled to a stop almost atop the fallen knight, even as the Huntsman's horn rang louder yet behind. Aikin slammed his fists over his ears to shut out that blast, but as he did, something sharp probed the small of his back.

"Three's the charm, they say in your World," came a too-familiar voice. Himself. The Huntsman. Herne. Cernunnos. He who wore man's shape and stag's antlers. "You may be the one mortal in eternity to have been hunted by me thrice in one night—in two different shapes, and three Worlds."

Aikin was too numb with fear to reply.

"Cleverness saved you once," the Huntsman went on, still with what was probably a spear point poking Aikin's back. "Rigantana saved you a second time, and my own word saves you now—but you should move aside, for you stand between me and my quarry."

"W-what're you gonna do to him?" Aikin managed, not daring to move lest he collapse in blind panic. He wished that bitch would stop gibbering.

"Why, kill him, of course! What good is a hunt without a kill?"

"And then?"

"We hunt again."

"Where?" Aikin demanded suddenly, as a ghost of a plan took form despite the insidious peals of insane laughter.

"Back up this Track. Nothing worthwhile runs past here. And courtesy precludes my hunting Rigantana's company on the other fork."

"What if I told you where other . . . prey is?" Aikin dared shakily, wondering where that notion had come from.

"What prey?"

"The guys we're after."

The spear probed deeper. Pain slid into Aikin's flesh. Godalmighty, that thing was sharp! Magically sharp, probably. Sharp enough to skewer him through before he was even aware of it.

"There *were* other prints," someone shouted from farther back. Aikin strained to follow the ensuing murmur, but the voices had shifted away from English—if they'd ever been that. And then something thrust against his foot, and before he could stop himself, he looked down—where the blackest dog he'd ever seen bared gleaming white teeth at him, the eyes above that inky muzzle red as coals.

"Lugh would consider it a favor," Aikin called over his shoulder.

"We do not *need* Lugh's favors!" someone—not the Huntsman—yelled back.

"I am mad," the Huntsman snorted, his voice as rough as the bark of his hounds, "but I am no fool. A favor here, a favor there: thus is balance maintained." A pause, then: "What might this favor be?"

Aikin told him.

"Those would be Rhiannon's men," a woman complained. "They would claim her protection."

"I swore only to preserve those of the royal house of Ys, and those *they* protect," the Huntsman snarled back. "Rhiannon's guard are never of her house, and her protection prevails only in her presence or that of her blood kin, else she could shield all of Ys from me."

"But—"

"Silence!" the Huntsman roared. "I will do this thing! The small fey flee Tir-Nan-Og, for a land that lies beyond Ys, and thus beyond Faerie. If they reach there, I cannot hunt them. And I *like* to hunt them. They fight better than the Sidhe; there are few repercussions if they are slain—and their souls, my spear tells me, are tastier."

Aikin was trying very hard *not* to think of wolves and cougars that killed many more rabbits, squirrels, and groundhogs than cattle, sheep, or deer; only hunting the latter when the rest became too scarce.

"We ride, then!" the Huntsman bellowed—and with that the pain in Aikin's back vanished. A crackling swish was the spear sweeping away.

"But my . . . friend," Aikin ventured.

"He will heal or not," the Huntsman growled. "We will not harm him, but you would be wise to leave him where he lies—for I seem to have come to like you, and you would be safer with us than otherwise. This swamp dislikes things that move and are . . . alive."

"But—"

"Follow or stay," the Huntsman snapped. "We are gone!" And with that he winded his horn, and reality shattered into noise.

Aikin shut his eyes and deliberately refused to watch as, with a roar like a hurricane, the Wild Hunt swept by. A few hounds loitered, one of which was nosing the motionless Eellar when Aikin finally dared open his eyes. "Git!" he yelled, as though he commanded one of his dad's 'coon hounds.

To his surprise, the beast responded, though it continued to stare at him with crazed, accusing eyes.

"You go too," Eellar hissed through gritted teeth, his handsome face tight with pain. "I will not die, though I may hurt for a time. When you may, send someone in search of me."

"You could ride with me . . ."

"It would not be wise."

"I—"

But Eellar muttered a Word that sounded different from any Aikin had ever heard, and the stag surged forward. "Here!" Eellar called as he passed, and somehow found strength to toss Aikin his sword.

Aikin caught it, courtesy of the red rags that bound his hands, and managed to fumble it into his belt beside the one he'd received from Alec, and then was off again. Of Eellar's elk there was no sign.

He didn't know how long he rode.

Aikin had heard of soldiers who could sleep in the saddle, but had never expected to be one. He had a pretty good idea he had been cutting at least tentative Zs, though, when something cold slapped his face and roused him several levels of consciousness—to see the last of the glittering moss sweep past the stag's rack.

And reveal a field of carnage.

The Track had emptied into a stretch of dryer, more open land than the swamps he'd been navigating, though stands of the odd gold-toned cypress still circled its three or so acres. Impossibly large birds perched on limbs here and there, none close enough to see clearly—which was a blessing, as the skies were already thick with dark shapes slowly spiraling down on vast dark wings.

Carrion birds, for certain—and there was definitely carrion. Rhiannon's troop evidently hadn't been far ahead of the Hunt at all—or had heard them coming and sought to meet them where the Track emerged— for the first body lay not ten paces inside the clearing. A man—a Faery man—it had been, and fabulously handsome as most of them were—had his chiseled features and beardless chin not been contorted in a rictus of something that clearly transcended pain, something that was probably linked to a large, neat hole in his chest from which blood had erupted in a perfect star to pattern his gold surcoat.

The next man had been dealt with even less pleasantly; indeed had been cloven nigh in twain, from the juncture of neck and shoulder. Fortunately, that part faced away from Aikin, so he was spared the full gory spectacle. Spared the sight, rather, for the air was rank with the stench of blood, viscera, and a nebulous something that could only be called fear.

The third body was a horse, and the elk went skittish at that, for the stallion's entrails twined in a sort of cat's cradle around its legs—and to his dismay, it still breathed faintly. He would have put it out of its misery, but the elk moved on, and he had little choice but to follow the Track toward the clearing's heart.

A warrior woman's corpse loomed into view to the right, face strangely peaceful for someone with the back of her head caved in. Her possible twin lay just beyond, crushed beneath a horse whose neck had been cleft in twain. A smaller shape sprawled beside her, a skinny feral-looking boy in motley of russet fur and emerald feathers: one of the lesser fey, a mascot perhaps. The sword that lay just beyond his outstretched fingers would scarce have made Aikin a dagger.

For some reason that affected him worse than the others, and his gorge rose unbidden. He lost it entirely when a vast crow lit atop that scrawny chest and poked its beak into an eye that had obviously been born to twinkle. He was barely able to turn his head in time to avoid soiling both his leg and his steed, and was only grateful that the elk seemed to sense his discomfort and strode past.

At which point a troubling thought struck him: *Supposing the ulunsuti was here: how did he find it?* And fast on the wings of that realization came another, that would have occurred far sooner had he not been so everlasting tired.

This was all his *fault!*

He, Aikin Daniels, had slain these folks as surely as Neman had caused the death of David-the-Elder! These folks had families who would hear of this massacre and curse his deeds, friends who might be prompted to seek revenge, who might cross the World Walls to effect it, as Dave had sought to do.

All because *he* was a coward. All because he'd tried to save someone who was no better than these folks from a similar doom.

He really *was* sick then—so sick he had no choice but to slide off his steed or faint. The ground was already soggy with his vomit when he fell upon it, and he doubled that amount twice over, heaving and groaning until there was no more to gag forth. When he looked up again, it was to see the dark lump of a fallen horse he'd not truly noticed before—and rising from where she'd evidently been crouching beyond its belly, a woman.

A survivor? He hoped? He feared?

But this was no warrior maid of Rhiannon's; this was another sort of woman entirely.

—Red dress, red hair, crazy eyes, blood on her face and arms clear to the shoulders . . .

Macha!

The reveler among the slain.

"A fine feast," Macha chortled, as she paused to wrench a crimson . . . something in twain and thrust it into her maw. She chewed noisily and spat out blood and gristle.

Aikin was too stunned to move.

"No," he mouthed silently—helplessly. "No . . . no . . . no . . ." The world reeled.

The ground hit him hard.

When he awoke, it was to see Macha bending over him, her mouth far too close to his own. He could smell her breath, hot and fetid. But her eyes, when he glimpsed them, were clear.

"Yes, look at me, boy!" she commanded. "Look, and see me sane, as I briefly am at the quarters of the day. Look, and hear, and know I speak true when I say that you had no part in this. I knew you were pursuing someone when we met upon the Tracks, but it was I who clouded your reason, I who bade you urge the Hunt to this slaughter. The knowledge that Rhiannon's host rode ahead was in your mind, but I brought it to your tongue."

"But . . . why?" Aikin choked, as he scrambled up on his elbow.

"Because Macha prefers many deaths to few, and thinks it better yet if a certain mortal goes insane. And best of all, if the folk of Faerie take the battle into his World. Then will Macha *truly* revel among the slain." She paused, and madness glazed her eyes again, all hint of rationality fled. "No, not Macha . . . *me* . . . *I* will revel among the slain!

"The slain . . . ! The slain . . . !" she went on in a kind of childish singsong, as she danced away across the field. ". . . Blood and gore and the brains of the slain . . . !"

And then distantly a horn sounded. And as Aikin watched in gut-twisting awe, the crazy woman raised her arms, flapped them twice, and became the largest crow he'd ever seen, which flapped away across the clearing.

Leaving him alone in a battlefield, trying to convince himself that all this grief was not his fault. The elk hadn't fled, but was not close to hand, so he gave himself to aimless wandering, knowing he should seek the ulunsuti, yet loath to come anywhere near those ruined bodies, among which there was no sound save the rustling wings of eerily mute ravens and the hiss of wind through bloodstained grasses.

And, to the right, an odd humming. He started at that, eyes narrowed, tired, and wary. There it was again: a steady buzzing drone that seemed out of place in this land of swamps, death, and Straight Tracks. His curiosity promptly awoke, and he stumbled toward it, stiff-legged from all that riding. He freed Alec's sword as he limped along: three feet of sloppily forged iron, that was also three feet of death past revival to anyone from Faerie.

The hum was louder now, easier to trace; and before he knew it, he was running back the way he'd come, but at an angle that looked poised to bring him upon what he now saw was another Track—likely that from which Rigantana's host should soon appear.

He almost stepped on it before he could stop.

It *was* the ulunsuti: humming like a crazy thing, where it lay in a pool of blood beside a young blond knight whose throat had been sliced open. It quieted as he squatted beside it, and more as he reached out to retrieve it left-handed. Yet something stopped him. *The thing was primed!* And who knew what would happen now? Could he simply ignore it and let it fall quiet? Or did it have to expend all that latent power he could practically feel? Certainly it'd had power enough already to sense him worrying about it and summon him. But what *could* he do besides wait? Yet how could he stand to remain here with all these dead bodies? How could he explain them to their kin? It was Macha's fault, she had herself admitted. But would anyone believe him if he repeated that tale? Even if it were true?

"God," he gritted, "I wish these folks hadn't died!"

And then, with absolutely no warning, the World turned to light and heat, and he knew no more.

Aikin awoke to the fine clear pain of a sword point lodged between his pecs, and to the sight of a grim-faced Faery man whose high-crowned helm was silhouetted against a brassy sky. Something warm pulsed in the fisted hand he pressed to the blood-soaked ground, and even without looking he knew it was the ulunsuti.

"I do not know who you are, mortal lad," the Faerie knight rasped blearily, "but I awoke here and found my fellows dazed as though newly roused, our horses running wild with a vast-horned stag, and only *my* brother still dead, in whose blood you seem to lie."

"Unnnhhhh!" Aikin groaned, and felt that more than sufficient reply.

"I seem to have lost something, however," the knight went on. "Have you perhaps found a certain . . . jewel?"

Aikin froze. *Lord, it was true!* He'd wished the dead alive, and here they were!—confused as much as he, and anxious to deliver the ulunsuti to Rhiannon's ships at the coast, but alive! Abruptly he followed the Faery's gaze to his left hand.

So what was he waiting for? Why didn't the guy simply *grab* the thing?

Because something lay beneath that hand, dropped clumsily when he'd fallen, but evidently sufficient to dissuade random pillaging: the hilt of Alec's sword. *Iron* sword, such as all in Faerie feared. And unless this guy killed him, he couldn't touch the ulunsuti while his hand lay upon it. Slowly, carefully, with the stone still in his palm, he eased his fingers part way 'round it.

"Raise your arm and live," the knight snapped, as his blade sliced through Aikin's T-shirt.

Aikin considered this. The guy had a point . . . far too sharp a one. Certainly he could kill Aikin before Aikin could fumble a useful grip. It would then be a simple matter to roll him away from the weapon. On the other hand, *he* had reinforcements in transit . . .

"I wished you alive just now," Aikin said, trying to sound formal and imperious, as he did in the games he ran. "I wished your souls free of the Wild Hunt, and so you live. I did it with the stone in my hand, but I could also wish you dead again—faster than you could slay me."

"You lie!"

"Wanta try me?"

The man paused. "Others will be joining me soon. I will wait."

"Yeah," Aikin shot back, daring to ease himself up on his elbows, careful to maintain his grip on both sword and ulunsuti. "Or perhaps I can wish them away as well. Perhaps there is no end to my wishes."

"You would be wise to wish yourself gone," the knight snarled, as he withdrew his blade but did not sheathe it. Aikin managed to sit upright. "Rhiannon will make short work of you," the Faery added with a smug smirk. "She will cast a glamour on you so fell you will do anything to be free of it, even release the oracular stone."

"No!" another voice countered, sailing clear across the field. "She will not!"

The Faery spun around. Aikin scrambled to his feet—to see riding from the woods a mixed company of Rhiannon's knights and Lugh's, with Rigantana in the van beside Eellar's second. Rhiannon's men were obviously prisoners.

"Rigantana," the Faery spat. "But you do not act in the name of your dam."

"I act in the name of Lugh Samildinach, High King of Tir-Nan-Og, whose land this is, and whose honor has been besmirched by my mother's subterfuge," Rigantana retorted, suddenly very close indeed. "And I act as the heir to the House of Ys."

"Your mother—"

"—Has no right to contravene Lugh's laws, which she has done, nor to risk Lugh's realm as she has done likewise. You will escort her back to Ys when Lugh arrives."

The knight did not reply. Aikin stared at Rigantana, who loomed above him: a beautiful woman still in mortal togs, astride an Irish elk. It took his breath away—and more when she smiled at him.

"You have what you came for?" she asked.

Aikin swallowed, then nodded awkwardly. "I . . . have."

"It is yours to return to your friend, to do with as he will; but I would ask you all to use it carefully. I doubt it can heal the World Walls, but perhaps it can prevent further damage."

"It's not my call," Aikin told her. "But I guarantee you: me and old Alec are gonna talk!"

"Perhaps I will too," Rigantana said, with an even wider smile. "I still have business in your World. And I must admit that my mother had the right idea about the ulunsuti—if not the right means of achieving it."

Aikin shrugged. "Yeah, well, I guess if our World's

wearin' through into Faerie, they've got a right to be pissed. And a right to emigrate."

Rigantana's brow wrinkled with thought. "It's a no-win," she sighed.

Aikin puffed his cheeks. "Maybe. But I think if you asked Alec nicely . . ."

Rigantana smiled again. "Well now, oh Mighty Hunter—and yes, I know whence comes that name—you soften him up for me, and then I will ask him myself!"

Aikin grinned back. "I will," he laughed. "Never doubt it."

The Heir of Ys gazed at the sunless sky and frowned. "I would love to continue this conversation," she murmured. "But the Tracks run strange this time of year, and if you would return whence you came in time to set your friends at ease, you must leave *now!*"

"But . . ."

"Now! I will summon your steed, but you must hurry. And tell Alec McLean and David Sullivan I will see them again—and not only on microfilm."

Aikin nodded mutely and pocketed the ulunsuti. By the time he'd located his mount, it was halfway across the clearing. By the time he'd retrieved his sticky squares, it was nuzzling the back of his neck.

Rigantana gave him a leg up.

He didn't look back when he left the meadow, but for all the tension, all the strange sights and experiences of the last few hours, his heart was strangely light.

He felt like Enya and Tori Amos, like Horselips and Clannad, like Pearl Jam and Live and Led Zeppelin—and like John Williams and Beethoven and Andrew Lloyd Weber.

Too bad he didn't have a CD player.

Chapter XXIV:
The Waking

(The Straight Tracks—no time)

"Is it my imagination," David asked Liz, the air, and his horse's mane, "or is the Track turnin' red?"

" 'Fraid not," Liz replied nervously, pacing her mount as close beside his as the encroaching briars allowed: they that looped and whorled in sullen copper-rust profusion along a Track too narrow to suffer riding abreast. "Or if it *is* your imagination, then I'm doing it too."

David scowled and tried to peer around the Morrigu, who rode vanguard of their odd company—a company that had grown increasingly grim and purposeful as their interminable trek progressed. Unfortunately, horse-plus-rider, plus his own mount's head blocked most of the forward view—that and an increasing number of what looked like branches of long-needled pines thrusting out above the briars past the middle of the Track. They would've been a comforting reminder of home, too—had their needles not been jet black, and the scaly bark that bore them the iridescent blue-green of a scarab's shell.

Never mind that the fragment of the Track he *could* see had definitely shifted from its usual luminous gold at least to orange, and—where the motes that comprised it floated nigh to their horses' chests—nearly to crimson. The effect was of heated metal cooling from yellow-white to dull, though incandescent, red.

Like dying stars, he thought—and shuddered; for

here, where the Tracks might be anything from cosmic string through points of frozen time to gears in a cosmic clock, even that was a real possibility. Shoot, that glowing carmine spark that had just bobbed past his stallion's nose could be someone else's Betelgeuse or Arcturus or Antares—which made him, Liz, Alec (with Eva the cat/enfield), and the Morrigu the four horsemen of some microverse's apocalypse. And even as he watched, the Track beneath the Faery's mare pulsed redder.

"Is this normal?" he ventured finally, pushing aside a particularly persistent bough of not-quite-pine. "Is it that Crimson Road you mentioned earlier?"

The Morrigu twisted around but did not slow her steady pace. "This stretch of Track lies very near your World," she answered tersely. "These branches that slow our progress are the shadows of trees in the Lands of Men frozen by Time and the World Walls and given substance. As for the Track: Iron rails lie in your World where it passes. It is not unlike the taint which forces our folk into your World near your family's dwelling."

"It's . . . . eerie," David gave back. "I usually feel good when I'm on the Tracks, but this is too damned spooky."

"The ghoul-haunted Woodland of Weir," Alec quoted, from the end of the file.

"Mr. Poe," the Morrigu called back, "and you are more correct than you imagine."

David didn't ask for elaboration; indeed, was increasingly unwilling to think about anything. So much had happened the last few days he barely knew which end was up. Simply making it through classes alone had been a pill; never mind agonizing over David-the-Elder; plus his friends' assorted crises—which latter, however, seemed slowly to be resolving.

But his own resolution loomed ahead, and he had no idea what form it would take nor how he would deal with it, only that it would occur, and a day from now it'd all be over and he'd finally get some peace. He wondered if Calvin had felt this way: there on the threshold of the Ghostcountry. Of course, Cal had *chosen* to go, and had known what he was getting into, and had talked about it afterwards; the Morrigu was as silent as the proverbial grave—and well-nigh as encouraging.

And for once he had nothing to say himself.

For a long time he simply rode, lost in reverie, his attention focused on the rump of the Morrigu's steed, the ears of his own, and the increasingly ruddy glow of the Tracks. Maybe he slept in place.

Certainly his consciousness had achieved *some* degree of separation from time, space, and his body when he found his mount slowing. He blinked, yawned, then stretched mightily—and blinked again when he saw that the briars had been superseded entirely by the shadowy pines, among the trunks of which the Track flowed like a river of luminous blood, a flood of cooling lava.

"We must go slowly now," the Morrigu advised, "or we will miss it."

David didn't ask of what she spoke, but very soon he knew.

It was a Track: *another* Track, that either intercepted theirs at an oddly oblique angle or else broke off at one. It was damned disquieting, too; and David couldn't help recalling H.P. Lovecraft's "alien geometries whose angles were slightly askew."

But even more troubling was that both sections of Track led beneath rough stone arches twice as tall as him and his horse together. Like the trilithons at Stonehenge, they were: massive fingers of glimmering granite set among the pines. But if both Tracks were still disturbingly red, there was something even stranger about the one on the right. It seemed to shimmer and waver, as though it were not wholly . . . *there*, but perhaps a reflection of the other mirrored in murky air. Abruptly, he looked away—trying to force it into focus was making him queasy as hell—but as soon as he did, the image clarified in the corner of his eye.

"*Closing* them might serve better," the Morrigu advised, "at least until you pass beneath the gate."

"What . . . is this place?" David asked shakily. "I've never seen anything like this on the Tracks. It makes me feel . . . weird.

"Better ask *when* is this place," the Morrigu retorted. "As for the rest, the Track on the right is the one you must take, but it only takes a form we can access on this one night of the year, and any business we have upon it must be concluded that same night or we are all lost—even me."

And with that she reined her horse to a halt and turned full around to face him. "This is *your* quest, David Sullivan," she intoned formally. "*You* determine where and when this gate leads; you must be first to pass through."

David stared at the dark archway dubiously. The eager pines grew close to either side: onyx and indigo; the upright stones gleamed gray and silver; the Track was the color of blood, but beyond was only blackness marked by one thin line of scarlet. He swallowed hard, paced his horse forward a step, then paused uncertainly, filled with deep foreboding. Suppose the Morrigu was lying. Suppose nothing lay beyond these rocks but death. Suppose all that fine talk about trifold sisters and madness and sanity had been a fabrication and this woman who styled herself the Morrigu was as mad as both her twins. Suppose he was already as beguiled as that poor bitter soldier had been, who'd veiled irrational jealous hatred with hashish.

"You will not know until you go," the Morrigu stated flatly. "And either way, you will have cause to rejoice and cause to regret."

"Yeah," David snorted. "I know!"

And before he had time to consider further, he kicked his horse in the flanks and surged ahead.

For an instant he knew cold past his nightmares of freezing, then heat washed up at him from the Track, which seemed wrought of sparkling embers: an endless road of dying fire. His horse's hooves crunched there, which had made no sound on the Track he'd abandoned. More crunchings behind spoke of his friends joining him, as he was not certain they had either courage or leave to do.

"This is your quest," the Morrigu repeated, her voice riding a rising wind. "You must lead. And whatever happens, you must not look back."

David didn't even nod, simply rode and let the stallion set its own pace. There was nothing to see: no whorling briars, no pines, no fantastic landscapes, merely an empty plain stretching endlessly to an absent sky. Lines of fire laced it like whip scars lashed into the earth, but there was no other color.

And on he rode.

Eventually a second gate appeared: another trilithon, beyond which he glimpsed a blur of nighted landscape: mountains that did not extend past that opening to either side. And he likewise felt a brush of air that carried the scent of life.

He kicked his horse to a trot.

The gate reared up.

He passed beyond . . .

. . . And almost cried out, for what he gazed upon was all too familiar.

He'd spent the first eighteen years of his life there!

Sullivan Cove. Enotah County. Georgia. Land his folks had dwelt on for nigh on two hundred years. Land that once had belonged to the Cherokee.

Somehow he was there again! A hundred miles north of Athens, riding down the logging road that snaked up to Lookout Rock, and not a hundred yards farther on became his parents' drive. Already he could see the barn roof to the right, the hilly pasture where his pa kept his rangy cows easing into view to the left.

A ridge loomed beyond: backdrop to the Sullivan Cove Road that ran past his pa's land through Great-uncle Dale's and thence to the lake that embraced Bloody Bald, where Lugh the Many-skilled hid his stronghold behind walls of glamour.

But . . . something was wrong! The barn was visible now, and other outbuildings, and the house itself; yet while the shape, size, and location were correct, all the details had altered to those of an earlier place and time, so that spirals and curves now danced along the heavy corner posts, while attenuated beasts battled upon steel-strapped doors. The tin roofs were now wrought of wooden shakes, and carved beams crossed at the gables, while the extensions that saluted the air had been shaped into knotwork dragons.

"Not your dream," the Morrigu whispered, "but his. This *is* Sullivan Cove, but you are in his World now."

". . . Whose?" David ventured faultingly.

"You know whose."

"My uncle's?"

"If that is whom you seek."

"Where . . . do I find him?"

"Where you saw him last."

"Not in the house?"

"He dwells in a darker house now."

David nodded grimly and swallowed again, ignoring a stomach that seemed intent on spoiling all this eerie solemnity by growling, and rode on down the drive, passing the house on the right to turn left along a wider road, along which he continued for roughly a quarter mile before turning left again, uphill. He paused there, saw the mountains lifting higher than they ought above a barren knoll, on the brow of which rose a mound that absolutely should not have been present. Torches flickered and smoked at intervals around it. It looked, he realized, like a Viking burial mound—or the rath of an Irish King.

"He whom you seek is within," the Morrigu mur-

mured at his shoulder. He wanted to turn, to look at
her, to gaze on Liz and Alec to see if they truly still
rode with him or were themselves now wraiths and
shadows. "You must continue afoot," she went on.
"And when you arrive, you must relinquish what the
dead desire most."

David swallowed again—and was suddenly very
light-headed. It was all too strange: he felt removed
from himself: drunk, stoned, dreaming—maybe even
dead. He had no past anymore, no future beyond what
rose atop that hill. There was only present. The eternal
now.

And still he hesitated.

"Not even the kings of Faerie can raise the mortal
dead," came the Morrigu's insidious whisper, bearing
threat, knowledge, and sympathy: all three. "The souls
of your kind linger but briefly when their bodies die,
then occupy fresh-born flesh—unless other Powers in-
tercede. There was no way to raise the kinsman you
loved—not in your World; you, therefore, must meet
him in his: in that moment between death and . . .
what comes after, when his dreams of his own past
deeds are most alive."

"So we've . . . traveled through time?"

"And beyond mortal space as well. We are neither
in the Mortal World nor Faerie."

Again David swallowed. "And my uncle . . . ?"

"He sleeps. He dreams. He awaits. He will have as
much life as you are willing to grant him."

But still David hesitated.

"You've gotta do it," came another voice from behind: Liz, this time. Calm, but with an edge that spoke
of deep control or raving terror.

"You'll never forgive yourself if you don't," Alec
added, his voice trailing into a sob.

"And the sooner I finish, the sooner it'll be over for
all of us," David sighed. Whereupon he slid off his horse
and onto familiar yet alien ground.

The turf was cold beneath his feet—his *bare* feet, he realized. Looking down, he saw that the rest of him was bare as well, save for rough woolen trousers that bagged low on his hips. His hair tickled his shoulders, brushed by the same nervous wind that whipped the torches. A horse whickered. Someone—Alec, probably—inhaled sharply.

Taking a deep breath of his own, he squared his shoulders and strode up that impossible hill.

His legs had started to tighten when he reached the summit, where a barrow rose higher than his head in the space that in his own time, place, and World would've been the family cemetery.

Of earth it was, overgrown with grass, with a ring of level ground around it and, facing east, two stone pillars that supported a lintel above another slab of stone that was surely a door. More carving showed there: snakes and leaves twining and reveling with each other, and over the center a boar was carved; and it came to him then that a boar rode the Sullivan coat of arms, yet this was older. In an alcove to the right, exactly at chest level, a vertical glitter of metal proved to be a short sword of the sort he'd seen in books about the Vikings. Its hilt likewise bore the incised likeness of a boar.

So what did he do now? Wait? Go up and knock? Summon He-Who-Lay-Within to parley in the frosty air?

He will have as much life as you grant him, the Morrigu had said. *You must relinquish what the dead desire most.*

And what was that?

Life, of course! The Morrigu had answered her own riddle.

Only . . . how did he do that? Obviously he was not supposed to die so that the dead could rise. But what *was* he to do?

And what was the cost of wrong choice?

All at once his courage abandoned him, puddling away like water from a punctured bag, leaving him nervous and cold and scarcely able to breathe. Impulsively, he stepped forward and rapped on the white stone door.

A hollow ringing answered—or was that the roar of the nearest torch as the wind whipped its flame toward him? His knuckles hurt, though he was surprised to find them abraded and gleaming with blood.

Nothing happened.

Nothing.

Not daring to think beyond the instant, but reacting to the image that had suddenly appeared in his mind, he reached for the sword by the door and closed his fingers around the hilt. It resisted. He yanked harder. It came free.

And then he lay down on the doorstep of his uncle's barrow—stretched himself out like he imagined a king or warrior or prince of the *Keltoi* would lie—seized that sword in both hands, and laid it along the length of his body from throat to thigh. The metal felt like ice against his bare flesh, but he didn't shift it; rather, he clamped his fingers around the blade midway down. And then he shut his eyes and squeezed with all his might.

It felt less like pain than cold, when the steel—or was it copper or bronze?—bit his flesh. And then fire awoke in his hands; and the distant warmth of blood puddling out across his chest and belly was a comfort against the chill air and the frigid stone beneath his back.

For a very long time he lay there, vaguely aware of his life ebbing out with that liquid. He wondered blearily how he would stop it—if he even could—and why it hadn't already, when it probably ought to have, given that there were no big veins or arteries in the hands. *Could* one bleed to death from hand wounds? Or was this the price? His own life? Was it a price worth paying? Would he for whom he made this sacrifice approve? Or would he call him fool—as more than once he had? Or even coward for refusing to let the past go?

He didn't know.

The only certainties were the stinging in his palms: the incessant flow of warm wet stickiness across his torso; the tang of iron in the air that had not been present earlier; heat and cold at war across his skin. And drowsiness.

Drowsiness . . .

Sleep . . .

Freezing to death was supposed to be like going to sleep, wasn't it? So maybe bleeding to death was like that as well, which was why so many people slashed their wrists in the tub: so that death would steal upon them unawares.

But *he* didn't want to die!

Yet he couldn't live either, not if he rose and bound his wounds on strips torn from his trousers and left what he'd come for undone.

But it'd feel so good just to . . . *stop*, to let it all go, to end the trials of this life and choose another in which he didn't have to deal with all this terrible knowledge that reality was not at all what most folks believed.

But that would also be a world without Liz and Alec—and Aikin and Calvin—and the Gang. Without his brother and his parents and Uncle Dale. And, he admitted, without the wonder of Faerie. He wasn't ready to face such a world.

So when would the bleeding stop? He was in control, something told him. Only he would know how much life he was willing to forsake.

All of it, something else supplied. *All but the very last drop; for if I die, the best remaining part of David-the-Elder dies with me.*

But there was still no movement in the barrow, and surely he would've sensed one now, with his soul already straining at whatever bound it to his clay.

And then he recalled something the elder David had read him when he was too young to know what it was: long before he'd discovered the Sidhe in Lady Gregory's *Gods and Fighting Men.*

A poem: a *Viking* poem the elder David had studied at Governor's Honors the summer before his junior year in high school. A poem whose form this experience emulated.

"The Waking of Angentyr," it was called, of which he remembered little save that it was eerie as hell and concerned a woman who sought a magic sword from the tomb of her ancestor, Angentyr. His uncle had read it to him first in the original Old Norse, and he'd understood not a word of the sound, and little of the sense. But one phrase he did recall, that had stayed with him from that day: the words of summoning.

"Vaku, Angentyr,—Vaku!"

"Wake-you, Angentyr,—Wake-you!"

And with consciousness starting to fade, and his body awash with blood, he took a deep breath and shouted to the torchlit sky.

"Vaku, David Thomas Sullivan—Vaku!"

And then he released the sword and fell back senseless.

He awakened into warmth. Clean skin and breeches. A dull throb in his palms that was pain veiled by something smeared there to banish it. There was a closeness to the air, too, that spoke of indoors, and with it the smell of leather, woodsmoke, and spices, under which hung the stench of mildew.

He opened his eyes and saw carved stone walls bearing spirals across which fire washed tints of orange, gold, and red, from a tiny hearth to his right.

He saw a stone table in the center of a domed room: a table draped in thick black fur. A table that might also have been an altar and a bed and a funeral slab.

And he saw who sat cross-legged upon it.

Almost he didn't recognize him: that fair-haired youth who grinned at him perplexedly, one dark brow veiled by a forelock so yellow-white it might've been his own.

Certainly the blue eyes were the same, and the dimpled cheeks, and the merry red lips above a smooth-angled chin.

But surely the bare-chested body was too slight, the limbs too slender for him to whom they should've belonged.

And he was certainly too young: David's own age, in fact, or just a *tad* older. He had no beard to speak of.

"However much I've changed, you've changed *more*," that one observed, his voice edged with a mountain twang David didn't recall, that seemed all at odds with their surroundings.

"Not . . . what I expected," David agreed, rising.

"Nor I," The Elder laughed, unfolding himself and sliding off the waist-high stone.

Suddenly they were facing each other a yard apart.

"You've grown," one said.

"You've shrunk," the other countered.

"You're almost as old as I am."

"And *you're* fixin' to be a whole lot younger."

"So they tell me."

They embraced: uncle and nephew, dead and living. Brother—almost—and brother. Hero and protégé.

"I'm not worth it," one whispered scarcely louder than the thudding of his heart.

"I'm not either," the other replied.

"I live in you, you know."

"And me in thee—"

An eyebrow lifted, askance. The embrace weakened. *"Thee?"*

"It rhymed better."

One giggled. It didn't matter which. They were too much alike.

"So what 'cha been up to?" the Elder asked eventually.

"Besides the obvious?"

"I wasn't surprised to see you, if that's what you're wonderin'."

"You weren't?"

"If anyone could transcend death for someone he loved, it'd be you."

"What's it like? Bein' dead, I mean?"

"It's an instant in time. *This* instant in time, in fact. Dying's no great shakes, but then it's over."

"So how long have we got?"

"As long as you need, I guess."

A stomach growled. "Long time since I ate," the Younger sighed.

"I got wine—mead, actually."

"I've never *tasted* mead, actually."

"Nor I. But this is how I dreamed bein' dead would be, how I'd have made the time after if I'd had my druthers, and so it is."

"Not bad," the Younger grinned, relaxing as he found a salt-glazed cup full of something hot and sweet-smelling thrust into his hands. He sank down on a pile of furs. "Didn't expect you to be a Viking, though."

"Didn't know enough about the Celts. You've surpassed me there, I guess."

"You don't *know*?"

The Elder shook his head and joined him. "You've got the advantage. You know everything after . . . *then*. I don't know anything past now—'cause it hasn't happened yet."

"Do you *wanta* know?"

"If you feel like tellin' me. Mostly I wanta know if you're happy. If you're still hangin' 'round with Alec—now there's a true friend for you. If you ever woke up and *looked* at that red-haired girl. What's up with my asshole brother."

"Pa?"

"Hard to think of 'im that way: as my bro and your dad. You're more my son than my nephew, and more my brother than either."

"Too bad you never had one—a son, I mean."

An eyebrow lifted. "How do *you* know?"

A chuckle. "You're kiddin'!"

A chuckle echoed. "I didn't die a virgin."

"I won't either."

"Good for you. Uh . . . might I ask?"

"The red-haired girl."

Another laugh: a little giddy, a little sad. And nervous.

"What's funny?" From the Elder.

"This isn't what I figured."

"So what did you figure? *I* wasn't lookin' for anything."

The Younger shrugged. "I dunno. High seriousness, I guess—to use that term you used to throw around. Not two guys hangin' out."

"So why'd you do it, then? If you wanta get serious."

" 'Cause . . . I wasn't finished. 'Cause I never got to say good-bye. 'Cause I hated that the world lost what you'd have been."

"You're a whole lot more! Doesn't take a genius to see that."

"Shit!"

"You're too young to—oh, hell, no you're not! I did at your age."

"I never heard you."

"I was careful."

Silence.

"I could never have done this. Much as I'd have wanted to, if it had been you who died . . . early, I couldn't have met you at the point of timeless eternity."

Silence.

"I wrecked the Mustang—once. It's fixed now."

"Still got the .308?"

"Of course."

"College?"

"Workin' on it."

"Major?"

"Anthropology. Minor in lit."

A yawn.

The Younger's arms prickled with alarm. "What happens when you sleep?"

"I dunno. I've never slept while I was dead—yet."

The Younger drained his mead. He stared at the bottom, saw fire reflected there in a glaze of liquid that was more than honey wine.

"Devlin ever get 'hold of you?"

The Younger started. "John Devlin?"

"The same."

"I got hold of *him*!"

A look of alarm. "When?"

"Couple of days ago. Why?"

"Shit! He never got the letter!"

"What letter?"

A long sigh. "Time for some straight talk, kid."

". . . Okay . . ."

The Elder cleared his throat. "You've *gotta* know by now that there's some weird stuff goin' on 'round the folks' place, right? Like, there's an odd streak of ground back in the woods and something screwy about Bloody Bald, if you look at it a certain way . . ."

"Yeah . . . but how'd you know that I know that?"

" 'Cause you're too much like me—all that crazy Irish blood, I guess. I mean, Dev just looked at *me* and knew."

"So what's the deal?"

"Basically that I told him a lot of stuff and he hinted at a couple of things, and I got to thinkin' about it, and decided that if I'd found out all that, you would too. But I'd also figured out it was dangerous, so I—I dunno—I had this funny feelin' I might not come back from where I was, so I wrote ole John a letter and told him to keep an eye on you, and tell you whatever he thought might be good for you to know, if he thought you oughta know anything. Had it in my pocket when—"

"What?"

"They *didn't* find it, did they? Or didn't want to puzzle out the pieces."

"Guess not. He didn't mention it, anyway."

"He would've."

"So . . . ?"

A sigh. "Basically I was scared you'd get tangled up in some stuff I was afraid to fool with, and it just didn't seem like stuff you could deal with alone."

The Younger fidgeted. "Yeah, well, I did, I guess—I mean, that's what all this is: how I got here, and all. But I *didn't* get into it alone. That's where we're different, you and me: you had to go solo. I had friends. Actually, there's a bunch of folks who at least know *something*."

"More'n you think, if what Devlin told me's true."

"Too bad about the letter, though. Prob'ly would've changed some things."

"Maybe, maybe not."

"Dev's a good man. You can trust him."

"Kinda thought so."

"Think of him as a surrogate me. Don't be afraid to talk to him. I wasn't."

"I'll keep that in mind."

"So . . . anything else buggin' you?"

A shrug. "School, friends . . . some stuff about the World Walls."

"World Walls?"

"Sorry. I figured you knew."

"I—"

Stone grated. Grit trickled down from the dome.

"Speakin' of walls . . ."

"Crap," the Younger groaned. "That must be a hint."

"Maybe so."

"Guess I can either split now or stay forever."

"Go for number one. The world needs you. I *love* you, but—I don't need you." A pause, a frown, then: "No, that's wrong. I *can't*. There's a difference."

"So it's over?"

"For this time and place. Not forever."

The Younger rose. "So what do I do now?"

"You say good-bye, we hug each other like crazy bears, you go out the door, and time starts up again— I guess."

"Like the Feast with the Head of Bran?"

"Uh . . . you got me there."

"The *Mabinogion*."

"Never got that far. It was next. 'Cept there *was* no next."

"Bran was a king of mythic Wales and he and his brothers fought a war with Ireland; Bran was killed and beheaded, only his head didn't die, and his buddies feasted with it for eighty years at Harlech, and as long as the outside door stayed closed, no one remembered their sorrow."

"Will *you* remember?"

A shrug. A wry smile. "I don't know. I didn't know what'd happen when I started down the road that brought me here."

"Do you *want* to remember?"

"I want to remember that you're a good man, that I owe you everything that's good in me, that you died before your time—and that I finally had a chance to say good-bye."

"Those are good things to remember and be remembered for," the Elder smiled. "And you're probably the one who's gonna have to close things down." He yawned again.

They hugged long and deep and powerfully, without self-consciousness, guilt, or fear.

"You really *are* shorter than you're s'posed to be," the Younger smirked.

"Not as tall as I wanted, that's for sure," the Elder growled—and stretched out on the slab.

" 'G-night."

"Sleep tight!"

"Don't let the bedbugs bite."

"It's not *them* I'm concerned about!"

"Love you, man."

"Never doubt it!"

And with that, David set his jaw, and walked to the white stone door.

It swung open at his touch. Cold roared in. Night rose above.

Chapter XXV:
The Wake

(Sullivan Cove, Georgia—
the Dreamtime—'twixt midnight and dawn)

The cat was the main thing keeping him sane, Alec decided. He'd been stroking its silky orange fur for what seemed like hours, and it had been purring blithely along the whole nerve-racking while. At the moment it sprawled across his lap with its chin and one forepaw athwart his left thigh, where he sat cross-legged on the cold hillside turf of what resembled a war between the familiar Sullivan Cove he'd been hanging out in all his life and an over-the-top production of Wagner's *Götterdämmerung*—complete with roiling lightning-lit clouds, flickering torches, and looming burial mounds. For that matter, it wasn't that far off some of the backgrounds for "What's Opera, Doc?," the Warner Brothers parody Aikin had been so keen to emulate less than a week gone by, which had engendered his Elmer Fudd costume.

—Which recollection was another much-needed distraction, like Eva the enfield/cat.

Trouble was, while the steady "burr" of Eva's contentment thrumming through his thighs was almost hypnotically relaxing, every flash of lightning made him tense up again, so that the beast was at best able to manage a holding action against the blind panic that had been hovering near ever since David had marched up that ridiculous hill.

Damn him! Damn the hill! Damn it bloody all!

332

Right from the start, he'd had to fight the urge to follow his obviously fey buddy, an impulse not alleviated when he'd seen David fumble beside the door, grab something that had flashed in the torchlight like metal, and lie down—which put him out of view even from horseback, and also, apparently, was the cue the Morrigu had been seeking to allow him and Liz to dismount.

They had: silent as pallbearers and as sober-faced. Liz had said nothing at all, simply folded herself down close beside him, and taken the hand that wasn't occupied combing fur. The Morrigu flanked him to the left, face impassive, though she'd been watching the eastern sky with increasing frequency of late. No one had spoken since they'd staked out their respective territories. Liz's hand was cold.

Alec suddenly felt as though he would explode if something didn't change. Waiting was not a thing he did well anyway—in common with David—and enduring it in what was in some sense a dreamworld was not a notion he wanted to contemplate, since he feared it really could stretch, objectively at least, forever. More to the point, he absolutely did not want to fret about David even one second longer. He'd therefore focus on another demon entirely.

"Uh—" he began, almost surprised to find his words audible in a place where the raw elements of reality were so overwhelming, yet so mutable. "Uh—" he dared once more, to the Morrigu, "I hate to ask this . . . but is there anything we can *do* about the World Wall thing? Assuming those folks Aik went off with recover the ulunsuti, that is. I mean, we only found out it was messing 'em up a couple of hours ago, and we've been busy ever since . . ."

The Morrigu scowled. Her jaw went tight, and Alec figured he was in for a tongue-lashing. Instead, she sighed and shrugged, for that moment more human than Faery.

"Waiting is no joy," she said tersely. "Nor do I blame you for seeking to divert your thoughts from your friend. But to answer your question: I know little about the oracular stone, and little more about the World Walls, save that they simply *are*. At times they are as transparent to us as air is to you, at others they are charged with Power, as rain and fog suffuse air yet neither negate nor change its intrinsic nature. Sometimes, in fact, they are so thick with Power that even the mighty of us cannot pierce them, either with the Sight, our bodies, or our art."

She paused to check the east, then continued. "No one will argue, however, that they have weakened in places—mostly where Iron lies deep and long in your World. And now we find that the gates wrought by the oracular stone can weaken them as well. Will they heal? Perhaps . . . given time. Certainly they have done so before, with new stuff flowing into their flaws like flesh overgrowing a wound. Yet we can neither speed that process nor hinder it. As for the oracular stone, my understanding of it is that it serves mostly to manipulate intangible forces: the soul, the mind, time—such things as that. A knife may make a wound, after all, but it cannot close one; even so the stone may create a rift in the World Walls but not repair it, so it seems to me. Your wisest course, then, should you recover it, is not to use it again in such a way as to weaken the World Walls more."

"You'll get no argument from me," Alec agreed. And would have said more, had not the whole eastern horizon suddenly strobed with a flash of blue-white lightning.

He inhaled sharply, as did Liz. The bolt left yellow afterimages like a colossal tree reaching from the mountainous horizon halfway across the writhing sky. It took an instant to realize that the bolt had jagged *backward*: a solid trunk of white fire at the earth, fanning out like limbs into the heavens.

It was slow in withering, too, for the ridges at its root continued to flare and flicker with ghostly blue sparks, as though the land there was wrought of dark velvet that had caught fire and was slowly burning through, revealing an eerie pink-blue *nothing* like a black light as big as the world.

The Morrigu sat bolt upright, eyes wide, face shadowed in indigo from that hell glow. She looked, Alec thought, very alarmed indeed.

"What's wrong?" he demanded. Liz's grip tightened on his hand. The cat hissed and dug in its claws. He ignored it.

"I have been a fool!" the Faery snapped. "I should never have let him come here, for once he entered the Realm of the Dreaming Dead, time runs at its own pace, and *his* time will neither be ours nor that of the rest of this World. Oh, I warned him, I know," she went on vehemently. "I *told* him that if we did not conclude our business tonight we would be lost—still, I should have given him some means to know *our* time, but it has been long and long since I walked the Crimson Road, and now dawn has found the borders and will soon devour all—"

"But we can still take the . . . Crimson Road back to our World, right?" Liz broke in.

"Wrong! Dawn will dissolve this World and sever the Crimson Road from the Tracks in your World, my World, and this World—all three—not to be rejoined until those forces that flow between the Worlds realign so as to recall it from the nothingness it will become— which will not occur until another year has died. In the meantime, the *Road* will continue—but nothing above, beneath, around, or upon it will remain, for there will be nowhere *to* be—Oh, it is too hard to explain in words you will understand, when even the mighty of Faerie scarce comprehend it!"

"So," Alec said, "the bottom line is that we've gotta split real soon."

"Not without David!" Liz protested, rising and turning to glare at the barrow-mound.

Alec mirrored her reaction. Did it look brighter up there he wondered? Were highlights of violet fire dancing upon it, as though roof and wall and lintel were limned by lasers?

"If he does not appear very soon, we will have no choice," the Morrigu informed them flatly.

"And of course you didn't tell *him* this would happen!" Liz flared. "He'd never have come here if he'd known there'd be this much risk!"

"It would not have mattered," the Morrigu countered. "His anger—and desire—were mightier than you know. And tonight—this night of all nights—the Road would have reached out to him. The best we could do was accompany him. At least we were able to ensure that he arrived with his mind intact. Many have not. Sometimes I think that is what drove my sisters mad: having spent too much time escorting the death-obsessed down the Crimson Road. I—"

She did not finish, for the world went blue-white again. The air throbbed with infrasound thunder as the sky tree reerupted, this time with twigs to fill the gaps 'twixt its branches. The flickering spread along the horizon to totally embrace the east. The mountains that had first sustained it grew even more tenuous. Some had raveled away.

The Morrigu joined them afoot, as wired as Alec had ever seen someone from Faerie. "Maybe there is time," she muttered. *"Maybe!"*

"For what?" From Liz.

"To flee! To save eight lives, if not nine!"

"Not without David," Alec insisted. "He went after Aik, and helped me. I can't desert him!"

The Morrigu glared at them, then at the sky. The lightning was constant now, but with each stroke, more phantom twigs stretched farther across the heavens, and more mountains caught fire. The gap from which it rose was a pulsing lake of blue-pink luminescence.

A horse whickered, threatening to bolt. The Morrigu calmed it with a Word. Already she was striding that way.

"Goddamn you!" Alec spat, tossing the cat from his lap and stomping after her, on the vague assumption he could actually restrain someone as Powerful as she.

"No!" Liz shouted. Then: "Oh, God, there he is!"

Alec whirled around. Liz was already running. He paced her shadow, overtaking her halfway up, as they both strove to reach that figure who, scant seconds before, had appeared in the sudden gap between the barrow's stone portal and one massive doorjamb, looking like nothing so much as a wraith escaped from ultimate night. It—David—had stared out, stepped forward—and collapsed, lost, for the nonce, to sight.

The ground shook again. Alec was flung forward onto all fours, in which mode he scrambled the remaining yards to the summit. Liz was right beside him, as was the cat. Dimly—distantly—he heard the trampling of hooves, the neighing of frightened horses, and the Morrigu screaming at them from the base of the hill: "Fools!"

Alec ignored her. Reality had tunneled down to instinct and reflex and the single desire to drag his best friend to his feet and get as far as they could as fast as they could and trust luck, which seemed so far to be their ally, to see them through.

And then he was off the turf and onto the quarter arc of pavement before the now-closed door, and Liz was with him, and they were kneeling by David's either side, where he sprawled facedown, shirtless and barefoot upon those cold, trembling flagstones, while the whole world growled and groaned as the tectonic plates of dreamstuff ground each other to glowing dust.

"Is he . . . ?" Alec panted, reaching for David's nearside arm to hoist him up.

"Thank God, no," Liz sighed, as she followed his example. And then he caught the slight rise and fall of his buddy's shoulders. Yet that breathing was shallow—so shallow—and escaping in something between a gasp and a moan.

"Fools . . . fools . . . fools . . ." came the Morrigu's frantic chant—or was that merely an echo of her earlier cries, or thunder playing mimic from cosmic spite?

Somehow they got David onto his knees. A nod at Liz, a jerk, and they wrested him to his feet. He swayed there unsteadily. His eyes were closed, though his lids twitched constantly. His breathing was better, however, and his lips worked. Between gasps, he managed to rasp out what might have been ". . . weak."

"Yeah, man, I know," Alec gritted, as he dragged his friend forward. "C'mon, Davy," Liz urged in turn. "Oh, Davy, come *on*—you've gotta! I know you're weak, but we've gotta get outta here, gotta go just a little farther."

"Yeah," Alec took up as they reached the edge of the slope and started down.

The ground promptly shook once more, tumbling them into a jumble of arms and legs a dozen yards down the hill. When Alec righted himself, it was to see the fire-tree in the east rear up again—this time with a crackling roar and the scent of ozone—and the far more welcome sight of the Morrigu on horseback charging toward them with two other mounts in tow. The third was nowhere around. Likely she had shied.

Alec regained his feet and pulled David up with him, though he recalled neither grip, tug, nor effort. Liz took up the slack as they stagger-ran toward their Faery companion.

The Morrigu met them halfway down, and a moment of utter confusion ensued in which it was determined that David wasn't able to sit a horse alone, and that the Morrigu was the only one competent to manage someone on the verge of unconsciousness *and* a near-panicked stallion at once. In the chaos another horse bolted. The Faery's Word of recall was lost in a clap of thunder, and then it was too late.

By the time they were all reseated—David ahead of the Morrigu, and Alec hanging on to Liz, with the cat squeezed in between—lightning had conjured the world-tree twice more, and the aftersparks had claimed three-fourths of the horizon, leaving only the west unassailed. Fewer ridges than ever showed to the east—south of which the gate to the Crimson Road lay.

"If we can gain Dreamer's Gate before this World dissolves, we will have a little time," the Morrigu shouted, as they galloped down the hill.

"Be faster to head straight overland," Liz advised, nodding to the right. "We cut across this field and a couple of pastures and save a quarter mile."

"And maybe our lives," the Morrigu added—and dug in her heels.

Though he mistrusted horses like the plague, Alec had no choice but to hang on for dear life as Liz did likewise, and the next few moments were the most frightening—and jumbled—of his life.

Reality had gone insane. The lightning was constant now, and so intense it really was like a vast strobe light distorting everything: landscape, distance, even Liz's head and their mount's flowing mane as it stretched out its neck before him. Nor was that all: the ground shook constantly, and the rise and fall of the terrain further screwed his sense of location, as did the spinning clouds and the glowering mountains to the right, which themselves had now begun to grow lines of dancing blue fire around their edges. The east was almost gone: the black-light nothingness having eaten its way much closer in just the last few seconds, so that it now seemed centered no more than one valley beyond that which cupped this World's Sullivan Cove.

Never mind that he'd just seen a cow acquire a crackling halo around her horns, that quickly spread across her body—until, in a clap of thunder, she dissolved. A tree beside the Sullivans' house did likewise. Black light showed in the earth where its roots had been.

The Morrigu was still pounding onward, however, with Liz and Alec right behind. And as best he could tell, there was only one pasture to go, and then a fence to vault and they'd be on the road to the gate. Already he'd caught a flash of crimson uphill to the right. Or maybe that was a trick all this pulsing light played on his poor tortured eyes.

Never mind the jolting and the effort it took simply to keep his seat—no smooth-gaited Faery steeds now!

And then they were careening downhill, and the barbed wire fence at the bottom was rushing toward them, and he had just time to recall that he'd only ever jumped a horse twice in his life, and both had been on Faery steeds too, when he felt the horse's body tense and stretch and fly smoothly into the air, only to touch down far harder than he'd expected.

Almost he flew from his precarious seat, and was certain his tailbone would never recover; but by the time he'd snatched a stronger hold, the mare was scrabbling for footing as she sought to follow Liz's frantic yanks on the reins and turn uphill.

Blessedly, they made it, and the gate was there: no more than an eighth-mile distant.

But the speed of dissolution was increasing rapidly, and worse, seemed to be eating its way toward their particular piece of road faster yet, as though it sought to cut off their escape. It had crossed the main highway now, and was reaving the woods where, in another World, a certain Straight Track lay.

But there was the trilithon!

—Only . . . something was wrong! No darkness laced with bloodred chasms lay beyond; rather, that landscape was lit with white so bright Alec could scarce bear to look at it. Yet even as it rose up before

them, he saw a shape moving in there: moving
quickly—

—A shadowy figure on the back of some kind of preposterous huge-horned animal galloping straight toward them. And even as the Morrigu yelled out a
frantic "Ride for your lives!" that figure burst through.

—And resolved into a wild-eyed Aikin Daniels
astride something between an elk and a moose.

"Turn now, you fool!" the Morrigu hissed, and
kicked her stallion savagely.

Alec heard Aikin swearing at his unlikely steed, and
the crunch of gravel as he got it slowed, and then,
much more clearly, a desperate, "Oh bloody fucking
shit!" and then they were all charging the gate, with
the Morrigu in the van.

By the time the Faery had passed through, Alec had
realized that his glance back at Aikin had shown the
Viking dream that had transfigured Sullivan Cove now
on the ragged edge of dissolution. The lightning was a
constant flash, and every building, tree, and blade of
grass wore Saint Elmo's fire around its edges—but *this*
phantom ornamentation also consumed. The mountains across the road were gone, the road thin as gauze
in spots, and the house a blue-black silhouette limned
in cobalt neon—and then . . . *not*.

Lightning struck a tree right in front of them. The
cat yowled. Their horse reared. Alec slipped back over
its haunches, grabbing for Liz frantically.

No good. Fabric tore. Liz screamed, and then he was
falling, and all he could see was the aft end of a white
horse rising to fill the sky, and Liz fighting to retain
her seat—

—And failing, as she too slipped off.

And then he struck the ground with a force that
drove the air from his lungs and made him see stars
dance across a stroke of lightning—whereupon Liz
landed atop him, evoking yet another constellation.
His butt hurt like hell, as did his hands where he'd

scraped them raw; there was also something up with his elbow. Claws dug into his chest as Eva found him. Liz kicked him as she struggled to rise.

A dark shape loomed above: Aikin, reaching impossibly far down to yank Liz to her feet, even as she tugged at his own torn and bloody hands.

"Run, you fools!" the Morrigu cried from safety. "Forget the beast! Make for the gate—or die!"

Alec did, vaguely aware that the ground felt uncomfortably insubstantial, as it had not when he'd landed on it, and how his every step left a web work of glowing cracks.

And then the gate rose ahead, and hooves were thundering past, and Liz was gasping along beside him, and the cat was clutched to his chest with his one good arm.

Abruptly he was under the stone arch—and through.

The thunder vanished; the world turned cold.

"Thank God," Liz gasped, slowing to a stagger. "We made it!"

"No," the Morrigu called back, "we did not!"

Chapter XXVI:
The Last Gate

(The Crimson Road—no time)

"What do you mean *we didn't make it?"*

Those were not the first words Aikin would've chosen to hear from Liz after far too long on the back of a beast he'd never in his wildest dreams expected to *see*, much less ride. Certainly not what he'd have chosen after dealing first with the weirdness of the Tracks themselves, then with a screwy stone gate that had jerked him from twilight into the insane glare of an endless blasted white plain fissured with crimson, all beneath a sky whose impossible brightness transcended color yet was lit with flickers of something brighter still. Never mind another gate beyond which black, blue, white, and whatever color lightning was strobed across what *might've* been a version of Dave's folks' farm, and then passing that gate and seeing his friends, only to be ordered to a return engagement in what he'd termed the Fucking White Hell!

"Yeah," Alec echoed Liz. "What's the deal?" It was strange, Aikin realized distantly, to hear conversation again. "Oh crap," Liz added, with a groan. "The horse didn't make it."

The Morrigu reined her steed to a halt and twisted around to regard the three who followed her: one on elk-back, two plus a cat panting along afoot. "The dreamworld is all but gone," she announced. "Before long, dawn will devour this place as well, and if we are here, we will also be devoured."

"Huh?" Aikin blurted out, likewise halting his mount as he finally blinked reality back to some sense of stability; his eyes—shoot, his whole head—aching from the glare and the noise and the insistent pounding of his interminable ride. "Oh Jesus!" he added, having finally gotten his act together sufficiently to make a body count and come up missing Dave—until he'd noted the figure lolling ahead of the Morrigu; clad, it seemed, in some odd mix of the running shorts he'd worn earlier and baggy checked sweatpant-things.

"Welcome to hell, preacher," Alec called, quoting *Paint Your Wagon*. He sounded, Aikin thought, totally fried.

"Been there, done that," Aikin retorted from reflex. "What's up with Dave?"

"Too much dreaming," Alec breathed, gaze flitting from Aikin to his cervine mount and back. "That's the short form. We'll save the long one for later, if you don't mind. 'Scuse me while I catch my breath."

"Yeah, but is he gonna be all right?" Aikin persisted. One look at Liz staring fixedly at the witch-bitch showed that she, at least, was bloody concerned.

"He gave his life to raise the dead," the Morrigu retorted. "He gave all but the last drop of blood he could give."

"Christ!"

"—Gave all he could too," the Morrigu observed, unexpectedly.

"And us?" From Liz.

"We double up—or triple up—and maybe we reach the gate, and if we do not, this brightness waxes until it transcends light, and then this place will vanish, and us with it, until it manifests next year to point the way to some other poor fool's dream—without us."

"But—"

"We must *ride*, mortal, if any are to survive! One of you sit behind me, the other go with Aikin! I dare not shape-shift here."

Liz and Alec exchanged glances, obviously torn between choices. Alec took a deep breath. "You're lighter," he told Liz. "You go with the Morrigu, so her horse won't have to carry as much." Without waiting for reply, he jogged toward the elk, his face a mask of despair as he realized just how high the beast's back was.

"Grab hold and jump," Aikin advised, and when Alec caught his hand, jerked with all he had. It took two tries, but Alec made it. And as soon as he'd settled into place, the Morrigu kicked her stallion to a gallop.

Aikin had no choice but to follow, but even flat out, the pace was less than his mount had dared once or twice—which was the first thing that had gone right in ages. And at least it bought him leisure to puzzle out what in blazes was going on. "Got your rock back," he called over his shoulder to Alec, patting his vest where the ulunsuti lurked in an inside pocket. "Pot was gone, though."

"No big deal," Alec grunted. "How'd you find us, anyway?"

"Rigantana started me off, but then I met Lugh and his crowd, and that old guy—what's his name? Oisin? Anyway, he held back and told me to ride north as fast as I could, then ride the red road as fast as I could, and then ride the road to the right as fast as I could—and keep on ridin' no matter what."

"Sounds like him," Alec grumbled. "Lay a bunch of cryptic bullshit on you that doesn't make sense until you're so far in you can't get out again."

"Yeah," Aikin agreed, but then had to break off as the Morrigu drove her stallion faster.

The glare worsened. Heat rose with it. Aikin was sweating like a pig; his eyes were squeezed nigh to slits. As often as not, he closed them. Alec's arms were a vise around his ribs. The cat had found its way into his lap.

Abruptly, the elk faltered. He kicked it, urging it back to its steady ground-eating pace.

No go.

"Hold up!" he yelled, to the Morrigu, who was already obscured by heat haze. He heard her swear, then had no time for such considerations, for the elk took a dozen more stumbling steps, vented an agonized wheeze, and crumpled onto its knees. "Jump!" he shouted, as he tensed to leap free. As soon as Alec released him, he pushed off—and the elk collapsed utterly. Aikin hit hard on his right shoulder, and rolled, barely missing an antler. Something yowled and hissed. Alec uttered a muffled "Oh hell!" His nose filled with glowing red sand.

But already he was struggling to his feet, dusting himself off as he helped Alec up. The latter retrieved the cat as Aikin stared at his fallen mount. By the way its eyes were dimming, he knew the creature was dead. "It ran half the length of Georgia tonight," he sighed. "And twice that back again—mostly at a gallop. Don't blame the poor critter a-tall."

"No mortal steed could have done as well," the Morrigu murmured, joining them, her face as darkly grim as the pervasive glare was bright. "Would it had lasted longer, though; for by dying it has doomed us all."

"What do you mean?" Alec demanded. "You can still shape-shift, can't you? If you turned into a horse—"

The Morrigu shook her head. "I have already *changed* too many times today—which, though you may not believe it, is wearying beyond belief; I have no strength left for such Workings, for a while. And even if I could, to dare that sort of thing here, on the Crimson Road, where the balance between Powers is already perilous—it could hasten the dissolution tenfold."

"Then take Dave and Liz and fly."

The Faery glared at him. "In the name of my kin I

owe him one life. I will not have others laid upon me! I—"

She paused abruptly. "What did you say a moment ago?" she asked, fixing Aikin with a piercing stare.

"When?"

"About Oisin."

Aikin told her.

"And you recovered the oracular stone?"

"Yeah . . . but . . . so what?"

"Oisin would not have directed you to the Crimson Road unless you had business here. Therefore, he foresaw some reason for your presence."

Aikin blinked at her—easy enough in the glare. He could barely see her white horse against the blazing sky. "Huh?"

"Think, boy!" the Faery demanded. "What is there about you that Oisin would send you to a place that could easily mean your death?"

Aikin shrugged and glanced at his friends for support. Liz shrugged back. Alec scowled, but then his eyes widened. "The rock!" he cried. "That's the only thing I can think of that separates you from the rest of us!"

"R-right," a weak voice agreed. Aikin started, then realized who had spoken. "God, Dave, you're alive!"

"But not well—yet," David gave back in a raspy whisper. ". . . too tired to talk, but not to hear . . . or think."

"So there's something we can do? Some way to use the ulunsuti?"

" 'Course . . . there is," David managed, but Aikin could tell it took all his strength to continue speaking. "Gate . . ." David mumbled—and fainted.

The ensuing silence filled with three gasps, and, more distantly, a low rumble like thunder. The sky turned black for a slivered second, like a TV switched off and on.

"It will be soon," the Morrigu hissed.

Alec gnawed his lip. "Gate," he mused. "Of course!

We use the ulunsuti to gate the hell outta here. Un-less"—he spared a scowl at the Morrigu—"that'll hasten the dissolution too!"

"But what about the World Walls?" From Liz.

"Fuck 'em," Alec snapped. "They'll live, we won't."

"It will likely not damage them anyway," the Morrigu put in, looking as though she thought their plan might actually succeed. "The Tracks—even this one—*transcend* the World Walls. They are *already* between; therefore, we should do no harm—*if* we gate to another place on the Track beyond the outer gate! And," she added pointedly, "even if it *does* hasten the dissolution, we will not be there to observe it."

"Let's do it," Alec agreed.

"Do we have the stuff?" Liz wondered.

Alec patted his backpack. "I've got the gear I took when I went to rescue Eva. All we need's a fire, something to put the blood in . . . and blood."

Aikin eyed them dubiously. "Human? Or—"

"We've got the horse—and whatever crazy thing that is we were riding," Alec gave back.

"Right!"

The Morrigu scanned the horizon, face going grimmer by the second. "Whatever we do, we must hurry. If one of you will help me with your friend . . ." Aikin was beside her in an instant, as was Alec. Together they lowered David to the ground. He looked, Aikin thought, deathly pale—or maybe that was simply the glare. The Morrigu joined them, then paused to whisper something in her horse's ear. That accomplished, she gave it a swat on the rump and sent it galloping down the Crimson Road.

"What'd you do that for?" Liz cried furiously.

"We could not all ride it, and there was no way to choose one life above another. But if the horse reaches the outer gate in time, it can pass on what has happened. At least our deaths will not go unmarked."

"Great," Alec growled, kicking at the ruddy dust.

Thunder rumbled, closer. No one dared look at the sky.

"Let's to it," Aikin sighed, kneeling by the fallen stag. "Anybody got anything to put blood *in*?"

"In my pack," Alec grinned, already fumbling through it. Liz set the ulunsuti down beside Aikin. "Fire?" she asked the Morrigu.

"Fabric?" the Morrigu gave back with a sigh. "This velvet you see upon me is but a glamour I raised lest my nakedness offend you."

Liz rolled her eyes, but stripped off the khaki vest she'd been wearing. Alec added his own vest, his shirt, and the patch pockets from his fatigues. Aikin donated his T-shirt, wadded it with the other material, and placed it on the ground.

A sharp glare from the Morrigu, and it sparked, then smoked, then smoldered, and finally erupted into flame. The heavy padded vest burned slowly—which was fortunate. Alec dug into his pack for the appropriate herbs to add to the blaze, as well as a small salt-glazed bowl, which he passed to Aikin, who produced the ulunsuti from his vest and set it in it. At Alec's nod, he slit the elk's carotid. Blood oozed out: a slow drip that nevertheless quickly filled the container. The stone promptly began to glow. "You should've seen what this guy did earlier," he offered, offhand.

"What?" Liz wondered, from where she sat beside the unconscious David.

"Remember when we were wonderin' what'd happen if the thing tasted Faery blood? Well . . ." Aikin went on to relate a short version of what had transpired in the distant battlefield.

"God," Alec breathed, when he finished. "You mean it can raise the *dead*?"

"The *Faery* dead," the Morrigu amended, "not yours. Our souls are both more firmly linked to our bodies and more independent from them."

"More Faery paradox," Aikin muttered, staring at the stone. "How do you know when this thing's ready?"

"When it won't glow anymore," Alec replied, then noted his scraped and bloody hands. "Guess *you'd* better do the honors," he added. "When the gate appears in the stone, you stick the rock into the fire—and we jump.

"Aikin frowned. "And the gate itself . . . ?"

Alec puffed his cheeks. "We stare at the stone and visualize where we want to go—I'd suggest the place we saw those two archways. And when it appears, you do the fire thing, and when the gate flares up, we jump. Somebody'll have to carry David. Liz, you wanta take Eva?"

Without having to be caught, the cat leapt into Liz's lap. Alec and the Morrigu eased their arms under their unconscious companion.

"Remember! Visualize!" Alec told Aikin. "Oh, and it's gonna hurt like hell!"

Aikin nodded, set his jaw, and, as the others settled into a circle around it, stared at the ulunsuti, where it sat glowing in its bowl beside the fire. And tried to recall those twin trilithons that had marked the juncture of the Track and the actual Crimson Road. And waited . . .

. . . waited . . .

"No go," Liz groaned at last. "Won't work. The image forms, then shatters—probably 'cause we're all too wired."

Aikin wrenched his gaze away from the glowing stone, and blinked. Was it his imagination, or was the glare around them brighter? And did the endless plain seem . . . less endless?

"Shit," Alec spat. "We're up the creek now!"

"No!" the Morrigu countered, "we are not!"

And with that, she swept forward and seized the ulunsuti from where it still glittered wetly atop the burning cloth. Before anyone could stop her, she slashed her breast with one long fingernail, and, when bright blood burst forth, pressed the ulunsuti there. It flared once more: brighter than ever.

"Think of the outer gate!" she cried. And then she shouted a word in a language none of them knew, and flame rose up around her.

"Goddamn!" Aikin yipped. *"Shit!"*

"Stop her!" Liz screamed. "Don't let her!"

"My choice!" came a shriek from the heart of the fire. "I owe David Sullivan a life. Use it—or waste your own!"

And with that, the fire raged hotter, and almost as bright as the impossibly brilliant sky. And then, within the heart of those flames, a darker center formed: the ghostly wavering shape of twin stone archways surrounded by lurking pines.

Another shriek followed, then another, the last of which sounded strangely like a caw—and the gate flared up man-high.

"Now!" Alec yelled, as he struggled forward with David in awkward tow. Aikin helped him, then a white-faced Liz, and together the four of them leapt toward it. The fire beat at them, but coolness lurked within, from that place beyond the gate.

And then the world turned to light and heat and they were through.

Light became dark. Waste became woodland. Day turned back to twilight; while the Track, that had been crimson, was once more orange fading quickly to gold. In lieu of sand, they stood upon pine needles.

As soon as Aikin got his bearings, he helped Alec ease David down, then surveyed their surroundings. Behind them rose the two archways, with a brightness behind one and blackness inside the other. But there was no gate glimmering in the air. No Morrigu—and no ulunsuti. Even as they watched, a brightness that transcended bright exploded beyond the right-hand arch then winked out, leaving only wavering no-color. An instant later, the stones themselves turned hazy and dissolved.

"Is she . . . ?" From Liz.

"I think so," Alec nodded.

"And your magic rock as well, looks like," Aikin added.

"No big deal," Alec told him. "How's David?"

"I'll live," came a blessedly familiar voice. Aikin whirled around to see David easing up on his elbows, blinking back to awareness. "I'm not sure what's been goin' on," he croaked. "But I think the Morrigu gave me some of her strength, or something, there at the end. I know that for a minute I was seein' through her eyes. I . . . I know what she did, too, and why . . . and while I don't think she should've done it, I guess it *is* done. And . . . I think she really *is* gone—in that body, anyway—and so's the ulunsuti." He shot Alec a weak smile. "One less thing to worry about, huh?—Mr. Reluctant Wizard!"

Alec rolled his eyes. "Yeah, but . . . we're still lost."

"Maybe not," Liz countered. "Check out Eva."

They did. The cat was running back and forth between them and the remaining trilithon, as though urging them to follow.

"Do it," Aikin said. "I've seen her do that come-on thing before, back when she was an enfield."

He glanced down at David, and was surprised to see his friend rising to his feet—with Alec's aid, granted, but getting up all the same.

"You make it, man?" he wondered.

"Got to," David grinned, and shuffled forward.

They hesitated before the remaining gate, for only darkness lurked beyond, and the merest glimmer of yellow Track. But the cat—who didn't look quite like a cat just then—trotted primly forward and pranced through. Aikin exchanged smirks with Liz, then eased back, bowed, and told his three friends, "After you."

"Don't trust magic, huh?" David chuckled, and followed Eva.

Aikin was the last to dare the gate. For an instant it was dark and cold, but then he felt warmth and the brush of wind, and scented wild things growing—and a moment later, found himself marching out of the woods atop Lookout Rock.

The sun was rising beyond the mountains to the east.

Alec was holding an honest-to-god enfield.

Liz and David were holding each other.

And from every tree, bush, and stone outcrop thousands upon thousands of crows, ravens, and starlings gave forth a raucous, unearthly keening. Yellow eyes glittered balefully—everywhere. Aikin's hair prickled.

The enfield trilled back, something that sounded close to language. The keening persisted, but the birds slowly parted, opening a path away from the cliff and toward the logging road that lower down became the Sullivans' drive.

The sun was fully risen now: a disk of red perched atop the ragged horizon like an immense burning ruby in the crown of a sleeping giant-king. Its rays lanced across the land like tangible things, to strike the quartzite cliffs of Bloody Bald.

And though the pointed cone of the mundane mountain did not alter for anyone save Second-Sighted Dave, all of them heard one sound, clear above the keening.

Horns, softly blowing: the horns of elfland greeting a Faery dawn.

"Wanta stand on my feet, big boy?" David stage-whispered into Aikin's ear.

Aikin grinned back but shook his head. "I've seen enough."

"Repeat that in a month," Alec snorted. "Then we'll know you're not lying."

Aikin cocked his head, listening. "The splendor falls," he murmured, eyes shining.

"On castle walls," Alec added.

"And snowy summits old in story," David finished

Tennyson's line, in a tone that betokened finality. And for a minute more they listened. The keening ended with the last trumpet call. The blackbirds as one watched—and waited.

"So," David sighed, when the morning light had shifted back to normal, "what'll it be? Go down the mountain and lay *another* wild tale on my folks, and get 'em to take us back to Athens . . ."

"Or . . . ?" From Liz.

He kissed her.

She pinched his butt.

The enfield stretched and whistled—which segued into a purr as the beast became a cat once more.

Alec patted his grumbling belly. "C'mon, folks, I'm starved."

"I could always *hunt* something," Aikin suggested wickedly. "Got four-and-twenty blackbirds right here!"

"Dream on," Alec shot back promptly. "But not till we get back to Athens."

"I've had too much death," David shuddered. "Come on, guys, let's do some livin'!"

And with that, they marched past the black-winged multitude—and raced morning into the valley.

Epilogue:
Treasure Trove

(Jackson County, Georgia—
Monday, November 2—evening)

The phone rang six times before David collared it. "Hello?" he ventured, half-afraid it would be a panicked Cammie, as the last call he'd answered had been—when was it? Barely two days ago, though it seemed like half a lifetime.

Instead, it was Uncle Dale. He felt a twinge of nerves when he recognized his kinsman. Dale Sullivan *never* called to chat.

"How's it goin', boy?" the old man asked without preamble.

"Fine, I reckon," David answered carefully. "How's things up in the cove?"

"Fine as frog hair," Dale gave back. "Just thought I'd pass on a couple things you might wanta know."

David raised an eyebrow at Alec, who was peering in from the hall, cat in hand.

"Like what?"

"Like I had company today."

"Wanta tell me who?"

"Guess."

"The Pope—Nuada—hell, I don't know."

"John Devlin."

"Oh!" Then: "What'd he want?"

"Brought me a poem he'd written. Said he should've been by a lot sooner, but just wanted to see where

355

David-the-Elder came from. And that it was never too late to make new friends."

"Ah-ha!"

"Said he'd see *you* one of these days."

"O-kay."

A pause. "Something else, too, boy: something kinda strange—nothing to worry about, but . . . well, I thought you'd wanta know."

"I'm listenin'."

Another pause. "Well, that Devlin guy wanted to go see David-the-Elder's grave, so me and him went over there. And . . . we found something."

"What?"

Dale cleared his throat. "It was right at the headstone; couldn't hardly see it, 'cept Devlin stubbed his toe on it. But . . . it was a sword."

David's heart flip-flopped.

"A . . . sword?"

"Viking, Devlin thought, or a damned good copy. I've got it here waitin' for you."

"Yeah," David laughed, "some things are worth hangin' on to!"

THE MAGICAL *XANTH* SERIES!

PIERS ANTHONY

QUESTION QUEST
75948-9/ $5.99 US/ $7.99 Can

ISLE OF VIEW
75947-0/ $5.99 US/ $7.99 Can

VALE OF THE VOLE
75287-5/ $5.50 US/ $7.50 Can

HEAVEN CENT
75288-3/ $5.99 US/ $7.99 Can

MAN FROM MUNDANIA
75289-1/ $5.99 US/ $7.99 Can

THE COLOR OF HER PANTIES
75949-7/ $4.99 US/ $5.99 Can

AVONOVA PRESENTS
MASTERS OF FANTASY AND ADVENTURE